PRAISE FOR
A LADY'S GUIDE TO FORTUNE-HUNTING

"*A Lady's Guide to Fortune-Hunting* is a sharp, modern, and absolutely delicious take on the marriage plot. Sophie Irwin's debut is one of the most fun, romantic books I've read in a long time."
—Taylor Jenkins Reid, *New York Times* bestselling author of *Carrie Soto Is Back*

"This book captivated me. What a sassy, witty, delicious tale."
—Sophie Kinsella, #1 *New York Times* bestselling author of *The Party Crasher*

"Plucky, witty, and bright . . . Readers of Jane Austen and fans of *Bridgerton* will swoon and fan themselves as they devour this fun, frolicking romp."
—Nita Prose, *New York Times* bestselling author of *The Maid*

"A complete joy! Irwin's fresh take on Regency romance is a timeless masterpiece featuring a whip-smart heroine who shares sizzling chemistry with a reluctant lord, and an ending that I promise will move you to tears. Irresistible."
—Fiona Davis, *New York Times* bestselling author of *The Magnolia Palace*

"*Bridgerton* fans will devour Sophie Irwin's delightful Regency debut. . . . A confection to be savored!"
—Kate Quinn, *New York Times* bestselling author of *The Diamond Eye*

"Move over, Mr. Darcy! Readers of Jane Austen, Georgette Heyer, and my own novels will adore this hilarious, sparkling debut! Utterly irresistible."
—Eloisa James, *New York Times* bestselling author of *Not That Duke*

"I cheered for Kitty as she continually confronts the whole of polite society in her outrageous pursuit of a rich husband. . . . An impressive debut novel."

—Mary Balogh, *New York Times* bestselling author of *Remember Love*

"Georgette Heyer fans will devour this fun, fast-paced comedy of manners."

—Erica Ridley, *New York Times* bestselling author of *Defying the Earl*

"I have not read such a satisfying and entertaining book in a very long time. . . . It reminded me a little of my favorite author, Edith Wharton."

—Santa Montefiore, *New York Times* bestselling author of *The Secret of the Irish Castle*

"A Regency romance with a bit of twenty-first-century wisdom. Delightfully well written."

—Charmaine Wilkerson, *New York Times* bestselling author of *Black Cake*

"A fun and biting historical romance that isn't afraid to put its leading lady first."

—*BuzzFeed*

"Delicious—frothy, gossipy, and glamorous. A Regency romance with Jane Austen and Georgette Heyer as literary touchstones."

—*Daily Mail* (London)

"Shades of Heyer with a dash of modern roguishness that belongs to Sophie Irwin . . . In short, I bloody loved it."

—Beth Morrey, international bestselling author of *The Love Story of Missy Carmichael*

"[This book] was like finding a long-lost Georgette Heyer, only better. Stayed with me after, keeping a smile on my face. A triumph."

—Susan Lewis, international bestselling author of *I Have Something to Tell You*

PENGUIN BOOKS

A LADY'S GUIDE TO SCANDAL

Sophie Irwin grew up in Dorset, England; after university, she moved to London to work in publishing. *A Lady's Guide to Fortune-Hunting* was her debut, and *A Lady's Guide to Scandal* is her second novel.

A LADY'S GUIDE TO SCANDAL

Sophie Irwin

PENGUIN BOOKS

PENGUIN BOOKS

An imprint of Penguin Random House LLC
penguinrandomhouse.com

First published in Great Britain by HarperFiction,
an imprint of HarperCollins *Publishers*, 2023
Published in Penguin Books 2023

LIBRARY OF CONGRESS CATALOGING-IN-PUBLICATION DATA
Names: Irwin, Sophie, author.
Title: A lady's guide to scandal : a novel / Sophie Irwin.
Description: New York : Penguin Books, 2023.
Identifiers: LCCN 2023005726 (print) | LCCN 2023005727 (ebook) |
ISBN 9780593492000 (trade paperback) | ISBN 9780593491997 (ebook)
Subjects: LCSH: Upper class—Great Britain—19th century—Fiction. | London (England)—
History—19th century—Fiction. | LCGFT: Romance fiction. | Historical fiction. | Novels.
Classification: LCC PR6109.R94 L335 2023 (print) |
LCC PR6109.R94 (ebook) | DDC 823/.92—dc23/eng/20230210
LC record available at https://lccn.loc.gov/2023005726
LC ebook record available at https://lccn.loc.gov/2023005727

Printed in the United States of America
1st Printing

Set in Berling LT Std

For Freya
(the liquor in our cocktails)

"She had been forced into prudence in her youth, she learned romance as she grew older—the natural sequel of an unnatural beginning."

Persuasion, JANE AUSTEN

A LADY'S
GUIDE TO
SCANDAL

1

HAREFIELD HALL, 1819

C ome now, Eliza, surely you can manage one tear?"
Mrs. Balfour whispered to her daughter. "It is expected from the widow!"

Eliza nodded, though her eyes remained as dry as
ever. However many years she had spent playing the part of
obedient daughter and dutiful wife, weeping upon command
was still beyond her.

"Recollect that we may have a fight on our hands today,"
Mrs. Balfour hissed, sending a meaningful glance across the
library to where the late Earl of Somerset's relations sat. Nine
months after the funeral procession, they had all gathered
again at Harefield Hall for the reading of the will, and from
the frosty glances being sent their way, it seemed Mrs. Balfour
was not the only one preparing for battle.

"Eliza's jointure was agreed in the marriage settlement: five
hundred pounds a year," Mr. Balfour reassured his wife in a
whisper. "Somerset has no reason to dispute that; it's the veri-
est fragment of the estate."

He spoke with bitterness, for neither he nor Mrs. Balfour
had fully reconciled themselves to Eliza's severely changed circumstances. A decade ago, the marriage of timid, seventeen-
year-old Miss Eliza Balfour to the austere Earl of Somerset—five

and twenty years her senior—had been the match of the Season, and the Balfours had reaped its rewards quite comprehensively. Within a year of the wedding, their eldest son had married an heiress, their second had been secured a captaincy in the 10th Foot, and Balfour House had been recarpeted entirely in cut-velvet.

But no one had expected the earl, with so strong a constitution, to succumb so quickly to an inflammation of the lungs last spring. And now, widowed at seven and twenty years, and without a child to inherit the title, Eliza's position was far less desirable. Five hundred pounds a year . . . Persons could and did live on far less, but on this subject Eliza agreed with her father. Ten years of marriage to a man who had shown more affection to his horses than his wife, ten years of near isolation in the cold, forbidding Harefield Hall, ten years of yearning for the life she might have had, if only circumstances had been a little different . . . Given exactly what—given exactly *who*—Eliza had been forced to give up, five hundred pounds a year felt a pittance.

"Had she only given him a son . . ." Mr. Balfour bemoaned, for perhaps the fifth time.

"She *tried*!" Mrs. Balfour snapped.

Eliza bit her tongue, hard. Miss Margaret Balfour—Eliza's cousin—pressed her hand under the table, and the clock struck half past twelve. They had now been waiting half an hour for the new earl, whose presence would allow the reading to begin. Eliza's stomach clenched in anticipation. Surely—*surely*—he would arrive soon.

"Disgraceful," Mrs. Balfour muttered, her face still fixed in placid, smiling repose. "Nine months late already, and late today, too. Is it not disgraceful, Eliza?"

"Yes, Mama," Eliza said automatically. It was always easiest to agree, though the unnatural delay was truthfully the fault of the old earl, not the new. For it was the old earl who had stipulated his will not be read until all parties named within it were assembled. Since the new Earl of Somerset—Eliza's husband's nephew, previously the heir presumptive Captain Courtenay—had been stationed in the West Indies when his uncle died last April, and since sailing conditions in '18 had been unprecedentedly slow, his delayed return was understandable. Torturous, but understandable.

All assembled in the library had already been waiting many months and the lateness of the hour today was taking its toll: the Honorable Mrs. Courtenay (sister-in-law to the old earl, mother to the new) had her eyes fixed on the door, her daughter Lady Selwyn was tapping her fingers impatiently, while Lord Selwyn sought to soothe his own nerves by regaling the room with various tales of his own superiority.

"And I said to him: Byron, old boy, you simply *must* write the thing!"

Beside him, at the center of the room, the Somerset attorney, Mr. Walcot, shuffled and reshuffled his papers with a pained smile. Everyone was impatient, but of all of them, surely none more so than Eliza, who felt—with every tick of the grandfather clock—her nerves reach new, dangerous heights. After ten years—ten long years—today she would see him again. It did not feel real.

He might still not come. A lifetime of disappointments had taught her the virtue of preparing for the worst: perhaps he had mistaken the date, or perhaps his carriage had suffered an awful crash, or perhaps he had decided to return to the West Indies rather than have to see her again. It was unlike him to be late, he had always been so punctual. Or, at least, the gentleman Eliza had once known was punctual. Perhaps he had changed.

Finally, however, as the clock struck quarter to the hour, the door opened.

"The Right Honorable, the Earl of Somerset," Perkins, their butler, announced.

"My sincere apologies for the lateness of the hour," the new Lord Somerset said, stepping into the room. "The rain has made the roads treacherous . . ."

Eliza's reaction was instantaneous. Her heart began to beat faster, her breath became labored, her stomach clenched, and she stood, not because it was polite, but because the force of recognition reverberating through her meant she simply had to. All the months she had spent imagining this moment—and she still did not feel at all prepared for it.

"Oliver, darling!" Mrs. Courtenay hurried over to her son, eyes shining, Lady Selwyn close behind, and Somerset embraced his mother and his sister, in turn. Mrs. Balfour clucked her tongue in disapproval of this breach of etiquette—he ought properly to have addressed Eliza first—but Eliza paid no heed. In many ways, he appeared the same. He was still very tall, his hair was still very fair, his eyes the same cool grey as the rest of his family, and he still carried himself with an air of calm assurance that had always been decidedly his own. Under the effects of a decade-long naval career however, there was a greater breadth across the shoulder which had not existed in him as a younger man and his pale skin had darkened under the sun. It suited him. It suited him very well.

Somerset released his sister's hands and turned to Eliza. She was suddenly horribly aware that the years had not been nearly so kind to her. With a small stature, brown hair and uncommonly large and dark eyes, she had always resembled some sort of startled nocturnal animal, but now she feared—with the all-black ensemble of her widow's weeds, and a figure drawn and tired from the uncertainty of the past months—that she appeared positively rattish.

"Lady Somerset," he said, bowing before her.

His voice was the same, too.

"My lord," Eliza said. She could feel her fingers trembling and fisted them in her skirts as she curtseyed shakily, bracing herself to meet his eyes. What would she see in them—anger, perhaps? Recrimination? She did not dare to hope for warmth. She did not deserve it. They rose from their bows as one, and at last, at very long last, their eyes met. And as she looked into his eyes, she saw . . . nothing.

"My most sincere apologies for your loss," he said. His words were civil, his tone neutral. His expression could only be described as polite.

"Th-thank you," Eliza said. "I hope your journey was pleasant?"

The pleasantries tripped off Eliza's tongue without thinking, which was a good thing indeed, because at this moment she was not capable of thought.

"As much as could be, with such weather as we have had," he said. There was no evidence, in his manner or deportment or tone, that he was sharing in any of the turmoil churning through Eliza's mind. He appeared, in fact, totally unaffected by seeing her. As if they had never met before.

As if he had not, once, asked her to marry him.

"Yes . . ." Eliza heard herself say, as if from a great distance. "The rain . . . has been most vicious."

"Indeed," he agreed, with a smile—except it was not a smile she had ever seen directed at herself before. Polite. Formal. Insincere.

"Good to see you, old boy, good to see you indeed." Selwyn had come forward, hand outstretched, and Somerset reciprocated the handshake with a smile that was suddenly warm again. He moved toward the middle of the room, away from the Balfours—leaving Eliza blinking after him.

Was that it? After all their years apart, all the time Eliza had spent wondering over his whereabouts, his happiness, poring over every memory of their time together, of all the hours spent regretting every single one of the events that had conspired to keep them apart—this was to be their reunion? A single, short exchange of commonplaces?

Eliza shivered. The January chill had pervaded the air all morning—her late husband's diktat that fires remain unlit until nightfall had outlived him—but now it seemed to Eliza veritably icy. A whole decade of existing literally oceans apart and yet Oliver—*Somerset*—had never felt more distant to Eliza than in this moment.

"Shall we begin?" Selwyn prompted. Even before Selwyn had married the late earl's niece, the two gentlemen had been close friends, for their lands shared a border—but for the same reason their relationship had also been temperamental. Indeed, their last business meeting before the old earl's death had deteriorated into a quarrel loud enough to deafen the whole household—and yet, from the eagerness in Selwyn's face, he was clearly expectant of a great bequeathment today.

Nodding, Mr. Walcot spread out the papers in front of him, and the Balfours, Selwyns and Courtenays watched from their respective sides of the room, wolfish and hungry. The scene would make for a dramatic tableau. Oils, in high color, perhaps. Eliza's fingers twitched for a paintbrush.

"This is the last will and testament of Julius Edward Courtenay, tenth Earl of Somerset . . ."

Eliza's attention faded as Mr. Walcot began to list the many ways in which the new earl was about to become very, very rich. Mrs. Courtenay looked about to cry in delight, Lady Selwyn was biting back a smile, but Somerset was frowning. Was he daunted at the vastness of the hoard, perhaps even surprised? He should not be. Even despite the late earl's austerity, Harefield Hall was still a veritable shrine to the family's affluence: from its walls of horns, hides and hunting trophies to its

exquisite porcelain tea sets, from the parade of Persian hel-
mets and Indian swords along the great staircase to the oil
landscapes displaying sugar plantations they had once owned,
Harefield wore its loot proudly. And in the work of a few short
sentences, this new Somerset owned it all. He was now one of
the richest and most eligible men in England. From this moment on, every unattached lady in England would be falling at
his feet.

Whereas Eliza . . . After today, she could remain at Harefield,
to act as the new earl's hostess until he married, remove to the
Dower House on the edge of the estate, or return to her childhood home. None of these options was particularly thrilling. To
return to Balfour to live under her parents' watchful eye once
more would be ghastly, but to remain here, in such close proximity to a man who clearly felt nothing for her, while she had
spent a decade yearning for him? It would be its own kind of
torture.

"To Eliza Eunice Courtenay, the Right Honorable Countess of Somerset . . ."

Eliza did not even focus her attention at the sound of her
name—but from the way Mr. Balfour had leaned back in his
seat, whiskers relaxing, it was clear that everything Mr. Walcot
had reported was in line with the marriage settlement. Her
future—such as it was—was secured. In her mind's eye, the
years stretched out ahead of her, grey and uninteresting.

"In addition, and in respect to her duty and obedience . . ."

How depressing, to be described in such terms, as one
might a faithful hound, but her mother visibly perked up, eyes
brightening with greed, clearly hopeful that the old lord had
bequeathed Eliza something additional—an expensive jewel
from his collection, perhaps.

". . . and conditional upon her bringing no dishonor to the
Somerset name . . ."

How like him to attach a morality clause to whatever small

bequeathment he had thought appropriate—ungenerous to the very last.

"All my estates at Chepstow, Chawley and Highbridge, for her use absolutely."

Eliza's mind came to sudden attention. *What* had Mr. Walcot just said?

All at once, a room that had been quiet and still became very loud.

"Repeat that last, would you, Walcot? Must have misheard!" Selwyn boomed, taking a step forward.

"Yes, Mr. Walcot, I'm not sure that can have been right!" Mrs. Courtenay's voice was high and piercing as she raised herself from her chair. Mr. Balfour stood, too, hand reaching out as if about to demand to read the document himself.

"To Eliza Eunice Courtenay," Mr. Walcot repeated obediently, "in respect to her loyalty and obedience—and conditional upon her bringing no dishonor to the Somerset name—I bequeath all my estates at Chepstow, Chawley and Highbridge for her use absolutely."

"Preposterous!" Selwyn was having none of it. "Julius was to bequeath those lands to our younger son, Tarquin."

"He told me so, too!" Lady Selwyn insisted. "He *promised* me."

"Lady Somerset's jointure was agreed at the marriage settlement, was it not?" Mrs. Courtenay added. "There was no mention of this, then!"

"Are the Somerset lands not all entailed on the title?" Margaret said, puzzled, only to be loudly shushed by Mrs. Balfour.

"If that is the late earl's bequest, if it is in the will, then you can have no issue with it!" Mr. Balfour insisted to the room in general.

They seemed to have entirely forgotten Eliza was there.

"The estates at Chepstow, Chawley and Highbridge were

inherited by the earl through his mother's line, and therefore were his to do with as he wished," Mr. Walcot said calmly.

"Preposterous!" Selwyn said again. "That cannot be the correct document!"

"I assure you, it is," Mr. Walcot said.

"And I'm telling you it is the wrong one, man!" Selwyn said heatedly, all pretense of joviality gone. "I saw it before—and it named Tarquin, I saw it!"

"It used to," Mr. Walcot agreed. "But the late earl instructed me to amend this line only a fortnight before his death."

Selwyn's puce face turned white.

"Your quarrel," Lady Selwyn whispered.

"We were discussing a loan—it was just business," Selwyn breathed. "He cannot have, he would not have—"

Ah, so *that* was why they had argued: Selwyn had requested a loan. Eliza could have warned him against such foolishness—indeed, Selwyn must have been desperate for he would most certainly have known that the incurably frugal and exceedingly proud late earl considered appeals to his purse the very height of impertinence.

"I assure you that on this—and every other matter—the late earl was quite clear," Mr. Walcot said calmly. "The lands are to go to Lady Somerset."

Selwyn rounded upon Eliza.

"What poison did you whisper in his ear?" he snapped.

"How *dare*—" Mrs. Balfour was swelling with indignation.

"Selwyn!" Somerset's voice rang out, cold and remonstrative, and Selwyn took a step back from Eliza.

"My apologies—I did not mean . . . A—a regrettable lapse in manners . . ."

Lady Selwyn was not cowed. "What of the morality clause? Did my uncle give any other elaboration—any indication of what kind of behavior was meant?"

"I do not see how that is relevant," Mrs. Balfour said, "given my daughter's reputation is unimpeachable."

"Given that my uncle felt it appropriate to include in his will, it feels *very* relevant, Mrs. Balfour," Lady Selwyn said sharply.

"We intend no disrespect," Mrs. Courtenay interjected. "Lady Somerset knows we are very fond of her."

Lady Somerset very much did *not* know this.

"All the late earl specified is that the interpretation of the clause is at the discretion of the eleventh Earl of Somerset— and no one else," Mr. Walcot said.

Selwyn, Lady Selwyn and Mrs. Courtenay all opened their mouths to argue, but Somerset interrupted.

"If the bequeathment was my uncle's wish, I certainly do not have an issue with it," Somerset said, voice firm.

"Of course, of course," Selwyn had clawed back some geniality. "But, my dear boy, I think it would behoove us to discuss what sort of behavior would constitute—"

"I disagree," Somerset said, speaking in a quietly confident manner and seeming not at all bothered by the glares of his family. "And unless Lady Somerset has changed a great deal since I was last upon British soil, she is incapable of causing even a raised eyebrow."

Eliza looked down, her cheeks reddening. In times past, while she had admired Somerset's conviction, in her he had bemoaned the opposite.

"Exactly," Mrs. Balfour agreed, her voice satisfied.

"But given the unusual nature of such a clause," Somerset went on. "I think it ought to remain amongst us, only. None of us would want to cause any gossip, after all."

There were nods of agreement from around the room—the Balfours enthusiastic, the Selwyns reluctant, while Mrs. Courtenay looked about to cry again.

There was a long, long pause.

"How much income do the estates yield yearly?" Selwyn asked.

Mr. Walcot made a brief reference to his notes.

"On average," he said, "they yield an income of just above nine thousand pounds a year. With her jointure, altogether it is an income of ten thousand annually."

Ten thousand pounds a year.

Ten *thousand* pounds. Every year.

She was rich.

She was *very* rich.

Richer than Lady Oxford or Lady Pelham, those celebrated heiresses, the diamonds of their respective Seasons; richer than many of the lords in Whitehall. Could it really be true? Her husband had never given any indication that Eliza was anything other than a perpetual disappointment to him. Inferior to his first wife in every way, and yet similarly unable to give him a son. And yet now, his spite—his displeasure at Selwyn's behavior—had caused him to show Eliza a generosity that she had never felt in his lifetime. Ten thousand pounds a year. He had made Eliza a very wealthy woman.

Eliza felt as if the thread tying her to normalcy had just been cut, and she was spinning away and away. She could not have repeated a single thing else that happened in the rest of the reading, only registering its conclusion when everyone began to stand and, mechanically, she too followed suit. The refrain of "ten thousand pounds a year" was rebounding around her mind like the loudest of echoes, preventing her from thinking of anything else.

"Ten thousand pounds!" Margaret whispered excitedly in her ear, as they filed out. "Do you understand what this means?"

Eliza twitched her head, whether in a nod or shake, she did not know.

"It will change *everything*, Eliza!"

2

⁂

The following afternoon found Eliza standing upon Harefield's front steps, ready to bid her guests farewell. Only Margaret, who had acted as Eliza's companion since the earl's death and would continue to do so for a fortnight longer, was to stay, and Eliza could hardly wait for Harefield to be their own again. Eliza heard her parents before she saw them, Mr. Balfour barking commands to the footmen, Mrs. Balfour reprimanding the maids, and as they appeared through the oak front doors, she took in a fortifying breath.

"You can do it," Margaret whispered in her ear. It had been plain, in the hours since the will reading, that Mr. Balfour fully expected to hold the purse strings of Eliza's new fortune. This would be Eliza's final chance to disabuse her parents of this notion.

"We shall see you in a few weeks, of course," Mrs. Balfour said.

"You mustn't tarry, the roads will only worsen," Mr. Balfour instructed.

"I wondered if—" Eliza began tentatively.

"By then, all your most pressing financial business will be managed," Mrs. Balfour said. "Won't they, husband?"

"Yes, I have already spoken to Mr. Walcot."

This being the most heartfelt farewell Mr. Balfour could

muster, he gave Eliza a sharp nod and disappeared down the steps, leaving Eliza with her mother—the more forbidding opponent.

"I thought perhaps . . ." Eliza said.

"We think it best if you make Hector's boy your heir," Mrs. Balfour said briskly.

Hector was Eliza's youngest brother.

"I don't know that—"

"Rupert, I think, would benefit most," Mrs. Balfour's voice overrode Eliza's.

Of all her brother's entitled weasels, Rupert was the worst.

"I think I would prefer—"

"Mr. Balfour can organize the papers as soon as you return home." Mrs. Balfour patted Eliza's cheek in a concluding sort of way.

It is not yours, Eliza might say to her mother, if she were braver. *It is not your fortune to spend, or to assign or to organize out of my reach.*

"Yes, Mama," Eliza sighed, defeated.

"It is decided. Goodbye, then—we shall see you anon. And recollect that you are still the countess, darling: you oughtn't to allow those Selwyns to run roughshod over you."

The irony of Mrs. Balfour issuing such advice was not lost upon Eliza—nor Margaret, who only barely suppressed a choke of laughter—and with this final instruction delivered, Mrs. Balfour left.

"I know she is your mother and my aunt," Margaret said, as they watched Mrs. Balfour climb into the carriage. "But if I saw her balanced precariously upon the edge of a cliff— perhaps about to fall into the ocean—I would hesitate to act. I wouldn't push her, but I would most definitely *hesitate*."

Unlike Eliza, Margaret's general manner of conversation was to say exactly what she thought, at exactly the moment she thought it, a trait their family deemed as the reason she had never married. Eliza was just sparing a moment of thanks that Mrs. Balfour was at least no longer in earshot, when a quiet cough had them both turning. Somerset had appeared in the doorway and, by the humorous cast of his expression, had overheard Margaret's less than respectful remark. Eliza flushed pink on Margaret's behalf.

"Ah," Margaret said, not sounding particularly worried.

"I shall pretend I did not hear that," Somerset responded, amused. In their youth, he had stood upon friendly terms with Margaret and it appeared his indulgence of her incivilities remained.

"If you could," Margaret said.

Somerset grinned, his smile breaking through his reserve just as the sun shone through clouds, and Eliza's breath caught—but then he turned toward her, and the warmth vanished as swiftly as it had appeared.

"Your father has informed me that you intend to return to Balfour, my lady," he said, and though he was making direct eye contact, Eliza felt as if he were gazing straight through her.

Look at me! Eliza wanted to shout at him. *I am here, look at me!*

"Yes," she said instead, voice as quiet as a mouse. "I do."

Ladies did not shout, no matter the provocation.

Somerset nodded, his expression giving away nothing. Was he relieved? He must be.

"If that is what you wish," he said.

It was not. It was not what she wished at all. But what other choice was there?

"You may of course have any of the carriages for the journey," he went on. "And if you wish to take any of the household servants . . ."

"That is kind," Eliza said.

"It is nothing," he said, and he sounded as though he meant it. Could there be anything more excruciating than this apathy?

"Nevertheless, you have my thanks," Eliza pressed.

There was a pause.

"You need not thank me," Somerset said quietly. "It is no more than my duty, as head of the family."

A remark which was, in fact, more excruciating than his apathy. *Duty. Family.* The words burned.

"Farewell, my dear Lady Somerset!" Lady Selwyn sang with affected sweetness, as she swept through the doorway. "We cannot thank you enough for your hospitality."

"Farewell, my lady." Mrs. Courtenay, not so skilled an actress as her daughter, did not smile.

"You behave yourself, now!" Selwyn said, wagging a finger in Eliza's face. "We wouldn't want to take that fortune away from you, would we?"

"Selwyn!" Somerset said, in sharp remonstration.

"Lady Somerset knows I am only funning!"

"Of course she does," Lady Selwyn agreed. She looked from Somerset to Eliza, and her expression tightened. "Somerset— may I borrow your arm to climb into the carriage?"

"Will your husband's arm not serve, Augusta?" Somerset suggested mildly. "I have a few matters to discuss with Lady Somerset."

Lady Selwyn shot Eliza a stinging glance, as if this were her fault, but reluctantly retreated with her husband and mother.

"I will be in town for the next fortnight," Somerset said to Eliza. "If there is anything at all you need assistance with, please do not hesitate to write."

Eliza nodded.

"Good day, Lady Somerset," he said, bowing his head over her hand.

"Lord Somerset," she said in return. There was something dreadfully ironic about their sharing the same name, now. Fate's cruel jibe at what they might once have shared, had Eliza's mother not been so eager to secure a title for her daughter— and had Eliza's will not been so very easy to bend.

As Somerset raised his head from her hand, their gazes met. And whether Somerset had lowered his guard, now that he was about to leave, or whether he was simply surprised by the sudden proximity of her face to his, as their eyes met, his neutral mask slipped. His polite expression turned abruptly arrested, even stricken, and his gloved hand tightened convulsively upon hers. And Eliza felt, at last, truly seen.

Not just looked through, as if she were some peripheral stranger, or looked upon, as if she were a mildly inconvenient duty, to be resolved, but *seen*: she as Eliza and he as Oliver, two people who had once known each other as deeply as it was possible to know someone. And though the moment could not have lasted for more than two seconds—the length of three quickened heartbeats—it was as if someone had thrust a hand directly into Eliza's chest and squeezed.

"Somerset! Do hurry up, old thing!"

And then it broke. Somerset dropped her hand as if it had burned him.

"Farewell, Miss Balfour," he said hurriedly. "Though I would wish it to be under happier circumstances, it was good to see you both."

He ran quickly down the steps and into the carriage.

"And I you," Eliza whispered to the empty space he had left behind—as ever, a little too late.

"Shall we go inside?" Margaret said quietly, her eyes watchful on Eliza's face. Eliza nodded.

They retreated to the first-floor parlor. It was the least grand of all the rooms, its drapes moth-eaten and brocaded carpets faded, but Eliza's favorite, for upon the wall hung a seascape that had been painted by her grandfather. An artist of superior talent and some renown, the painting—of a tiny boat sailing through cold, unfathomable ocean—had been brought to Harefield by the previous countess and it was a daily comfort to Eliza. An enduring reminder of the golden afternoons she had spent with her grandfather, learning to paint, in the simpler days of girlhood, before her skirts had been let down and her hair put up, when Eliza had naively believed she might follow in his artistic footsteps.

"Would you care for a pot of tea, my lady?" Perkins asked quietly.

"Oh, I think we need something *considerably* stronger than tea," Margaret declared, as she wrenched the lace cap from her red hair and the satin slippers from her feet. "A drop of brandy, if you will!"

Not by a flicker of an eyebrow did Perkins betray any surprise at such an unladylike request, and he returned promptly with a tray bearing the late earl's finest cognac.

"Thank you," Eliza said, as he poured them each a ladylike tipple. She would miss Perkins, when she left for Balfour.

"Famous!" Margaret agreed, though as soon as Perkins departed the room, she was reaching for the crystal decanter and liberally topping up both glasses.

Eliza would miss Margaret most of all. The last nine months, trapped within Harefield's walls for the strictest period of her mourning, might have been interminable, had not Margaret been sent to accompany her. Having her cousin—her dearest friend—at such close proximity after so many years apart, had been an unexpected joy, but now . . .

"Are we to toast our imminent return to the loving bosoms of our families?" Eliza asked, accepting a glass.

"Certainly not," Margaret said. "I think it a terrible idea."

"I know," Eliza said, for Margaret had made this opinion quite plain. "But I cannot remain here, Margaret. He was perfectly civil—but I think I might have preferred hostility to such nothingness."

Eliza did not have to clarify who "he" was.

"It has been ten years," Margaret said. "Surely you cannot still . . ."

Eliza sipped at her glass. The brandy burned her throat on the way down.

"I know it is foolish," Eliza said. "But when I saw him again . . ."

She remembered the jolt that had run through her, body and soul, as soon as he had stepped into the room.

"I might have been struck by lightning," she said, flushing to hear herself speak such a high-flown sentiment aloud.

"How uncomfortable," Margaret observed. "It makes me rather glad I have never been in love. Did he look the same as you remembered?"

"Better," Eliza said morosely. "Unnecessarily handsome, in fact. Could he not have returned just a little ugly?"

"Are you sure he is handsome and not simply very tall?" Margaret asked. "I have often noticed the two are confused."

"I am sure," Eliza said, taking another draught of the brandy.

"The Dower House is a little way from Harefield," Margaret said. "You might easily avoid him from there. Could you truly not abide that?"

Eliza shook her head.

"To linger on the outskirts of his life," she said. "Always wishing I were sharing it with him, while he thrives and marries and has children with someone else? No, I cannot."

Yet once more, as she considered the alternative—Balfour with her mother—she shuddered.

"But to return to being badgered and bullied by my parents," she said. "I—I think I will simply disappear. There is not enough of me left to endure it."

"Have you truly been so miserable, these past years?" Margaret said quietly.

Eliza did not answer. She had avoided telling Margaret, in their weekly letters and infrequent visits, details of her marriage, not wanting to be thought dramatic or spoiled. And, truthfully, while the late earl had not been the husband she would have chosen, nor life as Countess of Somerset one she enjoyed, the years had not been without their pleasures or joys. It was just that, in a life spent trying to please a man whose natural inclination was to disapprove, Eliza had had to find small pleasures, quiet joys. Until she had begun to worry that she herself had become so small and quiet that she might easily be tidied away into a cupboard with the crockery—and left there until she was required to adorn the table once more.

"There is no point worrying over it," Eliza said, after a pause. "I shall return to Balfour. I have no other choice."

She felt a pathetic, forlorn figure and hoped Margaret might say something appropriately soothing, perhaps while stroking her hair.

"I must say, I think you are making a great cake of yourself," Margaret said acidly.

This was not at all what Eliza had in mind.

"Excuse me?"

"Have you forgotten that you are now one of the richest women in England?" Margaret sat up and flapped an accusing hand at Eliza, who watched its progress with some alarm—it was straying dangerously close to a very expensive Ming vase.

"I have not forgotten," Eliza said, "but I am not sure it makes a difference, Margaret. I am just as trapped as I was before."

"Then the fortune is wasted on you, if you are going to act so damnably defeatist," Margaret said, shaking her head.

"Where else would you have me go?" Eliza demanded. She had thought Margaret understood.

"Anywhere!" Margaret snapped back. "You can most certainly afford to set up your own establishment, now. Have you never considered it?"

In truth, Eliza had not. Mrs. Balfour had always said the only unmarried women who set up their own establishments were either very eccentric, very elderly or both. Eliza was neither.

"Margaret, be serious."

"I am perfectly serious," Margaret said.

"What would I even *do*?" Eliza asked.

"Oh, only anything you want, Eliza!" Margaret said. "Have you really become so downtrodden that you do not *want* anything anymore?"

Eliza stared at Margaret, shocked at the venom in her voice.

"Not want anything?" she repeated. "Not *want* anything? Margaret, I want . . . endlessly."

"Is that so?" Margaret asked, sounding so dubious that Eliza began to lose her temper.

"It *is* so," she insisted. "I want to wear gowns of my own choosing—I am sick of being such a dowd—and I want to paint all day if I so choose. *And* I want to spend money as frivolously as I like!"

Eliza could not seem to stop, the words spilling out of her.

"I want to light fires in the daytime and to go where I please, and most of all—most of all, Margaret—I want to have married the man I loved, not the one duty required. But I did not. And nothing can change that, so you'll forgive me if, after a lifetime of being denied every single one of my desires, I seem defeatist now."

Eliza gave an angry swipe at her eyes. Mrs. Balfour had her

wish for tears at last, but it was far too late for them to be of any use.

"Well," Margaret said, after a short silence, "you may not be able to achieve *all* of that, but in your own establishment, you could certainly try—"

"They would never let me," Eliza interrupted. "I am a widow in my first year of mourning. The rules . . ."

"E-li-za," Margaret said, drawing out each syllable in remonstration. "You are not mousy little Miss Balfour, anymore. You are a *countess*. You own ten thousand acres of land. You are richer than our whole family put together. Isn't now the time to break the rules?"

Again, Eliza found herself staring at Margaret. Nothing she said was wrong, exactly, but the way she had arranged the facts, to make it seem as if Eliza now held some power . . . It did not feel true.

"This is your chance to finally have a life of your own," Margaret said. "I cannot bear you to waste it—oh, what I would do for such an opportunity!"

Margaret was leaning forward now, her hands clasped tightly before her, and Eliza wished, suddenly, that the fortune could have been gifted to Margaret, not her. For Margaret, braver, cleverer—and certainly more outspoken than Eliza—would surely make the most of such a chance. She deserved it, too. Deserved more from life than being shipped around the family to look after their various children, overlooked and unimportant—trapped, indeed—as the last unmarried sister. It might not be said aloud, but Eliza knew their family considered Margaret irredeemable, on the shelf: a spinster. It was not fair.

The injustice of it all began to burn in Eliza's chest, hotter than the brandy. "Obedient and dutiful," her husband had called her in his will. "Incapable of causing a raised eyebrow,"

Somerset had announced to the whole room. And that is how everyone had always seen her. It was the chief reason the late earl had wanted to marry her in the first place, perceiving Eliza's timidity to be proof of her malleability—and in all the years of their marriage, Eliza had never once given him reason to disbelieve this. But perhaps Margaret was right. Perhaps now was her chance. Perhaps now was *their* chance.

"I could not do so alone," Eliza said slowly. "To live alone would be most improper."

"Oh, society is positively riddled with spinsters and widows that you might invite to act as your companion," Margaret said, dismissing this at once. "Any respectable female would add to your consequence—*I* would come, but Lavinia is with child again."

"Lavinia is a shrew," Eliza pointed out.

"But a very fertile shrew," Margaret said. "As soon as the child is born, she will require me, and my mother will insist I go and—and that will be the end of that. You will have to do this without me."

Without Margaret, Eliza's resolve would crumble within a week.

"When is the child expected?" Eliza asked.

"Mid-April, all being well," Margaret said. She looked at Eliza contemplatively. "Though . . . Lavinia will not need me until then."

"If I wrote to your mother," Eliza said, "begged your company for three more months . . . ?"

"Just until the baby comes," Margaret said, a smile beginning to form around her lips. "Three more months is not so great a request."

A silence lay between them for a moment.

"We would have to be very, *very* careful," Eliza said.

A veritable grin now spread across Margaret's face.

"I am serious, Margaret," Eliza said. "If the Selwyns catch

a whiff of impropriety, they will start caterwauling about the morality clause. We need to think of a reason we are not going to Balfour—one everyone will accept."

"Where shall we go?" Margaret asked. "London?"

"London . . ." Eliza said wistfully. Eliza had barely visited the metropolis since her own first (and last) Season. She imagined herself and Margaret living there, free and independent to take in as much art and as many museums as they liked. In May, it would be the opening of the Royal Academy's Summer Exhibition, a sight Eliza had not seen since she was seventeen . . . But no.

"It cannot be London while I am in full mourning," Eliza said. "We would be in immediate disgrace."

"Another town, then," Margaret suggested. "A town, with enough entertainment to occupy us, even if you cannot attend any public occasions. What about Bath?"

Bath. Eliza considered it.

"Yes," she said at last. "For I believe there is entertainment to be had there of a quiet nature and I could say I had been prescribed a course of the waters by the doctor. No one would know it was a lie."

"I will visit the libraries, and attend concerts, and meet interesting new persons," Margaret said, voice dreamy.

"Yes, indeed," Eliza said. "And I will . . . I will . . ."

Eliza's voice faltered, doubt crept in. In her mind's eye, all at once appeared Mrs. Balfour's disapproving expression, and Eliza wilted under the imagined glare. She would be so disappointed. Her father, too. Eliza bit her lip and looked up to her grandfather's painting, hanging upon the wall—that tiny, brave boat that remained afloat only by overwhelming effort. Margaret made a gentle encouraging noise, as one might soothe a spooked horse, and Eliza took a deep, deep breath.

"While I will become . . . a lady of fashion?" Eliza suggested.

"Yes," Margaret said at once.

"And I will paint," Eliza went on, firmer now.

"All day if you should choose it."

"And—and I will never again marry for duty!" Eliza said, throat very dry all of a sudden. "That—that is behind me, now."

Across from her, Margaret swept her glass up into the air.

"Now *that* is a toast I like," she said. "To Bath!"

3

In her seven and twenty years, Eliza had done very little to offend, displease or even surprise polite society. There was something exceptionally thrilling, therefore, about their escape from Harefield Hall; although it took two weeks to plan, though each member of the Balfour family had been warned by letter of their decision, and though they were to travel in a sedate Somerset carriage, it still felt to Eliza quite as illicit as if they were hightailing to Gretna Green on a mission of elopement.

"Did your mother write again today?" Margaret asked, as they climbed into the carriage, Eliza's lady's maid, Pardle, following behind. As the journey was not long—under twenty miles—and the February morning so bright, Eliza had opted to have the barouche deliver them to Bath, so they might enjoy the warmth of the sunshine upon their faces. Their luggage had gone ahead of them in the company of Perkins and two housemaids, who were the only other members of the household Eliza had taken with her. Having deprived Harefield of its butler—which she should not have done had Perkins not specifically requested it—she had felt too guilty to claim any more of the hall's servants than this.

"There will certainly be a letter waiting for us when we arrive," Eliza said.

Predictably, none of the Balfour clan had been pleased with

their decision, but bolstered by Margaret's rallying and the fictional excuse of a doctor's recommendation, Eliza had remained steadfast. And when none of Mrs. Balfour's letters—ranging from the scolding to the pleading—had proven effectual, permission for Margaret to accompany her had been given, however reluctantly, until Lavinia's child emerged and Margaret would be fetched away.

"And have you had anything yet from Somerset?" Margaret asked.

Eliza did not reply, pretending to arrange her skirts around her. With hot bricks at their feet and blankets upon their laps, they would be comfortable until they paused for refreshment, but Eliza had still worn her warmest—and dowdiest—dress for the journey: another black robe, long in the sleeve and high in the neck, with a thick woolen cloak and an unwieldy traveling bonnet that made it rather difficult to turn her head.

"You still have not written to him?" Margaret guessed. "Eliza!"

"I will!" Eliza promised defensively. Somerset's approval of the scheme was, of course, of equal importance as Mrs. Balfour's, for only he had the power to remove her fortune; and yet, though Eliza had sat down to pen the letter a dozen times, on each instance she could not write a single word. How was one supposed to write a formal note to a gentleman with whom one had once exchanged love letters?

"I will write as soon as we arrive," Eliza vowed.

She took one final look back at Harefield's intimidating sprawl. She could remember, vividly, how alarming it had appeared to her, on the first time she had arrived—seventeen years old and trembling with nerves, worrying that she might be murdered within it. But she had survived and today she was emerging not as the timorous Miss Balfour, nor a diffident wife, but as the independent Lady Somerset.

"Let us go, Tomley," she instructed with as much command as she could muster and they set off at a brisk, slightly lurching pace. Eliza's usual driver had been taken ill, and the more youthful Tomley had a more cavalier way with the reins—Eliza winced a little as they jolted over a divot in the road; it was a good thing neither she nor Margaret were prone to travel sickness.

"What are you desirous of doing first?" Eliza asked Margaret a little way into the journey, as she opened her portfolio. It was expected that any lady of quality should cultivate accomplishments, but under the influence of her grandfather, a respected member of the Royal Academy, Eliza had received an unusually advanced artistic education—though it had not equipped her to draw in a barouche that was bumping over every irregularity of the road.

"Of course we will be severely limited by your mourning— not that I blame you, of course . . ."

"Your understanding is appreciated," Eliza said absently. Ought she to advise Tomley to slow down? This would be the first significant journey she had undertaken without either her father or her husband to manage proceedings, and she was not sure how involved she ought make herself. The road had truly become very narrow—surely such speed was inadvisable?

". . . but that still leaves a great deal open to us. The Sydney Gardens, of course, and the Pump Room—I say, Tomley, look out!"

There was a large pothole in the road ahead, just ahead of a sharp turn. Tomley pulled the horses wildly to the right in order to avoid the pit at precisely the same moment a post chaise came thundering around the corner. The collision was at once fast and slow: Tomley wrenched the horses around and the other driver tried desperately to pull his to a stop, but it was too late, contact was inevitable. Their wheels scraped sickeningly together, splinters of wood flying into the air above, and Eliza and Margaret grasped desperately onto each other as the barouche ricocheted in the opposite direction, and their seat cushions, blankets and reticules went flying over the sides.

The barouche teetered once, twice, and seemed on the point of turning completely . . . before it at last righted itself with a resounding crash. Both carriages came, at last, to a standstill, and there was silence—save for the comically peaceful noise of birds twittering in the trees above.

"Are you all right?" Eliza gasped.

"I—I think so," Margaret said, reaching up to adjust her crooked bonnet.

"Pardle? Tomley?"

"Yes, milady," Pardle whispered, clutching the sides of the barouche with white knuckles.

"My apologies, milady, my apologies," Tomley babbled, as he leapt from the carriage to see to the horses, who were dreadfully spooked, their eyes rolling and their mouths frothing. Across the road, the other driver was doing the same.

Eliza ran her hands down her arms, as if—nonsensically—to check all her limbs were intact. Miraculously, both she and Margaret appeared uninjured, though Margaret was pale under her freckles and Eliza felt herself begin to shiver violently.

Into the silence came the slow creak of a door being opened, and a man stepped out of the other carriage. He was tall, with dark curling hair and a brown complexion and—unlike Eliza and Margaret's dishevelment—the only evidence of the crash upon his person was the angle of his hat, which had slipped from rakish to precarious. He looked about the scene with an expression of mild astonishment, taking in first his driver, then the barouche and then, finally, Margaret and Eliza.

"Do you mean to rob me?" he asked, more curious than alarmed. "Is this a stand-and-deliver moment?"

Eliza stared at him. Had she hit her head in all the commotion?

"N-no, of course not!" she stammered out.

"Do you mean to *murder* me?" he asked.

"Certainly not!" Eliza said. What on earth . . . ?

"Then what the devil do you mean by it?" the gentleman said, brows furrowing. "I was in the middle of a very peaceful nap, you know."

Eliza gaped at him, speechless. Who on earth was this man? His skin suggested Indian descent—unusual in so rural a setting—and the private chaise spoke to affluence, so perhaps he was a wealthy merchant, en route to a nearby city? But a merchant would not speak to her in such a way.

"We did not *intend* to!" Margaret said indignantly.

"He was driving at a shocking pace, milord!" The man's driver, having calmed his horses, was now jabbing an accusatory finger at Tomley.

"So were you!" Tomley retorted.

"Shall we agree the fault was shared?" Eliza suggested hastily, before tempers could rise any further.

"That verdict feels a trifle premature," the gentleman said, a smile beginning to curl his mouth, as if he were tempted to find the whole incident rather amusing. "Ought the jury not properly hear the evidence before we deliberate?"

"I am glad you are finding this so entertaining, sir!" Margaret said tartly.

"As am I," the man agreed. "A sense of humor truly is man's greatest treasure."

Eliza reached up to adjust her bonnet, dazed. This was not at all the serene journey she had planned, and if she had thought tears would help matters, she might have begun crying already. By now they ought almost to have reached Peasedown and be looking forward to a restorative repast—not stranded in the middle of nowhere, having conversations with a strange gentleman so unusual as to border upon the lunatic.

"Tomley?" she said. "Are we able to continue?"

The coachman shook his head.

"The spokes on the left wheel are quite snapped," he said, examining them with a critical eye. "But not to worry, my lady, Peasedown is only three miles away. I shall take one of the horses and return directly with a wheelwright!"

"And leave us here?" Margaret said. Even if Eliza were not in widow's weeds, it would not be ideal to be left stranded and unprotected on an open road—as it was, it felt distinctly improper. But what choice did they have? Eliza raised her eyes to the heavens.

She would not weep. She *would not* weep. But why was it today that such a disaster had to occur, just when she had resolved to make a new start?

"Far be it for me to insert myself," the gentleman's voice interrupted her reverie. He still, infuriatingly, sounded a little amused. "But as my carriage seems to be wholly intact—indeed, mortifyingly so—may I offer you ladies transport to, ah, Peasebury or Peaseton, where you might rest out of the cold?"

It was tempting, and even as Eliza considered it another shiver ran through her—as if her body was in agreement with him—but she shook her head in refusal.

"You are kind to offer, sir, but I cannot accept," she said.

"I am kind to offer," the gentleman agreed. "And I am afraid—and I beg you will not think me boorish—I must insist. I cannot leave you here upon the road."

"But you must," Eliza said.

"I cannot," he said. "It is against the gentlemanly code of honor they made us all memorize at Eton. 'One shalt not leave damsels on the road, to be eaten by bears.'"

Eliza wondered vaguely if she was concussed.

"There are no wild bears in England," Margaret pointed out.

"You will have to take that up with Eton," the gentleman said gravely.

"You are a stranger to us," Eliza said. "It would not be proper."

"Why, that is easily resolved with an introduction," the gentleman said, sweeping a magnificent bow. "I am Melville."

Margaret gave a start. Tomley made an audible choking noise.

Oh. Of course.

The Melville family was one of the oldest lines in British aristocracy, and each new generation seemed to eclipse the last in infamy: the seventh earl, "Mad Jack," was famed for frittering a fortune away at cards; the eighth earl for first running away upon his eighteenth birthday and then for returning a decade later with an Indian noblewoman for a wife. In keeping with family tradition, the ninth and most recent Lord Melville's romantic entanglements appeared almost weekly in the gossip rags, yet he and his sister, Lady Caroline, had become just as renowned for their literary exploits: Lady Caroline for a loosely fictional political novel and Melville for the romantic verses that had held women throughout the *ton* spellbound.

Eliza looked Melville over, deciding that he was certainly as handsome and as well-formed as so often described, though not—as she had always imagined—carrying a cutlass. She could see now, too, that while he was dressed casually rather than elegantly, the exquisite cut of his riding coat, the shine of his top boots and the high crown of his beaver hat all proclaimed the *beau monde*. Her eyes traveled back up to his face, at which point she realized, from the raise of his eyebrows, that in her shock she had made no attempt to mask her obvious perusal of his person.

"Well?" Melville said, spreading his arms as if to encourage inspection. Eliza flushed. "Do you accept my benevolent and generous offer?"

"My lady, if I may—I do not think it proper," Tomley said in hissing undertones. Pardle gave a fervent nod of agreement.

Eliza hesitated, at an utter loss. On the one hand, association with such a notorious flirt—one might even say rake—was certainly undesirable. On the other, they could not very well linger here on a public road, in the cold, for the hours it might take Tomley to return. She looked over to Margaret, who gave a tiny, helpless shrug. It was up to Eliza to decide, then.

"His late lordship would not want—" Tomley pressed, which clarified matters.

"His late lordship is not here, however," Eliza said. "It is my decision, and . . . and I would not like to tarry any longer. Tomley, if you would help us alight from the carriage you may follow with the horses and procure the wheelwright's services."

"Allow me . . ." The earl offered Eliza his hand and, in a trice, both the ladies and Pardle were handed into the chaise which was blissfully comfortable, and after a brief pause Melville followed, handing Eliza her mud-splattered portfolio before settling himself in the seat opposite.

The carriage drew off. There was silence, as Eliza and Margaret stared at Melville. Eliza cudgeled her mind for something of interest to say but drew an utter blank.

Fortunately, Melville seemed more than able to carry the conversation.

"Where are you ladies traveling today?" he asked politely.

"Bath," Margaret supplied. "We are removing there for the remainder of my cousin's mourning."

"Oh, of course—I ought to express my sympathies," Melville said.

Eliza was not yet sure how to respond to such condolences. To make a parade of loss, when her grief so differed from society's expectation, felt crass—and yet to make no display at all would be considered unseemly.

"Thank you," Eliza said after a pause. "And where are you bound, my lord?"

"Oh, hither and thither," he said. "Today, of course, it has been more thither than I should like—you are an artist, then, my lady?"

Eliza did not immediately comprehend the change in subject, until she followed the direction of his gaze to her portfolio.

"I should not describe myself in such lofty terms," she said.

"Whyever not?" he said. "You clearly have talent."

"However do you suppose that?" Eliza asked, surprised.

"The book was open," Melville said. "I could not help but see. You capture the likeness of . . . ?"

He paused, a questioning lilt in his voice, and Eliza realized with a jolt of mortification that they had not introduced themselves.

"My apologies!" she said, her cheeks reddening. "I am Lady Somerset, and this is my cousin, Miss Balfour."

Melville inclined his head.

"You capture Miss Balfour's likeness very well," he said.

Eliza did not know what to say to this, so opted instead to change the subject.

"We admire your poetry very much, my lord," she said.

It must be the thousandth time he had been told such a thing, but Eliza was not literary enough to think up a more insightful compliment.

"How marvelous of you to say so," Melville said courteously.

"We are most impatient to read your new work," Margaret added, a cajoling note in her voice. "Do you know when . . . ?"

Melville had published *Persephone* in '17 and *Psyche* in '18—both romantic retellings of ancient texts—and all were on tenterhooks for his next publication.

"It appears your flattery was simply a ploy to incite me into a revelation," Melville said. "I am afraid my answer will not please you: I have not written anything new."

"Why not?" Eliza asked before she could prevent herself—an impertinence she immediately regretted, for Melville's brow was now raised.

"Inspiration eludes me," he said briefly.

"Perhaps you might be inspired by today's adventure," Margaret suggested slyly. "And we will find that your next volume begins with a carriage crash—or a chariot crash, I suppose."

Eliza shot Margaret a remonstrative look. Could she not see that Melville wished the conversation at an end? But Melville appeared more comfortable with Margaret's line of questioning than Eliza's.

"Oh, even a chariot crash should be too pedestrian for my heroines," he said, amused. "Perhaps after the chariot crash they might be rescued from a murderous mob by an erstwhile warrior? If my fair lady will forgive the artistic license?"

He looked toward Eliza, lips curled and eyebrows raised in playful inquiry. Eliza stared. Was he flirting with her? Surely not. Regardless, he seemed to expect a reply, waiting expectantly as if he thought Eliza about to pull a suitably amusing, or coy—or even interesting—remark out of thin air, but alas . . .

"I am not fair," she said.

"So you are not," Melville agreed. "Though you will forgive me for not being able to tell, under such—ah—magnificent headwear."

He gestured toward Eliza's hat. Beneath it, she flushed, feeling dowdier than ever.

A thump on the roof of the carriage had them all look-ing up.

"It appears we are drawing into Peaseton," Melville said.

"You have our thanks for the aid," Eliza said, in a conclud-ing sort of way.

"Oh, you shan't be rid of me so easily, my lady," Melville said. "I shall escort you inside to see you settled, while your man sees about this wheelwright."

They drew to a final stop and Melville made as if to leap out.

"No, no," Eliza said hastily, for as much as she truly had appreciated the rescue, she still did not think it wise that they be glimpsed by the whole village in the company of an unmar-ried man—and certainly not one with such a storied repu-tation.

"No, we shall not delay you any longer. We are perfectly capable of arranging matters ourselves," she said.

Melville looked consideringly at Eliza for a moment.

"Very well," he said, leaning back in his seat. "If that is what you would prefer."

Margaret opened the door, and a postboy sprang forward to assist them down.

"I hope," Eliza added, as Margaret and Pardle climbed down from the carriage, "I hope we may count upon your . . . discretion regarding today's events."

Melville's eyebrows flew upward again.

"Do you think me likely to gossip?" he asked gently and Eliza felt abruptly sure she had offended him, now.

"N-no—it is just that," Eliza stammered.

"I assure you, my lady," he said. "If I am to appear in the gossip rags this week, it shall not be for so dull a reason as this."

Eliza's face flushed at the edge in his tone and she hurriedly accepted the postboy's arm. Melville pulled the door shut behind her.

"Good day," he said out of the window. "And safe travels."

His driver set the horses off, before Eliza could respond.

"Goodness," she said, feeling stunned.

"I shall write to my sister as soon as we arrive in Bath," Margaret said, gleeful. "And you ought to write to Lady Selwyn—doesn't she fancy herself a patron of the arts? She will be positively *green* with jealously."

"I will certainly not be writing to Lady Selwyn!" Eliza exclaimed, coming back to herself and turning toward the inn. "We ought not tell *anyone*. Recollect the conditions of my fortune, Margaret, and his shocking character: my reputation is not a currency we can afford to spend."

"What is the point of exciting events occurring to one, if one cannot boast about it?" Margaret grumbled.

A warming fire, an excellent repast and the news that the carriage would be repaired in only a matter of hours did much to alleviate Eliza's unsettled nerves, and they arrived in Bath only a few hours delayed. As it was by this point dusk, they could not see much of the city as they drew through its streets, but as Eliza walked into the terraced house on Camden Place, their new home, she was overcome by relief. Perkins had selected lodgings that were so exactly suited to Eliza's tastes that she could almost believe they had been built and furnished exactly for her use: with a dining room, drawing room, parlor, three bedchambers and servants quarters set across four floors, the house was comfortably elegant, light and airy, and as far from the austere grandeur of Harefield as was possible.

"Everything is quite perfect, Perkins," she said, inhaling

the delicate fumes of a perfectly brewed cup of tea. Perkins, never one for grandiose displays of emotion, inclined his head.

"Will there be anything else?" he asked.

"No, thank you," Eliza said. Then, impulsively, she added, "Except—could the fires be lit? All of them?"

Eliza had had enough of the cold.

4

The *ton* no longer considered Bath quite as modish a resort as it had the century prior, and in recent years the city had become patronized more by the elderly, the unwell and the shabby genteel than the wealthy and the fashionable. To Eliza, however, it was quite the most splendid city she had ever seen. The whole town seemed to have been designed with elegance in mind: its grand amphitheatric crescents and beautifully spacious squares were all constructed in the same pale stone that, on a bright day, refreshed the eye with its shine. Surrounded by the lofty hills of the Claverton, the countryside was close enough that the air remained sweet, while the town itself was generously endowed with gardens, shops, libraries, and two impressive Assembly Rooms. It was a city that presented, in short, a breathtaking array of possibility for two women who were, for the very first moment in their lives, wholly in charge of their own time.

They eased their way quietly into Bath society that first week, and while Eliza wrote both her and Margaret's name in the subscription books of the Lower and the New Assembly Rooms, it was more out of courtesy to the Masters of Ceremonies than out of any real intention of availing themselves greatly of their entertainments. With Eliza almost ten months into her mourning, the strictest days of her seclusion—when she had to avoid all public society in its entirety—were already behind her, but the Countess of Somerset's arrival into town in full widow's regalia was still unusual enough to attract attention. With so many eyes upon her, she needed to remain above censure: Eliza could visit the Pump Room, peruse the shops of Milsom Street, quietly attend a concert or two and even host a few, very select, dinners—but until a year and a day had passed since the earl's death she could not attend large parties, or assemblies, nor display herself in too public a setting. Dancing, of course, was strictly forbidden for another whole six months after *that*. Mourning, for a lady of the first consideration, was a serious business.

With propriety at the forefront of their minds, therefore, Eliza and Margaret were conscious of conveying, as much as the reserve of good manners allowed, both Eliza's sorrow and frailty on their first excursions into Bath society. In this quest, Margaret's quick mind and silver tongue proved indispensable, for while deception threw Eliza into quagmires of uncertainty, Margaret had no issue embellishing the truth beyond recognition.

"The shock has rendered her weak," Margaret said in a hushed undertone to Lady Hurley, Bath's most glamorous dowager, on their first visit to the Pump Room, while Eliza—heavily veiled—choked down a glassful of Bath's famously healing (and foul-tasting) mineral waters.

"The doctor suggested an acute fluralgia," she explained to both Masters of Ceremonies when they had each paid a call of ceremony to welcome the ladies to Bath.

"What is fluralgia?" Eliza asked Margaret, once they were alone.

"I haven't the faintest idea," Margaret said cheerfully. "But it sounded good, did it not?"

By the time Mr. Walcot, the Somerset lawyer, paid them a

visit on the third day, Margaret had become so adept at explicating Eliza's emotional and physical delicacy, that he looked quite about to think Eliza on death's doorstep.

"Are you quite sure you are well enough, my lady, to manage your own affairs?" he asked, face alarmed. "I had thought your father . . ."

"Oh, I am feeling much improved already," Eliza hastened to say. Mr. Balfour would undoubtedly be better positioned to oversee her lands, for he had all the experience and knowledge that she lacked, but . . . But it was the first time that Eliza had ever truly owned property by herself and she found that she did not want to give it away in any capacity just yet. "If you will be so kind as to recommend me a land steward, and assist me with a few questions . . . ?"

She trailed off, flushing.

"I am already serving the new Lord Somerset in much the same manner," Mr. Walcot said reluctantly. "And there will be a great deal to learn, my lady. Are you sure you feel equal to such a task?"

Eliza gave Mr. Walcot a strained smile.

"I believe so," she said, trying to sound firm.

"If you are sure . . ." Mr. Walcot appeared unconvinced. "The new earl would be a safe pair of hands to count upon, if you ever find yourself worried, and I do wonder that he did not mention your arrival in his last letter," Mr. Walcot mused. "I should have called much sooner, had I known—but I'm sure his lordship had his reasons!"

That was certainly true, chief among them being that Eliza had still not written to him; her avoidance of the task was approaching the chronic.

"It is possible that my letter had not yet reached him," she lied. "Our visit was only recently decided upon . . ."

"Due to the fluralgia," Margaret put in helpfully. Mr. Walcot's worried frown reappeared, and throughout the rest of the visit Eliza was at pains to convey the precise balance of "capable but grief-stricken" that would most effectively reassure him.

Under the cloak of grief, Eliza and Margaret's first days in Bath were full, expensive, and thrilling. They made a complete exploration of all the Milsom Street shops: sampled scents at the *parfumerie*; feasted their eyes on the diamonds in Basnett the jeweler's and lingered over the shelves of Meyler's library. Here, they overheard a gaggle of twittering young ladies begging the harassed attendant for Lord Melville's next volume of poetry.

"I read in the paper that it ought to have been published by now!" one lady declared in the face of the attendant's denial.

"What would they say if they knew we had actually met him?" Margaret whispered in Eliza's ear.

"Don't!" Eliza said firmly and Margaret rolled her eyes.

A few doors down was Mr. Fasana's Repository of Arts, whose shelves were full to the brim of beautiful materials— easels, palettes, paintbrushes from the width of a pin to a branch and boxes of watercolors in shades Eliza could not name—and whose shop assistants were so knowledgeable that Eliza became a little overwhelmed. She wanted to purchase half of the shop, but as this would certainly raise eyebrows, she settled merely upon an array of pencils, a box of watercolors and a volume entitled *The Art of Painting* that she could remember her grandfather owning.

"Do you . . . do you mix oils here, too?" she asked shyly at the counter. Her grandfather had mixed his own colors—a laborious process that involved grinding the natural pigments and combining them with various media to achieve the desired consistency—but oils could be bought directly from merchants, or colormen, too.

Mr. Fasana, who had been roused from the back room to serve the lofty customer, appeared surprised at the request. It was common for a lady to partake in watercolors, but oils were a medium rarely used by amateurs, due to the mess they incurred and the skill necessary to use them correctly. "I can certainly do so, though may I suggest that a set of pastels might serve better for her ladyship's use?"

"Oh . . . yes," Eliza said, wilting under Mr. Fasana's disbelief, and the curious eyes of the other patrons. And, really, would not pastels do just as well? "Yes, thank you."

Last was their trip to the modiste. Eliza and Margaret were both well used to visiting milliners: displaying oneself in an array of ever-changing gowns was a key tenet of any lady of quality's life. Until now, however, their wardrobes had been ruled by the preferences of others: Eliza's by her husband's, who favored the old-fashioned style of gowns belonging to his generation, and Margaret's by her mother's, who believed that over-trimmed gowns in infantile pastels would gift Margaret eternal youth.

"I have resembled a trussed-up, over-puffed pie for years," Margaret said loudly, entering Madame Prevette's shop, and such was the state of their *toilette* that Madame Prevette clucked her tongue in agreement. In the blink of an eye, she had Eliza and Margaret standing upon dressing platforms in the back room, presenting fashion plates before them while her assistants flurried around them with yards of silk, crêpe and bombazine in every color imaginable, as if Eliza and Margaret were the center of a particularly fashionable hurricane.

They ran their hands over lace, muslin, cotton, gauze, and, under Madame Prevette's beady, discerning eye, chose dresses for every occasion imaginable. Eliza, of course, must dress only in black until April, but to Madame Prevette—who had first fled to England in the wake of the revolution—this was the most trifling of challenges and much instead was made of the style and cut of each gown: figured and embroidered and flounced to add interest where color would normally serve. Margaret, only distantly related to the earl through marriage, was long out of her mourning clothes, and so was measured for morning dresses in blue and green, evening dresses of deepest purple and walking habits in severe, military shapes—all with hats and shawls and gloves to match.

"I can have the first dresses ready in a week," Madame Prevette promised Eliza, when they had finally declared themselves finished, which was generously quick indeed and Eliza beamed her thanks. Looking around for Margaret, she saw her stroking a hand avariciously over a thick sable.

"Would you like it?" Eliza asked. The bill was already long and large.

"It is very dear," Margaret said, which was not a denial. Eliza checked the price and felt her eyebrows rise of their own accord. An indecent expense, her husband would have said. But he wasn't here. And it was for Eliza to decide, now, what expenses were worthwhile.

"We'll have two," Eliza said.

"They do say money cannot buy happiness," Margaret said, unable to hide her wide, delighted grin as they left, their new footman following behind, laden with boxes.

"A theory I mean to test," Eliza promised.

True to her word, Madame Prevette sent over the first box of dresses within a week, and so, by the second Wednesday after their arrival, Eliza and Margaret were finally ready for their first outing to a concert at the New Assembly Rooms— which they deemed perfectly proper as long as Eliza arrived unobtrusively, sat quietly during the interval, and left immediately afterward. Truthfully, even if it had not been perfectly proper, once Eliza had caught sight of her and Margaret's reflections in their new evening gowns she would have been tempted to attend anyway.

Rationally, of course, Eliza knew that the application of a new gown, however modish, could not have altered her appearance so radically. And yet . . . Seeing herself in the robe of black crêpe, ornamented with black velvet trimming at the hems, Eliza felt herself transformed: no longer a dowdy dowager hidden in a superabundance of black bombazine, but someone rather elegant. Under the gown's effects, she could notice too that her face had become less gaunt over the past weeks, her hair thicker, that the dark circles under her eyes had faded in prominence to now appear more piquant than frightened. In some indescribable way it was as if her whole being was taking its cue from the superior gown, standing taller, straighter and lighting up in a way she had not in years.

It might be a ridiculous power to afford gowns and hair and ribbons, but watching Margaret, who Eliza had never known to express even a passing satisfaction in her appearance, staring at herself in the mirror, eyes wide and vulnerable and so tentatively pleased with her reflection that Eliza thought her heart might break with tenderness, it did not feel ridiculous. The sea-green crêpe gown, short-sleeved, worn low on the shoulders, and trimmed only with a simple ribbon around the bodice, contrasted brilliantly against Margaret's red hair and pale, freckled skin, and became her tall figure to admiration.

"It almost feels too good to be true," Eliza said, with a sweep of her arm that she meant to encompass the dresses, the house, and the entirety of their new lifestyle. "Do you feel that way, too?"

Margaret snorted, her reverie with the mirror broken.

"Perhaps I might, if it were not for the constant letters from our mothers," she said. "Or if it were not for the Winkworths."

The Winkworths were their neighbors upon Camden Place: Mrs. Winkworth, a relentless social climber, her husband,

Admiral Winkworth, a surly gentleman with no discernible qualities, and their daughter, Miss Winkworth, the most silent young lady Eliza had ever encountered. Margaret had taken an immediate and violent dislike to them all.

"Mrs. Winkworth is one of the leaders of Bath society, we ought to make a little effort with her," Eliza reminded Margaret.

"I abhor effort," Margaret said darkly.

Wrapped in thick cloaks, they set out with only Staves the footman as escort. The hills of Bath made equestrian traffic difficult and therefore rare, but since most destinations were easily accessible on foot this caused no issue unless the day was wet, in which case one could procure a sedan chair or hackney cab. The New Assembly Rooms, situated in the recently built upper town, were a very grand set of buildings, boasting a hundred-foot-long ballroom, concert room and card room, all furnished extravagantly and lit with crystal chandeliers hanging from the lofty ceilings. Eliza gazed about with interest as they entered, for she had heard that portraits by Gainsborough and Hoare hung on the walls, but they had only taken a step inside when they found themselves hailed and turned to find the whole Winkworth family bearing down upon them. They were all distinctly ovine in appearance: Mrs. Winkworth a handsome sheep, Miss Winkworth a delicate lamb, and Admiral Winkworth a goat without any of the charisma.

"Good evening, Mrs. Winkworth," Eliza said, hiding her dismay under enthusiasm.

"You ought to have said you were attending tonight's performance!" Mrs. Winkworth chided. "We would have escorted you!"

Precisely why Eliza had not mentioned it.

"My apologies," Eliza said.

"Come, you must join our party—we are gathering in the

Octagon Room," Mrs. Winkworth said, beckoning them. Margaret stepped meaningfully on Eliza's foot.

"Actually, I think we ought to sit . . ." Eliza tried. It might not be wise to alienate Mrs. Winkworth, but neither would her set be Eliza's first choice of friends in Bath.

"I was very much hoping to make some introductions," Mrs. Winkworth said, a steeliness in her honeyed tones that so strongly reminded Eliza of Mrs. Balfour that she immediately capitulated and followed her into the Octagon Room where they were engulfed by the hum of many voices, the rustle of many skirts, and the sparkle of many jewels. Eliza sucked in a deep, steadying breath. One would have thought her tenure as Countess of Somerset, with all the hunting parties hosted at Harefield Hall, would have inured her to such nerves, but she had felt so vastly out of her depth amongst all the high-ranking peers the old earl had counted as friends, that the experience had detracted rather than added to her social confidence.

"Lady Somerset, Miss Balfour, may I introduce to you some of my dearest friends . . . ?"

As Mrs. Winkworth made the introductions around the group—each curtseying or bowing deeply to Eliza in turn—she skillfully contrived, without exactly lying, to give the impression that she and Eliza were far better acquainted than they truly were, perhaps desirous of using the borrowed glory of Eliza's title to boost her own social standing. Eliza, meanwhile, could only try to remember each name—Mr. Broadwater with the spectacles, Mrs. Michels with the enormous turban—and concentrate on not twisting her hands in nervousness.

"And this is Mr. Berwick, our celebrated artist . . ."

Eliza swung her eyes over to this gentleman, interest unfeigned.

"Oh, Mrs. Winkworth, you should not flatter me so," he said, with unconvincing humility and a bow to Eliza. "You are almost worse than Mr. Benjamin West—the President of the Royal Academy, you know, Lady Somerset—he sings my praises at every opportunity, to my mortification."

Under Mr. Berwick's bumptious speech, Eliza's interest wilted.

"May I express my very great sorrow for your loss, my lady," Mr. Berwick went on. "Though we artists are all true empaths, I still cannot imagine how you are feeling."

Eliza certainly hoped not.

"It has been a very trying time," she lied.

There were murmurs of sympathy around the group.

"If a little distraction would be beneficial," Mr. Berwick said. "I would be honored to have you sit for a portrait. Madame Catalani is sitting for me at the moment, but yours would be an even higher privilege. A haunting elegy to a widow's grief . . ."

He gazed into the distance as if to imagine it.

"I hardly think that would be proper, Mr. Berwick—" Mrs. Winkworth began crossly.

"Darling Lady Somerset, Miss Balfour, you both look divine!" Lady Hurley arrived just in time to interrupt Mrs. Winkworth mid-flow. She squeezed Eliza's arm in welcome, an intimacy that she, being a lady herself, felt comfortable indulging in though they had only met thrice, while Mrs. Winkworth looked on jealously.

"Your earrings are very fine," Margaret said. Lady Hurley—dressed today in a gown of ruby velvet, superbly ornamented with silver trimming—was a handsome dowager of indiscriminate age, lively humor and truly magnificent bosom.

"Oh, these old things? A gift from my late husband," Lady Hurley dismissed the nutmeg-sized diamonds with a graceful wave of her hand. "I must say, it is so lovely to see the rooms filled out at last."

"Splendid!" Mr. Fletcher agreed heartily. Lady Hurley's junior in age by at least ten years, the handsome Mr. Fletcher was nonetheless her loyal gallant, escorting her everywhere with utter devotion.

"Bath was almost at risk of feeling a little flat, do you not think?" Lady Hurley said to no one in particular.

"I cannot agree," Mrs. Winkworth said sharply. "As Camden Place is full year-round, we never feel deprived of company. Though I imagine it *might* feel a little flat on Laura Place, Lady Hurley. Has number four been let yet? It must have been a year since its last residents."

Even in the fortnight since their arrival, Eliza had witnessed a dozen such unsubtle jibes—Lady Hurley's late husband had picked up his title in the city, and Mrs. Winkworth's disdain of such commercial roots was well-known, but Lady Hurley only smiled.

"You will be pleased, then, to hear number four has indeed been rented just this week," she said. "Do you know Lord Melville? He and his sister, Lady Caroline, have rented the house for three months."

Mrs. Winkworth looked as though an artichoke had been thrust unexpectedly down her throat, Mrs. Michels's eyes expanded, and Mr. Broadwater made a shocked harrumph. Eliza and Margaret exchanged disbelieving glances. Since their arrival in Bath, their days had been so full that they had not had time to consider Melville a great deal and, as their bruises had long faded, the crash upon the Bath Road had assumed the quality of a dream. Melville turning up in Bath, of all places, seemed highly unlikely, and from the questions being pelted at Lady Hurley, they were not alone in this surprise.

"Is it really true, Lady Hurley?"

"Three whole months?"

"Is he as charming as they say?"

"Oh, you know I am far too discreet to indulge in speculation," Lady Hurley said, oozing self-satisfaction. "Though you may ask them yourselves, for I invited them to join us, tonight—ah, here they are now!"

5

Lady Hurley could not have designed a more perfectly dramatic moment. As one, they all looked to the doorway just as the Melvilles appeared within it: Lord Melville, dressed tonight in a long-tailed coat, knee breeches and silk stockings, and beside him his sister, standing almost as tall as he and exquisitely gowned in a gossamer satin dress of a celestial blue that shone beautifully against her brown skin. Lady Hurley beckoned to them with one heavily bejeweled hand, and as they walked languorously over, more heads began to turn and crane in their direction. From the excited murmurs and whispers that began filling the room, they had been recognized.

"Oh. My. *Goodness*," Margaret breathed from beside Eliza, speaking each word as if it were a separate sentence.

"Good evening, my lord, my lady," Lady Hurley said in loud, smug welcome. "I am so pleased you have come!"

"It is our pleasure," Lady Caroline said, in a low and musical voice. "I became acquainted with Madame Catalani in Rome last year—I am looking forward to hearing her perform again."

The tripartite power of Lady Caroline's literary reputation, her alluring air of fashion, and the reference to European travel proved immediately irresistible to Margaret, who opened her mouth eagerly, and stepped a little forward as if to immediately engage Lady Caroline in conversation—until Eliza laid a cautionary hand upon her arm. They had not yet been formally introduced.

"May I introduce you to my very dear friend, Lady Somerset?" Lady Hurley said, and Eliza forced herself to remain calm. Melville would surely recollect her request for his discretion at their last meeting—but as he turned and their eyes met, Eliza gave him a look of great meaning just in case. Melville raised his eyebrows, a faint smile at his lips.

"Lady Somerset," he said. "We meet again."

Oh, lord.

"You are already acquainted?" Lady Hurley asked immediately. "How so? Lady Somerset, I did not think you had visited London in many years."

"Would you like to tell the tale, or shall I?" Melville asked, a glint of mischief in his eyes. Eliza's heart began to gallop. "It is most amusing."

"We met very briefly many years ago, at a—a ball," Eliza blurted out, before Melville could utter another word.

"That does not sound very amusing," Lady Caroline said.

"Surely that cannot be the whole story," Lady Hurley agreed, with an intrigued flutter of her fan.

Eliza felt as if she were standing under a very bright light and tried desperately to think of a response to the question that would satisfy their curiosity, leave her reputation blemishless, and avoid insulting Melville all at once—but no such magical answer presented itself to her. Fortunately, just at that moment they were interrupted by the Master of Ceremonies, who indicated it was time to be seated.

"Shall we lead the way, Lady Somerset?" Melville said, with a flourish of his hand.

After a beat of hesitation, Eliza took it.

"I do not consider myself a forgettable man," Melville said, as they made their way to the concert room. "Perhaps you so frequently find yourself in carriage crashes that my memory has faded into insignificance?"

"I—I do not—it h-has not," Eliza stammered out. "It is just that—I should not particularly like the—the circumstances of our meeting to become public knowledge. Their being so particularly unusual, you understand, they would easily become gossip fodder. R-recollect I did mention the need for discretion, on the day in question!"

This last remark was said a little defensively, and Melville smiled.

"So you did," he agreed, escorting her toward the front rows of chairs rather than the retired location Eliza had planned. "My lamentable memory. May I compliment you upon your charming *toilette*, this evening?"

"Oh—yes," Eliza said, startled. "Yes, I suppose you may."

"I think it a great improvement that I can now see your face," Melville said. "It suits you."

"My face . . . suits me?" Eliza repeated slowly.

"Fortuitous, is it not?" Melville said.

Fleetingly, Eliza wondered if Melville were flirting with her before dismissing it immediately as improbable. Melville's flirts were usually found amongst the most dashing and charismatic ladies of the *ton*—Lady Oxford and Lady Melbourne, if gossip were to be believed—which Eliza most certainly was not.

As the rest of the audience filed in behind them, their row was the recipient of eager glances and craning necks, though as Melville did not appear perturbed, Eliza assumed he must be well used to such notice: the Melvilles, born to both Indian and British nobility, had been a source of national fascination since they were born.

Even as Madame Catalani appeared, the audience's attention seemed terminally divided—staring just as much to their row as the stage—until the moment the soprano began to sing, when her voice, so clear, so pure, so heavy with emotion, enraptured them all.

"Do you understand Italian?" Melville leaned toward Eliza so he could whisper close to her ear.

"No," Eliza admitted.

"Nor I," he said. "Of what do you think she sings?"

"I do not know," Eliza said limply, though this was not true. Catalani invested each note with such meaning, such sorrow, that Eliza did not need to understand the words to know of what emotion she was singing: heartbreak. One could not hear her without being reminded of times of such melancholy within one's own life and Eliza's mind went, inexorably, to Somerset, before she forced the thoughts away.

Too soon for Eliza's liking, it was the interval, and so distracted had Eliza been by the glorious music that she only remembered her intention to remain piously seated once she was already in the tearoom, and Lady Hurley had concluded the rest of her introductions. Fortunately, it seemed the mystery of how Eliza and Melville had met had been discarded in favor of a new line of interrogation.

"How long have you been in Bath?" Mrs. Winkworth had the first volley.

"A day," Lady Caroline said.

"And a half!" Lady Hurley interjected.

"Yes, you ought not overlook the half, Caroline," Melville chastised.

"And is this your first visit to our town?" Mr. Berwick asked.

"Oh no," Lady Caroline said. "I once spent a whole month here in my girlhood, on a whim from my mother to see me formally schooled."

"Oh, the Bath Seminary for Young Ladies?" Mrs. Michels asked. "Miss Winkworth, were you not educated there?"

"Yes, she was," Mrs. Winkworth said, speaking for her daughter as if she were a child.

"Why only a month? You did not care for it?" Admiral Winkworth said, moustache bristling in anticipatory offense.

"Rather, *it* did not care for *me*," Lady Caroline said, with an eloquent and elegant shrug of one shoulder. "But as I already knew everything in French a woman ought to know, my mother allowed me to withdraw."

Eliza badly wanted to ask exactly which French phrases in particular Lady Caroline thought essential, but refrained; whatever the answer, it would surely only end in Mrs. Winkworth clapping her hands over her daughter's ears.

"And are you pleased with Bath, on your second visit?" Margaret asked her, eagerly joining the fray.

"In so much as one can be, in only a day," Lady Caroline said coolly.

"And a *half*, Caroline," Melville corrected. "That is twice now you have neglected the half."

"How long do you plan to stay?" Margaret asked.

"Oh, only as long as we are welcome," Melville said.

"Careful, my lord," Lady Hurley said, with a flirtatious sweep of her fan. "If that is your only condition, you may find yourself staying here a very long while indeed."

"Would that be such a terrible fate?" Melville said, leaning in closer than was customarily considered appropriate. "Now that I have seen Bath's diamonds for myself, I am in no great hurry to leave."

Lady Hurley glowed at the attention. Beside her, Mr. Fletcher had puffed up like a disturbed pigeon, and beside *him*, Mrs. Winkworth was fanning herself with such aggression that she looked almost about to take flight. The scene was so delightfully ridiculous that Eliza tried consciously to etch every detail into her memory, so that she might attempt to capture it when she returned home. Pencil and watercolor, it would have to be, to convey the intricacies of expression.

"Do you mean to write while you are here, my lord?" Mrs. Michels asked.

"I do not," Melville said, and seemingly unruffled by the sea of enquiring eyes, took a snuffbox from his pocket and offered it to the person next to him—Miss Winkworth, who blushed as rosily as if it had been a ring box and hid behind her hair.

"You must put an end to our misery," Lady Hurley said. "When can we expect you next to publish?"

"We have come to Bath for a rest," Lady Caroline said.

"Well deserved, I am sure," Mr. Berwick interjected, "for *I* hear your industry has otherwise known no bounds, my lord— from Lord Paulet, in whom I believe we share a mutual friend."

"Indeed?" Melville said, the tiniest of frowns appearing between his eyebrows.

"I credit his patronage entirely for my acceptance into the Royal Academy," Mr. Berwick said eagerly. "I was very grateful that my dear friends Mr. Turner and Mr. Hazlitt saw to introduce us."

Melville appeared to regard the floor in some astonishment.

"Do be careful where you step, Caro," he said. "There are a great many names upon the floor."

At this, Eliza could not help letting out the tiniest choke of laughter—hearing it, Melville threw her a surreptitious wink. He *was* flirting with her—a wink was, after all, the most flirtatious act an eye could perform. Well. This was—this was highly inappropriate. Eliza was a widow in her first year of mourning, and Melville ought to know better. Clearly his libertine reputation was well-earned! But the outrage did not sound convincing even in the privacy of Eliza's own mind. It had been such a long time since Eliza had received any such regard from a gentleman—and certainly never from one as sought-after as Melville—she could not help but feel warmed.

"I believe we are to take our seats again," Mr. Broadwater said gruffly.

As Eliza took her seat, this time seated a little away from Melville, she could not help but glance at him sidelong; one could not deny he *was* very handsome, with such elegance of carriage, too!—but when she found her gaze caught and returned by the amused gentleman, she looked quickly away.

The performance finished to a general murmur of applause and cheer and Madame Catalani unbent to mingle with the audience members afterward, attaching herself immediately to Melville's side and engaging him in animated conversation that necessitated the frequent touch of her hand upon his arm. Eliza and Margaret, however, could not linger—they had stretched the bounds of appropriate behavior as far as they could and made instead straight for the cloakroom.

"Thunder an' turf!" Margaret declared improperly as their cloaks were being retrieved for them. Eliza empathized entirely. Their fortnight in Bath had felt more variegated and interesting than their entire lives up until this point, but the addition of the Melvilles to the city . . . It was as if an already delicious wine had been rendered abruptly sparkling, and as much as Melville's flirtatiousness ought to concern one whose entire life rested upon pristine behavior, she, too, was brimming with excitement.

"Later," Eliza promised. They would stoke the fire and ask Perkins for tea and discuss *everything*. But it took such a long while for their cloaks to be located that by the time they exited the building—Staves the footman striding ahead to hail a cab—they found that the Melvilles had overtaken them. They were standing on the cobbled street just ahead, Lady Caroline fiddling with the clasp to her cloak and Melville bouncing impatiently upon the balls of his feet.

"Let us bid them goodnight," Margaret whispered, making as if to walk forward, but before she could say anything, Melville's voice rang out.

"Do hurry up, Caroline," he said. "I wish an end to this tedious night. Never in my life have I endured such insipid company. I cannot comprehend how we are to survive here."

"There is less than an ounce of spirit amongst them," Lady Caroline agreed. "Let us hope for a swift return to London."

"Hope and pray," Melville agreed. "Lord save us from bumpkins, spinsters and widows—bores, the lot of them!"

Lady Caroline laughed, and then, clasping his arm, they walked off into the night.

"Oh," Margaret said, her voice small.

Eliza's face was burning. They stood there, blankly staring after the Melvilles.

"I suppose," Margaret said—and there was no excitement in her voice anymore, "I suppose we are dull in comparison to their usual set."

"We are *not* dull," Eliza said, trying to control the wobbling corners of her mouth. "A-and we would not deserve such disrespect, even if we were."

She felt hot and cross and as if she might weep, all at once. She climbed rigidly up into the carriage when it arrived, and clasped her hands tightly, holding herself together as best she could.

It was hardly the first time she had not been liked. On the contrary, a lifetime of slights and snubs meant that she usually navigated the world in expectation of such censure, but she had not expected it tonight. She had not expected it from him. Eliza's face was scarlet with mortification. She could not believe that such a short time before she had been so thrilled to receive the flattery of his attention, when all the while, that was what he was truly thinking. She was a fool.

By unspoken agreement, Eliza and Margaret took straight

to their bedchambers when they arrived home. There was no longer any pleasure to be had in discussing the evening, but neither did sleep appear at all likely. After Eliza had been helped to undress by Pardle, she sat motionless upon her bed, the Melvilles' words repeating in her mind like a children's rhyme being sung in the round: boring, insipid, spiritless. The insults might have hurt less, had Eliza been sure they were untrue. But as it was . . . "Obedient and dutiful," her husband had called her in the will; "incapable of causing a raised eyebrow," Somerset had deemed her at the reading; and now, after only two encounters, Melville seemed to think just as little of her. Eliza had thought, by coming to Bath instead of Balfour, that she had proved her bravery, but that was not true, was it? For it had been Margaret's courage, and not hers, that had led them here. And since they had arrived, had not Eliza been quite as much ruled by the opinions and wills of others as ever?

The sensible course of action to take, when one is feeling particularly worthless, is to try to cheer oneself up with happier thoughts and distractions. In that moment, however, Eliza was tempted instead by the more compelling idea of making herself feel a great deal worse.

Standing, she walked over to the writing desk that stood in the corner of her bedchamber and opened a drawer to extract the small wooden box that she had carefully placed inside weeks before. She placed the box on the table and sat down before it.

Eliza ought to have burned the contents a long time ago. Instead, she had smuggled it into Harefield at seventeen, and ten years later brought it to Bath. Perhaps the collection inside went some way to explaining why the flames of Eliza's affection for Somerset still flickered on even now—for whenever his memory risked growing faint, she could open this box, and be reminded of how terribly in love they once were.

On the top of the pile of papers that lay inside the box was a portrait. It was not Eliza's best work, just a pencil sketch of Somerset's face and torso, drawn from memory rather than in person, and it lacked detail and precision as a result. But even so, one could tell, just from a glance, that the artist had loved the subject. Eliza's grandfather always had said that Eliza drew as much with her heart as she did with her hands and it was there, plain as day, in the careful strokes of the pencil, the effort that had been invested in capturing every detail of his eyes . . . Their expression—well, the expression was everything. The soft way the sketch-Somerset was regarding her, as if she were something infinitely precious—exactly how he had used to look at her, before . . .

Eliza lifted the portrait out and placed it gently to the side. Underneath lay the letters, wearing thin and yellow from age. The ink had grown fainter with each year that passed, but Eliza did not need to be able to read the words. She could tell their story from handwriting alone: at the beginning, his script was neat and precise, on the notes that had accompanied the flowers he had sent her after their first meeting. Theirs had been as traditional a courtship as could be, and she had the dance cards, all littered with his name, to prove it. They met at one ball, danced at another, they spoke and flirted at garden parties and card parties and excursions to the races and in a matter of weeks they were penning each other sheets and sheets of heartfelt confessions in handwriting that was quicker, closer, more urgent—until the very last letter in the box, that ended with words that Eliza had traced with her finger more times than she could count. *The depth of my regard for you is such that I am driven to action. Tomorrow I shall pay a visit to your father.*

It was the last item in the box. One could almost fool oneself into thinking that was how the tale ended. A father's permission sought, granted, the question asked, and answered.

Marriage. Children. Happiness. But it had not happened that way. And the fact that their last, bitter words to one another had been spoken, rather than written, did not make them any less true.

"You must tell them you will not, Eliza," he had urged her, face as white as the moon above. "You must tell them you have a prior attachment."

"I have tried," she had whispered, voice choked. "They will not listen."

"Then *make* them listen!" he implored. "They cannot force you into accepting his suit!"

"I cannot defy them, you must see that," she had begged, trying to hold onto his hands even as he pulled them away. "The things such a match would do for my family—I cannot go against their wishes."

"My uncle, Eliza! You cannot—you surely cannot do this to me."

She had tried to make him understand—she thought she might die if he didn't understand—but he had not. All he could see was a weakness of character.

"You have no spirit," he had said, at last. "You have no spirit, Eliza."

Then, as now, the words had hurt because they felt true.

Eliza snapped the box shut. Enough. She could not allow herself to be haunted by Somerset's words any longer, and nor could she allow Melville's to ruin the life she and Margaret had been building here. And if she could not prove to either gentleman that she had spirit, then she could at least prove it to herself.

Eliza pulled out a fresh sheet of paper from a drawer. Perhaps her avoidance of writing to Somerset had been due to more than simply the awkwardness of such a correspondence. Perhaps she had known that it would feel so final, writing to him in such a formal manner, knowing he would respond in kind—knowing that she would be placing in the box a letter that proved, irrefutably, that their romantic relationship was truly and permanently at an end. But at an end it was. And she could not avoid that truth any longer. It was time to cease allowing events merely to occur to her, and to commence acting for herself.

Eliza dashed off a short note, wishing him well, informing him briefly of her decision to remain in Bath for the foreseeable future, and begging his pardon for the delay in her correspondence. This done, she folded the paper, waxed it closed, and wrote his address on the front. She would post it tomorrow. It was a small step, but it felt a good start. Eliza would not be spiritless anymore.

6

Eliza was not used to thinking of herself as a particularly angry person. She had felt anger, of course, and often, but it had always passed through her as a visiting emotion. Most of the time, there was no use remaining cross for long. Most of the time, one simply had to get on with it. It was to Eliza's considerable surprise, therefore, to find herself upon waking the next morning quite alight with rage. Sometime during her sleep her humiliation and sorrow and tentative feelings of resolution from the night before had mingled together in a curious alchemy to create an incandescent wrath she had never known before. How dare Melville say such a thing about her—about Margaret—when they had not done anything in the least to deserve it? How dare he try to ruin Bath for her, how dare he think himself so far above them, how *dare* he! The gall of the man was incomprehensible.

Wrathful indignation was oddly energizing. Eliza had no need, in fact, of the two fortifying cups of coffee at the breakfast table, though she availed herself of them all the same.

"Shall we remain at home today?" Margaret suggested morosely. "That wind looks awfully chilly."

Eliza and Margaret had, it appeared, traveled on radically different emotional journeys in the night, for Margaret looked distinctly downtrodden as she nibbled half-heartedly at a piece of toast.

"No!" Eliza declared. "We shall be going to Milsom Street as soon as you are finished."

They left Camden Place at a brisk trot that had Margaret grumbling and were the first customers of the day at Mr. Fasana's Repository of Arts.

"I should like to purchase some oils!" Eliza declared, as soon as they entered, startling the shop assistant half out of his skin. And when a harassed Mr. Fasana appeared, Eliza held onto her fury, which in some strange way seemed also to serve as a sort of emotional shield, and made a full order of oils in what felt close to every color under the sun, from vermilion and sepia, to Prussian blue and Indian yellow. Mr. Fasana promised delivery later that very day.

"Will that be all, my lady?" he asked.

"Yes," Eliza said. Then: "No."

And she proceeded to make such an order of such length— of easels and palettes, and a dozen squires of paper, and paintbrushes from the size of a pin to the size of a finger, jeweling pencils and bristle pencils, primed cloth, canvas and wooden panels that Mr. Fasana agreed to prepare for her—that Margaret commented, as they left the shop, that: "It might have been easier to inform Mr. Fasana what you *didn't* wish to purchase."

They went next to Duffield's library, where Eliza organized a subscription to the *Annals of the Fine Arts* magazine and borrowed every text on agriculture she could find.

"It cannot be so hard, to learn these things," she declared defiantly to Margaret, "whatever Mr. Walcot says!"

Then they stepped briefly into Madame Prevette's shop to place an order for two riding habits (they *would* keep a stable in town, for such a freedom would be worth a few raised eyebrows), before heading at last for the Pump Room.

"Tomorrow," Eliza decided, her walk even faster than it

had been on the outbound journey, "I might request from Mr. Fasana the name of a drawing master, for perhaps I will take up lessons again. Why should a woman's education cease after she is married? Would you like to take French lessons, Margaret? I know you have always wanted to, and we can more than afford the expense, now."

"Are you quite well?" Margaret asked. "You are looking swivel-eyed."

"I am very well," Eliza said. "I merely think it would behoove us to start pursuing our goals with a little *energy*, Margaret. I shall not be insipid any longer!"

"Ah," Margaret said. "I see what is happening."

"Lady Somerset!"

Eliza and Margaret turned to find themselves, for the second time in as many days, borne down upon by Mrs. and Miss Winkworth.

"Good day!" Mrs. Winkworth cried. "Are you bound for the Pump Room, as well? We shall join you."

"Wonderful," Margaret muttered under her breath, voice thick with sarcasm.

"Did you enjoy the concert last night, my lady?" Mrs. Winkworth asked Eliza. "It has not tired you out, has it? If I may say, you are looking a trifle fatigued."

No, you may not, Eliza thought testily.

"We enjoyed the concert very much," she said. "How did you find it?"

"Well," Mrs. Winkworth began with great emphasis, "I am not sure I think it wholly wise for Lady Hurley to have so encouraged these Melvilles. She cannot be aware of the family's reputation—Lady Hurley's husband acquired his title through trade, you know, so we cannot expect her to be well-versed in such intricacies."

Mrs. Winkworth made a great deal of her gentility in comparison to Lady Hurley's—that Admiral Winkworth's wealth had been accrued just as recently, from his time employed by the East India Company, she elected to overlook.

"The furor when the late earl chose such an . . . exotic lady to wife! I have never known its equal." Mrs. Winkworth paused, as if expecting Eliza or Margaret to beg her to continue. They did not. As much anger as Eliza felt toward Melville and Lady Caroline, she still did not want to hear such unpleasantness.

"And while I do so hate gossip," Mrs. Winkworth carried on in a lowered voice, "the whispers were that the late earl spent his time in India wearing the dress of a Musselman, attending *all* their festivals and goodness knows what else—"

"If the late Queen approved the match, I cannot think why anyone else should object," Eliza interrupted.

The Melvilles were distantly related to Queen Charlotte on her majesty's mother's line and her public friendship with the late Lady Melville had done much to smooth the lady's way into the *ton*.

"God rest her soul," Mrs. Winkworth said at once. Then, as if she couldn't help herself: "Whatever else, I do not believe that their reasons for visiting Bath can be as innocent as they maintain. And the London gossip will reach us eventually!"

Fortunately, conversation halted as they arrived at the Pump Room. A handsome building inside and out, with two ranges of large windows and a border of Corinthian columns, the Pump Room was where one could partake of Bath's famous healing waters, whether to bathe in them downstairs, or more commonly to imbibe them in the room above. However, its importance was social as much as medical, as residents and visitors alike gathered throughout the day to take a stroll about the room, meeting friends and surveying for any interesting newcomers.

For each of Eliza's visits thus far, the room had been pleasantly thrumming with people, with murmurs of chatter heard faintly over the violins that played every day from one o'clock, but today it was a veritable squeeze. And the reason for this change was all too apparent: holding court in the middle of the room were the Melvilles. Today, Lady Caroline was wearing a morning dress of green crêpe, its elegant simplicity making every other woman in the room look dreadfully overtrimmed by comparison, while the clinging fabric showed her fine figure off to perfection.

"And it appears we are to be seeing a great deal of Lady Caroline, in *every* sense," Mrs. Winkworth said cuttingly.

"I think she looks wonderful," Miss Winkworth said, so quietly that Eliza might not have heard her, had she not been standing so close. Unfortunately for Miss Winkworth, her mother heard her too.

"Her dress is indecent—and you ought not to admire it," Mrs. Winkworth told her daughter severely. "Do you want Lady Somerset to think you fast?"

Miss Winkworth looked up to Eliza with such big, frightened eyes that she might have been eight years rather than eighteen.

"I do not think her fast," Eliza said hastily. "I like Lady Caroline's dress, too."

"Good morning!" Lady Hurley and Mr. Fletcher had appeared behind them, followed within moments by Mrs. Michels and Mr. Broadwater. "What wonderful sunshine!"

"Splendid!" Mr. Fletcher agreed. In Eliza's brief acquaintance with the gentleman, it appeared that his opinions on all persons, situations and conversations could be split into three: "splendid," "not the thing" and, when the situation required, "damned if I know."

"Are you imbibing the waters, today, Lady Hurley?" Eliza asked.

"Yes indeed, Mr. Fletcher is about to fetch me a glass— would you like one?"

"Oh yes, if it is not too much trouble, Mr. Fletcher?" Eliza said. "Can you carry so many?"

"Damned if I know," Mr. Fletcher said, setting off with purpose, nonetheless.

"What language!" Mr. Broadwater said, disapproving. "In front of ladies, too."

"Oh, we don't mind," Lady Hurley said, taking a look around the room. "It seems my new neighbors are making quite the stir, indeed!"

"As esteemed persons always should!" Mr. Berwick agreed, appearing at Lady Hurley's left-hand side and bowing a greeting. His hair today, unlike its prim neatness the day before, had been fashioned into a kind of elegant disorder. It was not difficult to see where such inspiration had come from. "I myself shall be asking Lord Melville to sit for me at his earliest convenience—did you know he has not sat for a portrait since childhood?"

Murmurs of interest greeted this news and Eliza felt a pang of envy—not that she wanted to paint Melville, for after last night she frankly wished him at Jericho—but for the ease with which Mr. Berwick declared such a thing. She had only ever been able to draw and paint members of her own family, and while female artists of renown did exist, of course, scandal and slander still attended upon any woman who sought such public achievement. Even Eliza's grandfather, her guide and champion, had not felt it proper for women to join the Royal Academy.

"You may well paint him, Mr. Berwick," Lady Hurley said. "But it is I who shall host their first soiree in Bath. I can only regret that I am away from town Friday and Saturday, or I should have done so then."

"Is there such an urgency?" Eliza asked, amused at the fretful note in Lady Hurley's voice.

"Why, I do not want to be pipped to the post again!" Lady

Hurley said. "Lady Keith had the hosting of Madame D'Arblay when *she* arrived in Bath, Mrs. Piozzi had the Persian students last November—but *I* am determined to have the Melvilles!"

Mrs. Winkworth gave a soft snort, perhaps to intimate incredulity at Lady Hurley proclaiming herself a competitor of such distinguished ladies, but Eliza ignored her.

"Are you not at all worried to have such very—ah—dashing persons in town?" Mrs. Michels asked Lady Hurley, as Mr. Berwick bustled off in Melville's direction.

"A strong sense of impropriety surrounds them!" Mr. Broadwater declared.

"Oh, *pish*," Lady Hurley said scornfully. "It is a boon to have such fashionable persons in Bath, and especially two with such cleverness of mind."

"Cleverness is commendable—but an excess is fatal in females!" Mr. Broadwater said damningly. With crows of outrage, Lady Hurley and Margaret gave a spirited rejoinder, while Eliza's attention drew a little away from the commotion, eyes straying to the Melvilles once more. Watching the earl speak—his audience throwing back their heads in amusement around him—she felt an itch in her fingertips as she had last night. Would sketching Melville lost at sea, deprived of entertainment and approaching certain death, offer her satisfaction from her rage? Melville, as if aware of being watched, flicked his gaze up and over in her direction. Their eyes met. He lifted his arm in greeting.

And Eliza, who had never once in her life trespassed into rudeness, turned her shoulder on him, looking deliberately and obviously away, as if to deny his existence. The cut direct.

Even as she did it, Eliza could not quite believe her own daring, her heart quickening and her palms prickling. In seven and twenty years, she had never delivered the cut direct before. She had let countless slights and insults go unchallenged, unanswered, swallowing her pride again and again and presenting a placid smile to the world, but . . . No more. No more. Accepting a glass from Mr. Fletcher with a smile of thanks, she took a sip . . . Only to almost choke on it at the sound of a quiet but very familiar voice.

"Did you just cut me direct?"

Eliza turned quickly, to find Melville standing directly before her, head cocked. Her mouth fell open in horror.

"I—ah—" she stammered, her face growing hot.

"You did!" he crowed, intrigued and delighted.

Eliza stared at him, panicked. She had not expected to have to *converse* with him. Was not the whole point of cutting a person direct that one did not have to speak with them?

"May I ask why?" Melville said.

He did not seem offended, discomforted or even discomposed, and this fact, rather than calming Eliza, reignited her indignation. Did he truly believe himself to be so above her that he need not be touched in any way by the cut direct?

"Come, my lady," Melville prompted, when still she did not speak. "In what manner have I offended you?"

Eliza, every ounce of anger she had felt over the past day rising up, drew herself to her full height.

"Only in every possible way you could," she said, as defiantly as she dared whilst keeping her voice low—although everyone around them was busied in conversation, she did not want to risk being overheard.

"How terribly comprehensive of me," Melville said, blinking. "May I ask you to elaborate?"

Caution already thrown to the wind, it seemed pointless to try and retrieve it.

"We heard what you said to Lady Caroline last night, as you were leaving," Eliza said, turning her body slightly to draw him a little further away from the nearest group of potential eavesdroppers.

"You will have to remind me . . ." Melville said, slowly.

"'Lord save us from bumpkins, spinsters and widows—
bores, the lot of them!'" Eliza quoted.

". . . Ah," he said. "How unfortunate, for you to have heard
such a thoughtless—if pithy—comment."

Eliza gaped at him.

"Do you truly feel no shame?" she asked him.

"Why ought I feel shame," he said, still with that infuriat-
ing smile curling his lips. "It is you, not I, that has committed
the sin of eavesdropping, after all."

To Eliza's horror she found tears of frustration springing to
her eyes, and blinked them desperately back.

"And I am glad I did, for now I know how you truly think,"
she said, keeping her voice as level as she could. "Though even
if we were as dull as you and your sister seem to believe, then
we would still not deserve such unkindness."

Her voice ended a great deal wobblier than it began, and in
the face of such audible emotion, the residual humor faded
from Melville's expression.

"You humble me, my lady," he said, seeming, at last, to take
her seriously. "These past weeks have been . . . difficult for
Caroline and I . . . But that is no defense. You are correct, it
was most unkind. I am sorry."

The apology seemed sincere. Eliza took a moment to ap-
preciate it, for it was not often that a gentleman admitted
wrongdoing, no matter the crime. In all their years of marriage, the earl had not done so once.

"Thank you," she said at last, nodding her acceptance. Over
his shoulder, Eliza saw that they were beginning to attract an
audience of impatient ladies.

"I oughtn't monopolize your attention," she said. "I believe
Mrs. Donovan would like to speak with you."

"I care not," Melville said insouciantly. "I wish to speak
with you."

Eliza looked at him with uncertainty, suspecting a joke.

She may have accepted Melville's apology, but she would never again make the mistake of treating his flirtation seriously.

"Is that so surprising?" Melville asked.

"It was only yesterday that you deemed me a bore," she pointed out.

"My lady, you really must forgive the 'bore' episode if we are to be friends," Melville said.

"*Are* we to be friends?" Eliza asked, startled.

"Indeed, it is my dearest, lifelong wish," he said, clasping a hand to his heart. "You must dine with us at Laura Place—Miss Balfour, too."

"I cannot," Eliza said.

"Why not?"

"I am not yet dining abroad," Eliza said, gesturing to her widow's weeds. "And we have not even exchanged morning visits. It would be . . . odd. People would talk."

"And what a violent change of circumstances that would be," Melville said, drily.

Eliza stared. Could he truly care so little for the gossip and the rumors that followed him around?

"The *ton* have been talking about me since I was born," Melville said, as if able to read these thoughts from Eliza's face. "If I started worrying about their opinions now, I would have to immediately consign myself to a nunnery."

"Do you not mean a monastery?" Eliza asked, rather than acknowledge the more salubrious implications of his speech.

"No, the nunnery," Melville said. "Surely I must be allowed *some* fun?"

Before she could stop herself, Eliza let out a choke of scandalized laughter.

"She laughs!" Melville said, grinning victoriously.

"My lady, my lord—good morning! I do hope I am not interrupting?" Mrs. Donovan had finally plucked up the courage to approach, along with her three daughters. All were clutching volumes of *Persephone*, and clearly bent on receiving his signature.

"Not at all! Do excuse me," Eliza said, ignoring the dark look Melville sent her, and slipping away to find Margaret. She truly was grateful for the reprieve: one simply could not predict, from one moment, what Melville would say next, and while it was certainly diverting, Eliza was not at all used to having her wits so thoroughly tested.

"The cut direct? Eliza, you did not," Margaret said on their walk home.

"I did!" Eliza said, not even attempting to hide how pleased with herself she was now that she had only Margaret and, a few steps behind, Pardle as her audience. "And I made him apologize! I have never made a gentleman apologize before!"

As they reached Camden Place, Eliza noticed her boot lace had come untied and stooped automatically to fix it, still talking.

"Not my father, not my husband, neither of my brothers—"

"Somerset," Margaret said.

Eliza frowned as she tightened the lace.

"I am not sure about Somerset," she said, thinking.

"No, Eliza, *Somerset*," Margaret said.

And Eliza looked up from her stoop, followed the direction of Margaret's gaze and saw that indeed, a few yards ahead—utterly incomprehensibly—and exiting the front door of her house, was the Earl of Somerset.

7

It took Eliza several long moments to truly comprehend what she was seeing.

"What on earth . . . ?" she whispered to Margaret.

"Stand up!" Margaret urged her, but Eliza did not hear. The unlikeliness of Somerset, here, in Bath, walking out of *her* house, was such that she could not believe what her eyes told her. Eliza remained bent where she was, staring.

By now, Somerset had turned at the gate and within two steps he had seen them.

"Lady Somerset," he said, checking slightly—in surprise, presumably, at the sight of Eliza crouched so upon the ground. "Why are you . . . ?"

This, at last, galvanized Eliza into action.

She sprang up. "My lord! We were not expect—"

She moved so hurriedly that the blood rushed all at once to her head, and she tottered on her feet. Margaret made a hasty grab of Eliza's left arm to steady her and Pardle dashed forward, hands outstretched.

"Lady Somerset!" Somerset said, stepping swiftly forward. "Are you faint?"

The chilly reserve he had exhibited at their first meeting had vanished. His brows furrowed as he looked her over, appearing almost . . . concerned?

"I am—quite well," Eliza said, awash with embarrassment at her gracelessness. "It was just my shoe . . ."

"Perhaps we ought to take her inside," Somerset said, speaking to Margaret over Eliza's head as if she were approaching a hundred years old.

"Very well," Margaret said, exchanging a baffled glance with Eliza.

"Can you walk, my lady?" Somerset asked.

"Of course I can!" Eliza said. Could a lady not have one moment of precariousness without being deemed utterly incapable? "There is no need—"

She was about to declare herself perfectly able to walk unassisted, but at that moment Somerset slipped an arm around her waist to steady her and, with a jolt, Eliza found that perhaps she did not mind the assistance, after all.

"My lady!" Perkins exclaimed in alarm as they entered the hallway, at the sight of Eliza being thusly supported.

"Perhaps some cordial could be fetched for her ladyship," Somerset said calmly. "To be brought up to the drawing room immediately."

Pardle disappeared obediently toward the kitchen. Eliza was torn between bafflement at the unexpected turn the day had taken, indignation at the way Somerset was ordering her servants about, and reluctant admiration for the efficient way he was organizing matters. Why he seemed so sure she was suffering with a fainting spell, she could not know, but one could not argue that he acted with decision.

He did not withdraw his hold until they had climbed the stairs, entered the drawing room—Perkins holding the door open for them—and Eliza was seated upon the sofa.

"Well, I—I thank you for the assistance, my lord," Eliza said, a little breathless, deciding the best thing to do would be to brush past the whole encounter as if it had never happened. "I hope your family is—"

"Perhaps you had best not speak, until you have drunk

some cordial," Somerset said, firmly interrupting her pleasant-ries as Pardle re-entered with a tray.

Eliza accepted a glass, dismissing the maid with a smile.

"I am quite well," she tried again to explain to Somerset. "It was only my shoe."

"The poor honey is so confused," Margaret said, a spark of mischief in her eye. Eliza glared at her.

"Miss Balfour, could you lay your hands on some smelling salts, in case Lady Somerset feels faint again?" Somerset asked.

"I can try," Margaret said dubiously. "Perhaps Pardle will know where they are to be found."

She strolled out of the room at a pace that did not inspire urgency. Eliza—giving up on making sense of proceedings—sipped obediently at the cordial, while watching Somerset from under her lashes. He took a seat on the chair opposite, but remained tense upon the edge as if he expected her to faint again at any moment.

"We did not expect you in Bath," Eliza said, after a long pause.

"Nor I, you," Somerset replied. "I have come directly from Mr. Walcot, who informed me of your presence in Bath—and of your health. I confess, I had no notion of your being so ill."

Oh. Somerset's behavior began to make sense. She *knew* Margaret had overdone her description of Eliza's ill health to Mr. Walcot. Goodness knew how the man must have de-scribed her "fluralgia" in order to have Somerset come directly over, when at Harefield he could not remove himself from her company fast enough.

"It is not at all serious," she said.

"Mr. Walcot seemed to think it *very* serious," Somerset pressed.

"A misunderstanding, only," Eliza said. "It was not serious and I am quite well now."

She did not like to have to lie to him, but neither could she tell the whole truth.

"I am glad to hear it," Somerset said. "The way he spoke I—" He broke off.

"It was a little fatigue, only," Eliza said.

But Somerset was frowning again.

"Then may I ask," he said slowly, "why was I not informed of your departure to Bath? The seriousness of your condition would have explained the oversight—but if it is *not* serious . . ."

Oh dear.

"Did you not receive my letter?" Eliza asked, her voice the high squeak it always became when she had to lie on short notice. "I did write to—to inform you of the change in plan, but perhaps it was a little—ah—delayed."

Somerset raised his eyebrows with polite incredulity.

"When, may I ask, was this letter sent?" he said.

Oh *dear*.

"I am not quite sure," Eliza said. "There was simply so much to do . . ."

Somerset looked at her, his face chilly once more.

"My lady," he said after a long pause, "I am well aware that my uncle was disappointed to have me as an heir. He made it quite clear that I was a poor replacement for a hoped-for son, which is perhaps why he never invested in my education in the running of the lands. And perhaps that is an opinion you share. However, I cannot perform my duty as head of this family if you do not respect me."

"Oh goodness no!" Eliza said, quite horrified. "It had nothing to do with . . . I do respect you, indeed I do."

"And yet I had to discover news of your whereabouts from Mr. Walcot, who was much surprised to learn I was not already aware," Somerset said, voice hard. "My embarrassment was considerable, I assure you."

Under the chastisement, Eliza began to feel like a child.

"I ought to have written sooner," she said. "It was unconscionably rude."

Somerset nodded, somewhat mollified.

"Do you still intend, when you are fully recovered, to remove to Balfour?" he asked.

"I . . . do not yet know," Eliza admitted.

They were already halfway through February, and Eliza might have as little as eight more weeks of Margaret's company before she would be needed elsewhere. As much as Eliza felt more at home in Bath with each day, the idea of remaining without Margaret, of finding a new companion, was still far too daunting to contemplate.

"I see."

Somerset looked down to his hat, which he still held between his hands, and began to turn it slowly between them. The gesture was a familiar one. One he used to make whenever he was nervous but trying to contain it. Eliza could remember him, vividly, turning his hat the first time he had ever called upon her, at the Balfour's residence in London.

"I know that . . ." Somerset began again, staring back at his turning hat, "that the nature of our past acquaintance causes a little awkwardness, in our present circumstances."

"It is perhaps not an *ideal* situation," Eliza said, her mouth very dry.

"It is certainly not that," Somerset said, looking up. "And I should not like to think of that awkwardness preventing you from residing at Harefield, if you wish it. There will always be a place for you there, I promise."

It was so like him to make such a promise. He always had been incurably honorable.

"Thank you," Eliza said, and she meant it. "But we are happy here in Bath. It has provided a change of scenery that neither Balfour nor Harefield could have."

Somerset nodded.

"I can understand that—I can see that it would be difficult to be so constantly reminded of him," he said quietly.

Eliza remained quiet. She was conscious of a desire, improper in the extreme, to confess to Somerset exactly how little love there had existed between herself and her husband. To tell him that, in the years they had been wed, no warmth had grown between them, that the gulf separating them had only grown more glacial with every month that passed without a child. But it would be improper. And he would not want to hear it, anyway.

The sound of loud footsteps on the stairs heralded the return of Margaret, and as she entered, Somerset stood.

"No smelling salts?" he asked, a slight smile upon his face.

"Oh, my forgetful mind!" Margaret said airily. "You are not taking your leave already, Somerset?"

"I am afraid I am," he said. "Pray do not stand, Lady Somerset."

His duty seen to, his honorable mission achieved, he had no reason to prolong his visit. Eliza tried not to be disappointed.

"Do you return to Harefield tonight?" Eliza asked.

"Not tonight. I have more business to attend to with Mr. Walcot in the morning," Somerset said, after a brief pause. He turned his hat once more in his hands, then added: "Perhaps—perhaps I may call upon you again, tomorrow, if it would be convenient?"

"It would," Eliza said, tamping down excitement springing within her. "It would indeed."

Somerset bowed his head. "Then I will see you tomorrow, Lady Somerset, Miss Balfour."

The cousins waited until they heard the front door close. Then Margaret darted to the window embrasure to watch Somerset's departure down the street.

"He is gone!" she declared. "What did you speak of, when

I was absent? I tried to listen on the stairs, but your voices were too quiet."

"Not a great deal," Eliza said, feeling dazed. Had what just occurred, truly just occurred? "He reassured me I would be welcome at Harefield if I wished to return."

"Which you don't," Margaret checked.

"Which I don't," Eliza agreed. "Though it was most kind of him to suggest it. Did he seem . . . concerned to you, when he thought I was ill?"

"I should say so; most worried," Margaret said.

"And relieved, when he heard I was well?" Eliza said.

"Very relieved," Margaret confirmed with a sharp nod.

"And he means to return, tomorrow," Eliza said, half thinking she might have imagined it.

Perhaps, then, he did not *nothing* her after all. Eliza pressed a hand to her mouth, to try to prevent herself smiling. *Do not,* she tried to tell herself, *make the mistake of becoming hopeful now. He spent half the visit chastising you, for goodness' sake.*

But he was kind, a smaller, dreamier voice protested. *And he means to return.*

"Do you think—" Eliza broke off.

"Do I think . . . ?"

"It's just . . . his manner was so much the warmer, by the end," Eliza said. "Perhaps it is a sign that he might, one day . . . forgive me?"

"*He* forgive *you?*" Margaret said with a sudden frown. "Whatever for?"

"Margaret, you know 'whatever for.'"

"I do not at all understand why you still feel so guilty," Margaret said stoutly. "It was an impossible situation for you *both,* but it was only you who had to bear the consequences— marrying that old goat while he remained free and unencumbered."

"He joined the navy, Margaret," Eliza pointed out. "I do not think you can call that free and unencumbered."

"Oh pish, jauntering about the Atlantic with a boat of friends?" Margaret said. "Many persons would pay for such a diversion."

Margaret's understanding of the navy was demonstrably rather limited.

"I have always been fond of Somerset," she carried on. "But if he still bears resentment over the matter years later, then he is certainly not worth a single thought more."

"Perhaps we ought have a nuncheon," Eliza said, rising from the sofa to ring the bell.

She did not want to argue. Margaret had always been Eliza's fiercest defender and Eliza loved her for it—but she had not been there, when Somerset had heard of Eliza's betrothal. If she had, she might better understand why Eliza still felt such remorse.

"My lady." Perkins had appeared once more at the door. "A delivery from Mr. Fasana has arrived and it being—ah—a fair sight larger than previous, I was wondering where you might wish me to . . . ?"

"Oh!" Eliza said, recollecting the very large number and size of purchases she had made that morning. "Perhaps you ought to place them in here, for the time being."

Perkins paused delicately. "And the easel, too?"

Eliza looked around. The drawing room already boasted a pianoforte, and the addition of an easel would make the space rather crowded—and doubtless encourage questions from any visitor that entered. Visitors such as Somerset, tomorrow.

He means to return.

"Perhaps it ought to all go in the parlor, instead," she said, but abstractedly. "It is north-lit, after all."

Perkins nodded briskly. With characteristic efficiency, it did not take him above an hour to rearrange the first-floor parlor:

removing two chairs in order to accommodate the large easel which he had placed a little back from the window, so Eliza could enjoy the natural light whilst remaining unobserved from passersby; clearing the bookshelves to allow for all of Eliza's portfolios, full and empty, to be arranged neatly within; and purloining a small bureau from the drawing room to house her paints. With Eliza's mind full of agitation, it proved the perfect distraction, and while Margaret read her book, curled up upon the sofa, Eliza tested her new oils. At once, the room was filled with their sharp, acidic scent, a smell that transported Eliza so abruptly back to her childhood that she had to blink back sudden, joyful tears as she covered the canvas with a ground layer of yellow ochre. Soon she would capture Bath's evening light with that creamy roseate and begin a portrait of Margaret with the carmine that perfectly matched her red locks; but for now, in the fading afternoon light, Eliza resealed the oils—which came in strips of bladder tied at the neck as a suet pudding—with a tack and moved back to pencil and watercolor, sketching from memory the scenes from the concert: Melville's expression as he flirted with Lady Hurley, Mr. Fletcher's annoyance, Mrs. Winkworth's judging eyes.

By the time Eliza at last put aside her materials, the fire in the grate had almost burned itself out, her eyes were beginning to strain, and she felt calm enough, at last, to retire to bed.

Tomorrow, she vowed as she undressed, she would be prepared. She would not be found stooped on the ground as though she were some grubby urchin. She would be calm and collected and composed and all would go well.

8

Though the traditional hours of calling—between midday and three o'clock in the afternoon—left plenty of the day remaining, she and Margaret did not attend to any of their usual errands. Instead, to be sure not to miss Somerset's visit no matter what time he called, they arranged themselves patiently in the drawing room to await his arrival.

"What do you think you will speak of?" Margaret asked, from beside her.

"The usual subjects, I suppose," Eliza said. She had compiled just such a list that morning. "I shall ask him for news of his family, of London, of . . ."

Margaret made a face.

"What did you used to speak of?" she asked next. "When you were courting, I mean."

"When we were first acquainted?" Eliza said. "We spoke of books, our friends in common, the progress of the war."

"And then?" Margaret prompted.

And then . . . Somewhere through the snatched pieces of conversation, at the balls, at the garden parties, at the theater, his natural reserve and her natural shyness had eased sufficiently for them to discover not only the analogous turn of their minds, but the depth of their mutual regard.

"What has you so interested in the affair?" Eliza said, instead of answering. To indulge in such nostalgic yearning now would only serve to make her more nervous.

"Having no past loves of my own, I am left with no option but to take an interest in yours," Margaret said, shrugging.

"Have you truly never had a decided partiality for anyone?" Eliza asked.

"There were certainly those I enjoyed flirting with," Margaret said, considering the matter. "But certainly not enough to seriously consider any of them. I suppose, to be a rich widow, as you are, is aspirational—but could one ever be certain of the gentleman dying early enough?"

"Not without risking a rather long visit to Newgate Prison," Eliza said.

The clock struck twelve. There was a sound from below. The door.

Eliza stood. She had dressed very carefully today, in a robe of clinging black crêpe—made demure by its high collar—and she smoothed a hand down the front of her gown.

"You look very becoming," Margaret whispered.

Eliza could hear Perkins's murmuring voice, then footsteps upon the stairs. She had instructed him most firmly to bring up visitors as soon as they—*he*—arrived. She took a deep breath. Today, there was nothing to be nervous about. It was simply a morning visit. It was everything of the most usual.

Perkins opened the door.

"Lord Melville and Lady Caroline Melville, my lady," he announced.

"No!" Eliza blurted out, utterly thrown.

"Good afternoon!" Margaret attempted to cover this gaffe.

"Good afternoon," Melville said as he wandered into the room, a somewhat quizzical look in his eyes. "Were you expecting someone else?"

"N-no, of course not. We are not expecting anyone!" Eliza said, too loud by far.

"Melville, you said we had been invited," Lady Caroline said, turning to her brother.

"We had!" Melville said. "Though now I reflect on it . . . Perhaps only tangentially."

If that! Eliza had merely mentioned the possibility, in passing.

"Ought we to leave?" Lady Caroline asked, raising a brow in question at Eliza.

Eliza wanted more than anything to be able to answer honestly. Somerset might arrive at any moment and Eliza did not feel at all prepared to juggle two such disparate sets of visitors—let alone what Somerset might think, if he were to find Eliza sipping tea with two of the most accomplished flirts in England.

"No, no, of course not!" Eliza said instead, twisting her hands into her skirts. "Please, do sit down. May we offer you refreshment?"

"That would be very kind," Lady Caroline said, falling gracefully into the chair opposite Eliza, while Melville, ignoring Eliza's invitation, wandered over to the window to look out on the street below.

"Charming!" he said.

Eliza stared helplessly at Lady Caroline, without a single thought in her head. With other visitors, she might comment on the disappointing nature of today's pallid grey sky, but knowing Lady Caroline already thought her insipid did not endear such a subject to her.

"I owe you an apology, my lady, Miss Balfour," Lady Caroline spoke first, in the end. "Melville informs me that you overheard our terribly rude conversation at the assembly. How churlish we were—I don't know how you could ever forgive us!"

"We haven't," Margaret said promptly, before Eliza could answer. "Perhaps in time."

Eliza held back a groan, but Lady Caroline did not look offended. Rather, she was looking Margaret slowly over, as if recalculating her in some way.

"You have teeth," she said approvingly.

"Thirty of them, I'm told," Margaret shot back.

"And yet there were none to be seen on Wednesday night."

"On Wednesday night I was on my best behavior."

"A horrendous affliction," Lady Caroline said. "I am pleased to find you now cured of it."

They smiled at each other. That is, Eliza chose to think of it as smiling, and not, as might perhaps be more accurate, baring their teeth.

"May I offer you a refreshment?" Eliza said again, as Perkins swept back into the room. His tray of refreshments, normally a gloriously laden affair, was sparser than usual, with only a pot of coffee, and slices of cake and fruit. Seeing this, Eliza sent him a look of speaking gratitude, which he returned only with the slightest of nods—she could always trust Perkins to be awake on every suit. Now, she must hurry the Melvilles through the visit as quickly as possible. It was only twelve; there was no reason that the two visits need overlap in any way.

"Do you take milk, my lord?" Eliza said, handing Lady Caroline a cup.

"I am disappointed," Melville said, from where he was now examining the painting on the wall, a fine landscape she had purchased from an artist displaying his work at the Pump Room last week.

"Oh, well if you would prefer tea, I can . . ." Eliza began.

"I hoped to find the walls bedecked with your own art-work," Melville said, as if Eliza had not spoken. "But I do not think this is your hand."

"No, no, of course it is not," Eliza said, surprised that Melville had remembered such a detail. "That is far superior to anything I could achieve."

"You draw?" Lady Caroline said, regarding Eliza over the rim of her cup.

"A little," Eliza said.

"She paints too—beautifully," Margaret put in.

"Watercolors?" Lady Caroline asked.

"And oil, a little," Eliza admitted.

"Impressive. It is not a medium oft taught to women." Lady Caroline looked at Eliza and then to Margaret. "You are both a great deal more interesting than you first appear."

Eliza was not sure this was a compliment, so she sipped at her cup rather than answer.

"I am not sure that is a compliment," Margaret said.

"I am not sure I meant it as one," Lady Caroline returned. "You ought not to be hiding it."

The conversation was running away from them—and Melville had still not sat down; instead, he was now inspecting the bookshelves.

"My lord, can I interest you in some plum cake?" Eliza asked, desperately.

"Well, where are all these paintings?" he asked. "I see no sign of them here, at all."

"She has stacks of them upstairs," Margaret put in. Eliza glared at her.

"May I see?" Melville said immediately.

Eliza shook her head. "You will forgive, I hope, my reserve. I am not in the habit of sharing my paintings with those I barely know," she said.

"Then we shall simply have to get to know one another," Melville said, at last moving toward the sofa. Eliza looked to the clock. They were back on schedule. Everything would be fine.

Of course, it was at this moment that Eliza heard the unmistakable sound of hooves from outside and jerked her head wildly toward the door.

"Good lord, whatever is the matter?" Lady Caroline asked.

"That must be Somerset," Margaret blurted out. Eliza looked to her in panic—how on earth was she to manage such an encounter in front of the Melvilles? And would Somerset be shocked, disapproving even, to find Eliza in such unusual company? She wished Lady Caroline did not look so very beautiful, in her fashionable London dress—the likelihood of his falling immediately in love with her seemed very great indeed.

"Oh, a family visit, then," Lady Caroline said.

"He is not *family*," Eliza refuted instinctively.

Lady Caroline quirked a curious brow and Eliza flushed again at her rudeness.

"That is to say," she said hurriedly, "since he has been away so long, it does not feel . . ."

Eliza craned her ears, trying to make out sound from below, but to no avail.

"You are not well acquainted?" Lady Caroline asked.

"Not as such," Eliza said. "When he was Mr. Courtenay, wh-when he was in England," Eliza had turned into a gabster, it seemed, "but only a little! And that was of course many years ago now, and—"

"I shall be very interested to hear more of his travels," Margaret cut in firmly, before Eliza could offer any more unnecessary, nervous detail. "He will have some exciting tales, no doubt."

"Shouldn't get your hopes up," Melville advised her. "I hear he's a dreary fellow."

"He is *not*," Eliza said hotly and both Lady Caroline's eyebrows rose now.

There was the sound of a loud knock from downstairs and Eliza looked reflexively and eagerly toward the door.

"Oh, I *see*," Lady Caroline said, sounding very much as if she did. "Come, Melville, we must be going," she said, standing.

"But I have not yet had any cake," Melville objected.

"Oh, do not feel you have to leave . . ." Eliza said.

Somerset's voice could be heard below, and Perkins's too.

"I have recalled some errands I must fulfil urgently," Lady Caroline said firmly. "Come along, Melville."

Eliza could not tell if she were more mortified or grateful. How embarrassing it was to have been read so easily, and yet how kind of Lady Caroline to help.

"The Earl of Somerset, my lady," Perkins announced.

Somerset hesitated on the doorway for a moment, seeming startled by the fullness of the room.

"Good day, my lord," Eliza said, voice tremulous. There was no way to avoid it. "May I introduce you to Lord Melville and Lady Caroline Melville?"

"Good day," Somerset said. Halfway through a bow, the name seemed to register properly in his mind. "Melville?" he repeated.

"Yes, do you know me?" Melville said, inclining his head in return.

"Only by reputation, my lord," Somerset said obliquely.

"Ah, it stretches all the way to the Americas, now, does it?" Melville asked. "How marvelous to have transatlantic reach at last."

Somerset's expression flattened. He had always disapproved of gentlemen who trifled with women's affections.

"Marvelous is not the word I would have chosen," Somerset said slowly.

Eliza could not tell if Melville had perceived the coldness in Somerset's voice, but if he had he did not seem at all bothered.

"I admire a man with strong views on vocabulary," he said, in apparent compliment. "What think you then of 'remarkable'? Or 'pioneering'?"

Somerset's expression hardened even further.

"No—I have it—'*extraordinaire*'!" Melville said. "If you don't mind borrowing from the French?"

"We were just taking our leave," Lady Caroline said, cutting in.

"Not on my account, I hope," Somerset said.

"No, we are in pursuit of an urgent—though as of yet unnamed—errand," Melville said, affording Eliza a jaunty bow. "Lady Somerset. Lord Somerset. Miss Balfour."

They left. There was a long, long pause in their wake.

"I had not realized Lord Melville was in Bath," Somerset said, frowning toward the door as if the Melvilles were still standing there.

"He and Lady Caroline arrived only recently," Eliza hastened to make clear. "Would you like to take a seat?"

"And you are well acquainted?" Somerset said, sitting.

"Not at all," Eliza said.

"Though they appear bent on changing that," Margaret added, a pleased curve to her lips.

"I see," Somerset said.

"Is everything at Harefield well?" Eliza asked, adding quickly, "I forgot to ask, yesterday."

Pleasantries would surely settle the strained atmosphere in the room.

"Yes, very well," Somerset said, though his brow was still furrowed. "We are renovating the East Wing—the damp was getting a little . . ." Perceiving that this could be taken as an insult by Harefield's former mistress, he hastened to add, "So common, of course, in these ancient houses!"

But it was not that part of the sentence that she had noticed.

"We?" she asked, unable to help herself.

"Yes," he said. "The steward is overseeing, of course."

"I'm glad to hear it," she said, much relieved. Of course: he couldn't have married, or even become engaged, without her knowing—what a foolish fear to have crossed her mind. "Though I hope it shall not make you uncomfortable, to have such industry around you."

"I should not think—" Somerset started to say, before abruptly changing tack. "That is, yes, it is like to be most disruptive. I shall be remaining in Bath for the fortnight, to avoid the worst of the disorder."

For a moment, Eliza thought she might have misheard.

"You—you will?" she stammered. "I did not know; you made no mention of it yesterday."

"Yesterday, I did not yet know of the extent of the repairs," he replied.

"What fortuitous timing," Margaret said blandly, and Eliza knew that she, too, suspected Somerset of some dissimulation. But why should he lie? Unless it was because—unless it was for—

But that was surely wishful thinking.

"It will be easier to conduct business from here, anyhow," Somerset said calmly. "And I should like to be close to . . ."

There was the tiniest of pauses and Eliza caught her breath.

"My sister," Somerset finished. "She lives only five miles south of Bath, if you remember."

"Yes, of course," Eliza said. "Well, I am sure we are most pleased to hear such news."

It was an understatement. Eliza's surprise was giving way to giddiness. A fortnight! Two whole weeks of his presence . . .

"My valet is to fetch more of my things from Harefield," Somerset said, and his voice was lighter now. "I did want to ask if there was anything you should like to be brought to Bath? You took so little with you, though it was your home for so many years."

Eliza felt a pang in her chest. He was so kind.

"I could not possibly," Eliza demurred.

"You could," he said. "In fact, I insist you must take something."

Eliza's mind went briefly to her grandfather's seascape hanging in her parlor, the finest piece of artwork in Harefield, not that it was displayed at all to its advantage, before dismissing it immediately. It was too valuable, and while Somerset might not know its worth, Lady Selwyn certainly would.

"What is it?" Somerset asked. He always had been able to read her so easily. "You must tell me."

But Eliza could not risk Somerset ever thinking her mercenary.

"The teapot in the East Drawing Room," she said, thinking of her next favorite item from the house. "If no one else . . ."

A smile spread across his face, his first of the afternoon.

"A teapot? You do know that was your opportunity to ask for the family diamonds, don't you?" he said teasingly. It was not a tone she had ever expected to hear from him again, and her cheeks warmed.

"If you'd ever drunk its tea, you would understand," she said.

"Perhaps then I ought to try it, before I agree," he said. Then, entreating, "Are you sure I cannot persuade you to take anything of greater value?"

She shook her head and his smile widened.

"How like you to ask for something so small," he said, "to want so little for yourself."

Eliza could have told him that it was not selflessness, that there was nothing she wanted less than the oppressive weight of the family diamonds about her neck, but she would not, not when he was looking at her like that. As he had used to look at her before everything fell apart.

"You have not changed," he said.

Their smiles faded as they looked at one another, the weight of all that had happened, all that they had once been to one another, seemed to press heavily upon them both.

"*I* should not mind the diamonds, if no one else wants them," Margaret said, breaking the moment.

"I see that you, too, are unchanged, Miss Balfour," Somerset said, shaking his head with a smile. "Your humor is as lively as ever."

"There are some things even the Bath waters cannot cure," Eliza said, and Margaret laughed, but Somerset's smile faded.

"And how is your health?" he asked Eliza seriously, as one might a bedridden and ancient aunt.

"I am well," Eliza said.

"Does she not *look* well?" Margaret asked.

Eliza shot her a quelling look.

"She does. You do," Somerset said quietly, looking Eliza over. "A new gown?"

"Yes," Eliza said, mouth dry.

"It suits you," he said, and it was a compliment no less valued for its simplicity. "Are you still partaking of the waters?"

"Yes," Eliza said. "Though as much to visit with our new friends as anything else."

"New friends," Somerset repeated. "And do you count the Melvilles as such?"

"No," Eliza hastened.

"Yes," Margaret said at the same time.

Somerset frowned again.

"That is," Eliza clarified. "We have only met them a handful of times, so I am not sure I would call . . ."

"I should not like to overstep, my lady," Somerset said. "But I would urge caution where the Melvilles are concerned. The tales I have heard . . ."

The deliberate way in which he was speaking, as if choosing his words very carefully, tickled Eliza's curiosity.

"These tales are scandalous in nature?" she asked, not wanting to seem too eager for details—but eager for them, nonetheless. What had Somerset heard about Melville, in so short a stay in the country?

"They are not tales I will repeat in front of ladies," he said firmly.

"How dull," Margaret muttered. And though Eliza admired Somerset's sense of propriety, she could not help but privately agree with her.

"I will merely say that I would not recommend such a friendship," Somerset said. "A woman of your . . . A woman in your position ought to be careful."

The protective concern was warming and Eliza was briefly tempted to encourage it—but no, that would be too unfair.

"The Melvilles are lively," she said. "But in our acquaintance, limited though it is, that is the extent of their impropriety."

There was no need to mention the carriage crash, nor the overheard insults, for both events seemed, all of a sudden, far in the past—irrelevant, even, in the face of the joy Somerset had just visited upon her. *Two whole weeks.*

"If you spend longer in their company I am sure you will agree," she added.

"I suppose I shall see for myself," Somerset said, though with a raise of his eyebrows that suggested he doubted it.

The clock struck one. Somerset stood to take his leave.

"I will bid you good day," he said. "You intend to visit the Pump Room tomorrow morning?"

"Yes, we do," Eliza said eagerly.

"I shall find you there," he said. He gave a short bow, then left.

"Oh, my goodness," Eliza said, once they had conclusively heard the front door close behind him. He was staying. He was staying and she would see him again—tomorrow. "Oh, my *goodness*."

"Matters in Bath are about to get very interesting, indeed," Margaret said, sounding quite as gleeful as a cat might, upon consuming a large jug of cream.

9

That Eliza slept at all that night was nothing short of a miracle. She could not, for the longest time, and ended up—as had become something of a habit, this past week—taking her portfolio to bed with her, hoping that the lull of pencil upon paper would soothe her mind. But though she intended to capture the elegance of Camden Place, or the exterior view of the Pump Room, both calming, warm images, every time she tried, she instead found herself sketching the drawing room that day: Margaret's sly smile as she sparred with Lady Caroline, Melville's attentive eyes upon her bookshelves, and Somerset . . . Again and again, Somerset. His hands clenching at his hat, the furrow of his brow, how he had looked, teasing her . . .

She fell asleep still clutching it in her hands, causing Pardle to cluck over the charcoal smudges it had left on her sheets.

"The bombazine, today, my lady?" Pardle asked.

"I think the silk, instead," Eliza decided. It was far finer than any Eliza would usually wear to the Pump Room, of course, but given the very special occasion that today marked, it seemed only appropriate. Her eagerness to have Somerset once again within her sights was unequalled, and she had twice to remind herself that the need for such urgency had elapsed. She might see him every day until March, now, at the Pump Room, the Assembly Rooms, at church . . . After years of scarcity, it seemed an embarrassment of riches, and ten o'clock could not come soon enough. As the clock struck quarter to, Eliza and Margaret set out, winding their way through Bath's cobbled streets with as much briskness as was acceptable in ladies of quality.

They stood at the entrance, bidding polite good days to half a dozen acquaintances, while Eliza scanned the room frantically for Somerset. At last, she laid eyes upon him, standing in the middle of the room, speaking with Mrs. and Miss Winkworth.

"Poor man," Margaret observed. Eliza heartily agreed and made as if to step forward, but Margaret seized her arm.

"Then we will be embroiled in conversation with her too," she said, shaking her head. "Let him come to us."

"How on earth have they been introduced so quickly?" Eliza bemoaned, trying to catch Somerset's eye. It was not considered good manners to simply walk up to a person and begin speaking, one waited for, or requested from a mutual acquaintance, a formal introduction. As this was a rule that Mrs. Balfour insisted upon in others, but believed herself exempt from, it was perhaps unsurprising that Mrs. Winkworth felt the same. Eliza could only hope Somerset had not been offended by her encroaching nature.

"I imagine Mrs. Winkworth only needed to notice his signet ring to make her own introductions," Margaret suggested, her thoughts having traveled in a similar direction.

"Perhaps I will invite him to walk with us tomorrow," Eliza whispered to Margaret, as they stood waiting. "Lady Hurley mentioned that she often walks in Sydney Gardens after the Sunday service and so we could all promenade, together."

The halcyon vision filled her mind's eye, just as Somerset looked up and noticed them at last. Excusing himself from the Winkworths, he approached, appearing to Eliza even taller and broader and fairer than he had the day before, the sun streaming in through the large windows gilding him in golden light.

"Good day, my lady, Miss Balfour," he said. His eyes moved briefly and—perhaps?—appreciatively over Eliza's dress. "You are looking well."

"Thank you," she said. The silk had been the right choice. "I see you have met the Winkworths."

"Your neighbors, as I understand it," he said, nodding. "According to Mrs. Winkworth, I have apparently met them both before, at the opera, though as I have no memory of that encounter—and as Miss Winkworth could not have been more than eight years old at the time, I cannot help but wonder at its veracity."

Margaret snorted.

"I hope they were not too forward," Eliza said.

"They were perfectly charming," Somerset said. "Though Mrs. Winkworth did criticize her daughter's posture, at great length." He paused, and added, delicately, "You know, I have the strangest feeling that Mrs. Winkworth reminds me of someone . . ."

Eliza saw a teasing smile quivering at the corner of Somerset's mouth and found her own lips curving in helpless imitation.

"I had the same feeling, upon first meeting her," Eliza said, trying to keep her voice steady.

"I thought you might."

Eliza, inordinately pleased to find that Somerset's reserve had eased even further since their last meeting, could barely contain a smile. The fortnight stretched ahead of her, and she imagined a hundred of encounters such as this, with Somerset all the while growing evermore easy in her presence.

"Have you met with Mr. Walcot today?" she asked.

"I have, yes, much as he might wish me at Jericho," Somerset said. "There is much to learn about the business of being a landlord, if I am to perform the duty well."

There were many gentlemen who valued land only for the wealth and privileges it afforded them, but far fewer who placed the duties they owed to their constituents in higher importance. It did not surprise Eliza that Somerset belonged to this second group.

"I am fortunate that Mr. Walcot has the patience of a philosopher," he added, with a self-deprecating grimace.

Eliza raised her brows. That had not been quite her experience.

"I have no doubt that I am the slower pupil," she assured Somerset, wryly. In her second meeting with Mr. Walcot, this had been made very clear to her.

"Is your father no longer taking care of your business for you?" Somerset asked.

"No, but I am to meet with a land agent next week," Eliza said. "I have a great many questions for him. He may think me particularly stupid."

Poring dutifully over the very dry texts she had taken from the library had impressed upon her quite how much there was to know.

"Don't be foolish, Eliza," Margaret said. "You are far cleverer than half the lords *I* know."

"Excluding present company, of course," Eliza added meaningfully, with a nod to Somerset. Margaret turned to regard him, as if she planned to evaluate his intelligence right there and then.

"I beg you spare me whatever conclusion you reach, Miss Balfour, for I feel sure you are not likely to flatter me," Somerset said, voice serious, but eyes humorous. He turned to Eliza. "I agree that Lady Somerset has a good mind, and a great deal of common sense, although, if I can ever offer any assistance . . ."

Eliza hesitated. She had once again refused Mr. Walcot's suggestion that her father, brother—or any man at all—might be better suited to overseeing the lands, and she worried that accepting assistance now would amount to capitulation. On the other hand, such a conference with Somerset—their heads bent closely together, going over accounts—might have its own appeal . . .

"That is very kind," she said. "The lands at Chepstow, in particular, are a little confusing."

Somerset frowned thoughtfully.

"Perhaps you would be better off consulting my brother-in-law on Chepstow," he said, "for the lands border with his own."

Since Eliza heartily disliked Selwyn and since Selwyn would undoubtedly resent such a consultation after all the unpleasantness surrounding the will, this was an unwelcome suggestion.

"A wonderful thought," Eliza said mendaciously. "I shall certainly do so at our next meeting."

"You may do so today," Somerset said, "for he has accompanied my sister on a visit to Bath—there they are now!"

Eliza turned and saw, with dawning dread, that they were indeed being approached by Lord and Lady Selwyn.

"Lady Somerset!" Selwyn boomed. "How wonderful to see you!"

They exchanged bows and curtseys and Lady Selwyn made a point of looking Eliza overtly up and down.

"We were so worried to hear of your ill health, my lady," she said with transparent insincerity. "But I see now we need not have. You look as fine as five pence!"

She made it sound an insult and Eliza flushed. The silk had been a mistake.

"I had not realized you were visiting Bath," Eliza said.

"Oh, just for the day," Lady Selwyn said, with a sharp smile. "As soon as I heard my brother intended to reside at an inn for a fortnight, I knew it my sisterly duty to come and fetch him away!"

"My sister believes the Pelican to be some sort of hell," Somerset said to Eliza. "But I am quite happy there. It is close to my lawyer, my agent and all my lands."

"As is Sancroft!" Lady Selwyn insisted. "And you will be amongst family. Here you know nobody except Lady Somerset."

"You are forgetting Miss Balfour," Somerset said.

"How remiss of me," Lady Selwyn said, resting her cold eyes upon Margaret for a moment, before seeming to dismiss her existence entirely. "You ought at least return with us for a short visit—the girls would be delighted to see you again."

At the mention of his nieces, Somerset visibly softened.

"And I hear . . ." Selwyn said, leaning in as if he were about to import a great secret, "that Cook is preparing veal tonight."

He gave a significant nod. Somerset laughed.

"I do like veal," he said.

Eliza looked on, frozen. The Selwyns were going to take him away! He had only just arrived, he had only just begun to act normally in Eliza's presence, and now, after only one day of the promised fortnight, the Selwyns were going to take him away. For a visit to begin with, perhaps, but Lady Selwyn's self-satisfied expression told Eliza that once Somerset was in his sister's home, he would not be returning.

"Come, Lady Somerset, you must add your entreaties, too," Lady Selwyn said. "Surely you will agree that Somerset ought not be dining alone at such a place? It would be far too tragic."

Eliza could not let it happen. The old Eliza might have done, might have meekly accepted her fate no matter how unhappy it made her, but the new Eliza would not.

"In truth," Eliza said impulsively, "I was about to ask—to invite Somerset for dinner at Camden Place, to introduce him into society a little. Tonight."

To counteroffer in such a way was impolite, and Somerset's

brows snapped together while Lady Selwyn's eyes flickered very obviously down to Eliza's black gown but Eliza plunged on.

"Now I am *ten* months into my mourning, my mother has suggested I ought host a few quiet dinners at home—just five or six close friends, nothing in the least formal."

Her mother had recommended no such thing, but if Mrs. Balfour, the highest stickler imaginable, felt it acceptable, then surely Somerset could have no objection.

"I should not, of course, like to deprive you of a visit to Sancroft," Eliza added. "But if it is dining alone that Lady Selwyn wishes you to avoid . . ."

Somerset's brow cleared.

"How fortuitous," Lady Selwyn said silkily. "May I ask who else is attending?"

Eliza stared at her, stricken.

"Why, of course, our very dear friends . . ." she began, mentally flicking through all the persons she could hope to depend upon for a dinner party that very evening and landing, unfortunately, upon . . . "The Winkworths! Our neighbors. And of course, also the, ah . . ."

"Melvilles," Margaret said smoothly.

"The earl?" Lady Selwyn demanded.

"In Bath?" Selwyn sounded thunderstruck.

"Yes—they are recently arrived," Eliza confirmed, trying not to sound alarmed herself. Somerset's brows had re-furrowed. *Blast.* Did Margaret have to say the one family Somerset seemed already to dislike? The only persons of their acquaintance with whom Somerset must certainly *not* want to dine!

"And we are serving veal, too," she added desperately.

"I should be delighted to join you," Somerset said. "And my sister can rest easy that I am not to be abandoned to the tables of the Pelican."

Eliza smiled in relief. There was a pause as the Selwyns and Somerset looked at her expectantly. Oh.

"We would have of course invited you to join us, had we known you were visiting," Eliza said reluctantly. "It is a shame you are returning to Sancroft tonight."

It was not a shame.

"Why, that is easily resolved!" Lady Selwyn said. "We shall simply delay our return until morning—the Pelican can easily accommodate us."

"A wonderful suggestion, my dear," Selwyn said, and he had stolen Eliza's smile. "What time shall we arrive?"

"With Bath hours being so early, I should not imagine you will seat us later than six o'clock," Lady Selwyn interjected.

Eliza could not see a way out. Her quick thinking had deserted her.

"Half—half past six," she said weakly. "How delightful that you are able to join us."

And after curtseying deeply, she and Margaret excused themselves.

"I beg you will not think me boorishly practical," Margaret said, as they walked away. "But may I ask why you have invited them to what seems, by all accounts, to be a largely fictional soiree?"

"You were there!" Eliza hissed back. "The Selwyns were going to—to tempt him away with veal and I panicked, Margaret, and I just *spoke*—"

The full force of the consequences of such a rash invitation began to dawn on Eliza.

"What have I done?" she said, stopping on the top step. "To host a dinner party, still in full mourning! My mother will have my head. We must cancel it, at once. Oh, but then Somerset will go to Sancroft and the Selwyns will be victorious . . . But how on earth can we not?"

"It will be all right," Margaret said soothingly, pulling on Eliza's arm. When Eliza did not obey her pressure, Margaret clucked her tongue as if she were encouraging a horse and pulled harder. Eliza began to walk. "It is in the privacy of our own home, and half of the attendees are practically family!"

That was stretching matters, though Eliza could take her point, except that . . .

"We *have* no other guests," Eliza moaned.

"You will go straight to the Winkworths and then to the Melvilles," Margaret said. "I will speak to Perkins and it will soon not be in the least fictional." Margaret nudged her. "Yes?"

"Yes," Eliza said, thankfully. "Yes! Did I—did I also say that we were serving veal?"

"You did," Margaret said, pressing her lips together as if she were trying not to laugh. "Even I thought *that* was bold."

It was almost eleven on a Saturday. The chances of their cook securing a cut of veal were slim to none and Eliza let out another disconsolate groan.

At Camden Place, she and Margaret parted ways. Eliza— accompanied by a perplexed Pardle—went first to the Winkworths, hoping the invitation could be quickly given and easily accepted, but no one was at home. Eliza left a note begging their presence and excusing the late notice—if Mrs. Winkworth received it in time, Eliza knew she would come. But if she did not . . .

Eliza hastened next to Laura Place, where she realized she could not, in fact, remember on which side of Lady Hurley the Melvilles lived. Was it number four or number eight? She paused, thinking wildly of demanding Pardle start banging on doors, when the sound of a door opening made her turn her head, to see Melville stepping out onto the pavement of number four, evidently speaking to someone over his shoulder.

"Melville!" Eliza cried, brightening immediately.

Melville gave a start.

"Good God," he said, looking around at Eliza and clutching a hand to his heart. "Do you mean to kill me?"

"My apologies," she said.

"To what do I owe the—somewhat dubious—pleasure, my lady?" Melville said, sweeping his hands down his topcoat as if to brush off his surprise. "I would invite you inside, but you find me on my way into town."

"May I escort you?" Eliza asked—instantly flushed at the awkward phrasing.

"Escort me?" Melville repeated, amused. "Do you mean to protect my virtue from bandits?"

But he offered an arm, and Eliza took it without answering. They fell into step together, and Eliza considered how best to word her invitation, ideally with charming spontaneity rather than hapless dilatoriness.

"I was hopeful, this afternoon, of paying you another visit," he said. "One that might last, perhaps, a little longer than the first."

In all the excitement of the day, Eliza had entirely forgotten about the rushed conclusion of the Melvilles' call and her face flamed now in renewed mortification.

"You have my sincere apologies," Eliza said. "It was not my intention to make you feel as though you had to cut your visit short."

"It's no matter," Melville said. "Caroline explained to me that you're in love with Somerset . . . I'm curious; would you call him your nephew?"

Eliza choked on air.

"I—I—I," she stammered. "H-how dare you! He is certainly not *my* nephew! And I am not in love with him!"

"I shan't mention it to anyone, if that is why you are concerned," Melville said.

"If that is why I am concerned?" Eliza repeated. "My lord, you seem to be going out of your way to ask me the most intrusive, most indelicate . . . many people would consider it a great impertinence."

"I hope you are not one of them," he said. "They sound tedious."

"Perhaps we might instead speak on more traditional topics," Eliza said, trying desperately to grasp back the reins of the conversation. "Such as the very fine weather we have been enjoying?"

"And how long must we speak of the weather," Melville asked, with a dubious look up to the sky, "before we can return to more interesting matters? What caused you to marry his uncle instead? The title?"

It was decided. Eliza could emphatically not, in good conscience, invite this man to dinner. She would have to cancel the whole endeavor. Perhaps she could pretend to Somerset that their guests had all called off due to illness . . . But that lie would have the immediate threat of discovery. She could pretend that *she* was ill, instead—Somerset already thought her so, after all—but even then, could she trust that the Winkworths, forward as they had already been to Somerset, would not mention the lately delivered and quickly retracted invitation? In all possible outcomes, Eliza was left humiliated. Eliza imagined the smugness upon Lady Selwyn's face, if she heard the dinner party had been called off at such a late hour, the frown on Somerset's face at such inelegant behavior.

She shook her head. She could not. She would simply have to try and make the best of it.

"My intention in visiting you today," Eliza said doggedly, "was to invite you and Lady Caroline to a small dinner party I am hosting."

"Will there be dancing?" Melville asked.

"Certainly not!" Eliza said. One could not dance in black.

"A shame," he said. "When is the blessed event to occur?"

"Ah—tonight, in fact," she said. "A spontaneous decision— I hope you will forgive the very short notice."

He looked at her sideways, as if suspecting there was far more to the story.

"Is anyone else attending?" he asked suspiciously.

"Somerset," she said. "And the Selwyns. And, I hope, the Winkworths."

"Ah," he said. "Well, after a great deal of consideration—and due attention paid to all my previous engagements—I am afraid I cannot attend."

"What previous engagements?" Eliza demanded.

"I have engaged myself to spend as little time with the Winkworths as possible," Melville said. "I find that I despise them—all save for Miss Winkworth, who I merely find dull."

"You have only met them once!"

"And I find that sufficient."

"It is not a proper excuse," Eliza protested.

"Why should I need an excuse?" Melville said. "The simple fact of the matter is that it does not at all sound like something I would enjoy. Why should we attend?"

Eliza stopped abruptly in the street, and turned to face Melville, feeling so frustrated with him—with everything—that she might just cry.

"I had thought you desired my friendship, my lord," she said, desperately. "And what is friendship, if not kindnesses such as this?"

He looked at her for a long moment.

"Perhaps we could strike a bargain," he suggested.

Eliza raised her eyes to heaven, silently asking the lord for patience.

"What kind of bargain?" she asked at last, still with her eyes upon the sky.

"If we attend . . ." Melville said slowly, as if he were trying to think of what he wanted, "then you must show me your paintings."

Eliza looked at him in surprise.

"Why, that is very easily done," she said. She would have expected something far more outrageous.

"That," Melville said, "is what I have been saying all of this time."

"Then I accept," Eliza said, ignoring this. "Please arrive at half past six."

She hurried away.

"Half past six in the *afternoon?*" Melville called after, horror plain in his voice. Eliza did not turn back to answer.

10

⚜

The evening was not an immediate disaster. Indeed, before the guests arrived matters were progressing beautifully: Eliza returned home to find a note of acceptance from Mrs. Winkworth, the dining room dressed beautifully with fresh flowers, and that Perkins and the cook had managed to concoct a delicious menu that did, miraculously, include veal. And once Eliza and Margaret had dressed for dinner—Eliza in a chemise of black Italian gauze, fastened in the center with a jet brooch, and Margaret in a gown of Berlin silk that matched her eyes—they were so well pleased with their reflections that Eliza began to tentatively hope that despite the impulsive nature of the plan, and despite the fact that a more ill-matched group of persons could not be found in England, the evening might not turn out too badly.

It was a hope that lasted until the Winkworths' arrival, ten minutes early. For when they learned the Melvilles would also be in attendance that evening, their pleasure at being invited to dine with so many members of the peerage subsided dramatically.

"Did you know of this?" Admiral Winkworth demanded of his wife.

"Lady Somerset made no mention of it in her note," Mrs. Winkworth said.

"Is there an issue?" Eliza said. Eliza had known the Winkworths did not like the Melvilles, but she had hoped their social pretensions would be sufficient motivation to overcome it.

Admiral Winkworth rustled his moustache with vigor enough to sweep the floor.

"When I was stationed in Calcutta, my lady," he said, "it was common enough for the soldiers to consort with native women, but for a member of our nobility to *marry*, to mix his British blood with that of—"

"Lord Melville and Lady Caroline are my *guests*!" Eliza interrupted, frantically. "I must request you treat them with civility."

"If I may speak plainly—" Admiral Winkworth began.

"No!" Eliza blurted out. "No—I am sorry, but I would prefer that you do not, sir."

Eliza's heart was beating with nauseating quickness. She exchanged panicked glances with Margaret.

"If you cannot be comfortable in their company, then . . ." Eliza trailed off. They could not ask the Winkworths to leave—could they? No. The clock was striking half past the hour, and she could hear the front door being opened again below—it was too late.

"Of course we can!" Mrs. Winkworth stepped in, shooting her husband a quelling look. "Can we not, husband?"

"The Right Honorable. The Earl of Melville, and the Lady Caroline Melville," Perkins announced.

"Good evening," Eliza whispered.

The Melvilles looked characteristically dashing: Lady Caroline in a gossamer satin robe of dove grey with white lace striping across the skirt, her hair dressed with pearls, and Melville in a close-fitting black coat, plain white waistcoat and pantaloons—his curls a little dampened by the rain that had begun to fall.

"Behold!" he said, with a flourishing bow before Eliza. "We are on time."

"You seem very proud of yourself," Margaret noted, with more calm than Eliza felt herself capable.

"Oh, it is a veritable coup," Lady Caroline assured her. "We have not been so punctual in years."

"In the navy, we flogged the late," Admiral Winkworth said. There was a beat of silence.

"It becomes instantly clear why military men are all so dreary," Lady Caroline observed.

Margaret laughed, Admiral Winkworth grunted, Mrs. Winkworth's posture was very tense, and her daughter stood silent, tremulous with anxiety—and so when Somerset was announced shortly after, Eliza could have fainted with relief. She was even pleased to see the Selwyns.

"Somerset, you have of course already made the acquaintance of Lord Melville and Lady Caroline," Eliza said. "But Lord and Lady Selwyn, I do not believe that—"

"No, we have not, and I consider it a veritable travesty!" Lady Selwyn declared, her face wreathed in smiles. "When we have so very many common friends who ought to have made introductions years ago."

Lady Selwyn could be charming when she chose and Melville was certainly falling for it, returning her curtsey with a bow and her smile with a grin.

"What friends are these?" he said with mock outrage. "We must berate them severely for such a failure."

"Southey, for one," Selwyn supplied, taking this enquiry literally. "Scott. Sheridan."

"Oh my, Sheridan," Mrs. Winkworth murmured, much impressed.

"Dead now, of course," Selwyn told her.

"And I believe you have met Mrs. and Miss Winkworth, Somerset," Eliza said. "Though perhaps not the Admiral . . ."

"No indeed, we have *all* met his lordship once before, have we not, husband?" Mrs. Winkworth said, stepping forward.

"The races, wasn't it?" Admiral Winkworth agreed.

"The opera, I am told," Somerset corrected mildly, catching Eliza's eye, and she ducked her head to hide a smile.

Would she ever stop feeling quite so flabbergasted by the mere sight of him? A moment before she had been miserable with nerves and now, with one caught glance, she felt suddenly seventeen, as tremulously excited as if she were about to dance for the very first time. A moment later, Perkins appeared to declare dinner to be ready and Eliza led the party downstairs, a measure calmer. The Selwyns, previously the villains of the day, seemed now her salvation—and so long as Somerset remained smiling at her, she could be satisfied.

They sat according to gender and rank: Eliza at the head of the table, with Melville and Somerset on either side of her, Lady Selwyn and Lady Caroline next to them, then Admiral Winkworth and Selwyn, Margaret and Mrs. Winkworth, and finally Miss Winkworth at the end. The foot of the table, of course, remained empty and as they seated themselves Lady Selwyn sent a sorrowful look down toward it.

"A melancholy reminder indeed," she observed to the room at large, "that my dear, dear uncle should rightfully be with us tonight."

Since Lady Selwyn had been perfectly content dining after the funeral, Eliza was hard-pressed to believe her sorrow genuine, but the comment cast an immediate pall over the table.

"I hear he was a great man," Admiral Winkworth grunted.

"The best," Selwyn said sycophantically.

Eliza cast about for a change of subject.

"Indeed, it is not I, but Lady Somerset, who merits your comfort," Lady Selwyn said, before Eliza could think of anything. "For rarely have I seen a couple more in love than she and my uncle."

The lie was so unexpected that it rendered Eliza speechless. Beside Eliza, Somerset shifted uncomfortably in his seat and Eliza cast him a quick, worried glance but his eyes avoided hers. Pressing her advantage, Lady Selwyn extended a hand in Eliza's direction.

"I admire your fortitude, my lady," she said, voice brimming with affected sympathy. "Merely looking at *his* seat renders me on the point of tears—I wonder that you can bear it."

At this, Eliza's voice returned to her.

"Your admiration is gratifying, my lady, but unnecessary," she said. "Since the last gentleman to claim that seat—a Mr. Martin, I believe—is very much alive and well, the chair does not cause me pain."

"Indeed, there is not the smallest need to weep over *any* of our furniture," Margaret agreed. "Unless it is the oak itself you find upsetting, Lady Selwyn?"

Her retort sent the smugness fading from Lady Selwyn's gaze and Lady Caroline gave an amused snort of laughter— but Mrs. Winkworth's eyes were darting around the table and Eliza could practically sense her composing the tidbits of gossip she would be circulating the next day.

"I think the rain is like to continue," Eliza said with forced brightness. The gentlemen began to serve out the first course: white soup, a cod's head, and the promised loin of veal, accompanied by a few larded sweetbreads, a raised pie and vegetables dressed in melted butter.

Outside, a loud knell of thunder sounded.

"I think you might be right," Lady Caroline said dryly.

"Only in England could rain be considered good conversation," Selwyn said unctuously. "In Paris, the standards are far higher, are they not, Lady Caroline?"

"Have you spent much time in Paris, Lady Caroline?" Margaret asked, ignoring Selwyn.

"Yes, it is quite my favorite European city," Lady Caroline said. "I was very much in favor of our removing there this spring, but Melville deemed it too expensive and so . . . Bath it was."

The disparaging tone of her voice had the effect of irritating both Margaret and Mrs. Winkworth—an otherwise unlikely alliance.

"I am sure we consider ourselves very fortunate," Margaret said.

"Perhaps there is still a chance you may change your mind?" Mrs. Winkworth suggested.

"Oh brava, Caroline, you have offended half the table in one thrust," Melville said. "Am I expected to act as your second if Miss Balfour calls you out?"

"Oh no." Lady Caroline shook her head. "You are a terrible shot, Melville."

There was a tinkle of laughter around the table. Easier ground having been achieved at last, Eliza asked Mrs. Winkworth, who was so closely acquainted with both Masters of Ceremonies, what concerts they could look forward to next month. This conversational essay went down well: Mrs. Winkworth warmed to the flattery and Selwyn was so equally delighted to display his musical prowess that the resulting discussion lasted until the second course.

"Now, Melville, I must ask," Selwyn began portentously, as plates of partridges and dressed crab were brought to replenish the table, accompanied by a fricassee of chicken and a cream of spinach, "when might we expect you to publish again?"

"We do await your next instalment with a great deal of impatience," Lady Selwyn added.

"Doesn't everyone," Lady Caroline muttered into her glass.

"It pains me to disappoint a lady," Melville said, "but I must: I am not writing currently."

"But why!" Selwyn exclaimed. "When you have the *ton* waiting on your every word?"

Melville gave a shrug and took a draught of wine.

"One cannot know when Lady Inspiration will visit."

"You have me jealous, Melville." Somerset spoke up for the first time in several minutes.

Melville turned to regard him.

"Sayeth more," he invited.

"It must be agreeable to always have such a ready explanation for impotence—in the military, such excuses did not fly."

"Have trouble with your musket, did you?" Melville asked.

Somerset choked on a mouthful of burgundy.

"Are *you* writing anything new, Lady Caroline?" Eliza asked loudly.

"I am," Lady Caroline said. "A sequel to *Kensington*, in fact."

"Truly?" Eliza asked, startled. It had been three years now since the publication of Lady Caroline's eyebrow-raising novel, *Kensington*—a satire that had so pointedly lampooned lords and ladies in political circles that she had reputedly been banned from Almack's ever since. Eliza would have thought this harsh consequence reason enough to prevent Lady Caroline from continuing.

"There are many figures in society that have yet escaped my pen," Lady Caroline said.

"Ought we to be frightened, Lady Caroline?" Mrs. Winkworth said archly. "If you are to write such a novel in Bath, do you plan to feature us in it?"

"That depends, Mrs. Winkworth," Lady Caroline said. "Do you plan on doing something interesting?"

Mrs. Winkworth snapped her mouth shut and Margaret gave a choke of laughter, while Lady Selwyn's eyes darted around the table and Selwyn shook his head in disapproval. Admiral Winkworth, thankfully, appeared too busy with the cod's head to attend the conversation.

"I wonder, Melville," Somerset said. "Was it only economy that made you choose Bath over Paris?"

Eliza thought this conversation long over—apparently not.

"The fine company was also a draw," Melville said. "And the—ah—scenery, too."

"Your estate could not offer you scenery?"

"Oh, Alderley Park is far too large for two. We have let it to friends, so that others might make more use of it."

"How extremely charitable." Somerset speared a floret of broccoli with unusual aggression.

"Why thank you, Somerset, I am flattered you think so."

"It was not necessarily intended as a compliment."

There was a new tension thrumming in the air—one Eliza did not fully understand.

"Nevertheless, I have chosen to take it as one."

"Then perhaps I worded it incorrectly."

"Ah, not everyone can be a wordsmith."

"I think we are ready for the final course now, Perkins!" Eliza said loudly. Perkins, Eliza's only true ally tonight, had the table emptied in a trice, setting out a simple dessert of preserved fruits, a Savoy cake, and a plate of roasted chestnuts.

Silence now reigned. All seemed a little fatigued from the tussle of conversation, and Eliza racked her brains for another easy, neutral topic on which they could speak, one that was neither dreadfully boring nor disturbingly antagonistic. Nothing sprang to mind. She could not bear to look at Somerset. He must certainly be regretting that he had ever agreed to such an invitation, as Eliza was wholeheartedly regretting issuing it.

Think of something, Eliza begged her own mind, *anything*.

Rescue came, in the end, from an unexpected direction.

"Is Miss Selwyn keeping well, my lady?" Miss Winkworth said, so softly she would surely not have been heard, had the table not already been so quiet.

"She is," Lady Selwyn said, looking up from her plate. "Are you acquainted?"

"They attended school together," Mrs. Winkworth boasted.

"Is that so, Miss Winkworth?" Somerset said, smiling down to her. Under his kind gaze, Miss Winkworth seemed about to muster sufficient courage to speak, but as she parted her lips Mrs. Winkworth interjected.

"Yes, indeed. Winnie is forever wishing they might meet again."

"You may be in luck," Somerset said, looking directly at Miss Winkworth as if it were she, and not her mother, who had spoken. "My sister is considering hiring rooms in Bath this spring."

"Is that indeed so?" Mrs. Winkworth demanded, leaning forward.

"It is not yet decided," Lady Selwyn said. "But we may bring out Annie a little into society here before we depart for the London Season in April."

"A famous idea!" Mrs. Winkworth said. "She would undoubtedly benefit from the experience."

"I agree," Somerset said. "A person's first Season can be so very . . . overwhelming."

Across the table, his eyes met Eliza's very briefly. She wondered if he, too, was thinking of the same memories she was: the dances they had shared, the confidences, the whispered conversations.

"You are bringing Miss Selwyn out already?" Eliza asked.

Annie had been just a girl when Eliza had last seen her, with huge eyes and tangled hair and a tongue so impertinent even Lady Selwyn had not been able to curb it.

"She is turned seventeen," Selwyn said.

"Oh, practically ancient," Margaret muttered under her breath and Eliza shot her a repressive look, though her heart did go out to the absent girl.

"We ourselves have had Winne out in Bath for a year now,"

Mrs. Winkworth said, "in the hope of curing her of some shyness before she is pitchforked into London."

Miss Winkworth flushed.

"One does not at all mind a little shyness, when one does it so charmingly as Miss Winkworth," Somerset said.

"Exactly so," Eliza agreed, with a rush of affection for his kindness.

"A little is fine," Admiral Winkworth grunted. "An excess is fatal."

Miss Winkworth's pink complexion turned saffron.

"Do you have a match in mind for Miss Selwyn?" Mrs. Winkworth asked.

Eliza hoped for Annie's sake that her mother was not quite so ambitious as Eliza's had been. The graduation from girlhood to womanhood was not an easy one in any case, as Eliza could easily recollect: the weight of expectation suddenly felt, the constant admonishment, the pressing need to be daintier, prettier, *more* in every way—the anxious, sick feeling one carried around in one's very soul, that it would not be enough.

"Certainly," Selwyn said. "One does not allow one's daughter to marry willy-nilly."

"No, no, of course not," Margaret said, deepening her voice into a clear imitation of Selwyn's bluster. "One cannot simply allow women to make their own decisions."

Eliza bit back a moan of despair. Did she have to imitate him?

"Stands to reason," Lady Caroline agreed. "Where on earth would it lead?"

Was it too soon for the ladies to retire for tea?

"Of course, Lord and Lady Selwyn would never want Miss Selwyn to marry where affection was not," Somerset interjected in swift defense. "Only to offer guidance!"

Eliza looked down. Guidance was so soft a word, but she

knew better than most how insistent it could be, how inexorable. Lord and Lady Selwyn might not order Annie to marry the man of their choice, no. No, they would merely push and prod her, advise her against selfishness, recommend she think of her brothers, think of her cousins, the *family*. They would decree that first love faded, that marital affection grew from familiarity, would promise that in a year's time she would have a baby on her knee and that by then the memory of that fellow she used to care for would have faded into obscurity . . . Guidance of that sort was not soft. It could not be resisted. It would be pressed upon one, over and over again until it was easiest, simplest—even a relief—just to capitulate.

"Oh yes, guidance is imperative!" Mrs. Winkworth said. "One would not want Miss Selwyn to marry beneath her."

Eliza felt her mouth twist in a rather bitter smile. Somerset's eyes skittered briefly to her and then away again. She wondered if he, too, was considering the irony of his now being on the other side of the argument, when once it was he, with no title or fortune to recommend him, who had been considered the inferior match.

"And what if her sentiments do not align with your guidance?" Margaret asked.

Lady Selwyn raised a brow and did not answer.

"I think it unlikely," Selwyn said.

"And should such a moment arise," Somerset added, "Annie would certainly speak her mind."

"Has everyone sampled the Savoy cake?" Eliza asked, deciding that she could not bear to listen to this any longer. She would rather they return to any of the fraught subjects of the evening, than spend another moment discussing Annie's future.

"Yes, delicious," Melville said, obeying Eliza's entreating gaze. "Perhaps I might offer it around again—"

"And in the event of such a moment arising," Margaret

pressed Somerset. "You would cede to her wishes—as the head of the family?"

Eliza tried desperately to catch Margaret's eye—she did not know what her cousin was trying to achieve, but it was not to Eliza's liking. If she was intentionally alluding to Eliza's own history, then this was not the time for it. For what purpose did it serve now?

"Certainly," Somerset said. Lady Selwyn's mouth thinned, but she remained silent—she was too well-bred to disagree with her brother in front of so many observers.

"And if she fell in love with a pauper?" Lady Caroline said.

"I—I . . . We—" Somerset broke off. Under the twin, judging gazes of Margaret and Lady Caroline, his neck began to redden.

"She would not," Selwyn asserted.

"Out of the question," his wife agreed.

"Because she would never think to disobey?" Margaret suggested.

"*Because*," Somerset interjected. "Because we would discuss it and—"

He broke off again, unable to answer satisfactorily.

"Parry, sir, parry," Melville encouraged.

Somerset sent him a burning look.

"Annie knows her duty," Selwyn interjected. "She'll come to heel."

Eliza squeezed her eyes shut for a moment, wishing she were able to do the same to her ears.

"It would never come to that," Somerset snapped. His gaze flickered to Eliza again, defensive and harried, and then back to Margaret.

"If Miss Selwyn is as I remember," Miss Winkworth said softly, sending a dimpling smile in Somerset's direction, "she has spirit enough to make her opinion known."

"Yes, exactly," Somerset agreed at once. His eyes locked

again with Eliza's. "A lack of spirit is certainly not *Annie's* issue."

It was as if a bucket of icy water had been thrown abruptly over Eliza. She sucked in a desperate, shocked breath, feeling as if all the wind had been knocked out of her. All nine faces around the table turned toward her, but she did not heed them—still staring at Somerset, stricken to her very bones.

"My lady . . ." Melville said very softly.

Eliza stood without making a conscious decision to do so, the legs of her chair making a dramatic screech against the floor.

"I think it is time for the ladies to retire for tea," Eliza said. She could barely hear her own voice over the sound of her heart pounding in her ears. "Margaret, if you will escort everyone to the drawing room, I will," she caught her breath on a slight gasp, "I will join you in just a moment."

11

E liza darted from the room and up the stairs, hardly knowing where she was going, only that she needed to be alone. Just a moment, to master herself unobserved. She pushed her way into her bedchamber, closed the door and leaned back against the wood, closing her eyes and trying to breathe. Even now, she could not allow herself to break completely, for the sobs burning for release in her throat were not quiet, ladylike tears that she could indulge in for a few minutes before wiping her face and reappearing seamlessly into the dinner party. These tears would be loud and ugly. They would make her eyes swollen, her cheeks red, and everyone would see, and although she had already made a scene, already had her distress witnessed by everyone, Eliza still pressed her hand against her mouth and held the anguish in.

He had not forgiven her. And Eliza had not expected him to, exactly, but to be presented with such irrefutable proof, as clear as day in the bite of his words, the damning fire in his eyes . . . It was a shock, that was all. He had not forgiven her. He could not, he would not—and whatever secret hopes she had been harboring over their reacquaintance were foolish. This dinner party was foolish. Had she truly thought that if she contrived enough reasons for them to spend time together, believed that if she could hold him here in Bath, away from the poisonous tongues of his family—that he might fall in love with her again?

She had spent the day dashing around Bath, spent hours in front of the mirror, teasing her hair just so, in eager pursuit of a gentleman who held her in such contempt. A gentleman who had insulted her at her own dinner table, in full view of all her guests, with words that might have been especially designed to hurt her. Eliza pressed a hand to her breastbone as if the pain there might be eased with physical pressure. All this evening had achieved was to reopen a wound that ought to have healed long ago . . . Still, at least she knew she could endure this. She had become adept, over the years, at enduring this kind of hurt.

Eliza took a deep, steadying breath. Pushing her shoulders back and her memories down, she opened the door and headed for the stairs. It was time to rejoin the fray. As much as she might want to send all her guests away now and hang the consequences, she ought to save some face: an hour more of tea-sipping and polite chit-chat and then she could bid the whole awful, humiliating endeavor adieu. Eliza made to enter the drawing room, when she saw the door to the parlor—her painting parlor—was standing ajar, a pane of light escaping into the hallway. Worrying that she might have left a candle lit, she pushed the door fully open to find Melville standing there, examining the pile of watercolors that lay upon the table.

"Lord Melville?" Eliza said uncertainly. What was the appropriate way to challenge someone, when they were so obviously caught not where they were meant to be?

"My apologies for trespassing," he said, not at all apologetic. "You did say I could see them."

"I did not think you meant tonight," Eliza said, voice hushed. She would have prepared if she had known, would certainly not have encouraged him to riffle free rein through all her pieces. "Have you left Admiral Winkworth, Selwyn and Somerset all alone to the port?"

"I had to," Melville said at his usual volume. Eliza shushed him, casting a worried glance over her shoulder—it would cause more than raised eyebrows if they were found here, alone together, and the drawing room was only a little way down the hall. Melville obediently lowered his voice as he continued, "Winkworth was enumerating upon his kills during the siege of Seringapatam, Selwyn was listing all the classical tales I should be inspired by, and Somerset had sunk into depressed silence. An interval had to be sought."

Eliza felt a sudden pang of guilt.

"I am sorry," she said. "What an awful evening! I should never have induced you to come. Had I known that Winkworth . . ."

She trailed off. She had known—a little—of at least Mrs. Winkworth's aversion to the Melvilles, but in the moment, she had simply cared more for her dinner party.

"We shall not break bread with them again," Melville said softly, hands still moving through the pages, and Eliza nodded.

"What an awful evening," she said again.

"The fricassee, I enjoyed," Melville said with a quirk of a smile.

"Oh well, then I may rest easy," Eliza said, returning it.

Melville held up another painting to the candlelight.

"You have such talent, you know."

Eliza paused.

"Are you . . . making fun of me?" she asked. One could never be sure, with Melville.

"Why would I?" he said. "I do not pretend to be an expert, but these are as good as any of the paintings I have seen at the Royal Academy. The emotion you are able to convey!"

He moved next to a landscape of a lurid storm hovering over Harefield Hall.

"Is this Harefield?" he asked.

Eliza nodded silently, a little dazed by the admiration in his gaze.

"I had not realized you hated it," he observed quietly. "The way you paint it—always so cold, so desolate. Have you considered exhibiting?"

Eliza let out a little huff of surprised laughter and shook her head.

"And yet this must have taken you hours," Melville said. "The effort . . ."

"It is just for me," Eliza said. "But that does not make it any less worthwhile."

Melville stared at her for a moment, before he carried on riffling through, hands careful, eyes admiring, and paying her compliments so gracefully that Eliza could forget her unworthiness as she drank them in. Any dread she might have felt at the sight of him, here, looking at paintings only Margaret had ever seen, elapsed—and so overwhelmed was she to receive praise, so eager was she to receive more, that she entirely forgot what he might find in the pile.

"Is that me?" Melville said, checking suddenly.

"Don't!" Eliza said, moving forward, hand outstretched.

But it was too late, he had pulled it from the pile and held it near to the candle for a better look: the painting of himself, leaning in coquettishly to Lady Hurley, while Mrs. Winkworth and Mr. Fletcher looked crossly on.

"It *is* me!"

"I—I . . ." she stammered. What could she possibly say? There was no way to deny it. "It was just, that first night at the concert you—and it caught my attention—and I often paint such scenes as have occurred in the day, I hope you do not mind . . ."

"Remarkably accurate," he said, considering it. "Though I fancy I am a little taller than this."

The floor, stubborn and useless and unhelpful, opted not to swallow Eliza whole.

"We ought to return to the party. Our absence will have been noted," she said.

"You know, Mr. Berwick has been attempting to persuade me to sit for a portrait," Melville mused, ignoring this last point.

"So I hear." Eliza placed a hand pointedly upon the door.

"I told him no," Melville said.

Eliza gestured toward the hallway.

"Though I have been advised that it might . . . help," Melville said, "to include a portrait at the front of my works."

"Perhaps we could speak of this another time . . ."

"Would you do it, if I asked?" Melville asked, his voice still low and his eyes suddenly fixed upon hers.

"I do not understand . . ."

"Would you be my portraitist?" Melville said.

He seemed serious—he could not be.

"I am not sure where the joke is in this," she said. "But I wish you will stop and let us return to the rest of our party."

"I am not joking," he said. "You are very good and you capture likeness—mine and others—with character, but not flummery."

Eliza stared at him. As a girl she had often imagined such scenes as this: a handsome young lord being so taken with her artistry that he at once requested a commission (and then, after, her hand in marriage). But such things did not happen in real life. It was preposterous. Even if she were skilled enough—which she was not—the talk it would generate, the impropriety of making such a spectacle of herself . . . Eliza passed a hand across her forehead, which was beginning to ache. This was too much. After everything this evening had already contained she could not manage this, too.

"I should very much like you to do it," Melville prompted, when Eliza did not speak.

"I am flattered, my lord, but you should seek out a professional," Eliza said.

"From what I can see, you *are* a professional."

"Have you not already admitted you are not an expert?"

"You see, I was being humble," Melville explained with a grin Eliza did not return.

"I must decline."

"Why?"

"There are too many reasons," Eliza said. "It is inconceivable."

"Is it?"

Eliza wished he would drop the matter: declining something she badly wished to accept was difficult enough to do once.

"You have been very kind, my lord," Eliza said. "But, indeed, I am not what your kindness esteems me. I am uneducated, untested, unproven. And it would cause such talk."

Melville tilted his head one way, then the other.

"Is it that you do not want to?" he said.

"I . . ." Eliza said, quite at a loss. If matters were different, if the world were different, she would have already agreed. She might even have asked it of Melville first, just as Mr. Berwick had. But just because she wanted to, just because this was the sort of opportunity she had been dreaming of since she could hold a paintbrush, did not mean she could simply *do* it. It was unthinkable—wasn't it?

"I ought not to press you," Melville said, when she did not speak. "If you do not wish to, that is absolutely—"

"No," Eliza interrupted him. "No, I *do*—I might—"

She broke off. Melville waited silently, with more patience

than she would have expected from him, as she struggled to marshal her thoughts—it was impossible to think clearly, under such roiling emotions. She could not.

"Perhaps we might . . . discuss it," she decided.

"I adore discussion," Melville agreed promptly, and at last obeying the open door, he followed her out and made his way downstairs.

Eliza entered the drawing room to find Lady Caroline on the point of concluding an amusing anecdote involving a Parisian nun, a glove, and a grandfather clock that had Margaret dissolving in laughter. Lady Selwyn and Mrs. Winkworth turned to watch Eliza as she came in.

"Are you feeling well, my lady?" Mrs. Winkworth asked.

"Quite well," Eliza said crisply.

"You were gone such a while, we had begun to worry."

"There was no need."

"Did I hear Lord Melville come upstairs, too?" Lady Selwyn wondered. "I could have sworn I did . . ."

"If you are concerned about hearing things," Eliza said with a snap, "I think that rather a question for your doctor."

"Lady Hurley swears by Mr. Gibbes, if you are in need of a recommendation," Lady Caroline put in, eyes mischievous over her teacup.

"Oh, I should not trust Lady Hurley's judgment," Mrs. Winkworth said at once, leaning toward Lady Selwyn. "The woman is one of Bath's oddities—she may dress herself up with airs and graces, but there is the distinct scent of the City about her. My husband sometimes refers to her as Lady Hurly-Burly."

Lady Selwyn gave an appreciative titter.

"Very clever," Margaret said flatly.

"Lady Hurley has been very kind to Melville and me," Lady Caroline said with a raise of one arched brow.

Lady Selwyn ceased her titter at once and Mrs. Winkworth

flushed, but the gentlemen joined them before any rejoinder could be offered. Eliza smiled up at them in placid welcome, though she could not look at Somerset, for she knew she could not do so without fresh mortification staining her cheeks.

"Did you enjoy your *digestif*?" Lady Selwyn asked.

"Very much so," Somerset said. "Admiral Winkworth and I discovered that we have been stationed in many of the same ports."

"Oh, how marvelous," Mrs. Winkworth said enthusiastically.

"I too have visited a great many of those ports," Melville added, as he sat beside Margaret, "though in, I would say, a different capacity."

Margaret laughed openly while Eliza suppressed her own smile.

"That is a magnificent pianoforte, my lady," Mrs. Winkworth said loudly. "Do you play?"

Eliza looked over to the instrument in question and shook her head.

"I'm afraid it is sadly neglected," she said.

"You are not musical?" Melville asked, pouring himself a cup of tea.

"I have neither voice nor skill," she said.

"Much to your husband's despair!" Selwyn said, with a chuff of laughter.

Margaret glared at him.

"Do you recollect, Lady Somerset," Lady Selwyn said, with a tinkling laugh of her own, "the night your engagement was announced, when he bade you to sing for us all at Grosvenor Square?"

"I do," Eliza said grimly. It was rare, after all, for persons to have to live out their very worst nightmare—one did not easily forget it.

"You were so reluctant!" Selwyn said. "And we soon understood why!"

Eliza did not think she had ever hated a person more.

"Selwyn . . ." Somerset said quietly.

"We are just funning, Somerset!" Selwyn protested.

"I am not laughing."

An hour ago, such a defense might have warmed Eliza, but now it only worsened the throbbing in her forehead. Was Somerset setting out to be confusing? To alternatively ignore her and tease her, snap at her, then defend her. It was dizzying.

"Oh, gentlemen cannot help but wish their wives accomplished," Mrs. Winkworth said. "Whomever Winnie marries will be fortunate on that account, for she was born singing so sweetly."

There was a pause, as the company murmured politely. Then, as if she had been suddenly struck with a Very Good Idea, Mrs. Winkworth added, "Why, Winifred ought to entertain you with a song, now, Lady Somerset!"

"Mama . . ." Miss Winkworth whispered, shaking her head.

"I am persuaded a little music would be just the thing!" Mrs. Winkworth insisted.

Was there to be no end to their torment, tonight? Or was there merely to be an endless stream of unpleasantness for Eliza to sit through, helpless to avoid or avert?

"Oh yes!" Selwyn agreed. "Perhaps a jig of some sort."

"The perfect end to the perfect evening," Lady Selwyn said slyly.

"Mama, I cannot," Miss Winkworth said.

"Lady Somerset, I beg you will add your entreaties to mine!" Mrs. Winkworth said to Eliza. "My daughter is too modest to perform without them."

"If Miss Winkworth would rather not sing for us, I am not sure I—" Eliza began, as firmly as she was able.

"Mere bashfulness," Admiral Winkworth said. "Come now, girl, do not keep us waiting any longer."

"Oh, do not compel her, sir." Melville joined the defense of Miss Winkworth. "For then I will feel myself similarly obliged, and that I am persuaded you would certainly *not* enjoy!"

Margaret and Lady Caroline laughed, but Eliza could not be distracted from the sight of Mrs. Winkworth hissing remonstrances into her daughter's ear. Miss Winkworth's breathing looked now alarmingly quick and the ache behind Eliza's eyes twisted higher.

"Please do not . . ." she started, as Mrs. Winkworth began to chivvy her daughter out of her seat.

Once again, Eliza wished fervently that she could end the evening here and now: flout all convention and breach all rules of hospitality, send her guests away, and not care for the possible ramifications of such ill-manners. Would that such a course of action were open to her!

Except . . . was it not open to her? It would be ill-mannered, yes, inelegant, certainly—shockingly bad *ton*, in fact, but . . . But this was *Eliza's* house. They were drinking *her* tea. Attending *her* dinner party. Why should she sit here and pretend the Selwyns' jibes did not offend her, pretend the Winkworths were not horrible, pretend that she wanted to be here at all? There was no one to reprimand Eliza for inelegance, anymore. She was a woman grown, with a mind—and fortune—of her own, and she did not want to sit here for one moment longer.

For the second time that evening, Eliza stood. Her heart was beating as quickly as if she were about to leap off a precipice.

"I am afraid I have the headache," she said briskly. "And so, while I am sure Miss Winkworth's performance would give considerable pleasure, I must now retire."

The shocked silence that lay in the wake of her declaration might have made her wince had Miss Winkworth not been gazing at her with the stunned air of a mouse unexpectedly freed from a trap.

"Thank you for a lovely evening," Eliza said.

Lady Caroline set down a half-drunk teacup with a clink and stood. Silently, still stunned, the rest of the party rose to take their farewells.

"Brava," Melville whispered, bowing over her hand. Eliza did not respond, instead extending her hand next to Lady Selwyn, whose eyes were flicking between them with more calculation than Eliza should like. Somerset was the last to leave, hesitating at the doorway and opening and closing his mouth as if he were a fish.

"My lady—" he started.

"Goodnight, Somerset," Eliza said.

Whatever he wanted to say to her, whether to apologize for his rudeness or castigate her further, she did not want to hear it tonight. Not when she was so close to falling apart.

In their absence, the house felt blissfully quiet and still. Eliza sat back down upon the sofa and closed her eyes with a sigh. She would no doubt one day be sorry for such a lapse in manners as she had committed tonight, but at this moment she could not bring herself to regret it.

"It was a very memorable evening, at any rate," Margaret said, and Eliza felt the sofa shift under her weight, too.

"Which was, of course, my chief object," Eliza said dryly.

"Oh, did you have an aim, then?" Margaret retorted. "You weren't motivated just by lunacy?"

"I think I have been," Eliza said, still with her eyes closed. "All that effort to keep Somerset here, to win something over the Selwyns . . . And for what?" She paused, swallowed, and added in a hoarser voice, "He has not forgiven me. I ought never to have expected—I knew it was foolish to hope, but . . ."

She heard a rustle as Margaret shifted, then felt her hand begin to stroke Eliza's hair.

"With the way he has been acting," Margaret said, "it was not foolish. I thought as you did."

Eliza's eyes pricked with tears as a wave of shame washed over her again.

"Why seek out my company if he holds me in such contempt?" she gulped. "I would never have—if I had not thought—"

"It was unjust," Margaret said. "And unpardonably rude in front of *everyone*—there is no excuse. And I am sorry for the part I played in bringing it about. I was trying to make a point."

Eliza chuffed a slightly bitter laugh.

"I think you did so quite successfully."

"I am sorry," Margaret said quietly, and Eliza gave a jerky nod.

Her headache had not elapsed, even in the quiet. It seemed, rather, to be taking over her whole body, moving down her neck and shoulders to meet the throbbing pressure in her chest. *You have done this before*, she reminded herself. *This time will be easier.*

"Well, he is only here for a fortnight," Margaret said pragmatically. "You may easily avoid him for such a time and then you need not see him ever again."

"Oh, do not say that," Eliza said. "That is not what I want."

"What *do* you want?"

Eliza didn't know. Her head was hopelessly tangled. She wanted to avoid Somerset forever. She could not bear to never see him again. Both were somehow, incomprehensibly, true.

"I just need some calm," she said. "It is all so much, with the Selwyns and Somerset and the Melvilles—"

"What have the Melvilles done?" Margaret asked, with a little indignation.

Eliza had not the energy to explain tonight about Melville's offer: not now, when her thoughts were so knotted that she could not tell if she were appalled or exhilarated by it.

"Nothing. I just—nothing," she said.

"I admire them very much," Margaret said staunchly. "Lady Caroline is quite the cleverest—the most amusing—woman I have met."

"Beautiful, too," Eliza added.

Margaret inclined her head, eyes flicking away.

"I wonder that she has never married," Eliza mused. "She must have had scores of offers."

"I am glad for it," Margaret said. "Most commonly, spinsters are without standing, consequence, or importance to society. It is a relief to see that is not always the case."

"You have standing, consequence and importance to *me*," Eliza said, turning to regard her dearest friend. "You are the most important person in the world, to me."

"I cannot decide if that is the most wonderful," Margaret said, "or most depressing thing I have ever heard."

But she squeezed Eliza's arm to take the sting out of her words.

"Shrew," said Eliza fondly. "That could have been a lovely moment, before you ruined it."

"That is my finest lady's accomplishment," Margaret said. "I may not be able to paint or sing or embroider, but I am certainly quite capable of ruining things."

Eliza laughed, and it was a relief to do so. Margaret could always be trusted to make her laugh—and Eliza had done so more in the past month than perhaps her whole life put together. It was worth remembering that.

And worth remembering that before Somerset had arrived

in Bath—before her world had narrowed again to the point of a single man—she had been happier than she had ever known herself before. She had Margaret. She had Camden Place. She had friends and, even, the possibility—perplexing though it might be—of an artist's commission. Losing Somerset was not the mortal blow it once was.

She just wished it did not have to hurt quite this much.

12

The Sunday services at Bath Abbey were always as dry as dust, but Reverend Green's ponderous drone the next morning was particularly unbearable. Usually, Eliza was able to sink into languor—perhaps idly deciding which of the congregation's dresses she admired most—but this morning such distraction was impossible. She had awoken just as unsettled as she had been upon going to bed, the events of the previous evening circling around her head, sharp and painful, and her agitation had been in no way eased by Somerset's decision to seat himself directly in the pew in front of her.

He might easily have chosen another row. For as much as the abbey was always busy—another place to see and be seen—it had space sufficient to choose a position to one's liking. As Eliza and Margaret had, ignoring Mrs. Winkworth's beckoning wave to slide in beside Lady Hurley and Mr. Fletcher, newly returned from their visit to the country.

". . . for God cannot be tempted with evil, neither tempteth He any man . . ."

Eliza shifted in her seat, Somerset turned his head a little and she averted her eyes. She felt sure that if she looked at him, she might burst into tears right here and now and she did not think it wise to feed Bath's gossips any more than Mrs. Winkworth had likely already done. Eliza instead resolved not to look at him at all. Though how she was to maintain this, when his shoulders were filling up her entire view with the kind of breadth that might well make an oak tree jealous, she could not imagine.

"Would you like to take a stroll around Sydney Gardens after the service?" Lady Hurley whispered in Eliza's ear—she had ceased paying attention, too. "Melville and Lady Caroline are game."

Eliza turned her head to look at Melville. He and Lady Caroline had arrived late, causing a flurry of heads to turn in their direction and Eliza to feel an unexpected surge of relief. For as much as she had been thinking obsessively over Somerset's words, last night, she had been musing upon Melville's, too. And though he might have forgotten—he might not have meant his offer seriously—she could not help hoping he might ask her again.

Melville's eyes slid from the Reverend to catch Eliza's stare—and he winked. Eliza turned hastily back around.

"Yes, that sounds very fine," she whispered to Lady Hurley.

The sound of a hundred persons murmuring a final "amen" indicated at last the end of the service, and Eliza stood with the rest of the congregation, willing the persons ahead of her to move swiftly.

"My lady?"

Eliza pretended she had not heard Somerset's voice, keeping her head turned forward. *Hurry up*, she urged the ancient Mrs. Renninson. *Hurry up*.

"Lady Somerset."

When still Eliza did not turn, Somerset touched her very lightly upon the arm and, though he was wearing gloves and she a thick pelisse, she drew back as if scalded.

"I did not mean to startle . . ." he said.

Eliza looked up at him, felt her eyes begin to smart, her throat tighten—and looked hurriedly away.

"Good morning," she said, regarding her shoes. "Did you enjoy the service?"

"My lady," Somerset said quietly, "I wish to apologize for last night."

Of course he did. Of course his sense of decency would not allow him to pass over such an evening without addressing it, but since she could certainly not maintain composure through such an ordeal today, it would have to wait.

"We are blocking the way," she said, moving down the aisle after Margaret.

Somerset followed close behind her as they spilled out into the courtyard, and Eliza and Margaret made a beeline for the spot where Lady Hurley, Mr. Fletcher and the Melvilles were gathered.

"What a tedious service," Melville was saying.

"*Not* the thing," Mr. Fletcher—who Eliza suspected to have been asleep for the entirety—agreed emphatically.

"The reverend does always run on when he's preaching against temptation," Lady Hurley said. "The poor man can't help himself."

"And now it appears he means to mingle," Lady Caroline observed, as the vicar emerged from the entrance and began shaking hands.

"He enjoys speaking with the congregation," Lady Hurley explained.

"What is there *left* to speak of?" Melville said.

"Damned if I know," Mr. Fletcher said.

Melville clapped Mr. Fletcher on the shoulder.

"We understand one another perfectly, sir," he declared. "Thank goodness you are here."

"Splendid!"

The dreariness of the service aside, Melville seemed in higher spirits than Eliza had ever seen him—eyes so bright and smile so wide that even Eliza's mood began to lift out of the clouds.

"I hear you are to join us in Sydney Gardens, my lady," Melville said, turning to offer his arm to Eliza with an extraneous flourish. "Shall we be off?"

"I had not thought you much interested in outdoor pursuits, my lord," Somerset remarked.

"Oh, you wrong me," Melville said. "Lady Hurley tells us they are pleasure gardens finer even than Vauxhall and I am most intrigued to see the labyrinth."

"I should not have thought the labyrinth a particularly appropriate activity for Sunday," Somerset said.

"Wrong again," Melville rebuffed cheerfully. "For I mean to read aloud from Fordyce's *Sermons to Young Women* as we navigate, which will render the whole activity pleasingly godly."

"Splendid . . ." Mr. Fletcher said dubiously.

"Would you care to hear one now, Somerset?" Melville asked, patting his pocket pointedly. "They do so clarify the mind."

"Thank you, but I do not lack for clarity," Somerset said, before turning to Lady Hurley. "A pleasure to make your acquaintance, madam," he said. "May I join your party?"

"Oh, how delightful," Lady Hurley trilled. "May I claim your arm? Mr. Fletcher is to visit his mother this morning and I do so suffer without a gentleman's shoulder to lean upon."

She wound her arm through Somerset's, batting her eyelashes up at him—Somerset swallowed—and set off at a decisive pace that he had no choice but to obey.

"I also walk very quickly, Lady Caroline," Margaret said in undervoice, shaking out her skirts. "Are you certain you will keep up?"

"I assure you, Miss Balfour," Lady Caroline said, "it is most certainly *I* who shall be setting the pace."

They followed swiftly in Lady Hurley's footsteps, leaving Eliza and a smiling Melville to take up the rear, with Pardle a few steps behind.

The Sydney Gardens were only a short distance from the abbey—across the Avon and down to the end of Pulteney Street—and with the leading couples walking at such a fast clip, once they were within the garden walls, they soon disappeared around the curve of the winding path ahead, leaving Eliza and Melville strolling behind. There were all manner of sights to admire: shady bowers, romantic water features and swathes of cultivated wilderness lining the serpentine paths, but Eliza dispensed with the view to regard Melville.

"Do you truly carry a copy of Fordyce's *Sermons* in your pocket?" she asked curiously.

"Dear lord no," Melville said, pulling from his coat instead a small leatherbound notebook. "The day I read Fordyce to Caroline will be the same day I die under suspicious circumstances."

"And what would you have done if Somerset *had* asked you to read a sermon?" Eliza said, smiling.

"I am surprised he did not," Melville said. "The man is so determined to challenge me on every suit."

Eliza's smile faded.

"I am sorry," she said. "I do not know why he does so."

That was not entirely true. She had thought, before, that Somerset's behavior might be inspired by jealousy, but after last night, that seemed less likely.

"He is jealous," Melville said. "As you are fully aware, and no doubt aptly exploiting."

Eliza jerked her head around, startled.

"I am *not*," she protested. "And he is not, either."

As much as she might wish differently.

"It is nothing to be ashamed of," Melville said. "We have all done much worse in love's name, and I myself do not mind in the least being used in such a way. In fact, I beg you use me more, my lady."

Eliza flushed a deep, deep red, her shoulders creeping up toward her ears, but Melville was not done. As he had on the day they first met, he dislodged Eliza's hand to spread his arms wide, as if encouraging inspection.

"I offer myself to your use," he declared, and Eliza looked wildly up and down the tree-lined path to check they were not being observed.

"You must stop," Eliza said. "You are being absurd."

Absurd and improper, even for Melville, and she hardly knew what to say in response to such outrageousness, whether she ought to laugh or—

"Perhaps we might today find ourselves caught alone in some romantic bower," Melville suggested, "leaving Somerset with no choice but to call me out. Or do you think there is an orangery in these gardens? I have always been partial to an orangery."

Now Eliza *was* laughing—it was impossible to do otherwise.

"She laughs!" Melville crowed. "At last."

He offered his arm once more, and as Eliza took it, she noticed that the cuffs of his shirt were faintly stained with ink.

"Were you writing letters this morning?" Eliza asked.

"Not letters," Melville said. He waved the notebook at her, again, before putting it back in his pocket.

"You are working again?"

"I have not told anyone," he said, "but yes. *Medea*. Vengeance, passion, heroic couplets, etcetera . . ."

His tone was flippant, but there was genuine pleasure in his face.

"I can hardly wait," Eliza said, with perfect truth. "Though I thought you were here to holiday."

"I tire of rest," Melville said. "It's terribly dreary."

"And so, the notebook is for ideas?"

"Of a sort," Melville said. "Phrases I like, words I wish to use—stuff and nonsense, really."

"My grandfather used to do the same," Eliza said, remembering. "Not words, but he would sketch scenes or objects to recall them more easily later. He told me that any artist worth their salt should do so."

"And did you take his advice?"

"I am not an artist."

"I believe we have already disagreed on that point once," Melville said—and there it was. They had finally reached the topic Eliza had been aching to raise all morning. She fell silent as the canal came into view ahead, pretending to admire the intricate Chinoiserie bridge gently sloping over it while mustering up the courage to ask the questions that had been playing on her mind since last night. To broach them, in so public a setting, felt a risk but then, with the thick verdure around them, the hills of Bathampton just visible in the distance, and only the sound of the breeze moving through the trees to accompany their footsteps, one could easily imagine she and Melville to be lost somewhere in the countryside, quite alone. Eliza took another sidelong glance at Melville.

"Were you being truly serious, about the portrait?" she asked. She would react with equanimity if he was not.

"Gravely," Melville said. "Will you agree to do it?"

"Its purpose is to be included at the front of your volumes?" she checked.

"Yes," Melville said. "I am advised that it might help broaden my reach."

"Is your current level of fame insufficient?" she asked. "Is there a lady in the *ton* who has not read your volumes?"

"The *ton*, little though we like to think it," Melville said, "makes for the tiniest proportion of England, my lady, and I should like my poems to be read more widely."

Eliza absorbed this silently.

"I realize such ungentlemanly motivation does not at all fit in with my careless *joie de vivre*," Melville added.

"But if it is so important, this portrait," Eliza said, "why ask me? I have very little formal training, and if convenience is my only advantage, you must know you could very well ask Mr. Berwick—he is said to be very talented!"

"And so I could," Melville said. "But that would require me to speak with him, my lady, and that I will not do. I'd much rather be painted by a beautiful woman than some bumptious gentleman."

"I think that is exactly why I oughtn't agree to such a scheme," Eliza muttered, half-flattered—for it was not every day one was called beautiful—and half-crestfallen, for if Melville had only picked her out of a desire to flirt . . .

"I would not ask you, if I did not think you capable," Melville said, his voice so suddenly serious that Eliza was almost shocked to see him without his usual air of flippancy. And, as it had the night before, hearing such praise—such confidence in her ability—made her feel as if she could breathe more deeply and more fully than she had ever done before.

"I want it to resemble *me*," Melville said, "not some puffed-up fool in a library holding a globe—and I do not believe anyone else could do that better."

Eliza could not imagine the Balfours, or the Selwyns—or even, truthfully, Somerset—thinking this the sort of behavior that befitted a countess in her first year of mourning. If it was discovered that she was spending so many hours with such an infamous gentleman, the safety of her fortune would unquestionably be at risk. To agree to such a scheme was an act of lunacy, but . . . To decline the kind of opportunity she had dreamed of ever since she was a child? That seemed an even greater act of lunacy.

"*Will* you paint my portrait, Lady Somerset?" Melville asked, again.

Eliza looked away. She *ought* not. She *wanted* to.

"I will," she said.

Melville let out a whoop of celebration.

"I have conditions!" she added hastily. "I insist upon discretion!"

"I am *very* discreet," Melville said.

"Nevertheless it must remain a secret," Eliza said, amused but impatient. "A permanent secret—my name must never be attached."

"Done," Melville agreed cheerfully.

"And we shall have to think of some pretext, to excuse your visits," Eliza said. "For you to haunt Camden Place without explanation would do as much damage as the truth."

"When shall we begin?"

Ahead of them, Somerset and Lady Hurley came into view—gathered before the grand gate pier with Margaret and Lady Caroline alongside. They had completed a circuit.

"Tomorrow?" Melville suggested, and Eliza hushed him.

"Tuesday," she murmured. "Early, so we are not interrupted. And you must bring Lady Caroline—I should like as much chaperonage as I can muster."

"Chaperonage?" Melville repeated, amused. "Lady Somerset, do you not trust yourself around me?"

Once again, Eliza's cheeks pinked.

"There you are!" Margaret called. "We were on the point of sending out a search party."

"Lady Somerset was just drawing my attention to a particularly wonderful orangery," Melville said, shooting Eliza a grin.

"I will escort Lady Somerset and Miss Balfour back to Camden Place," Somerset said authoritatively.

"Are you tired, Caro?" Melville asked his sister.

"Not in the least," Lady Caroline said instantly. "Shall we locate this labyrinth?"

And after a quick round of farewells, they strode off, leaving Eliza and Margaret staring after them.

"Come, Miss Balfour, I would have you accompany me now," Lady Hurley said, taking Margaret's arm and leading her back through the gates.

There seeming no way for Eliza to avoid Somerset this time, she joined him reluctantly, leaving an impersonal gap between their shoulders. He made as if to offer his arm—then after a beat, returned the limb to his side, as they began to walk, allowing the two ladies to draw ahead on the pavement. After the verdant peace of the gardens, Pulteney Street was grey and noisy, but Eliza stared determinedly ahead as if it were the most fascinating view she had ever clapped eyes on.

"Lady Hurley is certainly fast," Somerset said quietly.

Eliza did not know if he was referring to her walking pace or . . . something else.

"Isn't she marvelous?" Eliza said pointedly. Somerset frowned.

"I know it is not my place," he began, "but my lady, I wonder if you ought to be more careful, with the friends you make here. Lady Hurley is . . . Well. And the Melvilles—I do not trust them. I do not know what, truly, has brought them to Bath, but I do not think it so innocent a reason as they would have us believe."

"No, it is certainly due to a scandal of some sort," Eliza said. Didn't everyone know this by now? "Perhaps an affair."

"My lady!" Somerset said, and Eliza pressed her lips together. Walking with Melville had loosened her tongue.

"I am sorry, my lord, I did not mean to shock you," she said.

Somerset let out a bark of surprised laughter.

"Shock me?" he repeated, as if this were amusing. He looked down at her, shaking his head. "You did not used to be so worldly."

"I used," Eliza said, very quietly, "to be seventeen."

The smile faded from Somerset's face. They were no longer speaking about the Melvilles.

"My lady," Somerset began again, voice rougher now. "My lady, you must let me apologize."

"There is no need," Eliza said, voice shaking. If they could just reach Camden Place . . .

"There is," Somerset insisted. "I was unforgivably rude—"

"Indeed, I would prefer to move past the incident," she interrupted. Somerset's regret could only be for his ungentlemanly conduct, and to have to hear and forgive such an apology—when the pain it had caused was not truly due to its rudeness, but to its honesty—was more than Eliza could bear.

"I think it best we discuss—"

"I do not think that—"

"By Jove, would you let me speak?" Somerset demanded, drawing to a sudden halt. Eliza considered walking on without him, but stopped, too. She would have to hear him, it seemed.

"I am sorry—that was impolite," Somerset said. "*Again*. I—I have been so unpardonably uncivil to you."

Eliza could not trust herself to speak. She merely gave a jerky nod.

"I wish to apologize—for everything that occurred last night," Somerset continued. "I was unkind and disagreeable and any apology I make would be insufficient."

He took off his hat, unheeding of the cold air.

"But I am sorry," he said. "If you wish me to leave Bath today, I will."

Eliza raised her eyes to the sky, in the hope it would keep any tears unspilled.

"No," Eliza said. "I do not want you to leave."

It was true. Even when it felt impossible to remain in his presence, even if he could never reciprocate her feelings. She had spent ten years without him and she could not wish him away, even now.

"I had been enjoying our reacquaintance," she said, bracing herself, at last, to meet his eyes. Really, did anyone have a right to eyes so blue?

Somerset gave a grimace.

"I had been enjoying it, too," he said.

Eliza looked ahead to where Margaret and Lady Hurley had stopped and were looking back at them enquiringly. "We ought to catch them up."

Somerset did offer Eliza his arm, this time, and she took it. The air between them felt less fraught than it had done earlier, but no less heavy.

"I ought to apologize, too," he said. "For my sister."

"Is there anyone you are *not* to apologize for?" Eliza asked, with her best attempt at a smile.

"Selwyn too," Somerset said doggedly. "I had intended to berate them most severely this morning but they were up and out so early that I could not. They were most unkind—more affected, perhaps, by the change in my uncle's will than I had realized."

"They have never liked me much," Eliza said. "I have grown accustomed to it."

"I wish you had not," Somerset said, so softly that Eliza was not sure he meant her to hear. "I wish . . ."

He trailed off and they walked on in silence for a moment.

"I hope I have not ruined things," he said roughly.

Eliza caught her breath and let it out in a slow, long exhale. What ought she say? Things *had* been ruined—for her, at least. But . . . She still wanted him in her life, even if she would have to put to bed her other sentiments, would have to learn, once and for all, how to fall out of love with him.

"Perhaps we were foolish to think we could simply spend time together, again," she said, "without the subject of our past arising, on occasion." Eliza looked up at him, forcing herself to hold the eye contact. "But perhaps now it has, we may be able to start our friendship, afresh."

"Do you truly wish that?" he asked. "Even after . . ."

"Yes," she said.

It was better than nothing.

"Friends . . ." Somerset sounded thoughtful.

"Only if you wish it, as well," she added hastily. She would not again make the mistake of assuming she knew his feelings.

"Do you think," Somerset asked abruptly, "that friends, while in Bath, might meet at the Pump Room each morning?"

"I would," Eliza said cautiously.

"Perhaps they might attend concerts together, as well?"

Eliza could not read his expression.

"They might."

"And ride out together, when the weather allows it, do you think?"

A small smile was pulling at the corner of his mouth and Eliza returned it very, very tentatively.

"I do," Eliza said.

Was it only to her ears that such a friendship sounded so akin to courting? Eliza tried desperately to banish the hope that was trying to unfurl once again in her chest.

"Then yes," Somerset said, bowing over her hand in farewell, "I should like to be your friend very much."

Dear Eliza,

Though I received your last letter safe in hand, I will not answer here any of your questions regarding the family— you may assume all of their health—for a piece of most disagreeable news has reached mine ears.

I have received report—by way of Lady Georgina, by way of her cousin, and thence a Mrs. Clemens of Bath— that Lord Melville and Lady Caroline Melville have made their home in Bath. Can this indeed be true? If it is, you can only guess at my horror! And I wonder that I should receive such reportage from Lady Georgina—by way of her cousin, etc.—and not from you, yourself!

I must instruct you to act with great prudency around such persons. The disgraces associated with their name are numerous, disparate and, indeed, recent—there are whispers that an affaire d'amour *has been occurring between Lord Melville and Lady Paulet for years. Lady Paulet, you will recollect, is the female painter whose work was so lauded by the* ton *last year and the fury of Paulet—Melville's most loyal patron—upon discovering the cuckolding was reportedly great. With such a scandal as this brewing, I trust that you will give Lord Melville no encouragement as to any pretensions of friendship.*

You may expect more anon—there are a few expenses regarding Rupert's education that I have agreed to on your behalf. He is—though you have demonstrated a shocking lack of interest in your heir—in possession of a further molar.

Your affectionate mother.

13

"Will you try to sit still?"

"I am."

"You are fidgeting."

"If you count *breathing* as fidgeting."

Eliza gave Melville a hard stare over the top of her portfolio, trying to emulate her grandfather's implacable manner of staring down his most demanding subjects.

"Are you well?" Melville asked, with a glint in his eye as if he knew very well what she was trying to do and had decided to be as difficult as possible. "You look dreadfully uncomfortable."

Eliza hid a smile behind the page. It was Thursday morning and this would mark the second of Melville's sittings. Eliza had decided, dredging up her recollections of how Mr. Balfour Sr. had conducted his portraits, to spend their first hours together capturing Melville in a variety of poses in order to decide upon the painting's composition. It was more challenging than she had expected. Partly because Eliza had never met anyone who *sat* with more animation than Melville, but mostly because Eliza felt so flustered to be sitting with him quite alone. It had not been what she had imagined, upon Tuesday, when Melville and Lady Caroline had called soon after breakfast, and they had sat cloistered together in the parlor with Lady Caroline examining Eliza's paintings.

"Do we have to indulge in such a charade?" Melville had

protested, when Eliza had reiterated the need for some excuse for the hours he would need to spend at Camden Place.

"Yes," Eliza had insisted. "I cannot be seen making such a spectacle of myself."

This solution, in the end, had been Margaret's.

"What if Lady Caroline were teaching me French?" she had suggested. "Melville would be escorting her to and from the house and visiting with you during the lessons."

Lady Caroline had raised her eyebrows. "And I just . . . dawdle here, for the duration of the sitting? How thrilling."

"Or you could actually teach me," Margaret had said mildly. "I have always wanted to learn and . . . I should not think it your first time in the role of tutor, is it?"

At that, Lady Caroline looked hard at Margaret for a few beats. Margaret returned her gaze steadily.

"It is not," Lady Caroline agreed with a slow smile. "Very well."

Eliza had imagined that they would conduct their lessons in the parlor, too—Eliza and Melville seated at one end, Lady Caroline and Margaret upon the sofa—a cramped affair, yes, but warm and companionable. Today, however, Lady Caroline had thrown that idea out.

"We have not enough space," she said, beckoning to Margaret. "We shall have to station ourselves in the drawing room."

"But . . . what about chaperonage?" Eliza said. At her age and as a widow, chaperonage was not perhaps as essential as it was for a young lady, but given the intimate connotations of a portrait sitting, it felt only wise.

"We shall poke our heads in every half an hour to ensure nothing untoward is occurring!" Margaret suggested brightly, and they left.

And that was that. It felt very quiet, in their absence, and Eliza's face flushed for no reason at all. *Nothing untoward is occurring*, she reminded herself. *You are doing nothing wrong.*

She wished, unfairly, that Melville would not look at her so very directly—her hands were becoming unsteady, her lines wobblier than they had been for years.

She wondered, briefly, what Somerset would think if he knew what they were doing today—and immediately banished the thought. She and Somerset were *friends*, no more—and barely that, for their interactions these past few days had been . . . tentative to say the least. She banished that thought, too, trying to rescue her first attempt at Melville's face which had become sadly mangled.

"You must have had a prodigious drawing master," Melville commented, as Eliza began to sketch out his profile again.

"Yes," Eliza said. He had been a portraitist himself, in fact, a Mr. Brabbington, employed at the direction of her grandfather.

"And did your grandfather have a hand in your education, too?"

"Yes," Eliza agreed again. In her girlhood, the whole family would spend the summer at Balfour House, and while her cousins played on the rolling lawns, Eliza would sneak into her grandfather's painting room to watch him at work. He had tolerated her presence when she was small and quiet enough to not become a nuisance, and then slowly, as he started to recognize some aptitude in Eliza, he began to treat her almost as an assistant.

"Do you miss him a great deal?" Melville asked.

Eliza met Melville's gaze briefly, before returning her eyes to her paper. Melville's line of questioning encouraged Eliza to unburden herself, but to discuss such intimate subjects whilst *alone* did not sit well with her.

"Yes," Eliza said. The senior Mr. Balfour had passed away when she was only fifteen years old, taking with him the only ally she had in the family—aside from Margaret—who thought of her as something other than a bartering tool.

"And your late husband?" Melville said.

Eliza looked up from her page, stunned. The impertinence!

"You do ask a great many questions, my lord!" she said, in reproof rather than answer.

"No more than you evade," Melville pointed out. "I do wish you wouldn't."

"Why?"

"I wish to get to know you," he explained. "You are familiar with the concept?"

"And I suppose if I asked *you* a great many personal questions," Eliza retorted. "You would feel comfortable answering them all?"

"Why, of course," Melville said. "You may ask me anything."

Eliza let out a sigh. She ought to have expected he would answer with such a challenge.

"Since I know very little about you, aside from what the scurrilous gossips say, I would not know where to begin," Eliza said evasively.

"Let us then begin with what the scurrilous gossips say!" Melville suggested. "Don't be shy! I promise to answer truthfully."

When Eliza did not immediately speak, he made a chivvying gesture, as if she were a horse. Eliza was struck with an unbecoming desire to shock him; to rock his indefatigable good humor for a single moment. She put down her pencil and folded her hands.

"They say the Melvilles are mad," she said, the worst thing of which she could think.

Melville considered this.

"It is difficult, as I am sure you will allow, for me to say whether I am or not," he said. "I never met my grandfather so I can't speak to his sanity, but he was certainly a brute. It's why my father fled abroad as soon as he could and didn't come back until the old man was dead. What else?"

"They say you're a rake," she said, boldly. Her mother would faint to hear her speak so.

"I spent some years deeply studied in petticoats, I will admit," Melville said thoughtfully. "Though I should not think more than the other gentlemen of our circles."

"Is that so?" Eliza said skeptically. It was not what *she* had heard.

"Society delights to imbue me with preternatural charm," Melville said. "It deems any lady that dares speak to me as lovelorn, any woman with whom I dance my mistress, and every unmarried chit that crosses my path as needing protection from me. It has been so since I was a schoolboy."

He was still smiling, but an edge of rancor had entered his voice that had Eliza eyeing him uncertainly, wondering if their game had gone too far.

"What else?" he prompted.

She hesitated.

"Come now, Lady Somerset, you were doing so well."

"They say that you came to Bath because of a scandal," she said.

"My point exactly," Melville said with a sardonic twitch of an eyebrow. "They say I go everywhere because of a scandal."

"Well, this time, they say it involves the Paulets," she said, and the smile slid off Melville's face at last.

"Do they now," he said.

"They do," Eliza said triumphantly, picking up her pencil to recommence sketching. *That* he clearly did not want to answer. "Do you have anything to say on that matter, my lord?"

Melville let out a sudden laugh.

"You could be a little more gracious in victory, my lady," he said. "But I shall cede the ground nonetheless—for discretion, on that subject, does indeed forbear me from speaking."

"Exactly!" Eliza said, more triumphant still, and Melville held up his hands in playful supplication, laughing again.

"Stay like that!" Eliza instructed, rushing with her pencil to try and grasp the expression—but it had slid off his face as easily as water off sand. She gave a little sigh.

"Am I being *very* difficult?" Melville asked, more amused than apologetic.

"No, no," Eliza said. She did not want to be thought ungrateful and truthfully, while it might be simpler if he was an easier subject, the challenge of it all was rather thrilling. She would have to move faster, keep her pencils sharper and watch him more closely. Her grandfather used to say that the secret to art was not learning to paint, but learning to *see*. To be able to put his lessons to practice properly, after all these years, made Eliza feel as if she were back in the painting room at Balfour, as if his hands were still guiding hers.

"I shall get there eventually," she assured Melville, her hands steadier now.

"Of that I have no doubt," he said.

She blushed at the certainty in his voice and Melville laughed gently.

"That was not even truly a compliment," he teased.

"If you cannot sit still, my lord," she said, flushing harder and staring at her paper, "perhaps you might instead remain quiet."

"Can't do that," Melville said cheerfully. "Do you think you will cease to blush after a few sittings?"

Eliza doubted it. She did not reply.

"I hope not," Melville decided.

The sound of the clock striking quarter to the hour had Eliza startling—and Melville frowned at it as if it had personally offended him.

"Must we finish so soon?" he asked.

"I do not want to be late for the Pump Room," Eliza said, setting down her materials with a little relief.

"No, God forbid we leave Somerset waiting for more than a second," Melville said, standing obediently.

Eliza avoided his gaze. Somerset had appeared at the Pump Room every day this week, for no other reason, it appeared, than to speak quietly with her for a few minutes, and each day their tentative accord became a little less strained.

"You need not accompany us," she reminded Melville.

"Oh, but I must—Somerset does so miss me when I am absent."

Eliza did not reply. She could not be sure, but it felt more and more as if Melville reserved his outrageous raillery for Somerset, as if his entire life's purpose was now to infuriate him. It was for this reason that Eliza might have preferred she and Margaret not arrive at the Pump Room with the Melvilles, but there was no helping it.

Somerset was already there when they arrived, making his way toward the door as soon as she crossed the threshold, proffering a goblet of the waters.

"Oh you shouldn't have, Somerset!" Melville declared, intercepting the goblet and taking it for himself. "I do not deserve such gallantry."

Somerset inhaled very slowly, and then turned to Eliza.

"May I escort you to the Pump?"

She accepted at once, leaving Margaret with the Melvilles, Lady Hurley and Mr. Fletcher. The further Somerset and Melville were from each other, the more comfortable she would be.

"Have you had a pleasant morning?" Somerset asked.

"Yes," Eliza said carefully. "Margaret, of course, had another French lesson . . ."

"Accompanied by Melville, I perceive," Somerset said.

"And I received a letter from my mother," Eliza added quickly.

"How *is* Mrs. Balfour?" Somerset said. "She seemed . . . the same, when we met at Harefield."

"She is very much the same," Eliza agreed.

"She writes often?" Somerset guessed.

"Sometimes twice a day," Eliza said, smiling as Somerset barked a laugh. "She and my father have a volume of opinions on how I should be conducting myself and my lands. One letter would simply not do."

"My family is similarly preoccupied," Somerset said. "My sister demands such a minute account of all my doings that I should think her quite able to become my biographer."

"Do you think such a text would make for interesting reading?" Eliza asked teasingly.

Somerset shook his head.

"Not unless the reader desired a lengthy education in crop rotation," he said, "the subject in which Mr. Penney and I are currently immersed—one of my land stewards, you know."

"Oh, yes he shall be mine, too," Eliza said. "I am to meet with him upon Friday."

"Yes, he mentioned it this morning," Somerset said. He hesitated. "Mr. Penney wondered, in fact, if I ought join your meeting."

Eliza frowned. Mr. Walcot had had his qualms, of course, about Eliza's direct involvement in her estates, but she had thought he now accepted it, however reluctantly. For Mr. Penney to have contacted Somerset regarding her lands, without even consulting her . . .

"It is merely so we may discuss where we border," Somerset added swiftly.

Perhaps that was it. Perhaps Eliza was being overanxious.

"If there are matters that pertain to both our lands, then of course we must confer," she said.

Having fetched Eliza's glass of water, they completed their circuit slowly—he asking after her nephews, she after his nieces—arriving back at Margaret's side just as Mrs. and Miss Winkworth bustled up.

"Oh my lord, we hoped to find you here!" Mrs. Winkworth

trilled up at Somerset. "Winifred was hoping you might frank a letter to Miss Selwyn?"

Mrs. Winkworth nudged her daughter forward. With her simple muslin dress, straw bonnet and a blush lighting up her cheeks, Miss Winkworth looked very becoming; she might easily, indeed, have been the inspiration for one of Mr. Woodforde's shepherdess paintings and any umbrage Somerset might have taken at her mother's encroaching softened at the sight.

"I would be glad to do so," he said, taking the proffered billet carefully in hand.

"That is very kind," Miss Winkworth said quietly.

"Oh, you have made Winifred's week, my lord! She will be in transports over your amicability all day, I am sure!"

"*All* day?" Eliza said in a voice sufficiently lowered that only Miss Winkworth might hear it.

"Perhaps . . . perhaps only the morning," Miss Winkworth whispered back with a hesitant smile.

"Have you all heard that Mr. Lindley is to perform at the concert next week?" Mrs. Winkworth ostensibly spoke to the group, but her whole person was turned only to Somerset. "A coup, indeed, for Bath. Somerset, do you think Lady Selwyn should be invited? I am persuaded it is just the sort of thing she would enjoy."

"I am sure she would," Somerset said, shooting Eliza a quick look. "In her last letter, she bade me pass on her well wishes to you all."

"Did she?" Mrs. Winkworth looked pleased as punch.

"She also bade me deliver a message to Melville in particular," Somerset went on.

"Oh, yes?" Melville said. "Can you share it now, or is it of such a nature that I must receive it privately?"

Somerset's jaw clenched.

"Lady Selwyn has heard that you are writing again,"

Somerset said, "and wishes to express how pleased she is—and her impatience for news, when you have it."

"Is that true, Melville?" Margaret demanded.

"Did Lady Somerset not already tell you so?" Melville asked. Margaret turned on Eliza, frowning.

"I did not know if it was a secret," Eliza defended herself.

As if in proof, Melville raised his forearms up to indicate the ink stains marring the pristine white of his shirt cuffs, without any sign of embarrassment. And, indeed, why ought he to be embarrassed? For somehow, on Melville the blemishes only added to his elegance—and Eliza promptly decided that she would include them in the portrait.

"Splendid!"

"Are we truly meant to interpret such marks as accidental," Somerset asked. "Not an affectation meant to convey an artistic mystique?"

Lady Hurley and Mr. Fletcher looked on, startled. This being the first time they had witnessed Somerset and Melville sniping at one another, they had no context for Somerset's sudden sharpness.

"Do you really think I have *mystique*, my lord?" Melville said. "How wonderful. I was beginning to think no one had noticed."

"Once again, you take a compliment where none exists."

"It makes speaking with you more enjoyable, you see."

"Will everyone attend the concert next week? I think we certainly will, now Lindley is to play," Eliza interjected, before Somerset could retort. He only seemed to anger further the more cheerful Melville remained.

There were murmurs of agreement around the group.

"I will," Somerset said. "May I offer my escort?"

"I am afraid Lady Somerset has already agreed to join our party," Melville claimed and Eliza shot him a startled look, for this was entirely untrue.

"Did she? Before even she decided to attend herself?"

"Ah, I have long known her to be prescient," Melville said.

"You have not known her long at all," Somerset snapped.

"We ought to go, now, Max," Lady Caroline interjected before Melville could respond—to Eliza's relief. The men were beginning to give her a headache.

Naturally, it was just as they were on the point of exiting that the heavens decided to reopen.

"Oh blast!" Margaret said improperly, staring out into the mizzle of rain. "Just when we shall never be able to get a cab."

With so many persons streaming in and out of the Pump Room, hackney cabs and sedan chairs would be in short supply.

"Not the thing," Mr. Fletcher agreed.

"We shall be drowned!" Lady Hurley declared.

"Do you intend to lay face down in a puddle?" Lady Caroline said, amused.

"I think it would be best if we make a dash for it now," Eliza said, looking up at the sky, which was darkening ominously. "Before it becomes any worse."

"Brava, Lady Somerset the brave," Melville said. "It will make for a romantic vista, at least."

"That is all very well, my lord," Somerset said, pulling his coat around him. "But Lady Somerset is wearing silk."

He strode out into the road and they watched him go, skeptically.

"Perhaps this is the last time we shall ever see him," Melville wondered.

In a trice, however, Somerset was returning, and the sight of him striding purposefully back toward them through the rain, with a hackney cab following closely behind as if he had conjured it up by sheer force of will—well, it was certainly affecting. And once again, Eliza could not help but notice how admirably Somerset's dark frock coat lay across his frame. He, of course, had no need of the buckram wadding some gentle-men used to pad out their outerwear.

"The gentlemen will have to walk," he said, "but the ladies shall be dry."

"You are a magician, my lord," Lady Hurley said.

"Flatterer," Somerset accused her gently, and Lady Hurley chuckled, accepting his arm up into it.

Margaret and Lady Caroline followed, and then it was Eliza's turn. Somerset extended his hand, and as she took it, she thought she felt him squeeze her fingers ever so slightly. She turned her head to regard him, but his expression was smooth, unreadable. Perhaps she had imagined it.

"I shall see you tomorrow, my lady," he murmured, before shutting the door.

From the street, Melville raised a hand to give a cheery wave.

"Lawks," Lady Hurley breathed, as the cab drew off. "You'll have all of Bath's quizzes talking if that keeps up, Lady Somerset."

"I'm sure I don't know what you mean," Eliza said, avoiding her eyes.

"For a moment they looked about to duel," Lady Hurley said. "It was . . . most affecting." And though the carriage was not warm, she began to fan herself vigorously. "I should not mind seeing it again," she added.

"Do you need smelling salts, my lady?" Lady Caroline asked with an amused smile.

"Since their behavior is motived by dislike of one another," Eliza said, "it gives me no pleasure."

It was mostly true—what lady would not feel a fleeting enjoyment for being competed over in such a way, whatever the motive? But to witness such a competition and prevent oneself—by force of will—from taking any meaning from it . . . There was something slightly torturous about it. Melville was a flirt, Eliza knew this, and Somerset was . . . Eliza did not know what Somerset was, but she would not be reading into his behavior *again*.

Across the carriage, Lady Hurley regarded her for a moment, as if deciding whether she believed her—then cackled.

"If you say so!" she said.

14

As February drew toward March, the weather turned inclement. Each day brought fresh sheets of icy rain and vicious winds, filling Bath's streets with puddles and bending its trees to inconvenient angles. Inside Camden Place, however, life felt warm. To the undiscerning observer, the pattern of Eliza's days was no more variegated than it had been before, with most activities still prohibited by her mourning. Onlookers could not know, of course, that twice weekly found Eliza busy with the most unladylike employment of portraiture—outlining Melville's shapes and shadows upon canvas—nor that the most regular of excursions had been invested with much excitement now she was accompanied, almost everywhere, by Somerset.

Friendship had truly never been so pleasurable. As discussed, Somerset and Eliza met with the land steward, and though Mr. Penney spoke to her with a condescension that made her want to scream, Somerset so considerately listened to Eliza's opinion throughout that she still, somehow, enjoyed the appointment. It was very agreeable to finally have a person with whom to discuss the complexities of land ownership: she could not do so with her family, for they would certainly try to take over, and Margaret had neither an ounce of interest in farming, nor a single qualm about telling her so. Somerset, however, occupied the same position as Eliza: trying his best to learn a duty he had not been born to.

"You have a good head for this," he complimented her, once Mr. Penney had left Camden Place while he had remained for a further pot of tea. "Most ladies would find it a dead bore."

"Is that perhaps because most ladies are not permitted the chance?" Eliza suggested, archly.

"Ah, you may be right," Somerset said. "Though I still think your interest commends you. My uncle would have been proud that you are taking your stewardship so seriously."

"Perhaps," Eliza said.

"You disagree?" Somerset said.

Eliza dithered for a moment. While she had felt sufficiently unencumbered these past few days to ask after Somerset's life in the navy—where he had traveled, what he had seen, of the friends made—the subject of the old earl was one neither was yet confident navigating.

"I did not generally inspire pride in him," she said carefully. Even in the beginning—most especially in the beginning—the late earl had been frequently disappointed by her ignorance. The Balfours' family line was certainly genteel, but they were not from aristocratic stock, and there had been much—so very much—that Eliza had not known. *You foolish girl*, her husband would often say, when she had made yet another error, when despite her carefulness, she had done something wrong again. *You foolish girl*.

"In the will," Somerset began haltingly. "He mentioned your loyalty and—"

"Obedience!" Eliza snapped. "Yes, I remember."

Somerset blinked.

"I am . . . I am grateful, of course, for the lands I have been given," Eliza said more calmly. "But to think he was motivated merely to reward me? It would not be very like him, you see. He changed the will the morning after he and Selwyn quarreled, in anger. If he had lived longer, he might well have changed it back."

Most probably the very next time Eliza mixed up the Baroness Digby and the Baroness Dudley—a mistake that always sent him into a rage.

"He was not a naturally affectionate man," Somerset conceded.

"He showed more affection to his horse than he ever did to me," Eliza said, throat a little constricted.

There was a pause. On the sofa, Somerset's hands lifted, stilled, and then returned to his side.

"But then, I suppose, Misty *was* an Andalusian grey," Eliza added, and Somerset laughed gently, seeming to understand that Eliza wished to abandon the subject for now. And if, in this moment and each of the five days since—as he fetched her water at the Pump Room, promenaded with her whenever rain eased, escorted her around the livery stables of Bath to choose mounts for her and Margaret—Somerset proved himself to be just as kind, just as considerate, just as capable as he had been when Eliza first fell in love with him . . . Why, were such qualities not also those that one might admire in a friend?

"A friend you want to kiss, perhaps," Margaret remarked tartly, when Eliza voiced this thought aloud. She was sitting in the window embrasure of the drawing room, watching the street below through the rain-stained glass.

"Oh shush," Eliza said, walking over to adjust her hairpiece in the mirror. It was Wednesday evening and they had dressed for the concert in their finest gowns: Margaret's a blue crêpe dress over a white satin slip, ornamented with earrings, necklace and bracelets of sapphire mixed with pearl—a set that looked even more divine on than it had in the jeweler—and Eliza, now that she was almost eleven months into her mourning, had begun to incorporate some white into her wardrobe with a gown of black figured lace over a white robe.

"Are you prepared for how you might feel when he leaves?" Margaret said now. "For it is this week, is it not?"

"Tomorrow," Eliza said, keeping her eyes steady upon her reflection. "And yes, I am."

Her voice did not waver—Eliza knew it did not, because it took such an effort—but Margaret still snorted.

"You have your head firmly in the sand," she said. "On more than one front, I might add."

"Pray tell," Eliza said without enthusiasm.

"Have you given any thought to what you will do when I leave?" Margaret asked. "As little as I like to think of it myself, it will be April in a month, and Lavinia will be approaching her seclusion. You ought consider finding a new companion. There are plenty of respectable women in Bath who would also be agreeable choices."

"Such as who?" Eliza said grumpily.

"What about Miss Stewart?" Margaret suggested.

"She's too . . . brassy," Eliza decided.

"Mrs. Gould, then? She is amusing enough."

"In a very literal sort of way."

"When did you cultivate such a high standard for wit?" Margaret wondered. "Come, they would not be so bad."

"They are not you," Eliza said.

"That is not their fault, precisely," Margaret said, her smile turned melancholy.

Eliza rather thought it was.

"The Melvilles are here," Margaret said, with a glance out of the window. "Once more unto the breach?"

Eliza nodded, throwing on her cloak and picking up her reticule and fan. They set out for the concert, everyone on fine form, Melville regaling them with an amusing tale of a hackney cab he had once shared with a well-known actor and his pet monkey while Margaret and Lady Caroline heckled him good-naturedly. Only Eliza was quiet. She could not shake off her conversation with Margaret so easily and remained ruffled by unease. Her current state of content had been hard-won, and only recently reached; to dwell upon its very real precariousness was not pleasant.

They reached the Upper Rooms and cast off their cloaks and pelisses.

"A new gown?" Eliza asked Lady Caroline, re-engaging herself in conversation with an effort, to admire Lady Caroline's dress of shining white lace—its skirt festooned into a bell shape far fuller than any Eliza had seen before.

"Yes, *finally*," Lady Caroline said, casting a dark look toward Melville.

Melville cast his eyes to heaven.

"Caroline has liked to characterize me as a pinchpenny," he said to Eliza, as they began to walk through the hall, "ever since I once dared to query if diamond-encrusted shoes might be a little . . ."

"*De trop?*" Margaret suggested impishly and Melville gave a delighted laugh.

"I shall not have my lessons used against me," Lady Caroline told her severely, rapping Margaret's arm with her fan.

They paused in the doorway. In a perfect mirroring of the last time Eliza had attended a concert here, the whole room turned to stare at the entrance, only this time, she and Margaret were standing with the Melvilles. She peered through the crowd, locating Lady Hurley and Mr. Fletcher standing by the fire, Somerset and Lady Selwyn next to them. Eliza took in a deep, shaky breath.

"Oh lord," Margaret muttered, spotting Lady Selwyn, too.

"Do try to be polite," Eliza reminded her.

"I am *always* polite," Margaret said with a sniff. "Unless I am irritated."

Lady Caroline let out a low laugh and, twining their arms together, they strode into the room with all the conviction of an especially glamorous coven of witches.

"'Double, double, toil and trouble,'" Melville quoted softly in Eliza's ear and she laughed. Melville appeared in the highest of spirits, tonight, positively glittering with energy.

"Writing is going well?" she guessed, as they wound their own way through the crowd.

"A thousand lines done so far," Melville said. "I should have written more were I at Alderley; Meyler's and Duffield's stock only Porson's *Euripides*, and it is not my preferred translation, but I am pleased. How could you tell?"

"You are . . . liveliest, on such days," she said, half embarrassed to have noticed.

"Idleness does not suit me," Melville said. "Despite what Somerset might think."

He lowered his voice as they reached the fireplace. Eliza took another steadying breath as she curtseyed her greeting. She would bear Lady Selwyn's presence with grace and fortitude. *Grace and fortitude*, she repeated, as if it were a prayer.

"What a marvelous magpie you make, my lady!" Lady Selwyn said cattily, reviewing Eliza's black-and-white ensemble.

"Yes, 'magpie' was certainly my intention," Eliza snapped, vow instantly forgotten. "Or gull."

"Your gown is fine, too, Lady Selwyn," Margaret said sharply. "My mother had a very similar one last Season."

Lady Caroline snorted and Lady Selwyn flushed.

"You have a good eye, Miss Balfour," Lady Selwyn said. "I did not think it quite right to waste a new gown on so provincial an event."

"Such condescension is truly admirable," Lady Caroline said smoothly.

"I am not sure a Bath concert can ever have enjoyed such an esteemed audience!" Mrs. Winkworth chirped from where she hovered at the edge of the group.

As with Eliza's dinner party, it was plain that such an ill-matched party could only end in calamity but unlike her dinner party, Eliza found she did not care to prevent it.

"This evening's concert *is* certainly far more attended than any in recent memory," Lady Hurley observed, gazing about.

"I should think we have Melville to blame for that," Somerset said. "The scores of young ladies desirous of receiving his signature seem to climb by the day."

"My dear Somerset, while I may take blame for the ladies," Melville said, "I can assure you that the gentlemen are not here for *me*."

He turned to look pointedly to Eliza, who avoided flushing red only by sheer force of will.

"Whatever can you mean, Melville?" Lady Selwyn asked.

"Let me enlighten you, my lady," Melville said. "Bath is becoming quickly riddled with gentlemen desirous of fixing their attention with our own Lady Somerset. Once she throws off her widow's weeds, Bath will be besieged."

Losing her internal battle, Eliza blushed red and Melville grinned as if he had won something.

"Perhaps if I were a younger woman," Eliza demurred, "but I am far into my dotage."

This was greeted with cries of outrage from the group.

"*Not* the thing," Mr. Fletcher disagreed heartily.

"To mine eyes, you are still a very green girl," Lady Hurley said stoutly.

"I did think you had begun calcifying," Lady Caroline said, pretending to look Eliza over.

Eliza laughed.

"You are all very kind," she said, meaning it. Ten years of marriage to a husband more inclined to admonishment than admiration had not given Eliza much reason to believe in her own desirability—but with friends such as this, she was beginning to stand a little taller.

"It is not kindness but prophecy," Melville said. He looked to Somerset. "In the absence of Lady Somerset's father, are you to act as gatekeeper, my lord?"

Somerset's face was rigid.

"I do not need a gatekeeper," Eliza put in hastily.

"And I could not perform the role if I wanted to," Somerset said. "For this marks my final night in Bath."

Which Eliza knew, of course, had been counting down the days with rising trepidation, but nonsensically, it still felt a blow to hear.

"You are leaving?" Melville asked, clasping a hand plaintively to his chest. "But we have only begun getting to know one another!"

"There are some urgent matters at Harefield I must attend to," Somerset told the group, ignoring Melville. "And as my business with Mr. Walcot has concluded—"

"Oh, have you finally graduated from Earl School?" Melville interrupted. "You know, I am a little offended that you did not seek *my* tutelage on the subject, Somerset."

"Are you?" Somerset said flatly.

"Indeed," Melville said. "Having been an earl myself for almost five years, I daresay I know a thing or two about it."

"And why," Somerset bristled, "would I receive instruction from a gentleman who I doubt even knows his own acreage?"

Lady Hurley and Mr. Fletcher gasped at the insult while a smirk curled its way onto Lady Selwyn's face.

Melville merely smiled. "Twelve thousand," he said. "My acreage, that is."

"And your principal crops?" Somerset demanded.

"Oh, a quiz," Melville said. "Marvelous. Turnips, my lord— my answer is turnips."

Somerset glared at him as if he suspected Melville of naming the first vegetable that sprang to mind.

"You practice the Four Field System, I imagine?"

"Of course."

"And what are your views on the Tullian drill?"

"Good lord, man, I don't have any!" Melville said. "I concede—may I offer you a bushel of turnips as your prize?"

The whole company laughed, but Somerset, his face still flushed with anger, looked rather as if he should have liked to hit him.

"Are you still thinking of bringing your daughter to Bath, Lady Selwyn?" Mrs. Winkworth tried to reclaim the Baroness's attention.

"No, we have decided against it in the end," Lady Selwyn said. "If anything I should think Annie *too* confident and really it does—"

Eliza took a tiny, instinctive step back, trying not to listen. She twisted the ring upon her right hand, and then fussed with the clasp of her bracelet, which was not sitting *quite* right, until, under her anxious fingers, the clasp sprang open. Eliza made a grab for it, but it slipped from her wrist, only to be caught, just prior to it smashing upon the floor, by Melville.

"Oh—thank you," she murmured, accepting it back.

"Can I help?" he asked quietly, and they drew a little away from the rest of the group.

"I can do it," Eliza said—to have Melville's hands upon her wrist would feel too intimate. "Perhaps you might hold my fan . . . ?"

"By all means," Melville said, taking it from her.

Eliza wrapped the bracelet around her wrist. Next to her, totally unconcerned by the delay, Melville regarded the fan thoughtfully. It was a silk and lace creation held together with fine sticks of dark tortoiseshell—her most expensive purchase to date.

"I wish it were still the fashion for gentlemen to carry fans, too," he said. "They are such useful creations."

"Do you think so?" Eliza said abstractedly, as she struggled with the clasp. *Almost there*.

"Oh yes, the expression one can achieve! As so." He unfurled its leaves and began to flutter it close to his face so only his eyes were visible—dark and laughing. "Perceive, I am now shy."

"I perceive it," Eliza said, smiling up briefly, before returning her eyes to the clasp.

There!

She straightened. Melville swapped the fan to his left hand and rested it briefly against his neck.

"And now?" he asked softly.

Eliza pulled at the thread of her memory—the language of fans was old-fashioned, now, but her governess had instructed her just in case . . .

"You are desirous of my acquaintance," she said. "Melville . . ."

She cut her eyes to the room—their party was not attending them, but there were still many eyes gazing in their direction.

"And now?"

Melville flipped the fan upside down to press the handle against his lips—kiss me—and Eliza blushed fiery red.

"Melville, I know you are merely funning," she hissed. "But we are *observed*!"

"I am aware," Melville murmured, at last snapping the fan closed and handing it back to her. "Somerset blushes, too—not as charmingly as you, of course, but nonetheless I am hopeful he will turn puce this evening."

Eliza looked reflexively toward the fire where Somerset's eyes were now on them, heavy and frowning, and Lady Selwyn's, too, darting ravenously between her and Melville. She felt her face heat even further.

"I should prefer," she said, very softly, "that you keep me out of your squabbles; I do not care to be used as an intermediary."

"I did not—"

She rejoined the circle before he could finish his statement, finding even more faces turned toward her—Mrs. Winkworth's sour, Lady Hurley raising her eyebrows significantly. Eliza raised her chin determinedly.

"Yes . . ." Lady Selwyn said at last, turning back to Mrs. Winkworth. "And Somerset has promised us the use of Grosvenor Square for her coming-out ball."

She threw her brother a coy glance.

"One of many promises he will have to keep soon enough!"

Somerset jerked his head around to his sister.

"Not now, Augusta," he said in warning.

"Goodness, how intriguing," Eliza said, trying to keep her voice light.

"My brother," Lady Selwyn said loudly to the whole group, "has promised *this* will be the year he finally secures a wife!"

"My, my, Lord Somerset," Mrs. Winkworth said. "Are there any hats in the ring already?"

There was an odd roaring sound in Eliza's ears. She did not think she could bear to listen to a second of this.

"My lady . . ." Mr. King, the Master of Ceremonies, appeared at Eliza's elbow to speak in a funereal whisper, and Eliza had never been so glad to see a person in her life. "I have saved a seat at a retired spot for you and one other."

"I shall be happy to accompany you, my lady," Melville suggested quietly.

"Yes, Somerset, perhaps you might escort me—" Lady Selwyn began.

"That is quite all right, Melville," Somerset said. "*I* shall be escorting her ladyship."

He offered Eliza his arm and she took it automatically, her mind still reeling.

"My apologies, for Augusta," Somerset said in a low voice as they followed Mr. King. "She can be—"

Oh, was he truly asking her to *discuss* it, right at this moment?

"There is no need to apologize, my lord," she interrupted.

"Of course there—"

"You shall have to . . . to let me know when I am to wish you happy," Eliza said hoarsely.

Somerset's arm tensed under hers and he took a sharp intake of breath as if to speak but the Master was indicating the area he had demarcated with a flourish, and Somerset remained silent. It was a little retired from the rest of the audience, and therefore away from the prying eyes of the public, and though it was a few more minutes yet before the performance began, Eliza did not prompt him.

The music struck up. The first few pieces, performed by an accomplished soprano and tenor in turn, were unknown to Eliza, although well performed. Then it was the turn of Mr. Lindley and his quartet, shuffling their music and tweaking their instruments, and Eliza wondered if she might take this moment to flee the evening entirely. They began to play, and as the first notes soared through the air, Eliza realized that this was a piece she recognized. Not that she knew its name, or even its composer, for she had only heard it once before: at Lady Castlereagh's summer ball in '09, she had danced to it with the man sitting next to her.

As the violins began to sing that unmistakable melody, Eliza's breath caught. Pleasure and horror warred for dominance in her chest. Pleasure, for to hear such a piece was to be reminded of one of the happiest memories of her life. Horror, because she did not think she could bear to sit there, next to him, while she listened—close enough to touch and yet as far away as he had ever been.

Eliza closed her eyes and tried to master herself. It was just music. It was just a memory. She could bear this, as she had borne everything else. But just when she thought she had done it, just when she thought herself able to breathe normally once more, Somerset took in his own ragged breath, and spoke.

15

"We danced to this, did we not?" Somerset said, so very quietly that his voice almost seemed to blend with the lowest violin in the company.

"Yes," Eliza whispered, her eyes still closed. "At—at Lady Castlereagh's ball."

"I remember," he said. "You were . . . you were wearing a dress that seemed to twinkle, somehow."

"It was embroidered with silver thread rosettes," Eliza said. She had been so proud of it.

"I could not take my eyes off you."

"Nor I, you."

It was as if they had entered a different world. They were speaking so softly, their eyes facing forward, lips barely moving, their whispers hardly louder than a thought, as they confessed their memories into the air with the kind of honesty that belonged to dreams.

"I left Lady Jersey mid-word," Somerset said. "She never forgave me for such deplorable rudeness."

Eliza could hear the smile in his voice even as she kept her eyes directed forward and it felt far more intimate, somehow, than being able to see it.

Eliza breathed out a hint of a laugh.

"My mother had promised all my dances away. But you said that you did not care . . ."

"I did not. I have never cared about anything less."

"And the music started," she sighed.

"And I took your hand . . ."

"And we danced . . ."

She could see them in her mind's eye now, the memory playing before them, rather than the musicians. Two young persons, as impossibly in love as could be, with no notion that their days together were already so numbered. She could remember the firm press of his hands as well as if they were grasping hers now, the drag of her skirts upon the ground, the soar of the music overheard. How it had felt so impossibly perfect. How hopeful she had been.

"I have never been one much for dancing," he said. "Too tall, too ungainly . . ."

"You always danced so beautifully," Eliza disagreed.

"Age has altered your memory," Somerset said wryly, and she felt the press of his leg against hers on the bench. "I had all the grace of a tree."

"I do remember laughing a great deal," Eliza admitted.

"With me, I hope," Somerset said.

"Always."

"I could have danced with you forever that night."

"The music stopped too soon."

Eliza swallowed, her mouth suddenly dry. She wished they might linger there, in that moment and that moment only—the dancing, the joy, the sense their time was endless . . .

"And I asked if you wanted to take in the air," he said, softly.

"I agreed," she said, voice barely audible. "The moon was so bright."

She could still smell Lady Castlereagh's peonies. Almost too sweet on the air, but only almost. It was a night for sweetness.

"I can't remember what we spoke of," Somerset said.

"I think it might have been the weather," Eliza said. "And all I could think of was . . ."

"And then . . ."

They paused. Involuntarily, Eliza pressed a trembling hand to her lips, remembering. Beside her, she heard a catch in Somerset's breath.

"If I had known," Somerset said. "What was to happen . . ."

It had been the very next day that everything had fallen apart. They had not even one day to enjoy the promises they had given each other. It had only been that night.

"I would never have let you go," Somerset said, his voice low, hoarse.

Eliza could no longer see the musicians ahead through the tears building in her eyes, and a tiny sob broke from her throat.

"Eliza," he said, so quietly she did not know if she had imagined it.

"Oliver," she said, brokenly.

And though they were in public . . . though there were a hundred persons around them . . . she felt his arm move and just when she thought him about to throw caution to the wind and take her hand in his—

The music stopped. Everyone began to applaud. Eliza took in a gulp of air, and . . . Somerset dropped his hand.

"Everyone is gathering for tea," he said, his voice very rough.

Eliza nodded blindly and stood, but found she could not move. Looking toward the laughing faces heading to the tearoom she knew she would not be able to pretend all was well.

"Would you please," she began. "W-would you please inform Margaret that I have returned home? I am feeling a little . . . light in the head."

She disentangled herself from Somerset's arm without waiting for a reply and hurried toward the door.

"Lady Somerset!" she heard him call after her, but Eliza did not look back. She dashed from the rooms, and through the hall, not even pausing to collect her cloak before stepping out into the air. She found herself enveloped immediately into drizzle, but with another half of the concert to go there was a plethora of hackney cabs available to her, and she did not wait for a footman to procure her one.

"Camden Place, please!" Eliza called to the first she saw, climbing inside and breathing a sharp sob of relief to be finally alone. But the door barely closed before it was wrenched open again.

And Somerset was standing there, his arm bracing the door open against the wind. He was not wearing a cloak, his hair was already dark from the rain, and his chest was heaving as if he had been running.

"Are you all right?" he demanded.

And what was there left for Eliza to say, except the truth?

"No," Eliza said, her voice breaking. "I am not."

There was the muffled sound of a question from the driver, and Somerset abruptly climbed into the carriage after her and slammed the door. The carriage drew off.

"If you will let me explain—" Somerset started.

"At my dinner party you spoke to me in such terms," Eliza overrode him, "as I thought made any romantic feeling between us an *impossibility*."

"I lashed out with an anger I truly regret," Somerset said urgently, clasping her hands. "I must assure you, the sentiments I alluded to that evening—the ones I spoke to at the end of our acquaintance, so many years ago—are not ones I feel any longer."

"They are not?" Eliza asked.

"I understand now that your actions spoke to an abundance of duty, rather than a lack of spirit," he said.

"You do?" Eliza asked.

"I do," Somerset said emphatically. "I have for a long time, now."

Eliza stared at him.

"But at the dinner party . . ." she said.

"I cannot excuse my behavior," Somerset said. "I had thought, upon my return to England, that I had long ago overcome the . . . anger I felt toward you upon leaving these shores. But being in your presence again, I was not prepared for the feelings which would arise."

He grimaced, and added, with a defeated shrug, "At times it has felt just as if I am eighteen, again."

"For me, too," Eliza whispered.

"I am not alone in it, then?" Somerset said.

"No," Eliza breathed. "No, not at all."

The relief sweeping through her felt sufficient enough to knock her off her feet. She had not thought . . . She had not *hoped* . . .

"And I confess," he continued doggedly, "that the reason I have lingered so long in Bath—beyond anything that my duty required of me—is because . . . Because I still . . ."

And Eliza knew what he was going to say, even as he hesitated—knew too that if the words were spoken, they could not go back.

"I still love you, too," she said.

It was the bravest thing she had ever done. Somerset jerked back as if he had been shot.

"My lady," he breathed. "The nature of our locality prevents me from being able—"

But after ten years of waiting, Eliza would not allow herself to be inconvenienced by such a nonsensical piece of honor. She reached out and laid a trembling hand upon his shoulder, tracing her fingers down the front to grip his lapel.

"Somerset," she said, with clear instruction. Then, softly, "Oliver."

"*Eliza.*"

He kissed her. And though they had only shared such an embrace once before, they fell into one another as easily as if they had done so a thousand times.

"I missed you dearly," she whispered when they broke apart, their foreheads still pressed together, his breath still ghosting across her lips. "When I saw you again, I was sure you had quite forgotten all that had passed between us."

Somerset shook his head emphatically.

"Then I am a better actor than I thought," he said. "For I was *overcome*."

He embraced her again and she had forgotten what it felt like to be kissed in such a way. Not for duty, not for obligation, but with such intent that to stop even to breathe felt unthinkable.

"Oh, what are we to do?" Eliza said, when at last they parted.

"Well, I should hope that after kissing me in such a way, you would intend to marry me," Somerset said, laughing a little.

"We cannot become engaged before a year and a day has passed," Eliza said. "The disgrace . . ."

"Not until you enter your half-mourning, at least," Somerset agreed. "Until then, it shall have to remain a secret."

"And what about Margaret?" Eliza asked anxiously.

"What about Margaret?" Somerset said.

"She is needed by her sister, for the new baby," Eliza said. "But then—after—she will live with us."

"Will you have need of a companion when we are married?" Somerset asked doubtfully.

"I will *always* have need of Margaret," Eliza said.

Somerset picked up her hand and kissed it.

"You are very sweet," he said. "Of course. She will be my family too, soon enough."

This reassured Eliza only for a moment.

"Your family despise me," she said, covering her face with a groan.

Somerset could not disagree.

"They are protective," he said, drawing her hands down gently and covering them with his own. "And I think they will like you a great deal more now that Tarquin will inherit Chepstow again."

"Whatever do you mean?" Eliza said.

"Oh, just that it—well, it would go a long way to easing matters with my sister . . ." Somerset said.

"But Chepstow is mine," Eliza said.

"And when we are married, it will be *ours*," Somerset reminded her.

"But . . . but it was given to *me*," Eliza said. She did not know why, exactly, she was fixating on such a point as this—it was, after all, a minor one in comparison to at last marrying the person she had loved all of her adult life.

"It was given to me," she repeated quietly. Surely that counted for something?

Somerset's gaze flickered between her eyes as if he could not quite understand her expression.

"Eliza, is this not our second chance?" he said, when she did not speak. "It may not have been what my uncle intended, but is this not worth sacrificing whatever we need to?"

The look in his eyes was so tender, so vulnerable, that she was not sure she could bear to see it. And if this was their second chance, Eliza wanted nothing more than to grasp it with both hands and never let go, but . . . Try as she might to focus only upon Somerset, her mind was racing. There was so much they had yet to discuss. So much about her new life that he did not know. She had not even told him about the portrait, yet, but how to broach such a topic now, in a carriage, when time already felt as if it were running out.

"There is much we have not spoken of," Eliza said softly.

Somerset ducked his head to catch her eye.

"We have time," he said gently. "We love each other. Everything else, we can solve."

He made it sound so simple. It *was* so simple. Eliza's frown slid from her face.

"We can," she agreed.

"And while circumstances have not been kind to us, in the past," he said, "we have the means to change that, now. We shall do better."

She squeezed his hands in return.

"We shall do better," she agreed.

The carriage drew to a stop. There was a thump on the roof.

"Five minutes!" Somerset called in response. Then, cupping his hand to her jaw, he spoke urgently. "I still must leave tomorrow. I must take a tour of my lands—I am afraid with this recent rain of them becoming flooded out—but I will write. And in six weeks, I shall return."

"Very well," Eliza whispered, leaning into his touch.

She had waited ten years. She could wait six more weeks.

"And in six weeks, you shall be in half-mourning," Somerset said. "I shall ask you to marry me."

"In six weeks," Eliza said, lifting her eyes to his, "I shall say yes."

He pulled her toward him once more.

"Will you be all right alone, while I am gone?" Somerset said, feathering a kiss onto the corner of her mouth.

"I will have Margaret," Eliza said. "And Lady Hurley and the Melvilles . . ."

Somerset's jaw clenched under her palm.

"I do not at all like the way he looks at you," Somerset said.

"And how is that?" Eliza said, laughing a little because he *was* jealous and Melville had been right all along.

"It is the way that *I* look at you," Somerset admitted.

"Listen to me," Eliza said, tugging upon his hands. "Melville flirts with me, I won't deny it. But he does not mean it seriously. You must note he flirts as easily as breathing."

Somerset raised his brows in comical disbelief.

Eliza wrinkled her brow, wanting to reassure him but hardly knowing how. For Melville's attentions had been assiduous and she had been enjoying them, truthfully. How could one not enjoy being so flattered, especially by a gentleman who did it so well as Melville? But it was not real—he was amusing himself, only.

"Melville has had a mistress in keeping for several years," Eliza said. "Whom he has been very much in love with, and so I hardly think him likely to have reattached his affections to *me* on such short notice. His attendance upon me is motived more by dislike of you."

"He told you this?" Somerset said, a good deal consternated.

"No," Eliza laughed, shaking him gently by his lapels. "The gossip is everywhere."

Somerset appeared torn between amusement and disapproval at Eliza's reference to matters of which ladies were expected to have no knowledge.

"If it is true, I do not see that it makes him any more trustworthy," he said.

"But do you trust me?" Eliza asked.

"I—of course," Somerset said. "But you are still so much the innocent and I—"

"I am not such the green girl that you think me," Eliza insisted. "I am well able to look after myself, I promise."

Somerset picked up her hand and kissed it.

"I look forward to the day when I might do that for you," he said.

Eliza knew she ought to tell him now that she was painting Melville's portrait but there was another thump on the roof and Eliza bit the words back. There was simply not sufficient time—the explanation was one thing, but the reassurance it would require would be far lengthier. She would do so in her letters.

"Won't you come inside?" Eliza asked.

"No," Somerset said. "We both disappeared in the interval and there will certainly be talk unless I show my face again. Besides . . ."

His gaze was warm as he looked her over.

"I may be a gentleman," he said, "but even I am not immune to all temptation."

Eliza blushed.

"Ah, so my shy Eliza still exists, too!" Somerset said. "I am glad to see her."

He kissed her one last time, lips, hands and finally eyes all lingering upon her as if all were equally reluctant to let her go.

"Six weeks," he said, whether to remind her or himself, Eliza did not know.

"Six weeks," Eliza repeated, as she climbed out of the carriage.

Eliza—

I awoke this morning already smiling. Last night feels sweeter than any dream, and I write you this note for no more reason than to prove to myself that it truly did occur.

I already miss you more than I am able to convey here, and the only solace I can find over our parting is knowing that when next we meet, I shall finally call you my fiancée. My Lady Somerset.

Write to me as soon as you are able. I cannot promise to compose you beautiful odes in return—in truth I have always been an indifferent letter writer—but I would have you tell me fully and honestly of your days while I am gone. There is not a detail I should find too dull from your pen.

> *Please consider me yours, always yours,*
> *Oliver*

16

Bath dawned cold, bright and dry the next day. It was the kind of morning that felt like a beginning, and as Eliza and Margaret stepped out of Camden Place, Eliza was hard-pressed not to consider it a sign of sorts. She smiled. She had not been able to *stop* smiling since a boy from the Pelican had delivered her Somerset's note an hour previous, her heart so brimming with joy that she felt certain it must be spilling out of her to the rest of the street.

"The satisfaction might be approaching a *little* much, Eliza," Margaret said, regarding her indulgently, and Eliza laughed, twining their arms together and setting off at a brisk trot.

She had hardly slept the night before—too alight with emotion to do anything other than sketch idly until the early hours of the morning, her mind turning the night before over and over in her mind, and yet she did not feel tired, but rather restless with energy.

They were bound for Mr. Berwick's painting rooms, just off Monmouth Street, where he had begun exhibiting his new works. He had delivered the invitation to Margaret at the concert's interval the night before, and as soon as Margaret had let it slip this morning, Eliza was hurrying her into her pelisse and nudging her out the door, motivated as much by a desire to be out, to be moving, as by curiosity. The sun hit their faces as they passed onto Lansdown Road and Eliza lifted her head to be able to enjoy it all the more, smiling again. It was a *wonderful* day.

"Your engagement will not remain a secret for long, if you continue beaming in such a way," Margaret said, laughing.

Eliza shushed her half-heartedly.

"I am not engaged," she reminded her. "More . . . engaged to be engaged."

"*Very* different," Margaret said. "It is a good thing, then, that I had not yet badgered you into accepting Mrs. Gould's—very literal—companionship. This is a far superior state to leave you in."

"I am glad you think so," Eliza said. "For I had wondered if perhaps—once your sister's child is handed off to a governess—you might make your home with us."

Margaret gave a bark of laughter.

"I do not think Somerset would be happy to share your company, so soon into your marriage," she said.

"He has already agreed," Eliza said.

"Under duress?"

"No," Eliza insisted. "He is fond of you, himself—and he knows that you are important to me."

"We shall see," Margaret said dubiously. Then, nudging Eliza's elbow, she added, "I am delighted to see you made so happy, Eliza, but are you sure *you* wish to quit Bath for Harefield?"

Eliza could not prevent the instinctive shudder that ran through her at the thought. But—

"Harefield will feel different, with him," she said. "I am sure of it."

They would close up the state apartments, rid the house of its gloomiest memorabilia, light the fires—and besides, Eliza imagined they would spend most of the year in London, or on visits, or inviting friends for long house parties . . .

"What friends are these?" Margaret asked gently, when

Eliza voiced this aloud. "Lady Hurley? Melville? Would Somerset like to have such persons visit him?"

Eliza frowned. Lady Hurley, perhaps, for Somerset had softened toward her, but the Melvilles—the thought was laughable. The trouble was, when otherwise would she see Melville—and Lady Caroline, of course—if she could not issue such an invitation? Equitable rank they might be, but they hardly ran in the same circles, usually—that they had come across each other in Bath at all was utter happenstance. Or, perhaps fate, if one was feeling more poetic, that is.

"I think we are here," Margaret said, peering around, and Eliza shook the thoughts from her head. Somerset had voiced it correctly, after all. They would solve all such problems, once they were together again.

Mr. Berwick's showrooms at 2 Westgate Buildings had once belonged to portraitist Thomas Beach, and they were so magnificent in size and ambience—Mr. Berwick had employed a violinist to play whilst his guests browsed—that Eliza was immediately struck by jealousy. How she would love to have such spacious rooms available to her, a painting room with perfect light and a capacious showroom calculated to display her pieces to their utmost advantage—to feel confident to exhibit, rather than hide.

"It *is* impressive," Margaret said begrudgingly, as they began a slow circuit of the room, pausing to gaze at the landscapes and portraits they passed. Eliza had hoped to confirm that Mr. Berwick's self-satisfaction was entirely unwarranted, but that he had talent was not surprising. He had exhibited so frequently at the Royal Academy, after all, and though he was hardly an exciting artist, Eliza had to acknowledge, as she stood in front of a three-quarter-length portrait of a woman— Van Dyck–inspired, certainly, with the froth of fabric, lace and flowers all about her—his gift with a brush.

"Good morning, Lady Somerset." Mr. Berwick appeared eagerly at her shoulder.

Though it was still morning, he was turned out in prime style, a diamond pin stuck in his elaborately knotted neckcloth, and Eliza noticed he was now wearing his cuffs a little paint splattered, in Melvillian fashion.

"I am so glad you could attend! Ah, I see you are admiring Madame Catalani!"

Madame Catalani? Eliza turned back to regard the painting again. She supposed it could be her: her hair was the correct color, after all, and she was wearing the same dress she had when she performed at the Assembly Rooms, although as Mr. Berwick had rendered her skin paler and her frame far slighter than Eliza remembered, and bafflingly, as having far more décolletage than she possessed in reality, Eliza had not recognized her.

"Are you sure we are looking at the right one?" Margaret said, disbelief clear in her voice.

Fortunately, the fortifications of Mr. Berwick's ego ran too deep for him to notice.

"Everyone has praised the likeness most effusively," Mr. Berwick said. "Mr. Fletcher deemed it absolutely splendid."

Eliza smiled. Of course he did.

"But you simply *must* see the portrait I exhibited last year," Mr. Berwick said. "Come—the *Morning Post* praised its innovatory use of color . . ."

Margaret snorted quietly as they followed.

"Behold!" Mr. Berwick said, standing back and giving a rapturous sigh as he regarded the painting. It was larger than the others—the only full-length portrait in the room—oil on wood, the subject posed in a classical style. The whole effect was certainly accomplished, but the longer one looked, the more that seemed a little *off*. The proportions of the subject's

body were peculiar: the torso too long, the legs, on close ex-
amination, curved, like a wishbone. Eliza stepped forward. At
closer quarters, the pastoral backdrop was all wrong: a sheep
larger than a horse, a horse standing at the same height as a
chicken. It was a farmyard from a nightmare.

"Some have called it a masterpiece, of course, but I myself
think it is not above adequate."

If that. Eliza had assumed such a portrait—which had
stood among the great artists of the age, with eyes and importance and consequence afforded onto it—would be miles and
miles above her own work in quality. But had she shown such
a painting to her grandfather, he would have rapped her over
the knuckles with a paintbrush.

"Oh, Mrs. Winkworth has just arrived—if you will excuse
me . . ."

Mr. Berwick bustled off. Margaret stepped level with
Eliza, peering forward herself.

"I must say, this ought make you feel a great deal more
confident," she said.

"It does," Eliza said. "It almost makes me think . . ."

"Yes?"

"It is of no import," Eliza said, deciding not to voice the
thought aloud.

For what purpose would submitting her own portrait of
Melville to the Summer Exhibition serve, other than vanity?
She was tempting fate sufficiently by painting the portrait in
the first place, was she not? And even if her fortune no longer
felt quite so precarious—Somerset was hardly going to remove his fiancée's income—she still had to find a way of explaining the whole scheme to Somerset in a way he would
understand. It was more than enough to worry about, without
adding new pressure. Certainly, it would be the realization of
every childhood dream she had harbored, ever since her first

visit to Somerset House at ten years of age. It might constitute proof, finally, that she did have skill, did have talent. It might allow her to call herself, at last, an artist.

"Shall we be off?" Margaret asked. "I have a few books to fetch from the library."

"I think I shall return directly home," Eliza decided, as they stepped out of the saloon back onto the street—Staves the footman springing back to their side from where he had been waiting.

"Writing to Somerset?" Margaret guessed, grinning. "Very well, I shall see you anon."

They turned in opposite directions, and as Eliza wound her way through the streets at a leisurely pace, she looked around her with renewed admiration. Knowing that her days in Bath were numbered, Eliza felt all the more aware of its beauty, its shining stone, its hills upon hills, the regal curve of its town-houses: it was just so beautiful. She was crossing onto the Royal Crescent, just for the pleasure of looking upon it, when a wild clattering of wheels had her turning around, startled to see, careering down the street toward her at top speed, a shining high-perch phaeton. In it, resplendent in a riding habit *à la Hussar* and a tall beaver hat plumed with curled feathers, was Lady Caroline.

Eliza let out a genuine gasp. It was well known, of course, that Lady Caroline was a prodigious whip, but it was quite another thing to see it in real life.

"Lady Caroline!" Eliza exclaimed, both in shock and in greeting, as Caroline brought the horses to a prancing stop beside her—her groom jumping down to hold their heads.

"I ordered my phaeton down from Alderley," Lady Caroline said in explanation, her eyes sparkling. "Hang the expense! Do you like it?"

"It is *magnificent*," Eliza said.

"May I take you up for a while?" Lady Caroline said, extending a hand in invitation. "I have just taken Lady Hurley up for a few streets, but I should like to spread their legs properly out of town."

Eliza hesitated. The high-perch phaeton looked very precarious, the frail body of the carriage hanging directly over the front axle, its bottom a full five feet from the ground. And she was only barely dressed for walking—a sturdy pelisse thrown over her flimsy morning dress in her haste to leave the house. And, further, what would be considered typically eccentric of Lady Caroline in London might well, for Lady Somerset in Bath, be remarked upon as dreadfully unusual.

But . . . With her engagement—her almost engagement—were not the days of watching her behavior so closely behind her?

"I would love to," she said, feeling reckless, and after bidding her footman return to Camden Place without her, she accepted the groom's assistance into the carriage.

Eliza had ridden in a high-perch phaeton once before, invited by a gentleman in her first Season—but either her memory had failed her, or that young buck had been a far more sedate driver than Lady Caroline, for this felt like something different entirely. Exhilaration was too small a word for it. The carriage, so unlike its placid cousin, the barouche, offered no protection to its riders at all, and though the day had felt not overly windy while walking, perched above the spokes and driving at what must be ten miles an hour at least, it buffeted directly into her face. By the end of the street, Eliza was breathless. By the time they passed out of Bath and into the fields surrounding the city, she was clutching tightly to her bonnet for fear its ribbon was not strong enough to keep it upon her head and letting out involuntary shouts at every tight turn.

Lady Caroline took them on a wide loop around Bath, and only once they seemed to be on the return journey did she allow the horses to slow sufficiently for proper conversation.

"Oh, I needed this!" Lady Caroline said, shaking her head like one of her horses. "My mind simply does not work without exertion—I have been struggling to write since we arrived."

"It must be difficult, to write again after such a delay," Eliza noted, raising her head to the sunshine.

"Oh, there has been no delay," Lady Caroline said. "I am always writing—it is just publishing that I have avoided these past years. The brouhaha after *Kensington* was such that I had to retreat from society, for a while."

"*You*—retreat?" Eliza said, unable to mask her incredulity. Nothing in Lady Caroline's deportment—so fearless and glamorous—had given Eliza reason to believe she was bothered by scandal.

Lady Caroline navigated a tricky turn of the junction with an unhurried flick of her wrist.

"You cannot have been in London at the time," she said. "Our closest friends paid no mind to the outcry, but many hostesses would not receive me. And while it took Caroline Lamb two years to be readmitted to Almack's after *Glenarvon*—a far more improprietous text—they were slower to forgive *me*. But then, standards for Melville and me will always be different than they are for our cousins—as my mother so often warned us."

"You are related to the Lambs?" Eliza said, though it ought not surprise her, for the aristocracy did have a wretched habit of marrying their own relatives.

"And the Ponsonbys, though more distantly," Lady Caroline said. "Our family trees are all hopelessly tangled."

Eliza regarded Lady Caroline out of the corner of her eye.

"The . . . Irish Ponsonbys, too?" she asked tentatively. There had been another article in the newspaper that week about Miss Sarah Ponsonby and her companion Miss Eleanor Butler, dubbed together the "Ladies of Llangollen," that had made some scandalous intimations.

"If you refer to Miss Sarah Ponsonby, then yes," Lady Caroline said, seeing through Eliza with ease. "Though I have no gossip for you."

Eliza flushed pink.

"The sequel to *Kensington,*" she said in a quick change of subject for she did not want Lady Caroline to think her scurrilous, "you mean to publish it?"

"If I can," Lady Caroline said.

"And you are not concerned about the consequences?"

"Certainly I am," Lady Caroline said. "It is why I plan to seek refuge in Paris this summer. Distance should insulate me a little from condemnation."

"But . . . then why risk it?"

"Because I want to," Lady Caroline said, as if it were that simple. "It is the work I am proudest of and I'll be damned if I will be intimidated out of publishing it."

"You do not think it better to . . . wait," Eliza said. "Until a more fortuitous time?"

She thought, briefly, of the steadily growing murmurs linking Melville and Lady Paulet.

"I tire of waiting," Lady Caroline said. "I shall not do it anymore."

"You are very brave," Eliza said. "*I* could not . . ."

"Couldn't you?" Lady Caroline said. "And what of Melville's portrait?"

Eliza shook her head.

"It will always remain anonymous," she said. She was under no qualms that Somerset was likely to find the revelation of her painting Melville's portrait difficult enough, without it being publicly known. "I did think, however . . . I did wonder . . ."

Eliza looked at the side of Lady Caroline's face, dithering for a moment, before deciding that while Melville might be blindly supportive, Lady Caroline would surely answer her honestly.

"I did wonder about submitting the portrait to the Summer Exhibition," she said in a rush. "I saw the work Mr. Berwick is to submit, and I think—well, I do not think mine is all that much worse. But then, why should I do such a thing— even anonymously, it will only invite more inquiry, more spectacle, and for no gain other than vanity."

"And for what reason do you think Mr. Berwick submits his work?" Lady Caroline asked politely.

"For publicity, I am sure," Eliza said. "How else will he earn a living?"

"He has an independent income of two thousand pounds a year," Lady Caroline said. "As he told me himself."

Eliza digested this for a moment.

"Ambition and pride are not muscles women are generally encouraged to cultivate," Lady Caroline said. "But that does not mean we are incapable of learning. If your true qualm is a lack of talent, well, rest assured that Melville has known enough artists to know skill when he sees it."

"Do you refer to Lady Paulet?" Eliza asked, before she could stop herself.

Lady Caroline gave an incriminating pause before answering.

"Yes, we have often been in her way," Lady Caroline said.

"Is she as wonderful as they say?" Eliza asked.

A landscape artist of great renown even before her marriage to Lord Paulet—himself a great patron of the arts—Lady Paulet's praises were regularly sung across all the elegant drawing rooms of London's West End.

"She is as talented as they say, if that is what you are meaning, and quite as capricious," Lady Caroline said. She did not say "capricious" as if it were a compliment.

"And she is a beauty?" Eliza asked, unable to help herself. She was not sure what she would gain from knowing the lady was beautiful—of course Lady Paulet would be, to have ensnared a gentleman such as Melville—but she found herself ravenous for detail.

"She is certainly not the sort of woman one can easily look away from," Lady Caroline said.

Eliza nodded tensely. She wished she had not asked.

"The rumors say that she and Melville were . . . closely acquainted," she said, peeping at Lady Caroline from the corner of her eye.

"I had not realized that particular piece of gossip had already reached Bath," Lady Caroline said, voice neutral—which was tantamount to an admission, in Eliza's view.

"Rumor has it," Eliza decided to risk bluntness, "that Lord Paulet's discovery of the affair is what led you to come here."

"I cannot speak to my brother's private affairs," Lady Caroline said briskly, "though you may rest assured that all involved suffered a great deal."

Eliza subsided, feeling herself chastised, and they drove in silence for a while—Eliza admiring Lady Caroline's graceful handling of the reins.

"How came you to be able to drive so well?" Eliza asked.

"My mother taught me," Lady Caroline said. "My father taught her."

"I did not know that she drove, too," Eliza said.

"My mother was careful always to behave as the perfect lady of quality in public," Lady Caroline said briefly.

"But she was accepted into society, was she not?" Eliza said, brow wrinkling. "I thought the Queen's patronage had . . ."

"Acceptance was not so simply achieved," Lady Caroline said. "There were those who found her a fascination, but to others, she had to do much more than simply change 'Nur' to 'Eleanor.' Each day was an exercise in proving her refinement, her European sensibility, her knowledge of English custom." Lady Caroline's mouth twisted into a rather bitter smile. "While English ladies all around her bedecked their bodies in Bengal muslin, their shoulders in Kashmir shawls and their houses in chintz without a single thought."

Eliza had not known—well, she had assumed, naively, that save for a few spiteful persons, all had been resolved with the Queen's blessing.

"And you do not . . ." Eliza said, her mind flickering back to Lady Caroline's decision to hang social consequence. "You do not feel a similar pressure?"

"It is a little different for me," Lady Caroline said. "I was born here. I grew up with the sons and daughters of dukes and earls as my playmates. My skin is lighter. It is not easy—but it is different."

Eliza nodded, silently.

"At Alderley, though, we could always be at ease," Lady Caroline said. "It was there Mother taught me to drive."

"I always thought it would be a wonderful thing to know how to do," Eliza said enviously.

"You can always learn," Lady Caroline said.

Eliza laughed. "And who on earth would agree to teach me?"

"Why, I would," Lady Caroline said, quite casually. "Let us start now."

"You cannot be serious!" Eliza said.

"I am quite serious—you have been observing me do it for a little while now. Come, take the reins."

"Lady Caroline, I do not think this is at all—" Eliza began to object.

"Oh, do call me Caroline," she said impatiently, dropping the reins into Eliza's lap. Alarmed, Eliza seized them and pushed them back toward her, but Caroline whipped her hands behind her back so that she could not.

Eliza looked to Wardlaw, Caroline's groom, perched behind her, hoping he might offer assistance, but he merely gazed back at her, a hint of amusement in his eyes.

"Do not look to him for help, Lady Somerset!" Caroline instructed. "Come now, I thought you wanted to learn."

"I have not the faintest idea of what to do!"

"Do not look so frightened!" Caroline said. "Now, hold them as so . . ."

It was far less exhilarating, far more terrifying, to be the driver rather than the passenger, and Eliza hunched low over the reins, her eyes wide with nerves, feeling she might turn to stone with how tightly she held herself.

"Try not to look so pained," Caroline instructed. "It is not at all dashing if one looks pained."

"I am trying not to kill us," Eliza said through gritted teeth.

"At this pace, I think it far more likely that we perish from starvation," Caroline muttered. "The peril is part of the fun!"

She let Eliza have the reins for a full twenty minutes. As Bath began to rise up around them once more, Caroline took the reins back for the final few miles. They drew up outside Camden Place and Eliza gathered her skirts around her—bone-tired, but thrilled with herself—but Caroline laid a hand on her arm, stopping her.

"Lady Somerset," she said. "Eliza. You may ignore me if you wish, but . . . I think that to have the means and the opportunity, but to not act, simply because you are afraid—it would be the most terrible waste."

Her face was uncharacteristically earnest.

"Thank you," Eliza said. "For today."

"Please pass on my regards to Miss Margaret," Caroline said, gathering up her reins. "And inform her we shall be tackling the future tense upon the morrow."

And she set her horses briskly off once more, leaving Eliza in the dust with a great deal to think about.

Oliver,

The days without you draw long, but I have waited for too
many years to quail at six weeks. However long they take
to pass, I know our reunion will only be sweeter for its
interlude.

As I said to you on that night—I need not, I am sure,
specify which I mean—there is much we must speak of
still. So much that I wonder we wasted so much time upon
pleasantries, when there are such vast quantities of each of
our lives that remain a mystery for the other.

I do not think I mentioned, for example, that I am still
painting. Perhaps you do not even remember that I used to
do so, but I have received a commission while in Bath—to
be fulfilled anonymously, but a proper artist's commission,
nonetheless. And while you may think it sadly self-
indulgent—as you well know, I lack for neither income
nor diversion—even if vanity were my only motivation,
I should wish to see it through. I will see it through.

I await your reply—your thoughts—with truly
excessive eagerness, and remain

Yours forever,
Eliza

17

Eliza raised the subject with Melville the very next day. He and Caroline arrived at the agreed hour—two o'clock in the afternoon, today, for the best light—and while the ladies had cloistered themselves in the drawing room ("*je te trouve belle*" floating in through the open door) Melville had cast himself down upon the sofa, as normal. The canvas that stood upon the easel was coated in a mix of yellow ochre and white lead, but otherwise marked only by a charcoaled outline of Melville's form, and the first assays of color upon his face and torso. Eliza twisted her hands in her skirts. If he did not think the exhibition a good idea—if he did not agree, if he scoffed or thought her deluded—then Eliza would not do it. She took a deep breath, sat down beside Melville and opened her mouth . . .

"Somerset is gone, then," Melville said.

"Oh—yes," Eliza said. "I have something I should like to discuss . . ."

"Gallant of him to escort you home from the concert," Melville observed. "He returned looking mightily pleased with himself."

"Did he?" Eliza said, as if she did not care.

"I thought he might have proposed," Melville admitted.

Eliza inhaled sharply, choking back a shrill denial that would give her away immediately.

"You are outrageous," she managed calmly. "You may see for yourself that my ring finger is bare."

She waggled her hand at him and Melville took it in his own, pretending to hold it to the light, examining it this way and that as if a betrothal ring might be hidden in plain sight.

Eliza started a little, for that had not been her intention, and she was not wearing gloves—she never did, while painting—and neither was he: it felt shockingly intimate. His skin was warm and smooth, save for the calluses she felt on his fingers—from holding a pen, or riding a horse without gloves, she could only guess.

"So it is," Melville agreed at last. "And it is all the prettier for it."

He took a moment more to let go, and Eliza withdrew her hand, feeling a little discombobulated.

"Will you write to him while he is away?" Melville asked, still in that light, conversational way.

"If an occasion calls for it, I should think so," Eliza said carefully. "Letters of . . . business."

"I thought they might rather be letters of love."

Eliza inhaled sharply and willed herself not to blush.

"You thought incorrectly," she said.

"A shame," Melville said. "A good love letter is worth its weight in gold."

As Eliza could attest . . . But now was not the moment to dwell.

"I hear you receive piles of them from readers," Eliza said, trying to steer the conversation away from Somerset. "Is that true?"

"Not quite piles—perhaps rather a small heap," Melville said. "Have you ever written to me?"

"I have not!" Eliza said indignantly.

"You can tell me," he said. "I shan't make fun."

"You absolutely would—and I have not! I would *never*."

"Your horror is unwarranted," Melville protested. "Some of the letters are quite affecting: one lady created such an evocative idea of our life together, that I was on the point of agreeing to it until Caro pointed out the billet had come from Coldbath Fields Prison."

"You are not serious," Eliza protested.

"I am!" he said, grinning. "To this day I feel a little wistful about dear Mary, for she may well have been the great love of my life. But when I would not send her a lock of my hair, she vowed to murder me and I deduced this indicated the end of our affair."

"A wise deduction," Eliza said, laughing.

"Why thank you," Melville said.

There was a discreet knock upon the door, and Perkins entered with a tray.

"Marvelous," Melville said. Eliza took a moment to remarshal her thoughts.

"Did you attend Mr. Berwick's exhibition yesterday?" she asked.

"I did. And to think you would have had him paint my portrait. *What* that man would have done to my legs!"

"You do not yet know what *I* may do to your legs," Eliza said, biting back a smile.

"I know you are the better artist," Melville said.

There was not an ounce of doubt in his voice and hearing it emboldened Eliza.

"It made me wonder if I might submit your portrait to the exhibition," she said in a rush. "Only if you approve, of course!"

Melville tilted his head consideringly.

"It may invite spectacle," Eliza continued hurriedly, "though if I submit anonymously, the secret should be kept."

"A famous notion," Melville said. "I wonder I did not think of it."

He agreed with such ease—no question or hesitation—that Eliza was almost unnerved.

"It could be a fruitless endeavor," she said, feeling a strange need to clarify matters. "Selection may be more rigorous this year."

"Which might weed out Mr. Berwick," Melville said. "But you will certainly pass muster."

"If such a feat is even possible in so short a time," Eliza said reflexively.

The process for submission to the Summer Exhibition was the same in '19 as it had been in Eliza's grandfather's day: nonmembers of the Royal Academy could submit their work to a committee of academy council members, in a rigorous five-day selection process in early April. Eliza would have less than four weeks to complete a task that might ordinarily take four months.

"Why are you trying to convince me out of it?" Melville asked. "I should think you perfectly able to meet such challenges."

Rarely had Eliza encountered such unassailable belief in her abilities. Margaret's support, of course, approached the evangelical—but it felt profoundly different coming from Melville. Margaret had known Eliza her whole life, after all; it was positively her duty to support Eliza and Eliza her. But Melville had no such motive and nor did he offer praise blindly, as his frequent castigation of Mr. Berwick proved. His belief existed purely because he considered her deserving of it . . . and Eliza felt herself unfurl toward the light he offered.

"Do you wish to enter?" Melville asked, with a quizzical smile.

"Yes," Eliza said, finally allowing herself to feel the rush of excitement that had been building all morning. "I do."

"Then . . ." He spread his arms invitingly. "We have work to do, do we not?"

And that very day, with pale morning light streaming through the window, a fire dancing in the grate, the sound of Margaret's bright laughter filtering across the hallway and a paintbrush in her hand, they began in earnest.

Eliza had always painted quickly—one had to, when one was always on the point of interruption—but in the coming days she moved with a swift purpose, unhesitatingly, as if Melville's confidence in her was catching. She positioned Melville exactly as she wanted him—facing the window at an angle, for the best light, and began the next layer of the painting, intent and determined. She deliberated over the exact shades upon her palette, returning to Mr. Fasana's shop to consult him upon new mixes, electing to use as many with linseed oil bases as possible, for the quickest drying time.

Working to a new deadline, Melville had to lend Eliza far more of his time, and he did so without complaint. Indeed, within a se'nnight of Melville's agreeing to the exhibition, it seemed that she and Margaret were rarely without the Melvilles' company, so frequently did they encounter one another in Meyler's library (Lady Caroline and Melville loudly denigrating the poets they did not like upon the shelves), attend the same musical performances (Melville whispering such a wildly inaccurate translation of the opera that Eliza had to press a fist against her mouth to keep from laughing) and drive together in Lady Caroline's phaeton (for Eliza's lessons continued at pace).

It was enough, truly, to make Eliza feel a little guilty.

"I am grateful you are sparing so much of your time," Eliza told Melville the following Thursday, palette balanced in one hand, brush in the other. After weeks of working with oil now, Eliza's paintwork was becoming freer—in the cursive sweeps of her loaded brush, she could feel her body, her arm, her grip upon the brush were all looser. "I do hope we are not taking you away from your writing desk?"

"Fret not," Melville said. "I always write in the early hours and I am grateful, indeed, that your driving lessons take Caro away before breakfast, for it leaves the house so blissfully quiet. Long may it continue, I say."

"She may well lose patience with me soon," Eliza warned him.

"You are not a nonpareil yet?"

"Hardly," Eliza said. "I should not think I could drive as she does, if I spent years practicing. Has she always been so absolutely fearless?"

"Caroline?" he said. "About horses, yes, it is how we were raised. My parents were almost as mad for horses as they were for each other."

Eliza was startled, as always, by the frank and easy way Melville could speak of such warm subjects.

"They married for love, didn't they?" she asked. She was familiar with the story, of course, but Eliza knew better than to trust a fourth- or fifth-hand account of gossip from before she was born.

"At first sight, if my mother is to be believed," Melville said, his eyes resting warmly upon Eliza's. "My father visited Hyderabad in '85. He was already acquainted with the Company's Resident there and being the runaway lord gave him glamour enough to be invited to court. Mother never told us quite how they met. She was the youngest daughter of the *nawab*—the governor—and ought never to have come near him, but I suspect my grandmother helped arrange it."

"And then they married?" Eliza asked. Melville shook his head.

"Not for two more years; her father had to be convinced, and the Nizam—the ruler of Hyderabad—petitioned too," Melville said. "And meanwhile, they courted discreetly. They conversed first in Persian, which my father knew a little, before he learned Urdu and she English."

"It sounds most romantic," Eliza said.

"It did not come without trials," Melville said. "Her family objected until the last, and when my grandfather died they had to remove to England—to a disgraced family name, an estate on the point of ruin, and an England absolutely consternated to have its first Indian countess. But we were happy, despite it all."

"They were affectionate parents?" Eliza asked.

Melville smiled.

"Very much so. They told Caroline and me almost every day how precious we were—although it was a shock indeed to arrive at Eton to find it an opinion not universally shared."

"They were unkind?" Eliza said.

Melville shrugged.

"It is as you might expect. Roughhousing, name-calling: the 'piebald' lord they used to call me, amongst other *hugely* derivative epithets."

The lightness in his voice was forced. Eliza might not have noticed the change weeks ago, but she could hear the difference now. She lifted the brush from the canvas, to regard him with her full, careful attention.

"It would have been worse, I am told, if we had remained in India. The British there are increasingly hostile toward persons such as us. I would have been dreadfully out of fashion."

Melville's voice was beginning to wear at the edges and Eliza was not surprised when he changed the subject soon after.

"What of *your* parents? Are they happy?"

"They are well suited, I believe," Eliza said, considering the matter. "They share in each other's aims and beliefs, although I have never considered either of them particularly romantic."

"And are you? Particularly romantic?"

It was another terribly personal question, but given what Melville had just shared it did not feel so very strange to answer.

"As a girl, very much so," she said. "I scarce wished for anything more than to fall, truly and greatly, in love, independent of duty, circumstance, familial interest."

"The reality did not meet your expectation?"

"Oh, it did, in every conceivable way," Eliza said. "It was just that I did not marry him."

It was the first time she had spoken about her relationship with Somerset, however indirectly, and as if afraid she might clam up at any moment, Melville asked his next question very quickly.

"What made you develop such a partiality for him?"

"Oh," Eliza smiled even to think of it, "I cannot think when, exactly it began—the moment we met, I suppose. He called me beautiful."

"And?"

"And? I assure you, this was enough to make me notice him—while you, my lord, may be used to drowning in flattery, for me it is a novelty. And then, once I had started noticing, I could not stop. He always was so honorable, so kind, so conscious of his responsibilities."

"Responsibility is not a word I usually associate with love," Melville noted.

"I am not the writer," Eliza said, self-conscious. "I do not know how to say it prettily. We merely had a great deal of mutual admiration and respect a-and enjoyment of each other's company . . ."

"I shall do my best with it," Melville said, patting down his pockets. "The difficulty is going to be finding a rhyme for 'mutual.' A half rhyme will have to do—contractual, perhaps? I wish I had a quill to hand."

Eliza threw a small piece of chalk at him and Melville dodged it with a laugh. It was the sort of behavior that would have been unthinkable, not long ago, but one could not spend as much time together, as Eliza and Melville now were, without growing more comfortable in each other's presence. And in moments such as this Eliza found herself oddly glad for the circumstances that had required a delay to her and Somerset's official engagement. It was not just the act of working upon the portrait she would have missed out on—it would have been the company, too. As unlikely as it might once have seemed, she was beginning to count Melville as one of her dearest friends.

Dear Eliza,

Your letter took a veritable age to arrive and the sight of your handwriting, which has not changed in these ten years, had me breathing easier than I have this week past.

Your commission sounds a charming scheme. When I remember the darling little drawings you used to show me—and I do remember them—I can well believe that another has been similarly enchanted. Shall I guess the painting's subject or is it to be a surprise? Perhaps a view of Camden Place, or the abbey? I look forward to seeing it regardless—but seeing you, most of all.

I cannot now write more, for I am being called away— expect a longer note from me anon.

Yours ever,
Oliver

18

Mid-March brought with it a false spring; a brief spell of sunshine that had everyone fooled for the fortnight it lasted, improving tempers across the city and turning the attention of many to the London Season. For while most of Bath's residents remained year-round, many of the wealthier inhabitants—such as Lady Hurley and the Winkworths—would be removing to the metropolis at the end of the month. All seemed energized by the approaching Season, but none more so than Lady Hurley, for no sooner had she spotted Eliza and Margaret at the Pump Room, than she had bustled over, dispensed entirely with pleasantries and invited them to a party.

"Before I leave for London," she explained, with all the rapidity of an officer delivering a field report, "I have settled my heart on hosting a rout next week, with a little dancing, to bid farewell to Bath, and I absolutely insist you are in attendance."

Eliza hesitated.

"Do not, I beg of you, say it would be improper!" Lady Hurley said. "Why, Lady Somerset, it must be eleven months since your mourning began! If you are seated, throughout, and do not stay too late, I am sure it cannot be thought in the least remarkable for you to attend a small party at a private residence."

"Come, Eliza, surely you are allowed *some* fun, now?" Margaret said.

Oh, dash it. It was not so very improper—she had only a month left of full mourning, after all. She was sure that Somerset would recommend she enjoy herself.

"We should be delighted to attend," Eliza said. "I have a fancy for a new evening dress, anyhow, and this makes the perfect excuse."

"I have just come from Madame Prevette, and she has in some ravishing new black gossamer that would look divine," Lady Hurley said. "Though I did not enquire how much of it remains."

"Then we must hasten to the *modiste* before the other widows make a run on it," Eliza declared, smiling to imagine a flock of black-clad women dashing down Milsom Street.

But Lady Hurley was too busy casting about for the Melvilles to pay heed.

"If I can be sure of their attendance, too, it is likely to be the most modish event of the year, but I cannot find hide nor hair of them. Though perhaps"—she threw a roguish look toward Eliza—"it would be quicker for you to invite Melville, my lady, for I am sure you will see him before I!"

"I do not know what you mean," Eliza said.

Lady Hurley cackled. "Oh, we all saw you, whispering together at the concert last week," she said. "And riding together yesterday afternoon! *Very* cozy."

She bustled away, without waiting for a response, but Eliza's cheeks still pinked.

The day before, when Eliza had been suffering from a fit of the sullens—for no matter how carefully she painted, Melville's ears were still lying awkwardly—Melville had removed the paintbrush from her hand and suggested a ride would clear her mind.

"Now?" Eliza had said uncertainly. "Alone?"

"I would prefer your groom attend us," he had said, making

for the door so that he might change into riding dress. "I suspect otherwise you might attempt a seduction."

And while it might not be altogether sensible to jaunt about the countryside with an unmarried gentleman at such an unusual hour, even with her groom in attendance—in Bath, one commonly rode before breakfast—after an hour on the hills, breathless and laughing, she had not cared. Now, however . . .

"Pay her no mind," Margaret advised Eliza, but as they walked to Milsom Street, Eliza could not help but wonder if the gazes upon her had increased in number since last week—whether the ogles were more speculative, whether she could hear her name being whispered by the little flocks of ladies and gentlemen that passed them.

Perhaps it would be wise to keep Melville at arm's length, in public. For while Eliza might know herself to be as good as engaged to another man, Bath's quidnuncs did not and there was no need, truly, for them to spend any time in one another's company outside of sittings. Wise—but tedious. *Hang it*, Eliza declared to herself, as they pushed into Madame Prevette's shop. Eliza was not about to make herself unhappy for the sake of appeasing some imaginary gossipmongers. Let them stare, if they like.

The black gossamer was everything Lady Hurley had said it would be, and Madame Prevette promised to have a new creation ready for Eliza by the time of the rout.

"You will be wanting a whole new *toilette*, soon, will you not?" Madame Prevette asked Eliza, as Margaret considered the merits of primrose versus pomona-green silk. "For your half-mourning?"

"Yes, I suppose I will," Eliza said, a little surprised. With everything that had occurred with Somerset, she had almost forgotten that the ending of her full mourning meant more than being able to marry him. It would mean the re-entry, at last, into the world of color: very soon, she would be permitted to lighten her dresses and gowns to the greys and lavenders of half-mourning. "Yes indeed, Madame Prevette, I will most certainly need to buy *everything* new."

"Perhaps I may show you some of my latest plates from Paris," Madame Prevette offered, and disappeared briefly into the back. When she returned, it was to find Eliza running her hand enviously over a roll of bronze-green satin, newly arrived. The color was so beautiful.

"Perhaps something in that color? It would suit you very well," Madame Prevette suggested.

"I would love to . . ." Eliza said. "But even half-mourning would not allow such a rich hue."

"Not even to save, to look forward to the day you might wear it?" Madame Prevette was an astute saleswoman, and Eliza was immediately intrigued. The idea of the dress of her dreams, hanging in her wardrobe like a promise of better things to come . . .

"Perhaps over a satin slip," Madame Prevette wondered aloud. "And matching slippers to complete the ensemble?"

Oh, why not?

"You have my measurements?" Eliza said. "And I can count upon your discretion?"

"It will be our little secret," she said.

Eliza and Margaret bade her farewell with a smile before hurrying home to meet the Melvilles.

"I suppose I ought to have asked if you had a preference on style," Eliza mused to Melville later, regarding the canvas critically. She hadn't allowed him to look at the canvas out of an anxiousness that to do so would be to spoil it in some way—though she was pleased with her progress. Without sufficient time to dry the portrait between sittings, Eliza was painting *alla prima*—laying fresh paint onto wet canvas—and a fortnight in, the bulk of the work was already behind her.

"I'm not sure I have one," Melville said. "As long as it combines the grandeur of Thomas Gainsborough and the playful insouciance of Thomas Rowlandson, I will be well satisfied."

"Oh, you want both Thomases, do you?" Eliza said, smiling.

"If you could."

"I'm afraid it is not at all what I had in mind."

"No insouciance at all?" Melville checked.

"Not even a little," she said gravely.

"Alas—though if you can capture my new pantaloons, I shall be satisfied," Melville said. "Do not, I beg you, heed Caroline: they are the very height of fashion, you know."

The pantaloons in question were a bright yellow—Caroline had dubbed them, moments before, as "too natty by half"—and appeared to have been veritably molded to his leg in a manner that Eliza might have thought brave, had Melville's legs been any less fine.

She shook her head.

"I am fixed on the pose," she told him. "Torso and head, only."

"Is it a compliment to my face that it is the portrait's focus?" Melville wondered. "Or an insult to my body to have it ignored?"

"Neither," she said, smiling. "Merely a reflection upon my lack of study—my full-body portraits always have a somewhat dislocated appearance. To truly be able to convey the proportions of the human form, I would need to study it—fully, *privately*, as they do at the Royal Academy. But of course, this is certainly not a lesson allowed to women."

Melville leaned back in his seat, surveying her with a mischievous eye.

"Was this not a tutelage the late earl could offer to you?" he asked.

Eliza did not flush at the question, which she saw as proof of her increasing immunity from his outrageousness.

"The late earl would not have been at all receptive to such a request," she said. "Had I ever dared to make it."

"Yours was not a . . . passionate marriage?"

He raised his eyebrows at her, challenging—as if to communicate that he knew full well that this was another shockingly inappropriate line of questioning, and was waiting for her to put a stop to it. But, this time, Eliza would not give him the benefit of feeling smug.

"The late earl saw to his husbandly obligations in the same manner as all his other responsibilities," she said archly. "That is to say: faithfully, dutifully . . . and with a great deal of brevity."

Melville gave a shout of surprised laughter. Eliza grinned, giddy and irresponsible.

"Well, as your current subject," Melville said, "if a more—ah—natural style of deportment would be beneficial to your education . . ."

He lifted his hand playfully to his cravat.

"Please leave your clothes where they are," Eliza said hastily, though she was still smiling. "Perkins will arrive with refreshments soon, and the sight would only disturb him."

"I would merely explain to Perkins my altruistic motivations," Melville said earnestly. "I have long been a supporter of the arts—indeed, I have offered my services to actresses, opera singers, dancers . . ."

Eliza laughed again, loud and uncontrolled, and from the open door came the sound of Margaret cackling, too. The French lesson had been long abandoned—when Eliza had popped into the drawing room to locate her maulstick that morning, both Caroline's and Margaret's faces had been worryingly full of smirks. Eliza did not quite like to wonder what they had been discussing, but no doubt it was that particular sort of serrated humor these ladies seemed to enjoy with one another—since February it was as if they had been sharpening their wits upon each other as knives upon whetstones.

"Are you to attend Lady Hurley's rout?" Melville asked. "I am greatly looking forward to it. Dinner, cards, a little dancing . . ."

"I envy you that," Eliza said. "I have not been able to dance in such a long time."

"Is this your chance?" Melville suggested.

Eliza laughed.

"Dance? In full mourning?" she said. "I should be chased out of town with pitchforks."

"Who would lead the charge?" Melville wondered. "Mrs. Winkworth?"

"Almost certainly," Eliza said. "She is already regarding my driving lessons with a great deal of consternation—and no doubt squirrelling letters to Lady Selwyn about my behavior."

This prospect did not worry her as much as it might once have done.

"You believe Lady Selwyn to have recruited a spy?" Melville asked quizzically.

"I would be very surprised if she has not," Eliza said with a snort. "She will certainly be on the lookout for anything that could—" She broke off. For a moment she had forgotten that the morality clause was a secret.

"Anything that could keep you and Somerset at a distance?" Melville suggested. "I noticed she did not regard your reacquaintance with pleasure—but if your driving has Somerset running for the hills then he is blander than even *I* suspected."

"He is not bland!" Eliza protested. She had not told Somerset, yet, about Caroline's lessons, not out of fear of his reaction, but to ensure herself skilled enough to impress him.

"Then do you need worry over what Mrs. Winkworth writes?"

"I do not worry," Eliza said, "but it is my fortune that is Lady Selwyn's greatest interest."

Melville tilted his head in question—and really, what harm was there in sharing one more secret with Melville, now?

"My lands were originally intended for the Selwyns' second son," Eliza explained. "My husband bequeathed them to me, instead, but if I cause any dishonor to the family name, they revert back to Somerset."

Melville went very still.

"A morality clause," he said slowly.

"It was the only silver lining for the Selwyns," Eliza said, working another tiny fleck of color onto portrait-Melville's cuffs. "If the lands revert, I imagine they would wind their way back to Tarquin eventually."

"That is . . . diabolical."

Eliza's lips quirked at the horror in Melville's voice.

"You have met them," she said. "Do you not think it within character?"

"I thought them snide," Melville said. "And self-serving—but not so malignant."

He ran a hand distractedly through his hair, more stricken on Eliza's behalf than she had expected.

"How could they *do* such a thing?"

"Oh, I am long accustomed to the idea," Eliza assured him. She had not meant to upset him. "It has not caused me an issue yet."

"*Yet*," Melville said. "You are worried it still might?"

"I used to be," Eliza admitted. "But not since—"

She broke off, biting her lip.

"Since?"

Eliza hesitated. She did not like to lie, outright, to one she considered a friend—but the idea of informing Melville of such a thing filled her with disquiet rather than gladness.

"Since?" Melville pressed again, more seriously now.

There was no helping it.

"Since Somerset and I are . . . to be married," she said.

The clock struck the hour, and it was not until the last knell had sounded that Melville spoke.

"I see," he said. "Yes—I see."

His face and voice, so blank and rigid, were at curious variance with his hands, which appeared a little unsteady. Melville pressed them into the arms of his chair, as if to cease their minute shaking.

"Of course—I had suspected, as you know."

Eliza's stomach twisted.

"Melville . . ." she said, uneasy but uncertain why.

"I wish you very happy," Melville said. His voice still sounded off.

"Thank you," she said. Why did this feel so dreadfully uncomfortable?

"Right-o," Melville said, with insincere cheer, standing abruptly and adjusting his cravat. "I'm afraid I have business to attend to—letters to write, poetry to compose, etcetera, etcetera." He strode toward the door.

"Melville!" Eliza said, clutching her palette with tight hands. She did not want him to leave—not in such a way . . .

"Melville?"

But he was already gone.

19

Melville missed all of their scheduled sittings the next week. He sent over apologies, citing his work, but the excuse felt weak, and Eliza worried over the true reasoning as a dog over a bone. The portrait would not suffer—that was not the issue. By now, Eliza had spent so much time staring at Melville that she might well know his person better than she knew her own. She knew the exact shape of his deep brown eyes, knew the curve of each of his knuckles, the sound of his laugh . . . Even if she hadn't made such a full study, by this point in the proceedings, when she was merely fussing with the detail, other artists would have dispensed with the need for a subject altogether.

But though she might not *need* his presence, she felt the lack keenly. The parlor felt bigger, colder, less interesting without Melville. One did not laugh on one's own, and Eliza could not even be entertained by Margaret, for her appointments with Caroline continued uninterrupted and every moment that Eliza heard their bright voices travel up the corridor was one when she regretted her mishandling of her last conversation with Melville. She could not know quite what had upset Melville, whether it had been the lie, when she had first denied her engagement or . . . something else. Their intimacy with one another had taken on new heights since Somerset had left and Eliza, feeling so much the easier in his presence, had stopped checking him. Or herself. And she supposed that, under such circumstances, to warn a gentleman that his customary flirt was engaged was only polite, was it not?

Whatever the reason, over the next week, though Eliza looked for his dark curls in the Pump Room, tried to spot his yellow pantaloons upon Milsom Street, pricked her ears for his voice in Meyler's library, Melville was nowhere to be seen. And with no Somerset and no Melville, Bath felt exceedingly quiet. And at least with Somerset she had the comfort of his weekly letters to assuage any missing of him. Not that the two ought be compared, of course, given that one was almost her fiancé and the other . . . was not.

By the day of Lady Hurley's rout, Eliza was suffering from a severe case of the blue devils—even as she regarded the sight of the finished portrait standing before her. Well, almost finished. For while she could think of nothing further to do to it, now that she had fussed over the waistcoat buttons until they were just right, scraping away the paint and reapplying it four or five times at least, Eliza could not shake the feeling that something was not quite right with it. If only she knew what.

"We ought ready ourselves," Margaret said, knocking her knuckles on the open doorway to attract her attention. "Lady Hurley will be most displeased if we are late."

Eliza took one last look at the portrait version of Melville. *I'll make it right*, she told the portrait in her mind.

Upon arriving at Laura Place, it became immediately clear that Eliza's idea of an intimate gathering and Lady Hurley's were quite different. There were twenty persons gathered for the dinner party alone, with more to come for the dancing. And although Lady Hurley's grand townhouse was very large— the dining table alone was expansive enough to seat twenty and it was the only house in the whole of Bath with a terrace leading off the ground-floor drawing room—Eliza could not quite understand, as she joined the line of persons greeting their hostess at the entrance, how they were all going to fit.

"A veritable squeeze," Caroline noted, entering just behind them. In an exquisite gown of lilac silk and gauze, it would be difficult for a lady to appear any more elegant than Caroline Melville did that night.

"You look very fine!" Caroline said to Eliza and Margaret.

"Thank you," Eliza replied. She was very pleased with the effect of her dress that night: black gossamer net over a white satin slip, the short French sleeves edged with a rich Vandyke lace, and instead of the jet jewelry she had been confined to the past year, diamond earrings and a triple necklace of pearls lay about her neck. "I do not look like a magpie?"

But Caroline did not answer, as she was too busy taking in Margaret's gown of pomona-green crêpe. Eliza could not blame her, however, for it was Margaret's most striking *toilette* to date, and Eliza could only be pleased that Caroline seemed to think so too, her eyes lingering avariciously upon Margaret's satin bodice, so beautifully ornamented with white beads and drops *à la militaire*.

"You look *very* fine," Caroline repeated to Margaret, more seriously than she had upon the first instance.

"As do you," Margaret said, cheeks a little pink, while Eliza tried subtly to peek over Caroline's shoulder to where Melville was handing his cloak to a footman.

"Oh, don't you all look well!" Lady Hurley said, as the persons in front of them disappeared into the room. She was wearing a diaphanous yellow gown that made her appear as a voluptuous sunflower. "Dinner will be served presently: my François has outdone himself tonight. There are jellies, fondues and blancmanges enough to feed the five thousand!"

"How wonderful," Melville said as he appeared, not sounding at all enthused. Though he and Mr. Fletcher were both dressed elegantly—Melville in a coat of blue superfine, and a waistcoat of navy velvet subtly adorned with silver embroidery—they appeared distinctly careworn. Eliza tried, unsuccessfully, to catch his eye.

"Ignore him," Caroline said. "He and Mr. Fletcher dined together last night and were drunk as wheelbarrows. He is more moan than man."

"Splendid, but," Mr. Fletcher said, pressing a weak hand to his chest, "not at all the thing."

"You have it, sir," Melville agreed, rubbing his brow. "I think we are to be commended for attending this evening at all."

As the highest-ranking lady and gentleman in attendance, Eliza and Melville were paired together to walk to dinner. For the first time in recent memory, Eliza was not sure what to say to him—and for the first time in memory, Melville did not seem inclined to speak first.

"Have you been keeping well?" she asked.

"I have," Melville said.

"You enjoyed your evening with Mr. Fletcher?"

"Assuredly."

"*Medea* is progressing well?"

"Yes."

She had never known him to talk so little. Perhaps this is how Melville had felt, trying to make conversation with her at their first sittings. She wished she could wind back the past week and scrape off a layer as one could with a painting and resume the easy acquaintance they had used to enjoy. As soon as the first course was served out, Melville turned very properly to speak to Lady Hurley, seated on his right, while Eliza had to make conversation with a recalcitrant Admiral Winkworth. The loud sounds of Melville and Lady Hurley's enjoyment in her ear, as they began a rallying discussion of their favorite poets, did nothing to improve her mood. Under Lady Hurley's influence, Melville's effervescence seemed to have returned; Eliza tried not to feel too bitter, sipping instead at the delicious champagne in front of her.

By the time the second course was being placed—the Soup à la Reine and Chicken à la Tarragon replaced by dishes of baked carp, oysters in batter, a blanquette of fowl and a raised pie, reinforced by a bountiful array of vegetable dishes—and Melville turned reluctantly to speak to her, Eliza was feeling distinctly lightheaded.

"Have *you* read Dante's *Divine Comedy?*" he asked.

It seemed very important, all of a sudden, that Melville think Eliza quite as literary as Lady Hurley.

"Yes," Eliza lied recklessly. Margaret had read it, which came to the same thing.

"And what did you think?"

The unfortunate truth was, of course, that Eliza knew nothing of the volume save for its title and the fact that Margaret thought it very clever.

"I thought it was very clever," she said.

"But the latest translation . . . I myself found it a little confusing, no?" Melville asked. Eliza hoped the question was rhetorical, but by the lengthy pause—and the way he was regarding her patiently—this was not the case.

"I wonder if—if the point *was* to be confused," she proffered sagely.

Melville looked at her.

"You have not read it," he guessed.

"I have not read it," she agreed.

As if despite himself, Melville laughed.

"Why lie?"

"So that you might think *I* was very clever," Eliza admitted, taking another draught of champagne.

"I already thought that," Melville said. "Now I just think you a liar, too."

Eliza looked at Melville sharply. Was he . . . ? Was that a reference to . . . ?

"I did not lie," she said, quietening her voice to a murmur, hoping this was her moment to clear the air.

"You omitted," Melville said, catching on at once.

"Out of necessity," she whispered. "And only a little: we cannot be formally affianced until April. Until then, we are only . . . engaged to be engaged."

"Oh," Melville said.

A pause.

"How whimsically indeterminate."

He sounded so much his normal self for a moment, that Eliza found herself leaning eagerly toward him.

"I am sorry for the deception, nonetheless," she gabbled in a whisper. "I should not otherwise have concealed it to one I consider—one I consider a true friend."

Melville took a thoughtful sip of his glass.

"And I do read," she added defensively—for once again, this seemed important to establish.

Melville did not smile, but his eyes began to crinkle in amusement.

"I have not accused you," Melville said.

"I know *you* are awfully bookish," she retorted, so relieved at the tacit acceptance—for that is what it was, surely?—that she felt almost breathless.

"Awfully," Melville agreed. He paused, then added, in more of his usual manner: "I could hardly write as I do, were I not."

"The classics," Eliza said, as knowingly as she could. "You enjoy reading such books? Homer and . . . the other one."

"The other one most of all," Melville said, smiling. "The scholarly populace would have them seem daunting, but they are just stories—magnificent and sprawling, but stories, nonetheless."

"Before I read your *Persephone*, I did not understand them in the least," Eliza admitted. "My husband bade me read more classics to improve my mind but I could not hold my attention."

She had thought herself too stupid to understand all the unknown words, places and names—but Melville's poetry had a way of re-spinning the tales, elaborating upon the romance, hinting at the salacious that . . . Well, one didn't pause to worry if one was intellectual enough, in the hurry to gorge oneself upon it.

"There is more kissing in my versions, I will allow," Melville said easily.

"It is more than that," Eliza chided him. "It is a skill, to invite people in as you do."

Melville blinked, fiddling with the stem of his glass as if unsure of how to respond—as if, despite all the praise he lavished on her, he was not expectant of receiving any in return.

"I am glad," he said slowly, looking searchingly at her. "I was a boy, when I first read them—a swot even then," he said, as if confessing something. "And I fancy even now I could return to the texts a thousand times over and still find something new to inspire me."

"And is that what you mean to do?" Eliza said. "Write a thousand of such poems?"

"I . . . One day I . . ."

Melville's eyes glanced warily around the table—the first instance Eliza had seen him concerned for eavesdroppers.

"It was my intention," Melville said, quietly. "Once I had sufficient popularity, to write poetry inspired by classics of a different kind."

Eliza tilted her head in question.

"My mother was a great linguist," Melville said, speaking faster now. "Urdu, Persian, Sanskrit . . . She was educated in them all, and she would read to us, each night, from manuscripts she had brought with her from India. The *Shahnameh*, the *Mahabharata* . . . these are some of the longest epics ever to be written, as fascinating as the *Aeneid* and their warriors as great as Achilles or Ajax."

Eliza's eyes flickered over Melville's face, waiting for him to continue. Out of all the conversations they had shared, all the confidences exchanged, she had the sense that this was the most intimate of all of them—here, at a dinner party, with the incongruous swell of conversation all around them—and Eliza would not have interrupted him for the world.

"There are *thousands* of stories within them," he told her, hushed and reverent. "If I could just . . ."

Melville's eyes, bright and animated, dimmed suddenly.

"Find a publisher willing," he finished around a sigh.

His fingers clenched around his glass and Eliza fought the urge to brush his hand with hers.

"You will," Eliza said. "I am sure you will."

If anyone could, it was he.

"Perhaps one day."

They paused as the table was replenished once more, this time with fruits, creams and jellies of all sizes, shapes and colors. Eliza, impatient to resume their conversation, accepted a selection at random and she leaned back toward Melville as soon as she could. It would be proper, of course, to have instead turned back to Admiral Winkworth: correct dinner table behavior, as Eliza had been taught since childhood, was to alternate conversational partners with each course, but nothing could have enticed her to do so tonight.

"You speak so many languages," she said, marveling at how it would be to possess such accomplishments—her adequate talent at embroidery seemed very feeble in comparison.

"Not all of them well," Melville said wryly. "When our parents . . . Well, there were fewer opportunities to keep up with them."

Eliza wished that they were having this conversation in the

privacy of her parlor, so she might have captured the soft melancholy of Melville's expression in that moment.

"Thank goodness for Caroline," Melville said reflectively. "Or else I would have felt most alone."

Eliza's heart clenched. She was so used to thinking the Melvilles' singularity somehow prestigious—she had never stopped to consider it might also be lonely.

"You do not have a sister," Melville said, accepting a footman's refill of his glass with a murmur of thanks.

"I have Margaret," Eliza said. "But no sister by blood. I used to wonder if it might have made my mother . . . easier upon me, were there another to share the attention."

"She was firm?"

Instinctively, Eliza gave a little grimace. Melville laughed.

"I am sorry," Eliza said, strangely apologetic to have broken the mood in such a way. "She is very firm—her opinions so strong, so loud, that it makes mine shrink, just to be around them."

Though Eliza had not spoken untruthfully, she still found herself abruptly guilt-stricken to hear herself speak such words to one outside her family.

"I have made her sound all bad," she said repentantly. "She is not. There were occasions that her always knowing best, her taking charge, gave me so much comfort."

Melville waited, a faint question in his eyes that he did not voice. Eliza looked again to Admiral Winkworth—sucking busily upon his chicken bones—and then to the persons opposite— Lady Caroline, who she would not mind hearing anyway, and Mr. Berwick, staring dreamily into space.

"In the early days of my marriage," Eliza said slowly. "When I . . . When there was no child . . ."

When each month had brought the same gut-wrenching disappointment, and each month her husband had grown colder and more distant, ever more critical . . .

"I did not know what to do," Eliza said. "And . . . she helped me."

Without having to be asked—for Eliza would not know how to ask, how to frame such an awful fear—Mrs. Balfour had begun directing her, in the same no-nonsense way she had once dressed Eliza's hair. Her twice-weekly letters became a lifeline, each one offering a new panacea Eliza might try, divined from unknown sources—a doctor or herbologist or botanist, it had not mattered—and Eliza would find herself picking strawberries at midnight under a waning moon or some such remedy.

"She gave me something to do, when I might otherwise have . . . lost myself," Eliza whispered. Lost herself wandering Harefield's empty halls, ruminating upon her own inadequacy, speculating on what her family and the earl's might be saying about her, behind her back. But even then Mrs. Balfour had protected her. When each Christmas passed with still no child to be seen, Mrs. Balfour had countenanced no discussion of Eliza's failure from the family—the merest mention would bring on Mrs. Balfour's gimlet eye with truly alarming rapidity. When Eliza had been more alone than she had ever known herself before, it had been her mother who had held her to earth, more even than Margaret.

Eliza cleared her throat, blinking rapidly. Melville was watching her calmly, not at all alarmed, as some gentlemen were, in the face of feminine misery, but accepting, regarding her openly. He had a way, on occasion, of considering you with his whole being, all the movement and the chatter and humor pausing entirely, to focus the entirety of that bright mind directly upon you. It felt—now as it had the first time—rather as if one had stepped into warm sunlight.

"I have never told anyone that before," she said. "Not even . . ."

She did not finish the sentence and Melville was tactful enough not to ask.

"I am sorry that I have missed our sittings this week," he said instead.

"That is all right," Eliza said. "The portrait is almost finished, anyhow."

Melville's eyes lit up with curiosity.

"Can I see it?"

"Soon," Eliza promised.

A tinkle of a glass being tapped with a spoon had them turning toward Lady Hurley, who had stood from the table to announce the dancing would begin momentarily. The younger gentlemen and ladies began to chatter excitedly as they stood from the table, to move into the drawing room with Lady Hurley pairing partners. By now, Eliza was so comfortably full that she was almost glad to not be joining the dancing. Almost.

"It appears I am needed," Melville observed, as Lady Hurley beckoned to him imperiously. "If you will excuse me . . . ?"

There was a moment—a brief, wild moment—where Eliza was about to demand he stay, that he ignore the requirements of civility and stay by her side for a little longer. But she mastered herself before the hasty words could trip off her tongue. There were more ladies than gentlemen and Melville would be in demand all evening. It would be selfish to make such a request—tempting, but selfish.

"Of course," she said, and Melville flocked obediently to Lady Hurley's side to be partnered with Miss Gould. Whereas Eliza . . . Eliza sank into a cushioned settee with a dejected sigh, while the string quartet in the corner of the room struck up a lively jig. Watching as Melville and Miss Gould bowed to one another, Eliza did not think she had ever felt the constraints of her widowhood more keenly than this moment.

20

It almost makes one jealous for one's own youth, does it not?" Mrs. Winkworth said, coming to sit down beside Eliza.

Eliza managed to catch the indignant and instinctive squawk before it left her mouth, instead letting out a vague murmur. In the last few weeks, she had managed to avoid Mrs. Winkworth's company to some success and she had almost forgotten the lady's deft way of delivering such stings.

"I used to think the waltz a sad romp," Mrs. Winkworth said, her eyes tracking the figure of her daughter amongst the twirling figures. Miss Winkworth performed the steps gracefully, and Eliza thought she seemed to stand taller with her mother at a safe distance. "But if it is danced at Almack's then I should think it important Winnie gets her practice in!"

Eliza made another vague murmuring sound. The likelihood of Mrs. Winkworth being sent vouchers to Almack's was, she felt, rather low. They might hail from a respectable lineage—Mrs. Winkworth, as she was so fond of reminding them, was the granddaughter of a baroness—but only the very select were invited to enter the hallowed halls of Almack's Assembly Rooms.

"Lady Somerset," Mrs. Winkworth said, her voice suddenly steely, "I must indeed thank you for the kindness you have shown my dear Winnie. She quite thinks of you as an honorary aunt, you know."

If dear Winnie actually thought such a thing, when there

were fewer than ten years between their ages, Eliza would consider her the most egregious shrew of her acquaintance—but as she knew it was unlikely, she reserved such dislike for the true author of the remark.

"And it is only because of the affection you have shown her, that I should feel comfortable to make a request of you that I am afraid you might otherwise think a sad encroachment!" Mrs. Winkworth went on doggedly.

This could go on for hours if Eliza let it.

"What is it that I can do for you, Mrs. Winkworth?" Eliza asked.

"I am sure I do not need to explain to you, Lady Somerset, the importance of a girl's first Season," Mrs. Winkworth said. "I mean to do everything I can to ensure that my daughter makes as successful a debut as possible, but our acquaintance in London is not as large as I would like it. If you would be as kind as to offer me a few letters of introduction . . ."

Eliza raised her eyebrows. Mrs. Winkworth's instincts were correct: Eliza did think her sadly encroaching. If one was traveling to a town or city where one was unknown, one might indeed ask a friend to give one a letter of introduction to a few persons of their acquaintance in the locality, thereby vouching for the good character of the traveler, and smoothing their way for admittance into the town's social circle. But to make such a demand outright, to a person one did not truthfully know very well . . . Eliza would be within her rights to give Mrs. Winkworth a set-down. She looked to the dance floor, and to Miss Winkworth, so timid and innocent. As objectionable as she found her mother, she could not deny she wanted all the best for her.

"I shall have a think," Eliza began, already trying to consider who she might offer. It had been a while since she had been out in society, but she thought the Ashbys might very well have a daughter coming out this year, and the Ledgertons had several sons of marriageable age, all said to be sweet and friendly boys.

"You are related to the Ashfords, are you not?" Mrs. Winkworth interrupted.

Oh. Mrs. Winkworth was aiming very high indeed, then.

"*Very* distantly, through two marriages," Eliza said. "But Mrs. Winkworth, I do not think . . . Families with titles tend to marry within their own set."

It was as tactfully as she could think to phrase it, but Mrs. Winkworth still flushed.

"It is not always the case," she insisted. "Why, think of Lady Radcliffe!"

"There are exceptions, certainly," Eliza admitted. "But—"

"And Winnie will have a handsome dowry," Mrs. Winkworth said. "I do not like to boast of it—*I* am not so vulgar—but my husband made an ample sum in Calcutta and Winnie will have it all."

Eliza did not know quite what to say.

"You are related to the Ardens, as well?" Mrs. Winkworth had abandoned all pretense at subtlety now.

"My late husband's cousins," Eliza said slowly. "But you cannot be thinking of Lord Arden, for Miss Winkworth?"

Arden had to be almost thirty years the girl's senior, and while he was well known to have a taste for young ladies in their first bloom, Mrs. Winkworth would surely not be willing to sacrifice her daughter to such a gentleman? But Mrs. Winkworth's eyes were hungry.

"If your ladyship could offer a letter of introduction to the Ardens," Mrs. Winkworth said. "I should be most glad . . ."

Eliza stared. She knew better than anyone the machinations of the marriage mart, but for Mrs. Winkworth's calculations to be so blatant, so openly grasping! Perhaps it was the rich supper she had just ingested, but Eliza felt nauseous. She turned to gaze back toward Miss Winkworth, who was now laughing as she spun in a circle with Mr. Berwick. Her youthful cheer would not have been out of place in the schoolroom.

"Mrs. Winkworth . . ." Eliza said, knowing she would not have drunk quite so much champagne had she known she was to enter into quite such a delicate subject, but unable to hold her tongue a moment longer. "I understand the desire to see your daughter marry well, very much so, but if you will not allow Miss Winkworth the dignity of her own choice, I implore you to think of a gentleman better suited to her than Arden."

Mrs. Winkworth's face, as Eliza spoke, grew pinker and pinker with indignation.

"Lady Somerset!" she gasped. "I only have my daughter's best interests at heart—that you should think to imply otherwise . . ."

"I am not trying to offend," Eliza said hastily. "Just to speak truthfully, as one who knows what it is to be so bartered . . ."

"Bartered?" Mrs. Winkworth repeated. "*Bartered?*"

Perhaps "bartered" had been a poor choice of word.

"All I mean to say is," Eliza said, "surely Miss Winkworth's happiness is worth more than a title?"

Mrs. Winkworth dragged in a deep breath through her nostrils.

"Lady Somerset," she said with a decided sharpness, "I had hoped, in coming to you with such a request, to be treated with discretion and understanding. Much like that with which *I* have been treating *you* these past weeks."

"I do not understand your meaning . . ." Eliza said slowly.

"I am aware that your wealth came with certain requirements, my lady," Mrs. Winkworth said, vindictive triumph now in her eyes. "Requirements that should not, I believe, look kindly upon Melville haunting Camden Place with you still in your blacks—and yet I have given you the benefit of the doubt *thus* far."

Eliza's heart quickened.

"Lady Selwyn has looser lips than I had thought," she said, with more calm than she would have believed herself capable. "Do you mean to threaten me, Mrs. Winkworth?"

Mrs. Winkworth's cheeks were ruddy, but she surveyed her with a gimlet eye.

"Will you offer the letter of introduction, my lady?" she said meaningfully.

It might have worked on Eliza, not too long ago. It would not now.

"To the Ardens, I will not," Eliza said, gently. She stood. "Enjoy your time in London, madam. I wish you the very best."

She wished she could have done more for Miss Winkworth. But at least she had tried.

Eliza walked around the edges of the room—speaking idly to Mr. Berwick for a moment, who she noticed was wearing a waistcoat strikingly similar to Melville's—before heading toward the grand French windows that led onto the terrace. They had been opened to allow a breeze to waft into the room, for despite the coolness of the spring evening, with such vigorous dancing the room had become hot and close.

As Eliza drew near, she came across the Melvilles tucked into the window embrasure, in the midst of a rather heated discussion.

"I simply do not understand what can have so suddenly changed," Caroline was hissing to her brother. "All this talk of prudence, and economy, again—you change your mind faster than a whirligig."

Eliza checked herself, not wanting to eavesdrop, and wondered briefly if she ought to walk in the opposite direction until Caroline stormed past Eliza in the direction of the card room.

Eliza approached Melville slowly. He looked up, face drawn,

and Eliza was overcome with an urge to put a smile back on his face.

"Have you spoken with Mr. Berwick, this evening?" she asked, as lightly as if she had not overheard a moment of their conversation.

"I have not," Melville took a sip from his glass with hands that were a little unsteady.

"I admire his waistcoat very much," Eliza said. She tilted her head toward the gentleman in question and as Melville's eyes followed, she had the satisfaction of seeing his eyebrows fly upward, his strained expression replaced with incredulity.

"Are he and my valet in *cahoots*?" he demanded.

Eliza laughed, but the reprieve was short-lived: Melville's face had already relapsed into unease.

"Did you overhear us?" he asked, regarding his glass again. Ah.

"'Prudence and economy' does not sound like you," Eliza said, rather than lie. She meant the words as a tease, but Melville did not seem in the mood for teasing.

"Perhaps I have changed," he said shortly. "People *can* change, you know."

"They can," Eliza said. "But why should you need to?"

If Melville—brilliant, audacious Melville—were suddenly to doubt himself, what hope was there for the rest of them?

"I am without a patron," Melville explained abruptly.

He looked at Eliza, and then back down to his glass, and then up to her again.

"Lord Paulet is a prideful man," he said. "And I thought I had found another . . . but I was mistaken."

"Oh," Eliza said.

So it *was* true. Eliza had known it was, of course, but she could not help but feel discomforted to have such confirmation. Which was foolish. For what did it matter to her that Melville had been having an affair with Lady Paulet?

"Is that so disastrous?" Eliza asked.

"Without a patron," Melville said, "I cannot publish this year. And if I cannot publish this year, I cannot raise the funds that Alderley needs this winter—nor afford such luxuries as phaetons and Paris."

"Caroline said she would need to retreat abroad if she finishes her novel this summer," Eliza recollected. "To shield her from whatever unpleasantness will follow its release."

"Abroad, yes," Melville said, rubbing his jaw. "But we would do better somewhere less expensive."

We?

"You would go with her?" Eliza asked. It ought not be a surprise, for the siblings came as an obvious pair, but Eliza found herself dismayed nonetheless.

Melville scrubbed a hand through his hair.

"The gossip about me is rising, not falling," he said. "I do not think England will be very pleasant if I am to be blacklisted as well as cleaned out."

"It is not fair," Eliza muttered. Why, when one thought of all the disgraces Byron had perpetuated before having to leave the country—the numerous love affairs, sideslips and public excesses all before the last straw of his divorce—what did Melville's one lapse signify in comparison?

"Best not to pull at that thread," Melville said. "For it is not like to change."

"Perhaps I could be your patron," Eliza offered impulsively. "I am rich, you know."

"So I hear," Melville said, with a rather rueful smile. "And while it is very kind, I shall have to decline."

"Why?" Eliza said. "I may not know a great deal about it, but I could certainly find out."

"I have no doubt you could perform the role excellently," Melville agreed. "But I cannot accept your money. My pride—such as it is—prevents it."

"How bothersome," Eliza said, as lightly as she was able.

"Isn't it just?"

"Well," Eliza said, thinking, "if my portrait is accepted into the exhibition, it should be beneficial for publicity, should it not? And perhaps then you may find it easier to secure a new patron!"

"Perhaps . . ." Melville did not seem cheered by this prospect. "But have you fully considered what such publicity might mean for you, my lady? We can, of course, submit it anonymously, but there shall be a great deal of interest in the identity of the portraitist."

"I have," Eliza said quietly. "It was my idea. I have wanted this since I knew what it was."

Melville nodded. They stood in silence for a moment, until the dancers ceased spinning, and everyone began to applaud the musicians.

"I really am so tired of looking on . . ." Eliza said, watching them.

Melville took in a breath then, in a trice, drained his glass and set it down upon the mantelpiece with a decisive clink.

"Well, then," he said, holding his hand out expectantly. "Let us change that."

"Don't be foolish," Eliza said, batting his hand away with her fan and glancing around to check no one had seen.

"Why not?"

"I am in mourning."

"I don't think you've ever been in mourning."

"In mourning clothes, then."

He proffered his hand again. Behind him, other couples were taking the floor, readying themselves for the next set. It was to be a waltz.

"My lord, do not. It is so against convention, it might as well be against the law," she said, turning slightly away so as to affect that she hadn't seen it.

"And what is the purpose of convention, if not to be flouted?" he declared. "Laws, if not to be broken?"

Eliza laughed. Melville raised his hand higher. There was a challenge in his dark eyes, provocative and tempting, and yet a confidence too—suggesting that he did not doubt for a moment that she would be brave enough to meet it. And as if in a dream, Eliza placed her hand in his. Unlike the last time they had touched in such a way, their hands were both gloved, but Eliza could still feel the warmth—and strength—of his grip through the satin. With a quick glance about the room to make sure they were unobserved, Melville tugged her a step backward, through the doors and out onto the terrace.

"What are you . . ." Eliza started.

The terrace was not lit—in such changeable spring weather, Lady Hurley had not thought anybody would be brave enough to head outdoors—but here was light enough streaming from the windows that they could see one another, while they would remain hidden in shadow to the persons inside.

The musicians inside began to play their first, opening notes. They could hear it out here quite as clearly as if they were still in the room. Melville touched a finger to his lips, then bowed. And Eliza, understanding at last his intention, swept her skirts out in a curtsey as a smile spread across her face. As the gentlemen inside began to move, so too did he, closing the space in one gliding step until there was barely a hair's breadth between them. This close, Eliza could see he had tiny flecks of gold within the dark brown of his irises. She had never noticed that before.

The violins began to play in earnest and then he was sliding one arm around her waist, pulling her in, reaching for her right hand with his left, and though they had not even begun moving yet, Eliza was breathless. Together they began to spin. Melville was a good dancer. Of course he was—she ought to have known he would be. The kind of dancer, in fact, who seemed not even to mind his steps at all, who seemed to do it so naturally it was as if this was how he moved always and it just happened that tonight there was music. Eliza could hardly see her feet in the darkness; all she could do was follow the pressure of his hand upon her back, certain that he would not lead her astray, and she laughed, breathless and exultant, felt his answering laugh upon her neck. They rotated quicker and quicker, dizzying themselves from the constant rotation, and Eliza had never felt so wonderfully irresponsible, so impetuous and light.

She could not have said exactly when they both stopped laughing. Could not have said at what moment her breathlessness ceased to be caused by quick steps and started to be caused by . . . something else. But it must have been about the same moment Melville began to hold her tighter, pull her even closer—the same moment that he rearranged their hands so that, instead of the traditional clasp, palm to palm, their fingers were intertwined—and without quite knowing why, their giddy and reckless dance felt abruptly edged with a kind of desperation.

They did not stop moving until the very last violin strings had faded from the air, and even then they did not draw back from one another, remaining where they stood, entangled in one another, gazes locked, utterly still. Eliza was not sure of the expression on Melville's face. Having spent so long studying his countenance, she thought she had seen every shade of emotion upon it—but she had never seen him look as he did now.

Slowly, silently, by increments, they drew back from one another. Melville offered Eliza one final, very deep bow. In the silence the music had left, their breathing was the only sound upon the air, heavy with more than simple exertion.

"My lady—"

And she did not know what he was going to say but . . .

"We ought," Eliza said, clearing her throat when her words came out a little hoarsely, "we ought to go inside."

Melville nodded without speaking. They crept back into the drawing room, Eliza first, then Melville after a few moments, just in case anyone was looking in that direction. But they were not. No one had seen. No one suspected. The wildest moment of Eliza's life, and only she and he knew it had happened.

21

Eliza finished the portrait the next day. The next morning, truly, for no sooner had she woken from a disjointed sleep than she was jerking upright—falling into her dressing gown and down the stairs as if she were late for an appointment. Opening the parlor's door, Eliza crossed the floor and opened the bureau to rummage through the oils within. Seizing the yellow and the brown and the white, she squeezed out drops of each onto a clean stretch of her palette.

She did not put on her apron, nor fold back her sleeves, before setting to work, uncaring of any risk to her grey robe and nightgown. Finally, when she had reached exactly the right shade, she selected her tiniest brush of finest sable and approached the portrait. It was the work of a moment, the final touch she had not even known was missing: the tiniest fleck of gold within each eye.

There!

Eliza took exactly six steps backward, squeezing her eyes shut for a moment, so that she might look upon it with fresh eyes, as an audience would. The likeness, she flattered herself, was clear—and better than she could have hoped. It was a head and shoulder view. One hand rested lightly upon the chest, as if Melville were about to play with his collar—which he often did when he was thinking—and even in the stillness of the painting, there was somehow a sense of motion: his face set at a tilt, while the eyes remained directly regarding the viewer, a playful challenge within them. Exactly how he had looked at her last night as he asked her to dance.

It conveyed all she had wanted to: Melville's humor and slyness, but also his warmth and countenance. One hand upon a notebook—cuffs bedecked with ink—suggested he might be about to compose you a poem, the curl to his lips that he was about to say something outrageous. Eliza felt her own mouth twitch in response, as unable to resist this Melville's teasing as she was the real one.

Eliza took a step closer. Yes, now that she had seen Melville at . . . at such close quarters, she could be quite certain the likeness was *very* good. With the eyes finally right, the whole portrait seemed to come alive, and while it could never be as compelling as he was in real life, as he had been, hand in hers upon that terrace, his draw so palpable that she wondered it had not pulled more people out onto the terrace with them, it gave an impression of it.

She had been able to convey, too, as she did when painting Margaret, her affection for the subject. It was there, obvious to her even if to no one else, as clear as if it were another color on the canvas, the strength of the regard she felt for him. In a portrait that seemed all about touch—of fingers, of lips, of eyes, the paintbrush too seemed almost to be caressing its subject with warmth, with affection, with . . .

And all at once, as if it had always been there, it became very clear to Eliza that she was in love with him.

The revelation came slowly and yet instantaneously. As when one searches for a word that stands out of reach of the mind for days—but then, when hearing it, one knows immediately that it is the correct one. She was in love with Melville. And it seemed quite possible that she had been for a long time. She had felt drawn to him from the beginning, of course—but then, so very many people were, and attraction was not love, however thrilling. It must have crept up on her, stealthy and unobserved, born out of their long conversations, his regard and curiosity for her thoughts, opinions, skills, the laughter they had shared . . .

Eliza staggered back from the portrait and sank down onto the sofa. It was impossible! It was surely impossible. She was in love with Somerset. She was engaged to Somerset. She could *not* be in love with Melville, too. But when she looked at the portrait, the truth stared her in the face, as plain as day.

"Margaret!" Eliza called, her voice shrill. "Margaret, can I borrow you for a moment?"

"Is something wrong?" Margaret called back, though she appeared obediently in the parlor a few moments later, hastily dressed and red hair falling about her shoulders.

"Oh, Eliza!" she said. "It's wonderful! The likeness is superb."

Eliza searched her face closely, there seemed to be no evidence that she was undergoing any of the same revelations as Eliza.

"You like it?" she said. "It seems . . . normal to you?"

"Normal?" Margaret said quizzically. "It resembles him, if that is what you are meaning, most strongly. You ought to be proud of it."

Eliza breathed out a sigh. There was no need, then, to make a confession.

"I think I'm in love with Melville!" Eliza blurted out, her voice so loud it made Margaret jump backward.

"Goodness, Eliza!" she complained.

"Did you hear what I said?"

"Yes, for it was right in my ear," she said, rubbing at it.

"You do not seem shocked!" Eliza said, accusatory.

"Well, I am not," Margaret said.

"Excuse me?"

"Come, Eliza," Margaret said, as if Eliza were a small child refusing to behave. "The way you speak to one another. The way you *flirt*. You must have suspected something before now."

"I did not," Eliza said faintly. "I swear I did not. I have been so focused upon Somerset, I—I have always loved Somerset . . . I never considered this to be even the slightest possibility."

Eliza paced the length of the room, sat down upon the settee, stood back up again, looked at the portrait, closed her eyes and pressed her hands to her face. What had she *done*? In the light of such a revelation, her behavior over the past few weeks appeared very suspect—the flirtation, the teasing, the *dancing*! She had betrayed Somerset's trust in every way she could.

"What are you going to do?" Margaret asked.

"Nothing," Eliza said at once.

"You are not going to tell him?"

"Tell him? *Tell* him? Tell *him*?"

"I am sensing the answer is no," Margaret said.

"Margaret, you do not seem to understand the gravity of the situation," Eliza said. "I am as good as engaged to Somerset. I love Somerset. I love *Oliver*."

She felt a surge of powerful guilt that she had even considered she might love another—when she had promised herself to Oliver, she had meant it with her entire being. That had to count for something.

"*Do* you love him?" Margaret said, eyes narrowing.

Eliza took a deep breath. She thought of Somerset. She thought of his letters, the way they made her feel. How it had felt to see him again, in January. How it had felt to touch him, to kiss him, in the carriage on that night of the concert. As if something lost had been returned to her, long after she had renounced all hope of its restoration.

"Yes," Eliza said.

"More than Melville?" Margaret said.

"I . . ." Eliza started. "I do not know."

For how could one compare the two? One she had carried

with her, her whole life it had seemed. It was requited, and close now to being hers for perpetuity. The other she had only just stumbled across. And Melville? Every woman in England seemed to have a tendresse for the man. He could have his pick of *anyone*. And while he might—*might*—be fond of Eliza, yes, and flirt with her, that too, and sometimes look at her as though he was delighted by the mere sight of her . . .

"It does not matter," Eliza said. "I am promised to Somerset. He is the man I will marry."

"You are not engaged yet," Margaret pointed out.

"We are as good as," Eliza said fiercely. "And I will not—I cannot—jilt him for a second time, Margaret. I cannot."

The sound of hooves upon the cobbles outside had her looking toward the window.

"Caroline!" Eliza said. "I had forgotten."

She must have slept late this morning. She had not even had breakfast.

She looked down at herself as if expecting to find herself miraculously gowned in a habit. She was not.

"You could cancel," Margaret suggested.

"No, no! I—I do not want to," Eliza said.

She wanted everything to be normal, for all that had just occurred to be placed back from whence it came.

"Then I shall delay her," Margaret said easily. "While you change."

And although Caroline was notoriously impatient at such delays, when Eliza finally emerged from the house, wearing her black habit, gloves and velvet beaver hat, she did not seem irritated.

"She hath risen!" Caroline called, leaning up from where she had been bent toward Margaret.

"My apologies," Eliza said, as Margaret stepped back from the carriage and Caroline's groom threw Eliza up into the seat. "What are we practicing today?"

"Junctions!" Caroline said merrily, and she set the horses off.

For all of Eliza's abstraction, that day made for a good lesson, one of the few where Eliza felt as if she were properly driving with a measure of competency, rather than those where she felt she might cry from frustration.

"Very good," Caroline said, after a few minutes of watching. "I am persuaded that soon you might be able to have a phaeton of your own."

"Of my own?" Eliza said, startled by the thought. "I'm sure I am not nearly dashing enough for that."

"Well, you cannot always be borrowing mine!" Caroline retorted. "I am not nearly kind enough for *that*."

Eliza laughed. "I have seen ample proof of your kindness. Do you really think I am ready?"

"Indeed I do," Caroline said promptly. "You may not yet be driving to an inch, but you are not far off. Perhaps not a high perch, but I think you might manage something a little staider—though in a very fine color."

"Perhaps a violet, or a pink? As I am a very grand lady," Eliza suggested.

"Oh, why choose? Stripes, I say!"

Eliza laughed. The decision to come out today had been a good one. Out here, in the hills, she did not need to think of Somerset, or of Melville. There was too much else to concentrate on.

"But perhaps you may not want to make such a purchase," Caroline said. "Would you get enough use from it, at Harefield?"

Eliza's smile abruptly faded from her face.

"Margaret has not broken any confidences," Caroline said quickly and unnecessarily, for Eliza knew that Margaret guarded her secrets as closely as a dragon hoarding gold, just as Eliza did in return. "But the way she has begun speaking indicates that she believes your time in Bath to be soon at an end. And it is not difficult to divine why."

Eliza, navigating a corner, did not answer. For what could she say?

"Am I to wish you happy?" Caroline pressed.

"Such wishes would be . . . a trifle premature," Eliza said at last.

This Caroline appeared to accept. There was a silence for a moment, then, "At least you will not have to change your name."

Eliza could not help but laugh.

"Have you ever been tempted, my lady?" Eliza asked, once she had mastered herself. "By marriage, I mean."

"Tempted? Yes," Caroline said with a sly smile. "By marriage? No."

"Is it that you never met a gentleman you felt affection for?" Eliza asked, curious as ever for more details of the lady's life.

"After a lifetime of my name already coming second to my brother's," Caroline said, "I am in no hurry to relegate mine into third place."

At Eliza's inquisitive look, she added: "First Melville's sister, then Lord Whosit's wife—for if I am marrying, I assume him to be a marquis at least—and Caroline, third."

"I did not know that bothered you," Eliza said. "You and Melville seem to rub along so nicely together."

"Oh, it is an old wound—watch their mouths now!" Caroline said.

There was a little interval in the discussion as Caroline talked Eliza through looping the reins and then they were on their way again.

"I am the elder, you know," Caroline said abruptly. "People forget, but I am the elder. The first to begin writing. But in every other way, I have come second. He was the first to be published. The more successful. He inherited the title. And my name will always appear . . . second. Forever the postscript."

Eliza did not speak, for what could she say? She could not say it was untrue, for it was a fact; she could not say it might not be that way always, for it would.

"Marriage cannot offer me any advantage I do not already possess," Caroline said after a pause. "I already enjoy independence, rank and freedom. What motive would I have to marry?"

"You do not consider love to be a motive?" Eliza asked.

Caroline looked at her a little askance.

"I would have thought you knew a great deal better than most that marriage rarely has anything to do with love," she said.

"I do," Eliza acknowledged, "but knowing it has not prevented me from yearning for it, still—nor so many from venerating the idea."

"But why is romantic love to be so venerated?" Caroline demanded. "It is the greatest fraudulence of which I can think: one will do anything, forgive anything in service of love. One's lover can be cowardly, selfish, thoughtless, choose you last, always . . . and yet, in adoration of them, one will do almost anything, no matter how unhappy it makes one, no matter how unlikely they are ever to offer you the same, in return."

Caroline had lost, in the speech, the languor that usually characterized her. Her voice was vehement, bitter.

"You speak as someone who knows," Eliza said.

Caroline dismissed this with a flap of her hand—the languor returning.

"I endeavor to speak with confidence on all matters, that is all," she said. "Though it sounded good, did it not?"

It had certainly made Eliza wonder after the gentleman who had broken Caroline's heart so thoroughly.

22

That night, Eliza could not sleep. She had returned from her drive with Caroline, convinced that the whole business with Melville's portrait was a hallucination, only to find, when she had gone upstairs to regard it once more, that her love was still there, quite as clear as day and just as damning as it had been an hour before. It was so very blatant, even indecent, and Eliza could not even think of it now without a rush of heat flying to her face.

Her body was tired—so tired—but her mind had never been livelier, bounding from Melville to Somerset and back again with such rapidity that Eliza almost felt nauseous. In the end, when counting sheep and reading by candlelight and sketching in her portfolio had none of them worked, she resorted to a piece of comfort she had not sought since she was a child. She got up in her nightgown, walked across the hallway to Margaret's bedchamber, knocking softly upon the door, and peeked inside.

"Eliza?" Margaret's sleepy voice whispered.

"I can't sleep," Eliza said.

Margaret grunted. Eliza took this as invitation and lifted the covers to climb in next to her cousin. The bed was big enough that they need not even touch, but Eliza reached out and twined her fingers through Margaret's anyway, just as they had when they were children.

"If you snore, I shall make you leave," Margaret threatened

sleepily, though with a squeeze to Eliza's hand. "I do not care how upset you are."

Eliza gave a soft laugh. There was silence in the room, for a long while. For so long, in fact, that Eliza believed Margaret had fallen asleep, and when she spoke, it was almost more to ask her words of the night than it was to ask Margaret.

"Is it truly possible," she whispered, "to love two persons equally, at the same time?"

There was a silence.

"I do not know," Margaret said softly. "I have only ever loved one."

It took a moment for Eliza to realize the full implications of such a statement.

"I thought . . ." she said slowly, "that you had never had a particular *tendre* for anyone."

"I hadn't," Margaret said. "Before we came here."

A horrible possibility dawned upon Eliza.

"Not Melville?" she said urgently.

"No, you goose," Margaret said, not in her usual impatient way, but wobblier. Almost afraid. "Caroline."

It took Eliza a little while to understand. For a moment she thought she might indeed have misheard.

"Caroline . . ." she repeated slowly.

Margaret nodded her head against the pillow. The hand within Eliza's trembled slightly.

"Oh. *Oh.*"

Eliza's mind began to connect a thousand pieces of information. A hundred different moments she had noticed but never divined their true meaning.

"And you . . . ? It is of a romantic nature, this love?" she checked.

"It is as you said, Eliza," Margaret whispered. "When I see her, I feel as if I have been struck by lightning."

"And does she feel for you, the same way?"

"I do not know," Margaret said. "There are moments, so many moments, when I am so sure, so *certain* that she does, when I feel as if we understand one another perfectly, but . . ."

"But?"

"But she does not act," Margaret said miserably.

"Perhaps she is waiting for you to act," Eliza suggested.

Margaret gave a little snort of disbelief.

"When she is so much more worldly than I?" she said. "Why ought I risk myself first?"

"She is worldly, yes," Eliza said slowly, "and used to far more independence than we have been, certainly, but she does traverse the world differently to us, Margaret. They both do."

Eliza thought back to what Caroline had told her, so many weeks ago now, of the great variance of standards between her and Caroline Lamb—the same flagrant variance that existed between Melville and his closest contemporaries.

"Society judges them far more harshly," Eliza said. "Perhaps the risk feels even greater to her."

"I do not know," Margaret whispered. "And I am too afraid to ask."

Eliza could understand this. No one wanted to have to *ask* if their feelings were reciprocated—and under such circumstances as these, the risks stood far higher than mere embarrassment. But now that Eliza was considering each and every one of Margaret and Caroline's interactions with new eyes, she could only wonder that she had not noticed their thrumming tension before.

"She flirts with you," Eliza decided. "Most assuredly she does flirt. Perhaps there is a way we could find out—I could—"

But Margaret was shaking her head.

"Even if we could, for what purpose?" she whispered. "Oh Eliza, I have considered it. But we could never be together, not properly."

"Could you not?" Eliza asked. "Consider the Ladies of Llangollen."

"Believe me, I have considered the Ladies of Llangollen," Margaret said.

"The gossip suggests," Eliza persisted, "that their relationship is romantic in nature, but so long as they give society the excuse of friendship, meet proprieties on the surface, no one does a thing to stop it."

"Except from gossip," Margaret said. "And they stare and speculate and laugh—and the ladies may well be happy, but are they invited to dinner parties? Do their families still speak to them? Are they accepted by society?"

Eliza did not reply, for what reassurance could she give? There was a reason, she imagined, that the Ladies of Llangollen chose to live in such seclusion, and their romance was only rumored—and while the consequence of such a relationship being publicly confirmed was not fatal, as it was for men, social exile was still no trifling matter.

"Besides," Margaret said, "I have no independent means, and in a few more weeks, I shall have no home other than my sister's—and Caroline and I will not come across one another again."

It was unlike Margaret to sound so defeated, and Eliza's chest ached to hear it. Surely there was a solution, a way forward, something, that would give Margaret the future she deserved.

"I do not think you ought to give up entirely," Eliza whispered. "If it were kept entirely, strictly secret, perhaps . . ."

"I am tired, Eliza," Margaret said and Eliza did not think she meant just tonight.

Eliza subsided for a moment, closing her eyes, but Margaret's revelation had made her only more awake.

"Was it her purple dress that made you fall in love with her?" Eliza whispered.

Margaret snorted.

"I am offended you think me so shallow."

"I have nothing else to go on!" Eliza said. She turned quickly onto her side to try and see Margaret's expression better. "Start from the beginning," she instructed. "And do not leave anything out."

That night, they stayed up into the early hours of the morning, spilling all their thoughts into the darkness between them, small and large and myriad—confidences so grand that not another soul could be trusted with them, trivialities so small that not another soul would be interested in them. And if no conclusions were reached, no solutions divined, then at least by the time they closed their eyes, unable to fight sleep any longer, it was safe in the knowledge that whatever tomorrow brought, they would face it together.

"You did say you would never again marry for duty," Margaret said, her voice as thick as soup. "If that is what you are doing with Somerset . . ."

"I do love Somerset," Eliza said. "Whatever I feel for Melville . . . it is nerves, no more. A passing fancy."

"If you say so," Margaret said, dubious.

"It is a passing fancy," Eliza said around the shape of a yawn. "I promise."

23

I t was not a passing fancy. Eliza might have been able to convince herself, had she been able to avoid Melville for anything more than a single day, but as if to make up for his recent string of absences, Melville appeared at Camden Place the very next morning with Caroline. They were both full of vim, declaring their intention of escorting Eliza and Margaret upon a visit to the coach houses of Bath, in order that Eliza might purchase her own phaeton. Had Eliza been able to prepare herself for the visit, perhaps it might have been easier to act normally in Melville's presence, but as it was, she could not even look at him without blushing. Indeed, even in the space of their short visit, Eliza flushed so often and with such severity that Melville inquired as to whether she had perhaps caught a little sunstroke.

"It is March!" she responded, thrown.

"So it is," Melville agreed. "But then, *I* am not the one who has it."

Instead, Eliza authorized Margaret to act upon her behalf; she was a finer judge of horseflesh than Eliza, anyway, and it would save Eliza from expiring from an excess of blushing.

You are engaged to Somerset, Eliza reminded herself, *you are engaged to Somerset*.

She did not tell Melville that the portrait was finished—that it only had now to dry—but one look at Margaret's guilty face, when she returned from the livery, told Eliza that she had let it slip. The next afternoon, therefore, she prepared herself for Melville's call with grim determination. His presence would not undo her.

"Good morning!" she said, when he entered the parlor, trying to make her voice bright and sunny. "A lovely day we are having!"

He looked from her to the window, where rain was splattering against the panes.

"Oh splendid," he agreed. "Where is it?"

He was bouncing a little on the balls of his feet with excitement. Eliza tried and failed to not find this endearing.

"Over there," she said, gesturing toward the easel, which she had shrouded in a white cloth.

"Is it dead?" he asked, eyebrows flying comically up. "Or just sleeping?"

"It is just to hide it from view," she explained.

"And here I thought the point was for it to be looked at."

"It is," Eliza said. "Of course. So I shall show it to you—show it to you . . . Now . . ."

She paused a moment longer, rallied, and then lifted the fabric off.

Eliza turned immediately to watch his face as he took it in—she wanted to see his reaction before he had time to modulate it—but she had not been fast enough, for even in that shortest of moments, he had wiped his face clean of expression, as he only did when he was trying to hide his thoughts. It was the subtlest of shifts, one Eliza would not have noticed had she not spent the better part of a month studying his face in minute detail. What was he trying to hide?

"Melville?" she said uncertainly. "Do you not like it?"

He started a little.

"It is perfect!" he said quickly. "More than . . . more than I could have hoped."

He looked at her, then back to the painting, and then back

to her again. Eliza felt her palms begin to sweat. Why was he behaving so unusually? Was it possible . . . ? Could it be that Melville had been able to divine from it what Eliza had?

"Of course, with such a handsome subject, how could it not be?" Melville said. All at once, the puzzling atmosphere in the room broke.

"Now we must hope it sets quickly," she said, "for the sending-in day is fast approaching."

Eliza could not prevent a faint note of anxiety from entering her voice. She had made no substantial additions for over a se'nnight, and done everything—from carefully selecting the mixes to diligently ensuring the parlor's constant warmth—to assist the drying process, but even so, to transport a painting so far, so soon after completion, was a risk indeed.

"I shall have it collected next week," Melville said. "And direct my man to treat it with the utmost delicacy."

They had agreed Melville would see the portrait framed and submitted—on behalf of his anonymous portraitist—so as to protect Eliza's identity. Any news, of acceptance or rejection, would go to him.

"I cannot quite believe it is finished," Eliza said quietly, the profundity of the moment suddenly dawning upon her. In the horror of her realization, she had quite forgotten to take in the rest. "Thank you, for asking me."

She looked up at Melville.

"I thought you quite mad, when you did," she confessed. "But I am so glad I said yes."

"I am very glad, too," he said simply.

He held out his hand. Eliza hesitated, wondering wildly if he meant to dance with her again, and then placed hers in his. Melville brought her hand up to his face and pressed a kiss to her knuckles, holding Eliza's eyes all the while and there was a moment, one shining, brief moment, where Eliza almost forgot why she could not love him.

And then she remembered. She pulled her hand back.

"I shall have to wish you good day, my lord," she said, voice trembling a little.

It could not be. It simply could not.

Melville gave a quick—almost flustered—nod of his head, and left.

Eliza,

The shortest of notes—I can only apologize for such brevity—I have arrived in London, where the Season is in full swing and preparations are underway for Annie's ball. You can imagine, I am sure, the furor Augusta is creating—and it demands far more of my time than I had predicted.

Just a word on ditches—Mr. Penney wrote to me regarding the possibility of flooding in Chepstow, and I have authorized our trench to continue across the border onto your territory. As the lands are so soon to be rejoined, I am sure you will not mind such an overstep. Swift action on such occasions is, after all, essential.

I shall remain here seven days more and then I will return to you. I am counting down the hours!

Yours,
Somerset

Mr. Penney,

From your recent correspondence directly with Somerset,
I can only assume you must have mislain my
correspondence address. Please find it above. I trust
any questions regarding my lands will be applied to only
myself in future.

Yours sincerely,
Lady Somerset

24

The second of April marked a year and a day since the old earl's death. The date was a more bittersweet affair than Eliza would have predicted, months before. Any day now, they expected Margaret to be sent for, infusing each arrival of the post with a sense of jeopardy, and in a week, regardless, Somerset would return to carry Eliza off. With each passing day, Eliza felt more disturbed. She wished Somerset's letters might still have the tenor of that very first note, for to receive billets ever shorter in length, and more irritating in their high-handedness—did he truly think she would not mind such an interference?—was causing her apprehension at his return to build even higher.

At least, however, Eliza was at last able to shed her blacks and the most severe restrictions upon her. Madame Prevette had outdone herself with Eliza's new wardrobe—her skill in rendering even the sober colors of grey and lavender into the most dashing gowns imaginable was superb. Each day, Eliza sighed with delight to choose her dresses: there was the slate-grey silk, with its demi-train and the little lace ruff around her throat, the dove-grey crêpe, adorned with black ribbons to compensate for the lighter color, a clinging robe of lavender silk for evening wear, and a stone-colored riding habit, trimmed around the body with swansdown.

After the monotony of wearing black every day for the past year, even this muted palette felt a veritable explosion of color to Eliza, and after months of circulating solely through the same three or four locations in Bath, Eliza was finally to be invested with a little variety. Lady Hurley had already left for London and was sorely missed by them all—the Winkworths, too, had gone, though missed they were not—but Bath was still busy enough for Eliza's liking and by the fifth day of April, she had already attended a card party, a picnic expedition and a trip to the theater. But on the sixth of April, something of even greater excitement occurred: Eliza's phaeton arrived. It was not violet or pink, as she and Caroline had joked, but a gleaming black with red lining upon the body frame. Eliza was so proud of it she thought she might burst.

"Look at her!" she declared to Caroline, who had walked around to view it.

"I am glad you approve," Caroline said, smiling.

"We ought to name her," Margaret said.

"As one does a boat?" Caroline laughed.

"Such a grand lady deserves a name," Eliza agreed.

"Oh, she is a lady now, is she?" Melville asked. "What admirable social ascension."

"She is at the very least a duchess," Eliza declared.

"We must take her on a proper outing," Caroline said.

"Can it be Wells?" Margaret suggested eagerly. "I have yet to see the cathedral's mechanical feature, and I wondered . . ."

Melville wrinkled his nose.

"The cathedral it is," Caroline said promptly, and Eliza looked down to hide a smile.

"I shall drive my phaeton, and Lady Somerset may follow with hers. Today!"

They set out within the hour, and as Eliza wound her way through Bath's streets in pursuit of Caroline, she felt herself to be very dashing, indeed. Caroline had instructed Melville to accompany Eliza, in case they ran into any difficulty upon the road—Melville, of course, was quite as prodigious a whip as his sister—and Eliza resigned herself to a day of blushing. But as the carriage ran like a dream and Melville made all the appropriate sounds of admiration, lounging back in the seat, she could not bring herself to regret the arrangement.

Eliza swept onto Bennett Street and then bore a sharp right onto the Circus, where she had to check her horses in order to make her way carefully through this crowded thoroughfare. As they passed along, they were hailed by Mr. Berwick, who gaped, quite agog, at Eliza.

"*What,*" Melville said in great consternation, "is that man wearing?"

And Eliza had to spare a glance, as well as keep a weather eye upon the hackney cab drawing up on the other side of the road, to see that Mr. Berwick was wearing the exact shade of yellow pantaloon that Melville had been so proud of in his own wardrobe. Melville's outrage lasted all the way out of Bath.

"First my hair!" he complained to Eliza. "Then my waistcoat—and now my pantaloons!"

"You do not own a monopoly on yellow pantaloons," Eliza pointed out.

"That is not the point, Lady Somerset!" Melville said in spirited rejoinder. "It is where such criminal imitation will *lead* that concerns me. Perhaps one day he will appear at the Pump Room and you shall see he has stolen my skin and means to wear me as a suit!"

"That," said Eliza, "is the most revolting thing I have ever heard."

"I agree," Melville said emphatically. "It is not I who would be doing it!"

Eliza dissolved into laughter. A week on from her revelation, she knew the impossibility of repressing her feelings for him—she could no more unlearn her sentiments for Melville, than she could unsee the sun each day. Every moment she spent with him was to understand more fully why she felt the way she did:

how much she liked the way he made her laugh, even when she was out of sorts. Even when she was out of sorts *with him*, even when she did not want to. She liked his total and entire belief in her competence: whether at driving, or painting, or merely upon social occasions, he did not treat her with the gallantry or solicitation that she was used to from other gentlemen, asking constantly whether she was cold or warm or would like a drink or was feeling tired; nor did he assume in her a feminine delicacy so many persons seemed to take for granted from the mere sight of her. And that she still loved Somerset, that she was still as determined as ever to marry him, did not seem to signify one jot.

In deference to propriety, they avoided all of the public turnpike roads that might have made their journey quicker but would also have allowed every Tom, Dick and Harry from Bath to Wells to gawp at them and it therefore took over two hours to reach the cathedral town, which stood at more than eighteen miles from Bath across the Mendip Hills. Once they arrived, they rested the horses at an inn while they dawdled about the cathedral. It was certainly beautiful, and the famous clock did not disappoint Eliza: above the face, figures of jousting knights on horseback charged in a circle when the bells chimed on the hour, though Melville confessed that he had rather hoped they might spin at quarter past the hour, too.

They dawdled about the cathedral for only two iterations of the mechanism and made an excellent nuncheon before the rapidly darkening skies warned them that a swift return to Bath was advisable. Sure enough, a mere hour into their journey, it began to rain.

"Oh hell," Melville said. "Are you cold?"

"Not yet," Eliza said, huddling her cloak about her. But as the sky began to darken, and the rain worsen—the track getting muddier and muddier—Eliza did indeed begin to shiver.

"Not long now," Melville said encouragingly, throwing his own cloak around her as well.

It was not the cold that was bothering Eliza, but the poor visibility, for with sheets of drizzle coming down and the afternoon sky purpling, it was becoming more difficult to make out the road.

"Perhaps you ought to take the reins . . ." Eliza said anxiously, as they bumped over a divot she had failed to spot.

"You have it well in hand," Melville said calmly.

"Could you—speak to me," Eliza said, hands clenching.

"What do you wish to speak of?"

"Anything—how is *Medea*?"

"Vengeful," Melville said. "Demanding."

Eliza smiled abstractedly, as she tried to keep Caroline's carriage within her sights. She was breathing rather quickly.

"I am doubtful, however," Melville went on with a light voice, as if Eliza were not about to vibrate out of her seat with anxiety, "that *Medea* is like to see the light of day. Paulet has, very disagreeably, seen fit to block my every avenue to publication."

"But still you write it?"

Eliza reined the horses in to navigate a tricky corner, then gave them their heads again once they were back upon the straight and Melville gave an appreciative murmur before answering.

"Time was, I would have petulantly abandoned the endeavor if there was no chance to see it printed. But though it is just for me, I do not think it any less worthwhile."

The words were familiar, and Eliza puzzled for a moment over who Melville could be quoting, before realizing . . .

"*I* said that."

"So you did," Melville agreed. "I suppose you may consider yourself my inspiration: seeing the care you put into those paintings in your parlor, with no hope or expectation of their ever being seen, struck something of a chord."

And Eliza, predictably, blushed—all of a sudden quite glad

for the weather, to give her an excuse to stare fixedly forward. It seemed now the rain was at last beginning to clear, and as they progressed onto the firmer roads that surrounded Bath, Eliza was able to release her hunch over the reins. By the time they reached the town, it was long after they had meant to return.

Eliza drove Melville directly to his doorstep. There was no sign of Caroline—she had drawn ahead miles before and must now have gone to Camden Place to drop Margaret.

"Excellent driving," Melville said to Eliza, as she pulled the horses to a stop.

"Thank you," Eliza said, turning to face him properly for the first time in many miles. Melville had long since abandoned his hat upon the seat beside him—the rain had been such that headwear could not offer much protection—and his dark curls were slicked back off his forehead.

"You are quite soaked," Melville said, looking her over as well.

"I know," Eliza said ruefully. "I am not sure my hat will recover."

"A shame," Melville said. "For it is a very charming ensemble, though . . ."

He reached over and delicately lifted a damp curl of her hair from where it had become plastered against her neck, and with a few deft movements had tucked it back into her braid. It was the simplest of touches, the graze of his hand against her neck occurring only very briefly, and yet despite this, and despite the rain soaking her to the bone, Eliza had to try very hard not to catch entirely upon fire. She trembled, whether from desire, or guilt, or anxiety, she could not know.

Melville left his hand resting gently upon her neck for a moment. He watched her steadily and, almost involuntarily, she felt her body begin to sway toward his. It would be so easy, the most natural thing in the world, to allow herself this . . .

"Melville," she said, very softly.

"You might call me Max, if you wish," he said, just as quiet.

And Eliza clenched her eyes shut and reined herself in. She could not. She could not.

"My lady—" Melville said.

"Don't," Eliza said, before he could continue. "Don't."

For whatever it was—a declaration, or a proposition or what she did not know—and however much she was desperate to hear it with every muscle in her body, she could not. She could not allow him to speak when she was promised to another.

"Then I shall not," Melville said gently, taking his hand back.

"It is just," Eliza said, feeling she owed him some measure of an explanation, though he had not asked for one, "it is just that when one has not expected such a thing, and one cannot—because one has already—and one thinks of all the reasons it is impossible, even if one *wants* . . ." Her words were as garbled as her thoughts. "Do you understand my meaning?"

"One does not," Melville said gravely. "One wonders, even, if *you* understand your meaning?"

Eliza let out a watery laugh.

"I do not know," she said, and she suddenly felt as if she might burst into tears. "I do not know."

"That is all right," Melville said, more gently still. He picked up her hand in his and pressed a single kiss into her gloved palm, and even that set Eliza to trembling again. "I shall bid you goodnight."

He climbed out of the carriage and, with a last tip of his sodden hat, disappeared into Laura Place.

That Eliza made it home without crashing owed more to her groom's quiet reminders to watch the other side of the road than to her own skill. She handed him the reins when they reached Camden Place and descended from the carriage, resembling nothing more than a drowned rat, thinking that it was a good thing Mrs. Winkworth had long ago left for London, for she might have suffered an apoplexy to see her in such a state.

Eliza hurried into the house, sighing to feel its warmth around her, and feeling tears beginning to spring to her eyes.

"Margaret?" Eliza called. "Margaret?"

Margaret appeared almost at once, running down the stairs, her hair still dripping.

"Are you all right?" Eliza said. "Whatever is the matter?"

"Eliza," Margaret said. "It is Somerset. He is here, in the drawing room."

25

Somerset? Here? Now?" Eliza said.

"Yes," Margaret said, in answer to all three. "He arrived this afternoon, apparently, and insisted upon waiting for your return."

Eliza looked at Margaret, panicked. She had not expected him for a week more, and she had not at all readied herself. She had thought she would have more time.

"Do not panic," Margaret said firmly. "He is not an ogre."

But Eliza could feel her breath coming in sharp gasps. She could not see Somerset *now*. Not when her thoughts were so disarranged that she could believe she had left her mind there, with Melville, in the phaeton. She needed more time. She needed to think.

"What if—what if I see him, and realize I do not love him anymore?" Eliza whispered, pressing a trembling hand to her forehead.

What if Somerset saw her and realized exactly what Eliza had done?

"Then we shall think of a way through," Margaret said. "I promise."

Eliza dithered, looking despairingly down at her sadly muddied skirts. Margaret gave her a gentle push in the direction of the stairs.

"Go now, before you lose your nerve," she said. And Eliza

went. She might once have tried to delay but Margaret was right. However awful this might be, if she did not go now, she would not have the courage to do it. She pushed open the door to the drawing room. He was standing in front of the fire, hands clasped behind his back, and there was a moment, when he turned around to face her—backlit by the flames and his face half in shadow—where the resemblance to his uncle was so strong that Eliza almost gasped. Then, her eyes adjusted. The resemblance vanished. And it was just Somerset standing there, a half-smile upon his face as he regarded her.

"Good evening, my lady," he said.

"Somerset," she said shyly. "We—I did not expect you until next week."

"I thought to surprise you," he said. "But you do not seem very pleased."

"I *am* pleased," Eliza said. "Of course I am."

She found, saying it, that it was true. For as Eliza stood there, drinking in the sight of him, she could feel that her love for him remained. And all of a sudden, what had felt so large, so complicated a moment before, was rendered utterly simple in her mind. Whatever it meant, that she was able to love two men at once, it did not matter. Her feelings for Melville were undeniable, but this was the man whom she had loved faithfully, enduringly, foolishly, for years, and who had loved her all that time in return.

And if her heart did not beat quite as fast as it had begun to with Melville, and if she did not blush quite so frequently, nor breathe quite as quickly . . . What did that matter? This was the man she was to marry.

Somerset held out his arms, and she half ran across the room to him, laughing in relief. Somerset caught her hands in his, but did not use the grip to bring her closer, instead holding her a little away from him.

"What is this?" he said. "You are quite soaked through."

"I do not care," she said, leaning her face up toward his expectantly.

"I do," he said, pushing her back. "You will catch your death. You must run and change."

"I am not in the least cold," Eliza protested. "I will soon dry by the fire."

"I will wait for you here," he said, his voice brooking no argument. Eliza raised her eyes briefly to heaven, but obediently ran from the room. His solicitousness was incomparable, and though it was a little inconvenient at present, to be displeased at such protective concern would be churlish. In a trice, she had returned, dressed in the first gown she could lay her hands on, of lavender crêpe, and he smiled when she re-entered the room, holding his own hands out now.

"Your hair is still wet, my love."

"I am not going to dry it now," Eliza said. "So you may save yourself from asking."

She raised her head to his again, but again, he did not offer the kiss she desired.

"Where were you out in such weather?" he asked.

Eliza hesitated. She had not mentioned in any of her letters the driving lessons she had been taking with Caroline, nor the carriage she had recently purchased, wanting to surprise him. In her mind, she had imagined driving up to him in her best, most flattering habit and asking him, suavely, if he would like to come up with her for a few streets.

"Were you out driving with Caroline?" Somerset asked. "I hear she has been giving you lessons."

Eliza frowned.

"Who told you?" she asked.

"Mrs. Winkworth," Somerset said. "The whole family attended Annie's coming-out ball."

"How inconsiderate of her to ruin my surprise," Eliza said lightly, trying to decipher his expression. "I wanted you to be shocked and awed by how very dashing I have become."

"I was certainly shocked," Somerset said. He looked Eliza in the face for a long moment, then sat down upon the sofa with a sigh, pulling her down to sit next to him. "I ought not to have left you here, unattended," he said, running a hand through his hair.

"Unattended?" Eliza said, not sure whether to be more offended or amused. "I am not a horse, my lord. And I have Margaret."

"You do not know, clearly, what people are saying," Somerset said.

"What people?" Eliza said. "And what are they saying?"

"My sister reports that the Bath gossips are all aquiver with the news of Lady Somerset driving all over the countryside, attending routs and card parties and buying up half of Milsom Street."

Instinctively, Eliza bridled at the note of censure in his voice before forcing herself to focus only on the concern in his face. He was worried about her.

"Perhaps I have been a little high flying," she admitted. "But you know how gossips are. And my fortune is mine to spend as I wish. Do you not like my new colors?"

"I do," Somerset said. "But there are rumors that you have had Melville living in your pocket these past weeks. What of them?"

Eliza bit her lip. She could not lie to him. If he asked her whether she had feelings for Melville, she would not lie. But he had not asked.

"There is an explanation," she said. "The commission I wrote to you of—I must confess that it is Melville's. I have been painting his portrait."

"*What?*" Somerset gasped.

"I have been painting Melville's portrait," Eliza repeated. "That is why he has been so often in my company. So you needn't wor—"

"Eliza!" Somerset exclaimed. "How could you countenance such a thing and not tell me?"

"I did tell you," Eliza said defensively. "I told you I had received a commission. You seemed to think it a good idea, then."

"That is when I thought it was—painting some flowers, or someone's horse!" Somerset said. "I did not think it was a *portrait*! Of an *unmarried* man."

Eliza flinched. She knew he might not be pleased, but neither had she expected such unequivocal anger. He was pressing uncomfortably hard on Eliza's hands and now dropped them hurriedly.

"We were chaperoned," Eliza said, weakly. Which was true, at least in the beginning.

"Oh, by Miss Balfour?" Somerset said derisively. "Yes, a formidable duenna indeed."

"I would ask that you not speak of my cousin in such a tone, Somerset," Eliza said, with a coldness she did not recognize as her own. It was one thing for Somerset to express anger toward her, but she would not allow it against Margaret.

Somerset took a deep breath.

"You are right," he said. "I am sorry. I should not blame you—either of you. It is he who is to blame, of course."

"Melville?" Eliza asked.

"Goodness knows what he can have said to you in order to induce you to agree," Somerset was muttering, "what lies he would have woven."

It was so ridiculous that Eliza let out a burst of laughter. Somerset reared his head back, offended.

"I am sorry," Eliza said, still smiling. "I am very sorry, but it is just so very absurd. Melville did not induce me, and he did not lie. It was my choice, and even if you do not approve, I do not regret it. And I cannot see what is so wrong."

"You might feel differently," Somerset said ponderously, "if you knew what I have recently discovered."

"What do you mean?" Eliza asked.

Somerset ran his hand through his hair once more—it was looking sadly untidy now.

"I am not sure if I should tell you," he said.

Eliza felt a rush of irritation. Such slanderous aspersions had haunted Melville his entire life and were the precise reason he might soon have to leave the country.

"You have been making such declarations since the day you met Melville," she snapped, "but I am yet to hear of any proof. I should have thought unfounded gossip beneath you, Somerset."

"You chastise me for wishing to protect you?" Somerset said, bristling.

"I do not need protection from Melville," Eliza said.

She paused, took a breath, and mastered herself. It did not truly matter what other people were saying, what the gossip was. It mattered only what they themselves thought, what they felt.

"Let us not fall out with one another," she said gently, "for does any of it matter, now? I have begun half-mourning. You have returned. We can become engaged, at last."

Somerset visibly softened.

"That is true," he said. "*Finally.*"

The strange tension that had lain in the air since he had arrived melted. Somerset pulled gently upon her hands and she swayed toward him until their mouths, at last, met—and once again it was so familiar, so natural, that Eliza could hardly believe they had not been doing so all along. It was some time before they separated, but when they finally did, Eliza moved to lay her head upon his shoulder, and sighed contentedly. The fire was very warm, and his shoulder was very comfortable, and she could suddenly imagine them doing just this a thousand times more, in the years to come.

"When shall we marry?" she asked. "Soon, I hope. Before my mother gets wind of it."

She felt Somerset's shoulder tense underneath her and raised her head to regard him.

"You needn't worry," she said. "She has no power to compel me this time."

"It isn't that," Somerset said. "I have been thinking a great deal of how we shall manage our engagement."

"Have you?" Eliza asked, smiling.

"And I think it would be best if you returned to Balfour," he finished.

Eliza laughed, thinking he was making a joke. He did not laugh with her.

"Eliza, our engagement will cause a furor," he said. "You know it will. We cannot get around that fact."

"No," Eliza agreed. "But why should that mean I need return to Balfour?"

"Because the life you have been living these past weeks," Somerset said evenly, "is already causing talk. And so, it would behoove us to remove you from the public eye a little, before we make any announcement."

"You make it sound as if I have been cavorting around town in my petticoats," Eliza said. "I assure you, I would recollect having done so."

"Be reasonable, Eliza," Somerset said. "I am trying to protect you."

"I cannot return to Balfour," Eliza said.

"What is a month or two of quietude—if in exchange we have a lifetime of happiness?" Somerset said. "Then we will announce our engagement over the summer, and in the autumn we can marry quietly."

"In the *autumn?*" Eliza repeated. It was only April.

"It is when your mourning will be finally complete, in its entirety," Somerset said. "When did you think we would marry?"

She certainly had not thought he would insist upon such traditional propriety. Why, Lady Dormer had married on the year mark after her husband's death—and true, it was still considered something of a joke in high society, but . . .

"What if . . ." She clutched his hands. "Oliver, what if we just married, now? It is going to raise eyebrows no matter how long we wait—what if we married and bore the consequences *now*. We would at least be together."

Somerset was shaking his head.

"You know I cannot," he said. "I cannot risk doing such harm to my family."

Eliza stared at him. A decade later and it seemed they were having the same argument. They might as well be reading from the same script, only they had swapped parts, for she was urging him to bravery and he speaking of familial duty.

"Would it matter?" she asked. "Would the consequences truly be so bad? They cannot forbid it, they cannot keep us apart anymore, they do not have the power to do . . . anything, really."

"It would not be proper," Somerset said.

"Hang propriety!" Eliza cried. "I have lived my life by the rules of propriety and I do not wish to any longer."

"Do not talk in that way!" he snapped. "It does not become you. You know we cannot 'hang propriety.' Our lives would be forever dogged by it."

"I cannot return to Balfour," Eliza said, pulling insistently upon the hands still holding hers for emphasis. She could abide waiting until autumn, she could abide delaying her happy ending more months on still, but to exchange her life here for *Balfour*? No, that she could not do.

"You can," he said, eyes fixed on hers as if intensity alone would convince her. "You must. You will live quietly for a few months, while my sister ensures a good match for Annie, and then we will marry without fuss and retreat to Harefield. As long as we do not flaunt ourselves, or mix much in society, the upset will subside and our families will be safe."

"And now I am to live in isolation after we are married, too?" Eliza said, appalled.

She took her hands from his.

"Be reasonable, Eliza," Somerset said, growing irritable now.

"I *am* being reasonable," Eliza insisted. "It is just all so different to what I had imagined. I thought we would marry next month, that we might honeymoon abroad, spend the next Season in London, taking in the galleries and museums and seeing our friends . . ."

"But I despise the city," Somerset said, frowning. "Why on earth would we choose to spend time in London when we do not have to? We can attend local assemblies if we wish—what does London have, that Harefield cannot provide?"

"A thousand things!" Eliza said instantly. "Friends. Diversions. Dances. Art. You may pick any one of them!"

Somerset let out a quiet, disbelieving laugh.

"You are not serious?" he said. "I know you like to draw, Eliza, but it cannot surely serve as a reason to keep us apart. This is the only way we can be together. You must see that."

"I do not just *like* to draw," Eliza snapped, "it is part of me. An important part."

"It did not used to be."

"If you truly think that, then you were not listening."

Somerset scrubbed a hand across his face.

"Be reasonable," he said, again.

"You are not trying to find another solution!"

"You never used to be this stubborn," Somerset said.

"No, you used to think me spiritless," Eliza said. "Which would you prefer I be? I cannot do both."

"You are being impossible."

"These terms are impossible," Eliza said.

"I am not trying to make you unhappy!" Somerset said. "Sacrifices must be made."

"But why does it always have to be *me* who sacrifices?" Eliza said, casting her hands up into the air. "I have sacrificed enough, Oliver, and I cannot sacrifice any more."

"This is the only way," Somerset said, very emphatically, "for us to be together. You must see that."

Eliza stared at him for a long moment.

"Perhaps you are right," she said, at last. "Perhaps it is the only way. It is just that I cannot do it."

"It is only six months," Somerset said.

"It is only six months—and before that it was ten years," Eliza said. "And before that, *always*. I have had enough of waiting for my life to begin."

"What are you saying?" Somerset said, face paling. "Do you . . . Do you no longer wish to marry me?"

His voice broke in the middle of the question.

"I would marry you in an instant," she said hoarsely. "But not like this—I cannot go back."

"You would be my wife," Somerset said. "Would that not be worth it? After all the years we have both waited?"

Only a few months ago, Eliza would have said yes in a heartbeat. And she wanted to be able to say yes, now. But she did not want to make herself small again, in any way—not her character, not her desires, not her life. Not even for him.

Somerset seemed to read the answer in her silence. He stood and moved away from her, facing the fire, head in hands.

"I cannot believe you mean to break my heart for a second time," he said eventually, turning back to her, shaking his head bitterly. "I cannot believe you mean to do it again."

Eliza wanted to curl up on the sofa, to press her head against her knees and crumble—but she stood and looked Somerset in the eye as directly as she could.

"Back then, I could not say yes for my family's sake," Eliza said, as clearly as she could. She needed him to understand. "Now, it is for my own."

To say it felt as if she were wrenching some essential piece directly out of her heart, but Eliza gritted her teeth against the pain. It was the truth.

"And I suppose this has nothing to do with Melville?" Somerset asked savagely.

Eliza stared at him.

"Six weeks ago, you were ready to say yes to me; was it him who changed your mind?" Somerset demanded. "Do you love him?"

"I did not change my mind because of him," Eliza said quietly. "You have to believe me."

Somerset let out a derisive laugh. It was not a pleasant sound.

"I cannot believe he has had you so fooled," he said. "If you only *knew* . . ."

"I know everything," Eliza said. "And he is not the villain you make him out to be."

A light knock at the door interrupted them.

"My lady," Perkins said, eyes moving between Eliza and Somerset. "You have a visitor downstairs. Shall I tell them you are otherwise engaged?"

"At this hour?" Somerset said crossly. "Who on earth . . . ?"

"Lord Melville, sir," Perkins said.

"Oh lord," Eliza breathed. The only possible thing that could make such a situation worse.

"It needed only that," Somerset snarled.

"Tell him to go away, Perkins," Eliza said, quickly. "Tell him now."

"Oh dear," came the sound of Melville's voice, as he appeared beside Perkins in the doorway. He had not yet changed out of his damp, mud-sodden clothes. "Afraid I took the liberty—raised voices, you see."

"Taking liberties does seem to come naturally to you, Melville," Somerset said.

"Good evening, Somerset," Melville said, as if Somerset's salutation had been a normal one. "I thought I heard your dulcet tones. Is everything well, Lady Somerset?"

"Oh everything is *quite* well, Melville," Somerset said harshly.

Melville did not appear to hear him, instead steadily regarding Eliza, who became horribly aware of her own tear-filled eyes and the redness of her face. She opened her mouth to reassure Melville, to lie, but found she could not.

"Perhaps you could call at a different time," Somerset said, in a voice that would have been polite had it not been so very loud. "Lady Somerset and I were just in the midst of a rather personal discussion."

"Perhaps it is one I ought join," Melville said, setting his jaw. "Could we have some tea, Perkins? Calm the nerves."

"Yes, my lord," Perkins said, withdrawing slowly. He did not close the door after himself.

"Melville, you appear not to have understood me. I was politely requesting you leave," Somerset said.

"Yes, I understand," Melville said. "You see, I was politely refusing. I shall remain until Lady Somerset requests I do otherwise."

Somerset laughed again.

"You seek to protect her? *You?*" Somerset said.

"Somerset!" Eliza protested. "Melville does not deserve such rudeness."

"You might think differently, if you knew what I had just discovered about Melville," Somerset said. Then, looking directly at Melville: "Well?"

"What do you *want*, Somerset?" Melville demanded, his voice rising a little from its amused calm.

"Do you pretend not to know to what I am referring?"

"I'm sure I could guess," Melville said, "if you wish to quiz me again."

"Joke away, my lord," Somerset said. "I do not think you will find her such an easy audience once she knows."

Melville's mouth snapped shut. For once, he did not have a witty retort to offer.

"I wish you would cease speaking in such riddles!" Eliza said loudly. "Will you just tell me what you wish to say?"

"Would you like to, or shall I?" Somerset asked, with horrible politeness.

"My lady," Melville said, taking a step toward Eliza and holding his hands out entreatingly, "I do have something to tell you—something I ought to have told you long ago—but you must know, it does not truly change anything between us. I still feel—"

He sent a foul look toward Somerset, as if suddenly furious to have him in the room with them.

"I came here tonight to—to tell you how I felt, and make a clean breast of *everything*," he said, and there was a strange note of urgency in his voice. "I swear that was my intention."

"What on earth is going on?" Eliza said slowly. She had assumed that Somerset meant to inform Eliza of Lady Paulet, but then Melville—having already referenced the affair—would surely not appear so rattled. It was the most perturbed she had ever seen him.

"Do hurry up, Melville," Somerset said impatiently.

Melville took in a breath, then swallowed—apparently, for the very first time in his life, utterly lost for words.

"Oh, enough of this," Somerset said impatiently. "Eliza, Melville was sent to Bath by my sister. He was employed by her to embroil you in a scandal. To ruin you."

26

When Eliza was nine years of age, her grandfather had demonstrated to her the proper way to cut a quill, and as she had tried to copy his practiced movements, the knife had slipped, slicing her across the palm. It had been a deep wound, an angry slash of red more vivid than any pigment she had ever seen, but though Eliza had instantly understood what had occurred, and instantly perceived she was about to feel a great deal of pain, it had taken ten full beats of her heart before the hurt actually came.

It was the same now, in the wake of Somerset's declaration.

This is going to hurt, Eliza thought vaguely, though in that moment, she could feel only shock.

"Excuse me?" she said, very politely.

"Eliza," Melville said, "that is not precisely true—"

"She is still Lady Somerset to you, Melville," Somerset snapped.

"Excuse me?" Eliza said again, of them both.

"When Lord and Lady Selwyn came to Bath in February," Somerset said, still glaring at Melville rather than looking at her, "they devised an awful plan, to incite you into impropriety great enough that I would be forced to remove your fortune. They thought it likely you would be susceptible to an unpropitious flirtation, that I would react strongly given our history, and that Melville was just desperate enough to help them."

Eliza felt herself sway slightly. She looked over to Melville.

"Is that true?" she asked. "You . . . volunteered your services?"

Melville shook his head fervently.

"No," he said. "It was not—not like that. They visited me to discuss patronage, and we . . . brokered a deal, yes, but I did not know about the morality clause, I swear it. All they told me was that I should draw your affections away from Somerset, to court you publicly—and I did not think twice, because truly it was not the least burdensome. I would have done it anyway."

"When was this?" Eliza said. She was not sure why it mattered, why such detail had any relevance, only that she needed to know. "When did they visit you?"

"The evening of your dinner party," Melville said, reluctantly. "They sent a note around afterward—it was still early. I met Selwyn for a drink."

"You were in such high spirits that Sunday," Eliza remembered, with an awful, sinking feeling in her chest. "And—and that was when you began writing again. So . . . it was not my influence that caused such a change. It was theirs."

"Can it not be both?" Melville said, lifting his arms a little as if he wished to touch her—then dropping them.

"Everything from that moment on was a deception," Eliza said wonderingly.

"No, no, I swear—my motives may have been complex at first, but everything I said, everything we spoke of, it was because I wanted to. That was *always* me, all along."

"I could not believe it, either, my lady," Somerset said, contempt in his eyes as he looked at Melville. "Until my sister showed me the letters exchanged between them, I did not even think *he* could stoop to such low behavior."

Somerset had seen proof then. It was not just Lady Selwyn's word for it. There had been proof.

Melville was still staring at Eliza.

"It was always me," he whispered again.

"I should have known better than to expect more from a man who has never completed an honest day of work in his life," Somerset went on.

"Dear God, man, you served in the navy—we *know*," Melville said, his silence breaking as he looked angrily over to Somerset. "If you should like a pat on the back, you may simply ask, there is no need to continually remind everyone!"

Somerset stepped forward, fists clenched. Melville did not move away.

"Oh, are you going to hit me?" he said. "And what do you imagine that will achieve?"

"I imagine it would make me feel better," Somerset said through gritted teeth.

They were standing almost eye to eye, now, chest to chest. Eliza watched them as if she was standing a very great distance away. Once again, it was as if she were not here.

"All this time," Eliza heard herself saying. "All this time, you have been working for the Selwyns?"

Melville blinked away from the stare he was holding with Somerset.

"No!" he exclaimed. He made as if to move toward her, but Somerset's hand barred his way. He batted it aside but stayed where he was. "*No.* I ended the agreement as soon as you told me about the morality clause."

He looked back to Somerset.

"Lady Selwyn will have told you that, will she not?" he said. "That I ended the agreement?"

"That is not what she said," Somerset said.

"Liar," Melville said, shaking his head. "You and her, both."

"Who else knew?" Eliza asked. "Caroline?"

She imagined the pair of them, cloistered together and sniggering.

"No," Melville said. "Caroline does not know."

"And is that why you were so eager for me to paint your portrait?"

"The first time I asked," Melville said, "it was before the scheme had ever been mentioned."

"But after . . ."

Melville hesitated, and in doing so dashed an ugly black line through all of Eliza's halcyon memories of his regard, his respect, each of the portrait sittings now tainted beyond repair by this horrible new perspective. She felt, in that moment, as small as she had ever done. She had had it all wrong again. *You foolish girl*, she heard the old earl whisper in her mind. *You foolish girl*.

"Every time you offered your escort," Eliza said with dawning horror. "Every time you complimented, or flattered, or dared me into behaving carelessly . . ."

"It sounds so much worse than it was," Melville entreated. "My motives were not so reprehensible: I wanted to know you, to spend time with you, I truly did."

Eliza was shaking her head as if to clear her ears of water. Her mind was running through every single interaction that they had shared: their friendship, their flirtation, his encouragement, time and time again, to flout the constraints of her mourning. The clues had been there the whole time. None of it had been real.

"What a fool I have been," she whispered. "You never cared for me."

The pain came now. Throbbing through her in time with her heart, and with it came anger hotter than any she had ever known.

"I *do*," Melville said desperately. "It was just that—"

"As soon as I heard the news," Somerset interrupted Melville, "I knew I had to tell you. That is why I returned early."

"Oh, how dare you," Eliza began. Somerset nodded his head

grimly, looking to Melville. "No, how dare *you*!" She jabbed a finger at Somerset. "How dare you sit here and lecture me on propriety, when it is your sister that has been behaving so wickedly. How *dare* you! If I were to tell people, what they have been planning, it is not *I* who would be castigated!"

"You cannot tell anyone!" Somerset said at once. "Eliza, you cannot, the dishonor—"

"Oh I could," Eliza threatened. "And it would be no less than you all deserved."

"I am not the villain here!" Somerset said. "Let us remember it is he who—"

"I care not," Eliza said, stamping her foot in her rage. "You have *both* made a fool of me!"

With every word she spoke, her volume grew louder.

"Keep your voice down, Eliza," Somerset snapped. "The servants—"

"She has a right to shout, Somerset, you pigeon," Melville said angrily.

"Get out! Both of you!" Eliza cried.

Somerset and Melville both stared at her, unmoving.

"Oh, just get out," she said, voice suddenly small and cracking. "I cannot bear to look at you any longer."

The tinkle of crockery had them all looking to the door, where Perkins was standing.

"Gentlemen," he said, with more authority than Eliza would have believed possible in a man bearing a tea tray, "may I escort you to the door?"

"That won't be necessary, Perkins," Somerset said. He started toward the hallway.

"If I hear even a whisper of that morality clause being used against me," Eliza said to his back, her voice containing a venom it never had before, "I shall tell everyone what the Selwyns planned to do. I promise you I shall."

Somerset turned to look at her for a moment. There was no

warmth in their eyes as they stared each other down. Finally, he nodded, and left the room.

"My lord," Perkins said sternly. Melville had not moved. He was still standing there, staring at Eliza as if she held the whole world in her hands.

"I ought never to have agreed to it," he said. "But they lied to me, d-did not tell me—"

He was stammering. Eliza had never seen him so discomposed.

"You heard all my confidences," Eliza said. "You encouraged me to unburden myself. You flattered me and flirted with me and fed me nonsense about my worth—all so that I might hang myself out to dry."

Melville pressed a hand to his forehead.

"I am sorry," he breathed. "It was never my intent—it was not nonsense, you have to believe me!"

"I don't believe you," Eliza said, shaking her head slowly.

Melville squeezed his eyes momentarily shut as if to protect himself.

"I don't know how I can . . . fix this," he said. "I came here to . . ."

"Please just go," Eliza whispered.

Melville looked at her.

"I love you," he said.

It was the killing blow for Eliza. Tears began to stream down her face in earnest, and she gripped her elbows in her hands as if to let go would be to crumble into nothingness.

"I don't believe you," she said, her chin wobbling.

Melville nodded silently, looking up to the ceiling as if he, too, were fighting tears.

And he, too, walked away.

27

E liza did not leave Camden Place for a week. To leave would require assuming a socially acceptable veneer and Eliza . . . Eliza had been cut wide open. It was not a wound she could hide for the sake of small talk. And so Camden Place became her harbor, as it had been since the very moment of their arrival, and within its walls, Eliza crumbled as she had never done before.

The loss of both Melville and Somerset in one night, in one fell swoop, felt unfathomable, and at first Eliza could not parse which pain belonged to which loss. She wept for the loss of both of them, for the life she had thought she would have with Somerset, for the months of joy she had thought was hers with Melville, for the love she had given up and for the love that had never truly been real in the first place.

"It was all a lie, Margaret," Eliza whispered to her cousin, on that first night. "It was all a lie."

They were lying in Eliza's bed and Margaret was stroking her hair. She had not asked Eliza if she'd wanted company—indeed, since the moment she had found her, crumpled on the drawing-room floor, she had not left her side.

"I am so sorry," Margaret said, wiping the tears gently from Eliza's cheek with her thumb. "I am so sorry, my darling."

Eliza hung onto Margaret's hand as she fell asleep, in the vain hope it might anchor her, and when she woke the next morning—so early the sky outside was only just light—their

fingers were still wound together. Eliza stared vacantly up at
the ceiling as dawn broke, not moving a single muscle in her
whole body.

Who was she now, Eliza wondered, if the person she had
become was built upon falsities? What did it make her? Not
wanting to make herself small, for Somerset, seemed faintly
ridiculous, for she was smaller now than she had ever been.
Smaller than the mousy Miss Balfour he had fallen in love
with, smaller even than the feeble countess she had used to be
before Melville had dusted her off and made her feel shiny
again.

She was not an artist, really, for how could she know, now,
if she had any talent at all? Perhaps she was as bumptious as
Mr. Berwick, blundering about with no sense that she was
being laughed at behind her back. If she had ever thought herself desirable, for having two gentlemen fighting over her, then
what was she now that she had neither?

The ceiling had no answers for Eliza, but still she continued to regard it.

"Shall we go down to breakfast?" Margaret whispered when
she woke—seconds, minutes or perhaps hours later, Eliza did
not know.

"No thank you," Eliza said politely. She would stay here in
bed a little longer, she thought. Perhaps it might be her home
forever.

The ceiling turned yellow, pink, purple and blue with the
light as the day passed, Margaret returning at intervals with
tea or lemon cakes or a magazine she might enjoy—and Eliza
did her best to sip, nibble and leaf obediently, for it was not
Margaret's fault that things had turned out so dreadfully, and
really, she ought not be forced to caretake in such a way on her
remaining days of freedom. But neither was Eliza capable of
looking after herself—or rather, she probably was capable, it
was just that she did not *care*, anymore. She simply could not

fathom feeling anything but hurt ever again and there was, as yet, no part of her that felt ready to try.

It took two more days for Margaret to begin to lose her softly-softly approach toward Eliza's depression, and on the fourth day, Eliza found herself positively dragged from bed, stuffed into a loose gown and chivvied down to the drawing room.

"I might have an easier time with Lavinia's baby!" Margaret remarked tartly, trying to make Eliza smile, but Eliza could only look balefully about her.

Both Melville and Somerset had been in this room, frequently and recently. There was not a direction Eliza could gaze in that did not remind her of one of them, and she felt a hot rush of rage that they had managed to taint the sanctuary she and Margaret had built for themselves here. Hurt, at long last, gave way—very briefly—to fury. Eliza lasted only an hour downstairs that day before she was overcome by fatigue and had to retreat, once more, to her bedchamber, where she ordered the shutters to be closed and the fire doused, so that she might be left in the dark to try to find the sleep that was eluding her.

By the fifth day, Eliza was able to remain downstairs for several hours—and the kernel of pride she felt at the achievement was morbidly absurd. Sorrow had made her the invalid she had once pretended to be—indeed, never had there been a time when Eliza had felt more like wearing black and taking the Cure, than now. Either one of these heartbreaks would have felled her. Two—both—seemed frankly excessive.

The door nudged open, and Perkins came in, bearing a tray.

"Perhaps we might have the fire lit, Perkins," Margaret said.

"I shall send Polly up presently," he nodded. Then, after a brief pause, he added, "There is a visitor downstairs."

"If it is Lord Melville," Eliza said, "tell him to go."

Melville had called on Camden Place every day that week, and Eliza had refused to see him upon every single instance.

"It is not Lord Melville, my lady, but Lady Caroline," Perkins said calmly.

Eliza's refusal was on the tip of her tongue, but Margaret—seated across from her—was not able to hide the yearning in her eyes. Eliza took in a ragged breath.

"I will not stay," she said. "But show her up, Perkins."

"Are you sure?" Margaret began.

"Yes," Eliza said, though she could not tell if it was true.

She did not even bother patting her hair into place and when Caroline appeared in the doorway, looking predictably stunning in a gown of primrose-colored sarsenet, trimmed entirely around the bosom with a quilling of blond lace, she felt a rush of petty irritation toward her.

"Good morning, Eliza, Margaret," she said crisply. "What a fine mess my brother has made."

There was to be no dancing around the subject, then.

"I imagine you have a lot of questions," Caroline said, regarding Eliza directly.

"No," Eliza said. "No, I don't, actually."

If she had wanted more of an explanation, she would have accepted Melville's visit. She did not. For what could he say that would change the facts as they stood? And what could Caroline possibly tell her that might make Eliza feel better? Nothing. Eliza stood. She found she could not look at Caroline any longer. Blameless though she might be, she was still too much of a reminder of Melville to bear.

"I am afraid I cannot stay, Lady Caroline—do you mind if I leave you with Margaret?"

"Of course," Caroline said. "But—wait."

She pulled a letter from her reticule and offered it to Eliza. Eliza did not take it.

"What is it?" she asked guardedly.

"It is regarding the Summer Exhibition," Caroline said. "Your portrait has been accepted. Congratulations."

Eliza stared at the billet. It was so odd. Not a week ago such news would have thrilled her. She would have been delighted beyond belief. Melville would have been delighted, too—would have declared he had known, all along, that she could do it and here was the proof. Would he have been lying? Would his deception have extended even to sharing in Eliza's celebration?

Eliza's stare finally left the billet in Caroline's hands. Twenty years of desiring such an accolade and now . . . Now it was just one more thing that had been sapped of joy. Eliza forced her legs to move and made for the door without saying anything further. She shut it firmly behind her, but as she did so, her vision darkened just slightly at the edges—it had been so many days since she had exerted herself, and she had stood up far too quickly. Reaching for the wall, she steadied herself against it for a moment, breathing deeply.

"Did you know?" Eliza heard Margaret say, through the door.

"Of course I did not!" Caroline said. "I would never have agreed to it, which is exactly why I should imagine Melville kept it a secret. If she would just let him explain . . ."

"What is there to explain?" Margaret said. "We know everything. Melville was having an affair with Lady Paulet, Paulet discovered it and Melville was in dire enough financial straits to require a new patron. It may explain Melville's motive, but it does not excuse his actions."

Her indignant voice was a little muffled by the closed door, but still audible to Eliza from where she was leaning. Vision returning, Eliza straightened, about to make her way upstairs until . . .

"It was not Melville who had the affair with Lady Paulet," Caroline said quietly. "It was I."

Oh. *Oh.*

"Why then does everyone think . . . ?" Margaret said.

"We could not exactly tell the truth, could we?" Caroline snapped, as if Margaret were particularly stupid. "It seemed better to let Paulet assume Melville had been her lover, but we had not predicted his rage. It would take a large investment for any publisher to stand up to him. Hence, the Selwyns' arrange—"

"Do you still love her?" Margaret interrupted. "Lady Paulet?"

This was not for Eliza to hear. She moved quietly away from the door, toward the stairs, and was just about to climb them when she saw one of the housemaids, Polly, ascending from the other direction, heading toward the drawing room.

"Polly," Eliza whispered. "What are you . . . ?"

"Perkins said I am to light the fire, milady," Polly said, a little nonplussed to find her mistress lingering upon the stairs in such a way.

"There was a time," came Caroline's voice through the door, and though she had lowered her voice even further, her words were still faintly perceptible.

"We do not require it," Eliza hissed. "Not now."

Obediently, Polly turned back around. Eliza looked wildly up and down the stairs, with more energy than she had felt in days. How likely was it that another member of the household might be sent to the drawing room—to deliver refreshments or some other errand? Lady Caroline and Margaret's voices were quiet enough to not be overheard unless one was hovering directly outside, and Eliza trusted her servants to be above eavesdropping, but was it enough to risk such a discovery?

No. Eliza planted herself before the door, standing guard.

"There was a time," Lady Caroline was beginning again. Eliza tried not to listen, but . . . "When I thought I would love her for the rest of my life. But that was before I met you."

Eliza heard Margaret give a little sob and her heart squeezed with bittersweetness.

"You as well?" Margaret whispered. Her voice was shaking.

"Of course me as well," Caroline said, in an impatient way that was so quintessentially her that Eliza smiled, despite herself. "I have been *waiting*—"

But Eliza would never know for what Caroline had been waiting—for reasons Eliza could not hear, though she could well guess at, Caroline's words broke off abruptly in the middle of her sentence. At the very bottom of the stairs, Staves the footman crossed the hallway and just as Eliza was about to wave him away, he redirected toward the kitchen.

The quiet from within the parlor lingered for one, two, three more beats then, "I leave for Paris next week," Caroline said softly.

"Paris?" Margaret said.

"I have finished my novel," Caroline said. "I am hopeful of publishing this year. Paris was always my plan."

"Yes . . . of course," Margaret said, though she sounded as if the breath had been knocked out of her. "Perhaps when you return . . ."

"Come with me," Caroline said urgently. "You can practice your French, properly, and see Paris, and if we get bored we shall simply go to Brussels or Frankfurt or *wherever.*"

Eliza pressed her hand to her mouth, willing Margaret silently—but as powerfully as she could—to say yes. To seize such a future as Eliza had not been able to.

"I cannot," Margaret said. "My family . . ."

"You would give up a chance at happiness, with me, for a family you cannot stand?" Caroline demanded incredulously.

Eliza privately agreed.

"They would never forgive me," Margaret said. "And I would have nothing to fall back on if you and I—"

"You would have Eliza, would you not?"

Yes, Eliza thought fiercely, *she would*.

"It is not just that. How would it—how would we . . ."

She sounded very young, all of a sudden, as she stammered.

Caroline sighed, and her voice gentled. "To our friends—to those we trust—we might tell the truth. And to the rest, we would just be very, *very* good friends."

"And we would be accepted, by society?"

"We would be discreet, of course, but Paris is more liberal than London."

"Discreet enough to avoid rumors?" Margaret said. "To keep the secret from even the servants?"

"I trust my household wholeheartedly," Caroline said, a faint note of reproof entering her voice. "There will always be those who will not receive us, if they suspect, but I did not think you cared so much for others' opinions."

"I do not," Margaret protested quietly. "There is just so much to consider . . ."

"I have so much to show you," Caroline said. "Margaret, *come with me.*"

Eliza imagined Caroline would be holding Margaret's hands entreatingly—as she herself had done to Somerset, as Melville had tried to do to her. She squeezed her eyes shut against the memories.

Say yes, Margaret.

"I do not know," Margaret said, her voice small. "I . . . I must think. Can you delay going, even a little?"

There was a pause so long that Eliza half wondered if it would ever be broken.

"I have spent a very long time, waiting," Caroline said. She sounded very tired, all of a sudden. "I vowed never to do so again."

"You must understand my concerns," Margaret entreated. "Tell me you understand."

"I do understand," Caroline said. "But I cannot stay. I cannot wait."

"Not even a little? For me?"

"I love you, Margaret," and now there was a fullness to

Caroline's voice that spoke to tears. "But I just . . . For once, *I* should like to be chosen first."

"But—"

A long pause—a kiss?

"I hope we meet again," Caroline said.

"Don't—don't go!"

"I must."

The sound of footsteps upon the floorboards. Eliza sprang from her guard up to the next landing and watched as Caroline exited, pausing outside the door a moment to breathe deeply. And then she left.

Eliza walked slowly down, feet as heavy as her heart. Inside the room Margaret was sitting alone upon the sofa, eyes dry but face very pale.

"Are you . . ." Eliza began, hardly knowing what she meant to ask, but Margaret shook her head.

"I am all right," she said. Her voice was very high. "I am all right."

"Very well," Eliza said. She sat down next to her.

"I am all right."

"It would be all right, if you were not all right," Eliza said very softly.

"She would not wait for me," Margaret said, voice very constricted.

"She cannot stay here, if she is to publish again," Eliza said. "Her life would be made too difficult."

"I know," Margaret said, her chin wobbling. "I just . . . I just thought I was going to be braver."

And Eliza might not have felt, these past days, any real sense of who she was anymore: whether she had been right to refuse Somerset, whether her love for Melville had been at all *real*—but before all of that, she had been a friend. *That* she had not lost. She leaned over to wrap Margaret tightly in her arms and Margaret—who Eliza had not known to weep since she was ten years old—burst into great, gulping tears and pressed her face into Eliza's shoulder.

"I do not want to be in Bath anymore," she said into the front of Eliza's gown. "I just can't be here anymore."

"All right," Eliza said, squeezing her tighter.

"I don't," Margaret said again.

"All right."

"Can we just go? Anywhere else?"

"Of course," Eliza said; she would have agreed to anything Margaret asked, in that moment. "Of course, I shall think of something . . ."

Her eyes fell upon the billet Lady Caroline had left on the table—the acceptance from the Royal Academy.

"Perhaps . . . London?"

Eliza—

*Lavinia has entered her seclusion, so we are expectant
Margaret will be needed imminently. As your first year of
mourning has now ended, will you have the goodness to
inform your mother the date you mean to return to
Balfour? You must indeed have had your fill of the Cure
by now—I do hope you are not to become one of those
sickly women forever struck by ailments. One must press
on, Eliza!*

Your mother

28

Eliza and Margaret traveled to London by hired post chaise, only in the company of their maids; Perkins and the rest of the household were to stay in Bath, to await their homecoming—though Eliza could not yet conceive of when this might be. When one was running away, one did not like to consider such practicalities as the return journey.

When she and Margaret had traveled to Bath, Eliza's mood had been anxious but jubilant, as she was equal parts thrilled and fearful. This time, there was an air of manic determination in the manner with which she directed their hundred-mile journey to London as fast as she possibly could. Attending the Summer Exhibition when it opened in two weeks—seeing Eliza's portrait exhibited there, with their own eyes—was by far the least important reason for their departure. Far more pressing to Eliza was flinging herself and Margaret into so much distraction that they might be able to outrun both their heartbreaks.

When London crested on the horizon ahead of them, Eliza was more certain than ever that this had been the right decision. In the serene elegance of Bath, one could not help but turn one's thoughts inward, but in the insistent grandeur of London—Bath's noisier, messier, demanding older sister—one could not help but be distracted.

The post chaise took them all the way to Russell Square,

where they were greeted enthusiastically by none other than Lady Hurley herself.

"It is so wonderful to see you, both!" she sang, holding out her hands in welcome. "Hobbe, see to their bags at once!"

Eliza had written to Lady Hurley just as soon as Margaret had agreed, tearfully, to the scheme, and in her return letter Lady Hurley had at once invited them to stay at the lodgings she had taken for the Season. Lady Hurley was certainly not the only person of Eliza's acquaintance in London, and nor was she the grandest—her townhouse, while spacious and lavish, was on the less-established Russell Square rather than the more fashionable Grosvenor or Berkeley—but she was the only one whose acquaintance Eliza wished to renew at such a time.

"To allow yourselves to think would be disastrous," Lady Hurley said, clapping her hands—without being given any specific detail, she appeared to have surmised an accurate enough picture of what had occurred. "Let us go to the theater."

And though every bone in Eliza's body felt leaden with fatigue, she agreed at once: to think would, indeed, be catastrophic. Lady Hurley's box at the Theatre Royal was well situated both to regard the stage, and also—as was just as important, for not even *The Beggar's Opera* could hold Eliza's restless attention for long—their fellow audience members.

"Last night we saw the Duke of Belmond," Lady Hurley confided in Eliza and Margaret, as she brought her opera glasses to her eyes and began scanning the boxes across from them. "With a lady amongst his company who was most certainly *not* his wife, may I add."

"Not the thing," Mr. Fletcher said with smug relish. Mr. Fletcher, who had taken lodgings in Duke Street for the Season, appeared as much in evidence upon Lady Hurley's arm in London, as he was in Bath.

As Eliza gazed around at the ornate interior, she noticed

the glint of a fair number of opera glasses being turned in the direction of their box, too.

"Why are they looking at us?" she asked Lady Hurley.

Lady Hurley lowered her opera glasses and looked at Eliza as though she was denser than mud.

"My dear Lady Somerset," she said, sounding greatly amused. "You are an unusually young widow of great fortune. Did you imagine you could join the Season and *not* cause a stir?"

The words were so close to ones that Melville had remarked to her, not so many weeks ago, that Eliza had to press a hand momentarily to her breast to soothe its pang before she could respond.

In the two weeks they were to spend in London ahead of the opening of the Summer Exhibition, it proved that on this matter Lady Hurley and Melville were both quite right. The last time Eliza had spent the Season in London, as Miss Balfour, it was only by the sheer force of her mother's will that anybody had taken much notice of her. This time, however, she was the widowed Lady Somerset, and rich to boot, and not even her half-mourning prevented the *ton* from taking notice of her. By the next morning, they were besieged by invitations and very soon Lady Hurley was shepherding them from breakfast parties to morning visits, to picnics and promenades. In the evenings, they attended the theater, the opera and even a few balls—and if Eliza could not yet dance, she could certainly watch, she could certainly chat, and, as it happened, she could certainly flirt.

For while Melville had not given Eliza much reason to believe in any gentleman's trustworthiness, he had certainly made her a better flirt. And once she had overcome her incredulity at the number of unattached gentlemen who were now dancing attendance upon her, Eliza's overpowering need to keep her mind occupied made her quite motivated to engage in as many—somewhat frantic—flirtations as she could manage.

"One almost feels sorry for the poor lambs," Lady Hurley said, with a cluck of the tongue, as several such lambs reluctantly left their box upon their second visit to the theater, the bell having rung to indicate the end of the interval. "The competition is so dreadfully fierce."

"I do not feel sorry for them in the slightest," Margaret said. "From birth, they are overpraised, overindulged and overvalued by society."

Margaret had begun to regain some of her habitual sharpness.

"I notice that you, too, are not without your share of admirers, Miss Balfour," observed Lady Hurley, an amused sparkle in her eye.

This was true, and though Margaret dispensed snubs and set-downs with almost vicious liberality, she did at least appear to derive a manic sort of enjoyment from the exercise.

"Do you have a favorite gallant, yet, Lady Somerset?" Lady Hurley asked, not bothering to hush her voice as the curtain rose again. This time it was *The Two Spanish Valets* and Eliza averted her eyes from the stage—Melville had so enjoyed the play when it had been performed at Bath—to shake her head in response.

There was the sweet Mr. Radley, of course, who made up in compliments for what he lacked in liveliness; the grey-haired and distinguished Mr. Pothelswaite, an amusing conversationalist with pleasing manners; the handsome but tedious Sir Edward Carlton. But none of them—no matter how amusing, how interesting, how engaging—could inspire in her any fraction of the feeling she had held for either Melville or Somerset. And try as she might to be distracted by London, Eliza still found herself dwelling—as she lay in bed or watched the opera—on both these gentlemen, still, and one most especially.

Eliza had chosen to end her relationship with Somerset. She made that decision herself, and before anything else had happened that horrible night, she had thought it the right one. She would always have mourned him—mourned what they had lost, what they might once have shared—and though she would always carry a small torch just for him, she could understand it. It made sense why they could not be together. Whereas Melville . . . Until the very moment Somerset had revealed the truth, Eliza had still wanted him. Still wanted him, now, despite everything. And none of London's entertainments could take her mind off that fact for a single moment.

Eliza would just have to try harder. And if the very proper evenings of entertainment Lady Hurley had thus far been chaperoning them through would not serve, then perhaps some of the faster entertainments London had to offer might.

"I cannot thank you enough for your hospitality, my lady," Eliza leaned in to whisper to Lady Hurley.

"Think nothing of it, my child," Lady Hurley said with a wave of her hand. "Have you been enjoying yourself?"

"I have," Eliza said. "Though I was wondering . . . Tomorrow, might we partake of supper at the Royal Saloon?"

Under Mrs. Balfour's strict chaperonage, the Royal Saloon in Piccadilly had been one of the many locations Eliza had been forbidden to visit, but Lady Hurley was a very different sort of duenna. The very next night they spent a fabulous evening dining in one of the saloon's most public booths, in the company of Mr. Fletcher and a highly painted cousin of Lady Hurley's, before attending a rather rowdy card party at this lady's house, where Eliza and Margaret were introduced to the previously mysterious games of loo, faro and whist. The day after, the whole company took a steamboat to Margate with a different group of Lady Hurley's friends, and the day after *that* they spent a very diverting afternoon wandering around a spring fair in their plainest gowns, mixing amongst both respectable tradesmen and less-than-respectable tradesmen, and gazing at the attractions.

And if Eliza were beginning to turn more heads than was advisable, and if London were beginning to gossip of how *fast* Lady Somerset had become, and if each day Eliza were receiving fewer and fewer invitations to *tonish* parties, it seemed a satisfactory price to pay. For when she was laughing in a supper box, or dallying pleasantly with a crowd of gentlemen, or drinking far too much punch at the Opera House, she could pretend, for a few blessed moments, that she was still not missing a man who had been as good as paid to ruin her.

On the day before the exhibition's opening, when Eliza had exhausted all of these possibilities and more and could not think of a single other place left to visit, or a single other amusement left to peruse, she suggested they all attend the masked ridotto at Vauxhall Pleasure Gardens.

At this, even Lady Hurley had paused. Public ridottos of this sort were looked down upon by the Polite World as ghastly and vulgar affairs.

"They are not, perhaps, very genteel," she warned, but Eliza was not to be deterred. The more outrageous the diversion, the better the distraction—and the better the distraction, the less she felt as if she had been cut wide open.

Lady Hurley persuaded, they set out that evening in Lady Hurley's coach, and if Eliza felt more wan than excited, well . . . It had been a tiring few weeks.

"I received a letter from Caroline this morning," Margaret said, apropos of nothing.

Eliza felt her heart begin to race.

"Oh yes?" she said, striving for unconcern.

"They have arrived in London," she said. "For one day, before they travel to Dover for the crossing. Melville is going to Paris, too, now."

"I see," Eliza said, as if Margaret had just informed her that vegetal hats were back in fashion.

"He wants to see you," Margaret said. "He wants to explain."

Lady Hurley's eyes traveled from Margaret to Eliza and back again.

"That is all very well, but I do not want to see him," Eliza said savagely. "Goodness knows what lies he will have come up with, with so much time to prepare for such a meeting."

"Do you not think it might be easier," Margaret asked, "to speak with him, rather than try to busy yourself out of feeling this way?"

"No," Eliza said.

"Eliza . . ."

"No, Margaret," Eliza said. "No."

The sound of music upon the air alerted them that they were approaching Vauxhall, and Eliza leaned toward the window more out of a desire to avoid Margaret's conversation than anything else. Yet as she gazed out upon the acres of pleasure gardens, its intricate walks lit by a thousand golden lamps, the hundreds of persons streaming in and out of its pavilions and lodges, Eliza felt a stirring of genuine excitement in her breast. She turned to look at Margaret, her greatest friend in the whole world, and took a moment just to marvel at how very fortunate she was to have been born related to such a creature.

"Once more unto the breach?" she asked.

And Margaret grinned with shining eyes.

"Certainly," she agreed.

"*Splendid,*" Mr. Fletcher said with great feeling.

They placed their masks upon their faces and wrapped their dominos about them. Under these half robes, they were both wearing evening gowns: Margaret's a beautiful blue silk,

Eliza's the magnificent bronzed-green creation of Madame Prevette. While it was still months too early for Eliza to wear such a color, the mask would conceal her identity so that it did not matter. Lady Somerset might be in half-mourning, but tonight she was just Eliza.

They climbed out of the carriage and were immediately immersed into the sound of music and merriment, of loud voices and louder laughter, of more accents and languages than Eliza was accustomed to hearing. Outside the confines of the *ton*, this was an assemblage of classes and nationalities far more variegated than Eliza was used to: it was a London she had not seen before, and it was magnificent.

They went first to the supper-boxes, to partake of a simple supper of sliced meats, bread rolls and custard tarts with glasses of claret as accompaniment and then headed for the rotunda, to join the glittering, shifting throng of dancers.

Here, Eliza could see, for the first time, why public ridottos were considered by the *ton* as so very indecent. For the manners were so much looser than what she was used to, in every way: bawdy witticisms were shouted from one dancer to another, hands were clasped tighter and lower than would ever have been allowed in a high society ballroom, scuffles broke out over imagined slights between the young bucks, the punch was served freely and drunk with abandon. It might very well have been the most high-spirited evening Eliza had ever spent and, safe in the company of her trusted three, she danced quadrilles, cotillions, country dance after country dance, laughing as they tried to keep up with the music and swapping partners with abandon.

The first waltz, when it began, degenerated into chaos almost immediately. Danced closer and faster than any Eliza had ever done before, and so busy laughing her way through the steps that she was not paying attention, not even looking at her partners, really. For once, Eliza did not feel overwrought with thinking, and it was such a release that she felt almost giddy, hardly caring which arms caught her as she threw herself around the dance floor, spun first by a man in a black domino, then a red, then a purple, and then into the arms of a partner more graceful than the rest. A partner who did not merely clasp her hands, palm to palm, but deftly intertwined his fingers with hers. And Eliza looked up into dark brown eyes flecked, just in the middle, with the tiniest suggestion of gold—eyes she would have recognized anywhere.

29

Staring up into Melville's eyes, the smile slid off Eliza's face and her heart began to beat faster and faster. As the dancers swapped and exchanged about them, Melville, masked with a plain black domino, grasped Eliza tighter, refusing to relinquish her to the crowd, and she followed his steps automatically, instinctively, while her mind reeled. What was he doing here? The blissful thoughtlessness of the last few minutes was truly gone, and her thoughts bounced from one contradictory feeling to another: she was pleased to see him, she wished he had not come; she wanted to hear his voice, she would not speak with him. Finally, as the dying strains of the violins had everyone parting and bowing to one another, Melville let go, his hands dragging reluctantly from her waist while Eliza took two swift steps back. If she was going to have any chance of thinking clearly, she had to maintain some distance.

Silently, Melville held out his hand and Eliza teetered between the two sides of herself for a long moment, before she took it. She had too many questions. Melville pulled her gently through the dancers and the onlookers, only stopping when they reached the relative quiet of the lantern-lit paths.

A giggling couple dashed past, clearly bent on some sort of carnal mischief, and Eliza pulled her hand from Melville's grip.

"How did you know we would be here?" Eliza asked.

"Miss Balfour," he said. "She sent a note to Caroline by postboy—and so we came."

"I came to London to be away from you," Eliza said.

"I know," Melville said. "But I . . . I must be permitted to explain myself. I cannot leave England before I do."

He drew her over to a stone bench embraced on either side by trees and they sat.

"When the Selwyns approached me," Melville began, with no preamble and speaking rapidly as if he thought them about to be interrupted at any moment, "I was desperate. I had already spent weeks touring the country, trying to convince some wealthy patron to support me; the day we met, I was on my way back from just such a fruitless quest. No one wanted to defy Paulet: I had thought my career over, my aspirations squashed, thought that Caro and I were to be sentenced to the fringes of society and Alderley to crumble into disrepair."

Eliza hardened her heart against the sympathy that wanted to stir within it. He was a writer; she ought expect he would tell the tale well.

"When Selwyn explained what he wanted," Melville was speaking slower now—this part of the story was not so easy to narrate, "it did not seem so villainous. I already found you interesting and he made it sound as if all I had to do was . . . continue. Continue to spend time with you, and flirt, yes, and perhaps even tempt you into bending the rules of propriety a little—but only to hinder your and Somerset's relationship. I had no notion of the risk to your fortune. Selwyn told me it was only to prevent an alliance between you, and I was happy to stand in Somerset's way. I never thought he deserved you."

It was a piece of manipulation that *was* typical of the Selwyns, but . . .

"Did you, at any point, consider what harm you might cause to me?" Eliza asked. "A lady's reputation is a fragile thing."

Melville hesitated and Eliza watched him closely.

"Not for a while," Melville admitted. "I have never had much influence over my own notoriety: it exists, no matter what I do, and I have had to learn not to censure myself for what I cannot control. If the gossips spread lies about you and me . . . well, I suppose I thought the fault lay with them."

The slow way he was speaking, as if each word was one he was uncomfortable voicing, suggested that he was trying very hard to speak honestly—and, despite herself, Eliza softened, a little. She had seen for herself the way Melville had been dogged by whispers and rumors and prejudice from the moment he set foot in Bath, long before he had even met the Selwyns.

"It was not until you revealed the truth of the morality clause that I saw how I had been manipulated," Melville continued heavily. "I ended the arrangement that day, I promise."

He looked up and caught her gaze, misery and longing clear in his eyes. "And then, the night we danced I realized . . ."

"Realized what?" Eliza asked, breathless.

"That the reason I wanted to spend time with you, the reason I was so unsettled by the news of your engagement, had nothing to do with the Selwyns. It was because I was falling in love with you."

Eliza let her head drop to rest in her hands. To hear him say such words! It was painfully wonderful. She felt Melville's hand press gently upon her back, and it was so comforting . . . It would be so much easier to believe him, and allow herself to be held but—

"How do I know you are telling the truth?" she asked, straightening. "I cannot bear to be made a fool of again. You have lied to me so many times, so often and so well and so convincingly—and I have had to question so much since—"

"Eliza, look at me!" Melville pulled his mask off his face, so that she could see him, properly, and grasped her hands in his. "When it came to us, when it came to me and you, I never lied. When we spoke of our dreams, our families, our lives, I was not lying. I promise you."

"But Somerset said you never ended the arrangement, not until he did," Eliza said.

"He was lying," Melville said.

"But—"

"I love you," Melville said, interrupting Eliza before she could finish. "All you need to tell me is: are those feelings returned?"

Eliza paused and then knocked his hands away.

"What right have you to make such demands?" she said. "It is *you* who needs to answer *my* questions, Melville."

"Are my feelings returned?" Melville asked again, so bullishly that Eliza bristled even further.

"I will not be bullied into making a declaration, when you will not answer me," Eliza said, shaking her head. "How else am I supposed to know I am not being manipulated again? Lied to, again?"

"Why would I lie now?" Melville said. "What could I hope to gain from lying, now?"

"The same thing you stood to gain last time," she retorted. "Your circumstances have not changed, have they? You still need money, or a patron. For all I know it might be *my* fortune you're after now."

She had not even truly meant it—it had spilled out of her with her anger and frustration—but Melville flinched back, leaning away from her.

"Is that what you think of me?" he said. "That I am some common fortune hunter?"

"Can you blame me?" Eliza said, feeling a chill in the space his body used to warm. "After what you have admitted already to doing for money."

"You must know I would never—"

"Must I?" Eliza cried. "I thought I knew you; for months I

thought I knew you, and then I discovered everything to be false. How am I supposed to know, Melville? *Prove* it to me."

"If you cannot forgive me, then this is all fruitless," Melville said.

"If you will not prove it to me, then perhaps it *is* fruitless," Eliza said.

"You are not trying," he said.

"*You* are not trying!" she said. "It is you who is guilty. It is you who has led me so astray that my life risks being every bit as broken as yours!"

In that moment, all Eliza wanted was to hurt him as she had been hurt, and Melville's face twisted in pain and anger.

"Oh, yes, it would be much easier to blame me, wouldn't it," he snapped. "Tell me, what part of your life did I ruin? The part where you spent years pining for a man who doesn't even *see* you? Or the part where you waited obediently for society's permission to be happy?"

Eliza jumped to her feet, tears springing to her eyes.

"The part where I loved you," she choked out. "*That's* the part I regret."

Eliza turned on her heel, dashing back toward the rotunda, half blinded by sobs. Tearing through the crowd, she looked urgently about for Margaret but trying to catch sight of her in the sea of dancers was as fruitless as parsing a single drop of rain from an ocean. Every time Eliza caught sight of a woman in a pink domino, she was either the wrong height or the wrong shape or just plain *wrong*.

And then, finally, she caught sight of her. Margaret was in the center of the room, dancing a country dance, twirling around and around with her hands clasped with a lady wearing a red mask and domino. Caroline. Eliza watched them for several moments, spellbound, her tears paused. They were not the only ladies dancing with one another, for there were more women in attendance this evening than gentlemen, and under the safety of their masks and dominos—released from any fear of observation—Margaret and Caroline were spinning and laughing with abandon. As one does when one is dancing with the person that they love.

Eliza waited until the dance had ended to catch Margaret's eye. Margaret, unlike Eliza, had no trouble recognizing Eliza. She left Caroline's side immediately and hurried over.

"Did Melville find you?" she demanded.

"Yes," Eliza said.

"What did—" Margaret began, but Eliza interrupted.

"I am going home," she said.

"I will come with you!" Margaret said at once.

"No," Eliza said, gently. "Stay. *Dance.* Return safely."

"Are you sure?" Margaret said. Over her shoulder, Eliza saw Caroline hovering at a little distance, her eyes watchful.

"Yes."

"I do not know what I am doing," Margaret admitted shakily. "I do not know if this is even *possible*."

"Tonight, you are just dancing," Eliza said, her gut wrenching with the effort it took to speak calmly. "Now, off with you!"

Eliza turned and wound her way back toward the carriages to find herself a hackney cab, alone and unattended, and only once she was safely ensconced within did she give herself permission to weep.

30

Eliza walked slowly into Lady Hurley's home, untying her loo mask with clumsy hands and casting off her domino at last. She had never desired sleep so much in her life.

"My lady." Hobbe, Lady Hurley's steward, approached at a fast clip.

"Good evening," Eliza said tiredly. "Could I have some tea brought up to my room, please?"

"My lady, Mrs. Balfour is in the drawing room."

Eliza was sure she had misheard.

"M-my mother?"

Hobbe nodded.

"Here? Now?"

"In the drawing room, my lady," Hobbe repeated.

"When did she arrive?" Eliza asked, mouth drying.

"Around seven o'clock this evening."

It was now past eleven.

"Oh no," Eliza said faintly. Without knowing the whys and wherefores behind her mother's visit, Eliza was absolutely certain it could not be for a good reason—and that she hadn't been in to receive her made it far worse.

"I did explain you were attending a concert, and that you were not sure what time you would be back . . . But she insisted upon waiting for your return."

"Good lord!"

Eliza stood still for a moment, wondering what on earth to do, what *could* be done to alleviate this very unfortunate collection of circumstances. She stared down at her dress, at her *bronze-green* dress, and wondered if the sound of her voice had carried up to her mother or whether Eliza might be able to sneak upstairs to change.

"Eliza!" Mrs. Balfour's voice called from the drawing room, and Eliza was moved to obey its summons without consciously deciding to do so.

She paused at the door, took a deep breath and entered.

"Mother, what a pleasant surprise!" she said brightly.

Mrs. Balfour did not get up to greet her. She was arranged neatly upon the sofa, sipping tea. How she managed to look so intimidating in the pose was beyond Eliza, but one could not argue with its effects.

"I am so sorry that we were not at home to attend to you upon your arrival. We—"

"Do sit down," Mrs. Balfour said, cutting across Eliza. It did not matter that this was Lady Hurley's house, and she was only a guest—it had become Mrs. Balfour's room as soon as she had entered it. Eliza sat on the facing settee, hands clenched in her lap.

"When I first received your letter," Mrs. Balfour began, in a slow, considered voice, "declaring your intention to set up your own establishment in Bath, I had qualms."

Eliza knew this of course: the qualms had been documented at length.

"But I reassured myself," Mrs. Balfour continued, "by remembering that you have behaved well all your life. You have always done the right thing, always behaved with propriety, known your duty, honored your family. I have always been able to count upon you. I have never had to worry."

"I—" Eliza began.

"But entertaining a notorious rake in your home? Driving

a phaeton upon public roads for anyone to see? Coming to London the very moment you entered half-mourning to dally with every gentleman that crosses your path, your name being bandied about town as if you were some common jade and not a Balfour—not a *countess*? I should have worried more, Eliza."

She did not raise her voice—that was never Mrs. Balfour's way—but she had a manner of speaking, in crisp and damning tones, that made even more of an impact than if she had shouted.

"Mama," Eliza began, "you cannot listen to the gossips— they make everything sound so much worse than it is."

"Have you been visiting faro houses, Eliza? Have you been staying with a woman who reeks of trade?" Mrs. Balfour asked. "Where were you this evening, in a gown that is entirely inappropriate for your state of half-mourning?"

Eliza did not answer. To lie at this juncture would be fatal.

"It matters not," Mrs. Balfour said. "It does not truly even matter what I think—though I confess myself to be very disappointed. It matters what society thinks, it matters what Somerset thinks—both agree that you have become dreadfully, unforgivably, fast."

"Somerset?" Eliza repeated, thrown. Were Somerset and her mother *corresponding*? "What does he have to do with this?"

"Only everything, Eliza," Mrs. Balfour said, leaning forward. "No doubt you have a letter waiting for you in Bath, from Mr. Walcot. I shall add failing to have your correspondence forwarded to my account of your irresponsibilities. Fortunately, Somerset himself saw fit to write to your father a week ago, to warn us of what was to come."

"Wh-what did he say?" Eliza said, faintly.

"That given your recent behavior, he has no choice but to rescind your bequeathment," Mrs. Balfour said. "He is to take away all the estates, as soon as the paperwork can be fulfilled— and that should not take above a few days."

"But—but he can't!" Eliza protested.

"I assure you, he can," Mrs. Balfour said, and Eliza wondered how much her fury was tempered by vindication. "As the will so clearly stated: it is up to him to interpret your behavior and he has interpreted it, as I do, as deplorable."

"But he said he would not!" Eliza said. "He agreed not to, in exchange for—"

She broke off, feeling suddenly and certainly that there would be no benefit to Mrs. Balfour learning of the Selwyns' scheme. But it did not make sense—Somerset knew what Eliza could reveal about his family, knew the disgrace she could bring to his doorstep with just a few words. When last they spoke, he had seemed committed to avoiding such a circumstance—what had happened to change his mind?

"Then perhaps the sustained embarrassment to his family's name has changed his mind." Mrs. Balfour sat back, death blow now dealt. "One cannot live in a man's pocket, as you have been doing with Melville, entertaining him for hours in the privacy of your home, without accusations of the most grievous sort being levelled at you."

"I will go to Harefield," Eliza said, blinking around the room as if to find the answer upon the walls. "I shall make him see sense."

"No, you will not," Mrs. Balfour said briskly. "I have a suite of rooms booked at Pultney's. You will accompany me there, now, and tomorrow you will accompany me back to Balfour, Margaret will go to Lavinia, and then you will instruct Perkins to pack up your house."

"No."

"No?" Mrs. Balfour blinked.

"I cannot," Eliza said.

Mrs. Balfour stared at her.

"You cannot?" she repeated. She had evidently not considered it a remote possibility that Eliza would disobey her. In truth, neither had Eliza. She had always suspected, if such a moment as this were to come, that she would capitulate instantly.

"Eliza, I had not thought it necessary to explain exactly what your behavior has risked for our family's reputation. But perhaps it is." She leaned forward once more, eyes narrowing. "If word spreads that Somerset is taking away your fortune, and the reason for it, the shame will attach to us all. The best we can hope for now is to keep the whole thing as quiet as possible and beg Somerset to do the same."

"No, Mama—that is not the best I can hope for," Eliza said. Mrs. Balfour's nostrils flared and Eliza plunged on before she could be interrupted. "For tomorrow—tomorrow I will be attending the Summer Exhibition. I have had a painting accepted, a portrait of Melville."

Her voice held no shame at the admission, only quiet pride, and Eliza laid trembling fingers on her lips. She had thought all satisfaction at the achievement to have vanished, rendered impossible by Melville's betrayal—but there it was, still there. Hidden, until now, but not gone.

"Eliza . . ." Mrs. Balfour breathed. "What have you *done*? Have you—have you put your name to it?"

"It is anonymous."

"For now," Mrs. Balfour whispered. "But word will no doubt get out eventually and . . ." She pressed a hand to her head.

"I know this is beyond comprehension for you, Mama," Eliza said, "but I could not let such an opportunity pass me by."

Mrs. Balfour stared at her, as if she did not recognize her in the least.

"When did you start to believe your pleasures were above your duty to your family, Eliza? To risk all of us, for yourself, is beyond comprehension," she said at last. "You have brothers, nieces and nephews—it is your duty to act for their best interests, as well as your own."

"And I did!" Eliza cried. "For ten long years! I have given you most of my life, Mama! Made every sacrifice you have ever asked of me, gave up everything. I did it, for all of you, and I did it without complaining. But I am done now. I want more from my life than duty."

She was breathing hard. They were both standing now, though Eliza was not sure when it had happened.

"And do you not think *I* wanted more?" Mrs. Balfour asked. "That your grandmother wanted more? That any of the ladies on this street want more for themselves? We cannot. And so, we get on with it."

Eliza stared at her. She had never suspected Mrs. Balfour had ever wanted anything other than the life she had, the one she spent every day still fighting for. And Eliza wished, suddenly, that they might have reached this subject in another conversation, that they could have spoken with such honesty at another, softer moment. Eliza would have liked to have known this version of her mother, before.

Mrs. Balfour closed her eyes and visibly tried to calm herself. "All I want—all I have *ever* wanted—is what is best for all of my children," she said quietly. "Do you believe that?"

And suddenly Eliza's throat hurt.

"I do," Eliza said, and she could hear the tears in her voice. It was true. Overpowering and badgering and opinionated as she was, Eliza knew that everything Mrs. Balfour did was for the good of them all, and it had not always felt a trap. One never had to worry about the right thing to do, what the correct course of action was, for she would tell you. Eliza could simply rest her will against Mrs. Balfour's and allow it to prop her up—and there was part of her even now that longed to do it. To submit herself back into the familial fold that would berate her, and mold her, and push her around—but that would also protect her, shield her. It would be a smaller life, but it would be a safer one.

"Tomorrow we will leave for Balfour," her mother said, no doubt in her voice. "And Margaret for Bedfordshire."

Eliza took a deep breath.

"No, Mama," Eliza said. "Tomorrow I will attend the exhibition. It's a chance—an opportunity that perhaps you never had—and I am going to take it."

A safe life was not what she wanted. And if her fortune was to be taken away from her anyway, she might as well go out in whatever blaze of glory she could muster.

She swallowed and added with more difficulty still, "It does not mean that I am unappreciative of the sacrifices you have made for me. That I am making different choices is not to disrespect yours."

"I shall never forgive you, if you do this," Mrs. Balfour whispered.

Eliza squeezed her eyes shut, willing herself to hold onto her strength.

"I have to, Mama—I hope you will understand one day."

"Then we have no more to say to each other," Mrs. Balfour said, and in another moment she was gone, leaving Eliza quite alone.

31

Eliza awoke early the next morning, before the rest of the household, and Pardle helped her dress in a simple gown of dove-grey silk before they quit the house without breakfast. Eliza had decided she would attend the Summer Exhibition alone, this morning, for she did not know how she was likely to react upon seeing the portrait again. The last time she had seen the painting she had been sending it off for judgment, full of thrill and pride and *love*. Today, she was in a far more somber mood, for the pall of Mrs. Balfour's visit and the news of the loss of her fortune the night before had cast the future in a grim, uncertain light.

The difficult thing with acts of bravery, in Eliza's opinion, was that they did not feel nearly as good as one might imagine. In fact, in the aftermath, one could feel quite as guilt-ridden and as nervous and dreadful as one did after an act of cowardice. Only almost, however. For underneath it all, underneath the fear of what was to come, the concern that her family might never forgive her, Eliza could be reassured by one small kernel of satisfaction: even if this turned out to be the most egregious mistake of her life, at least it would be one that she had chosen, rather than one that had been chosen for her.

The cab slowed as they neared Somerset House. That the Summer Exhibition was held at a property which had belonged, two hundred years before, to her late husband's family, was a piece of irony that had, strangely, only occurred to

Eliza at this very moment. She wondered if she had submitted the portrait under her own name, whether this fact would have secured her a more favorable spot? The placement of paintings within Somerset House was at the discretion of the hanging committee, and the range of positions ran from the very good (eye level, in the first rooms, usually reserved for academy members) to the average, to the very poor (on the ceiling in the notoriously dark Octagon Room) and Eliza had no idea where her portrait was likely to be.

They pulled into the courtyard and Eliza squared her shoulders. It was time. When Eliza had visited the exhibition before, as a child, it had been thronged with people, but today Eliza must have been one of the very first visitors. She was offered, immediately upon entering, a copy of the catalogue, but although she knew this volume to be an indispensable guide to locating the pieces of art displayed, Eliza did not make the purchase. She felt the moment was too momentous to take a shortcut.

Instead, she passed slowly from room to room, followed by a silent Pardle, her eyes as wide and admiring as they had been upon her very first visit, so many years ago, her hand clasped in her mother's as they tried to locate her grandfather's pieces. The walls and ceilings were packed so tightly that it was difficult to know where to look, and Eliza's gaze traveled from portraits to landscapes to seascapes to historical paintings, all clustered and mingled together. She allowed her attention to wander freely, not paying too much heed to the artists of each work but lingering wherever she felt compelled to do so. She gazed upon miniatures and etchings and sculptures, and marveled at the myriad of skilled hands that could have created such beautiful objects.

She walked through the fifth room—taking in the vast historical battle scene on the east wall—and into the sixth, where she stopped abruptly in the entrance. For there, hanging opposite, in her direct eyeline, was her portrait. And although Eliza had come with the express intention of seeing it, she still felt as if all the breath had been knocked out of her. It was here. It was really here. Whole and undamaged.

She had done it.

And as Eliza stared, and the portrait-Melville returned her gaze a little quizzically (as if to say "who did you expect?"), Eliza felt a smile spreading across her face. Despite all that had happened, despite all the uncertainty of the future, in this moment she felt only exultation. A painting of hers was hanging here, amongst some of the greatest artists in Europe, at an exhibition she had thought, as a child, so above her she might as well be glimpsing heaven. It was almost beyond comprehension.

She could not have said how long she had stood there, in front of it, only that after a little while, a few persons began to trickle into the room around her. They seemed mostly—by the way they were speaking—to be exhibitors themselves, and from the way several came to linger at the same wall as Eliza, it seemed that her portrait had already begun to generate discussion.

"Who do you think did it?" one gentleman said to his fellow. The paint stains on his hands told Eliza that he, too, was likely to have a painting hanging on the wall. "Got the look of Jackson about it—do you think he's snuck it in anonymously as a joke?"

"No, no," his friend disagreed. "The colors are all wrong for Jackson—I think it far more likely to be an Etty. Look at the flair, my boy."

They examined it for a few more moments, guessing at the artist—all the names were, of course, men—before moving on. Melville's portrait looked sidelong at Eliza, eternally amused, and Eliza returned the smile a little sadly.

"Lady Somerset?"

Eliza turned her head to see Mr. Berwick

"Good day," she said, smiling in greeting.

"Good morning!" he said. "You are here early."

"I wanted to avoid the crowds," Eliza said simply.

"I see you have located this year's mystery!" Mr. Berwick said jocularly, with a nod to the portrait.

"I have," Eliza noted.

"I don't suppose you have any guesses as to the artist?" Mr. Berwick asked.

Eliza shook her head.

"It is a *very* good position," Mr. Berwick said enviously. "Though sometimes they have to give such spots to the more simplistic portraits—they would be quite washed out with anything more challenging, you see."

"I do see," Eliza said. "And where is your portrait, sir?"

"Oh, they gave me the location of my choosing, this year," Mr. Berwick said airily. "It is best viewed at an angle, you see—somewhere high is *essential*."

"Of course," Eliza said, smiling. "Well, it was good to see you, Mr. Berwick—I have enjoyed seeing another Bath face, here."

"I quite agree," he said with a bow. "And none of you thought to warn me of your arrival! I had to berate Somerset most severely . . ."

"Somerset?" Eliza said, her attention sharpening. "I thought he was in the country."

"No, no," Mr. Berwick said, smiling genially. "I saw him just an hour ago—he would have liked to linger and speak longer, I daresay, but he had an urgent meeting at Grosvenor Square—Lady Somerset?"

But Eliza, with unpardonable rudeness, had left his side mid-sentence. She had thought Somerset at Harefield. She could not believe that all this time he had been in lodgings not a mile away from where Eliza had been.

He must have heard she was in town, must have known where to find her. And he had sent such a missive by way of Mrs. Balfour, anyway.

The serenity that Eliza had found that morning had vanished. She stalked back through the rooms of Somerset House, out into the courtyard, and back into her hackney cab in a steadily climbing rage.

How dare he!

How *dare* he.

"Grosvenor Square, please!" she called to the driver. "And make haste!"

32

Eliza had not spent a great deal of time in her late husband's London house—the old earl, as did the new, preferred countryside isolation to city liveliness—but less than half an hour later she disembarked in the grandest square in all of London. As she stood in front of the grand, towering and terribly austere townhouse, Eliza was reminded of how inadequate she used to feel inside. For the second time that day, Eliza squared her shoulders and knocked. The expression that the footman made, upon recognizing his old mistress, approached the comical.

"My lady!" he gasped.

"Is Somerset at home?" Eliza demanded, walking into the entrance hall.

"He is hosting a breakfast party, m-my lady," he stammered. "H-he has guests."

"Wonderful! Inform him, will you, that I am here and desirous of having a moment of his time?"

The footman bowed and left, reappearing minutes later with Barns, the Somerset butler.

"Lady Somerset," he said. "This is an unusual time for a visit."

"And yet I'm sure we can cope," Eliza said briskly, her voice, for one moment, sounding extraordinarily similar to her mother's. "Please inform his lordship of my presence."

Barns hesitated, left, then returned after only a few moments.

"His lordship thanks you for the visit, and begs that you return later, as he is currently entertaining guests."

"You may inform his lordship that her ladyship will not return later, for she has urgent business to discuss now; in fact, her ladyship will very much go in to see him at breakfast if his lordship does not come out now," Eliza said, her smile wide and insincere.

Barns looked at her and then—briefly—to Pardle at Eliza's shoulder, as if hoping to find an ally there. Pardle returned his gaze with a basilisk stare.

"May I invite your ladyship to wait in the library, while I deliver the message?" Barns said, capitulating.

"You may," Eliza said graciously. She left Pardle waiting in the hall. This was not a meeting she wished to be observed, even by her.

Only a few moments after Barns's departure, the library door opened again and Somerset strode inside. Eliza had braced herself to feel something stir at the sight of him, but though her heart did beat faster, it was from anger rather than heartbreak, and this steadied her.

"Eliza!" he said. "I must ask you to return later, I am in the middle of hosting a breakfast party and—"

"How dare you?" Eliza interrupted him. "How dare you write to my father, to inform him of your plans, before you wrote to me! How dare you not deliver such news yourself, when you have been in London and must have known of my presence here, too—*how dare you* take my fortune from me? I assure you, my lord, I earned every penny of it."

"How—"

He tried to interrupt her, angry, but she was in full flow.

"You seek to punish me for rejecting your suit. I understand.

But is punishing me, is sentencing me in such a way—will that give you the satisfaction you seek?"

"It is—it is not about punishment!" he bit out angrily. "Though I would be within my rights to feel a little anger, it is not about that at all—you wrong me! The gall of you to accuse me of such a thing!"

"You castigated me once for a lack of spirit. Now your issue seems to be my excess of it," Eliza said. "It seems I cannot please you, no matter what I do."

He gritted his teeth. "Your fortune was given to you by my family, under conditions that you have flouted extraordinarily—to such a degree that I wonder that you show your face here!"

"How have I flouted it?"

"Only in every possible way you could, Eliza," Somerset said. "Flirting with every unattached gentleman in London—visiting all the most insalubrious venues in London while in half-mourning—dancing with Melville while you were still wearing black."

This at last brought Eliza up short.

"Who told you that?" she demanded.

"I see you do not deny it," Somerset remarked bitterly. "You were seen, Eliza, not that you seemed to care a fig for that at the time! I warned you that you cannot live in a man's pocket without setting tongues to wagging. Your reputation has been darkening by the day, and you were too busy mooning over Melville to care!"

"And I warned you," Eliza said. "What I should do, what I should tell people, if you tried to take my fortune from me. How might the tongues wag, once they hear what the Selwyns were plotting to do, my lord?"

Somerset looked at her, suddenly still.

"Who will believe you?" he said quietly. "Eliza, you have

hung proof of your affair with Melville in Somerset House for
the world to see. Marking the portrait as 'anonymous' will not
keep it a secret for long, mark my words. The rumor mill is
already beginning to churn, and once the truth is known, no
one will think any aspersions you cast at Lady Selwyn anything more than spite."

Eliza stared at him. "How can you be so cruel?" she whispered.

"Contrary to what you may think of me, Eliza, I have not
done this to punish you for rejecting my offer," Somerset said
heavily. "Your behavior has had very real consequences upon
my family—upon *me*."

"What consequences?"

He paused. The look in his eyes, as if he were working out
how best to say it, as if he knew it was going to hurt her and
even now wanted to avoid doing so . . . Eliza guessed what he
was about to say before he said it.

"I have made an offer of marriage, my lady. And her parents are reluctant to accept while you denigrate the Somerset
name—they are concerned, and rightly so, for the direction
you might take the family."

"You are to be married?" she asked, slightly short of breath.
"It has been only three weeks!"

"I must marry someone, Eliza," Somerset said, casting his
arms up helplessly. "And if not you, then . . . She is kind, and
sweet, and I hold a great deal of affection for her. And her
parents will not allow my suit until your behavior is dealt
with."

"Who is she?"

He hesitated again. Eliza frowned.

"I will find out eventually," she said. "You cannot expect to
keep it a secret."

"My lord?"

Eliza turned at the sound of a quiet, timid voice.

The identity of Somerset's breakfast guests became suddenly, horribly clear.

"Miss Winkworth!" Somerset started.

"I could not help but hear," Miss Winkworth said softly, her head peeking inside the room, one hand pressed against the wood of the door. "I was coming through the hall and you were speaking so very loudly. Good morning, Lady Somerset— I like your dress a great deal."

"Thank you," Eliza said automatically. It was the most she had ever heard the girl speak.

"Run along back to the dining room, now. I shall be in presently," Somerset instructed her, as if she were a very small child. Miss Winkworth hesitated, her eyes traveling between them.

"Hurry back," she whispered. "My mother is about to start critiquing my posture, I am sure of it."

She dimpled a smile up at him before making an obedient retreat, and Somerset visibly melted.

Eliza stared at him, open-mouthed.

"You are marrying *Miss Winkworth*?" she asked, too confused to be upset. "How can that be?"

"You, of course, introduced us at your dinner party . . ." Somerset began, seeming painfully aware of the awkwardness of such a beginning. "And then my sister invited them to Annie's ball, and we spoke a little, and danced at Almack's that week, and since you . . . since we . . . We have become more acquainted."

It was as traditional a courtship as any. As traditional as theirs had been. Except . . .

"Oliver, she is so young," Eliza breathed.

He flushed.

"She is wise beyond her years," he retorted. "She knows what she wants and . . . She is very precious to me already—in time, love will grow."

It seemed that the appeal of the young and timid was a family trait. For a moment, standing there in his full morning regalia, in this house, his resemblance to his uncle was very apparent . . .

But then Eliza's mind, which had very briefly paused, began to turn again.

"And Mrs. Winkworth said they cannot accept, unless you address my behavior?" she said slowly. "Because she hates me."

"No, because they are worried for their daughter," he argued.

"Let me assure you, that is not so," Eliza said, with a bitter laugh. "You are the finest catch in England—of course Mrs. Winkworth is not going to reject your suit! She is *manipulating* you, to revenge herself upon me, for not writing her letters of introduction."

"Revenge?" Somerset snorted. "You speak of her as if she is a villain from a melodrama!"

"She certainly seemed quite villainous," Eliza retorted, "plotting a match between Winnie and Lord Arden."

"*Arden?*" Somerset's jaw dropped. "Surely she cannot have intended—"

"Oh, she did," Eliza said. "She asked me specifically for an introduction, given he is related to *your* line. And when I suggested such a match might be unfair to her daughter, she flew into very high dudgeon."

"Arden, though . . . Surely not even Mrs. Winkworth . . ." Somerset said, the note of approbation as he said this lady's name making very clear his opinion.

"She is quite capable of it," Eliza said. "You cannot tell me she has not been pursuing your title most assiduously?"

Somerset did not reply.

"Or that Miss Winkworth is not entirely terrified of her?"

"The sooner I have Winnie out of her claws the better," Somerset muttered in agreement.

He eyed Eliza consideringly, hackles lowering.

"You did not tell me about Arden," he said finally.

"You did not tell me you had a *tendre* for the girl," Eliza said, raising her brows and having the satisfaction of seeing Somerset flush.

"Yes, well," he said. "Just because you might have a point regarding Mrs. Winkworth—it does not make your behavior any more honorable. Do you mean to continue parading yourself around the city?"

"I have not decided yet," Eliza said honestly.

She did not know much of anything about the future.

Somerset chuffed out a laugh.

"At least you are honest," he said. "If you . . . modulate your behavior, perhaps I can see my way to pausing this process. But . . ." He looked at her. "Eliza, you must agree to close all contact with Melville. I can find it within myself to forgive much, but that I cannot abide. Do we have an agreement?"

Eliza ran her teeth across her bottom lip. It was the most conciliatory offer she was likely to receive from him. And had the previous night not proved that she and Melville had no future together, anyway? But yet . . . Was she really to allow any man to make such demands of her, anymore? Allow her life to be ordained, in perpetuity, by their high-handed judgments or capricious moods?

"No, we do not have an agreement, my lord," Eliza said, gently.

It was foolish. It was reckless. It was necessary.

"I cannot allow what I want—or who I want—to be dictated to me," she continued. "And if my fortune is the price I have to pay for such freedom, then I will pay it."

Somerset gaped at her.

"Goodbye, then," Eliza said, gathering up her skirts in her hands. She took one last look at him, one last long look. Part of her would always love him, she knew. They had been too much part of each other's stories, for too long, for all that love to disappear. Their roots would always be a little tangled. But Eliza would have had to give up too much to be with him. And she could not do that anymore.

She walked toward the door. As she reached it, she paused.

"Be kind to her, Oliver," she said, without turning. "She is very young, and who she is . . . may yet change."

33

Eliza felt disjointed, on the journey back to Russell Square. The threads tying her to normalcy had been cut again, by herself this time, and though the world around looked the same as it had done minutes before, everything was different. Eliza was rich Lady Somerset no longer. It was done. There was no going back and she did not *want* to—but how was she to proceed from here? She still had five hundred pounds a year to her name—her jointure could not be taken away from her, and that was something. It was sufficient, at least, to rent a small house, and pay for her essential expenses, though the life she had so much enjoyed of late, of careless expenditure and new dresses and shining carriage horses, would be behind her.

Perhaps she could set herself up as a portraitist—earn a living, as some gentlemen did? Eliza bit her lip. She would not know where to begin. *I should think you perfectly able to meet such challenges*, Melville had said to her once, and though the mere thought of Melville had a rush of bitter anger rising up within her, Eliza still found herself sitting a little straighter. She could do it. She could—she *would*—do it all.

Whatever serenity Eliza had achieved by the time she walked into the breakfast room of Russell Square was shattered immediately by Lady Hurley.

"Oh, Lady Somerset, thank goodness you are home!" she moaned, jumping up from her seat to wring Eliza's hands.

"Whatever is the matter?" Eliza asked.

"It is Miss Balfour," Lady Hurley said, lowering her voice as a maid entered with a tray. "She did not arrive home last night."

For a moment, Eliza was sure she had misheard.

"From the masquerade?" she said faintly. "No, no! She was to accompany you home in the carriage."

But Lady Hurley was shaking her head, and Eliza felt her heart begin to pound, sickeningly.

"We left before her—she said she would be escorted by Lady Caroline once the dancing had finished," Lady Hurley said miserably. "But her bed was not slept in."

"You left her with Caroline?" Eliza demanded. "Does *she* know where . . . ?"

"I do not know where the Melville house is," she said. "And I cannot very well find out without all sorts of questions."

"Have the carriage brought around," Eliza interrupted, not caring if it was rude, and dashed up the stairs before Lady Hurley could reply.

There was nothing to worry over. Margaret had been with Caroline, and Caroline would not let anything happen to her. This was all a simple misunderstanding. Something they would laugh about in years to come, she was certain.

Eliza pushed open the door to Margaret's bedchamber, hastened over to the writing desk, and began riffling through it. She discarded a note from Margaret's mother and a theater program and—*there!* Caroline's handwriting—and, at the top of the billet, their address. Berkeley Square! She dashed back down the stairs and past Lady Hurley, who was wringing her hands in the entrance hall.

"I shan't be long!" she called over her shoulder and leapt into the carriage, calling, "Berkeley Square!" to the driver, willing him to go as fast as possible.

I ought not have left her there. This was not Bath, where every person was an acquaintance, every locale only a stone's throw away from their home, and every event as safe as houses. It was London, and even though Margaret was going to be all right—certainly, she would be all right—still, Eliza ought never to have left her.

Eliza veritably hammered upon the Melvilles' door to be greeted with the second baffled butler of the morning.

"I am afraid," the butler said, "that my lady is taking breakfast—and not yet accepting visitors."

But by now Eliza was quite *au fait* with forcing herself into homes. She could hear Caroline laughing somewhere close.

"She will accept me," she declared, ducking under the butler's arm and pushing the door open.

"My lady!" the butler yelped, scrambling after her. "My *lady*!"

Eliza had already walked inside, taking two hasty steps into the room and—

"Oh, thank goodness," she breathed.

For there was Margaret, sitting next to Lady Caroline at the breakfast table, sipping at a cup and leafing through a broadsheet. Neither lady was yet fully dressed for the day; they were instead both wearing very modish dressing gowns— had Eliza not been so dreadfully relieved, she might have blushed.

"Good morning, Eliza," Margaret said. "I did not know we were expecting you this morning."

"We were not," Caroline said. "How awfully modern, to barge in unannounced."

Her voice was just as languorously amused as usual, but today the effect was quite different for the curve of her lips was far softer, her eyes were brighter—and Margaret, next to her, was smiling so hard it looked as if it hurt.

"An early French lesson?" Eliza said, falling into a chair without asking, and laying a trembling hand to her brow.

It was all right. She was all right.

"Of a sort," Margaret said, cheerily.

"Did you not think a *note* might have been considerate?" Eliza demanded. "I was halfway to thinking you murdered!"

"Such dramatics so early in the day," Caroline murmured into her chocolate.

"I wasn't thinking," Margaret said—in explanation rather than apology. "A strategy that has served me rather well."

Caroline brushed her fingers softly over Margaret's wrist. Eliza sat up. She had intruded enough.

"I will let Lady Hurley know she may rest easy," she said. "That the hour was too late to wake the household—or—or something."

"Oh, send a note and stay to breakfast," Margaret entreated her. "There is far too much for just us to eat."

It was tempting, for Eliza had been awake for hours now, and the repast was a handsome one—soft bread rolls and several fragrant meat dishes Eliza did not recognize—but now the panic had faded, her heart had quietened, and her hands were no longer quite as clammy, she was cognizant that Melville might appear at any moment. When she was worried for Margaret's safety, such an encounter of course did not weigh with her, but now Margaret was demonstrably more well than Eliza had ever seen her, Eliza would rather avoid it. The day had been full enough already.

"He is not here," Caroline said, reading the direction of Eliza's thoughts exactly.

"Oh?" Eliza said, much relieved. Much relieved and yet also, somehow, the tiniest bit disappointed—which was exactly *why* she needed to leave now, because even to be here was to feel confused.

"He left for Russell Square only a few moments before you arrived," Caroline said.

"To speak to you," Margaret added, as if this was not clear enough.

Eliza's breath tried to catch—she would not let it.

"We have already spoken at length, last night," she said stoutly. "There is nothing further to discuss."

"If you say so," Margaret said dubiously. "I shall see you at Russell Square anon."

Eliza slipped past the butler a little sheepishly—he was standing guard at the bottom of stairs as if concerned she might chance a robbery—and out onto the street. Lady Hurley's driver had disembarked from the carriage to confer with one of the footmen across the street, and, catching sight of Eliza, he hastened back toward her, just as a curricle came clattering around the corner, drawn by a pair of prancing greys, and driven by Melville.

"Let us leave now, quickly," Eliza called to the driver, holding out an arm expectantly to him—the steps to the carriage were too high for her to reach alone.

Melville pulled to an abrupt stop ahead of her and leapt down. He was wearing no hat, and in his hand was clasped a sealed billet.

"My lady," he said breathlessly. "I have just come from Russell Square."

"Congratulations," Eliza said. "I am just going there."

"May _I_ escort you?"

"I already have a carriage."

Melville took a hurried step forward. He looked drawn, tired and—though his caped driving coat, Hessian boots and buckskins were all very fine—a little disheveled, for his neckcloth was loosened as if he had been tugging upon it. This, however, inspired irritation rather than sympathy in Eliza; when she had not slept well, she appeared drawn and jaundiced, and it was unjust that Melville in fatigue should remain so appealing

"Eliza—" he said quietly.

"Lady Somerset," she corrected.

"Lady Somerset," he agreed. "I only wish to apologize."

"Your apology did not go well yesterday," Eliza pointed out. Melville winced.

"I behaved abominably," Melville said. "I only wish to speak with you—with no expectation of forgiveness—and I come with hat in hand."

Eliza's eyes flicked up to Melville's bare head.

"Metaphorical hat," he added, with the tiniest of smiles— and Eliza scowled. She would not be appeased by humorous chatter and a becoming appearance. She was not so easily manipulated, anymore.

"I would have refused to see you, had I been home," she said.

"I expected as much," Melville replied. "It is why I wrote a letter, too."

He held out the billet. Eliza did not take it. She knew well what a beautiful writer he was; no good could come of reading such a letter. Melville let his hand drop.

"Lady Somerset—please, could I just escort you back to Russell Square?"

Eliza sighed, fiddling with the buttons on her pelisse. She was so tired, but . . . After all the bravery of this morning, was this to be the moment she quailed? Eliza nodded without looking up. She spared a moment to inform Lady Hurley's driver of her intention, bidding him tell his mistress that all was well, before accepting a hand up into the curricle without further words.

"Would you like to drive, or shall I?" Melville asked, very politely.

"They are your horses," Eliza said.

"So they are," Melville agreed.

He set them off at a brisk pace. Melville inhaled sharply as if he were about to begin speaking, paused—subsided for a moment—and then began again.

"I owe you . . . many apologies," he said. "Last night, I was so afraid you might run off at any moment, that I became overcome with a sense of haste. Of course, *of course*, you may demand of me any question you wish."

Eliza eyed Melville narrowly. His words were too fluent.

"I have breached your trust. I must earn it back," he added when she still did not speak.

"Who has knocked such sense into you?" Eliza asked.

"Ah—Caro," Melville said. "Then Margaret. Then Caro again."

Eliza snorted.

"And are you merely repeating lines they have fed you?"

"No, no!" Melville said. "It is how I feel: I want you to ask me whatever you need."

Eliza pressed her hands to her face. It was far more difficult to remain angry with a calm, humbled Melville, and if Eliza could not hold onto her anger, then she would instead have to be dreadfully afraid. She could not bear to feel any of her hurt renewed. It was already painful enough.

"It does not have to be now," Melville said, as they drew onto Russell Square and he slowed his horses.

"Oh, but it might as well be," Eliza said, face still half-hidden. It was pointless—truly pointless—for to repair even a friendship on so rotten a set of foundations was inconceivable, but Melville would plainly not cease until they had lain the whole to rest. It would at least, surely, spare them from having to revisit the conversation yet another time.

"Perhaps not quite the spirit I was after," Melville murmured, unable to prevent himself from funning even now, but he turned the horses obediently and headed instead for Hyde Park.

"Everything you told me," Eliza said, "about my talent—about your admiration for me . . . Did you mean it?"

"I did," Melville said, jolted back into seriousness. "I do.

What you have been able to achieve, even in the short time we have known each other? I think it glorious. And I don't just mean the portrait."

Eliza gave a little jerk of the head—not quite a nod, not quite a shake.

"And did you . . . did you tell the Selwyns about the portrait?" she asked.

She was not sure why this mattered so—the idea that while she had believed this a secret shared between her and Melville, Lady Selwyn might have been smirking and aware the whole time—only that it did. There was a beat of silence in the carriage. Eliza regarded the side of Melville's face. If he tried to sell her on a pretty untruth, then she would know.

"I was going to," Melville said, slowly. "I cannot pretend otherwise, I was going to. But I did not. It felt too much a betrayal."

It would have been. Eliza let out a slow breath. The image playing in her mind's eye, of the Selwyns and Melville cloistered, sniggering, together, faded a little—as oil paints did, under direct sunlight.

"You said you loved me," she whispered, so softly she could barely hear herself over the rattling of wheels and hooves.

"Yes," he said.

"Did you mean it?"

"Yes."

"When did you . . . when did that begin?" she asked.

"I do not know that there was one single moment," Melville said softly. "I was drawn to you from near the moment we met. That was never a lie. You were so guarded and I wanted to know you. To find out what you thought—what you wanted—under all that propriety and carefulness."

Eliza could not have torn her eyes away from him if she had tried. She did not try.

"It took me a while to understand. It was far too easy to lay the cause at the Selwyn scheme's doorstep, but I began to realize that—that it was your eye I wanted to catch, when something amusing occurs; your opinion I wanted to hear, always. It's with you I want to share all my secrets, you I wanted to walk with, sit beside, dance with," Melville continued. "It was always you—big and small—and the hours we spent together, in that tiny parlor, are amongst the happiest of my life."

He looked at her sidelong.

"Does that answer it?"

And it did, but . . . Eliza was not sure it was enough.

"I want to believe you," Eliza whispered, her eyes full. "I just . . . don't know how."

"What if I tell you again? However many times you need to hear it."

"Difficult to do from Paris," Eliza noted, swiping a hand across her face.

"I am not going to Paris," Melville said.

"You are not?"

"How could I—when you are here?"

Eliza's breath caught. He was saying everything she most wanted to hear—everything that she had not known she needed to hear, too.

"I have no fortune now," she said, because part of her, even now, still wondered if *this* was why. "Somerset has taken it away."

"He has?" Melville demanded. "*Why?*"

"The gossip, the rumors—someone saw us dancing," Eliza said. "And I have not been well-behaved, this fortnight."

"I shall go to him. I shall make him see it is all my fault," Melville said at once.

"I already have," Eliza said. "He said he would restore it, if I promised to relinquish all ties to you. I told him I would not."

Melville pulled his horses to an abrupt stop, in the middle of Hyde Park.

"Eliza . . ." he said, rather wonderingly. He did not sound dismayed, or unsettled or alarmed. He was looking at her as if she had just offered him the most precious gift in the world.

"It was not for you," she said. "It was for my freedom—my independence—*myself*."

"And brava indeed," he said. "But . . . was it for me, just a little?"

Eliza stared at him. He was very still, hardly looked to be breathing. She had that feeling again, of standing upon a precipice, of making a decision that would affect all that came after. It was hers to make, hers entirely.

"Yes," she whispered, her heart beating so loudly it almost drowned out her voice.

"Oh, thank God!" he said. "I had thought, after last night, there was no hope at all."

"So did I," she admitted.

He dropped the reins to reach for her.

"Would you think me the worst brute alive if I said I was glad that your fortune is gone?" Melville said, squeezing her hands between his.

"No," she whispered, throat constricted. "But it might make you the worst fortune hunter in history."

She smiled, tremulously, to show she was joking.

"Impossible," Melville said. "I am the very best in everything I do."

The curl in Melville's mouth was back. Eliza had missed it.

"Perhaps it is a very good thing I was not painting your ego," Eliza said. "It would never have fitted upon the canvas."

Melville laughed, louder than the joke warranted.

"Marry me, you darling thing," he said.

"I have only five hundred pounds a year to my name, now," Eliza warned him.

"I don't give a flying fig," Melville said, eyes searching hers. "Marry me."

"We shall be dreadfully purse-pinched," Eliza said.

"We are two of the most extraordinarily clever, talented and beautiful people I know," Melville said. "I am confident we shall find a way through. *Marry me.*"

"Very well," Eliza said.

"Very well?" Melville repeated, grinning. He let go of her hands to grasp at the reins again and set the horses off at a rollicking pace that had Eliza grasping for her bonnet.

"Where are we going?" she asked, laughing.

"I have somewhere in mind, don't worry," he said. "Somewhere out of view of any gawpers."

"Are you taking me to your assignation spot?" she said indignantly.

"It is either that or I don't kiss you, so I am not quite sure what you expect from me," he said.

"How many women have you taken there?" she demanded.

"Ah—I should prefer not to say," he said, drawing up between two trees, in a private little copse. "Though I assure you, you are the only one of them I have proposed marriage to."

"Melville!" she said, half laughing, half berating.

"That is not my name," he said, taking her hands in his, and tugging her very gently across the seat toward him.

"Max," Eliza said, shyly.

He grasped her head gently in his hands.

"I am going to do my very best," he said, "to make you the happiest woman alive."

"That sounds a little unrealistic," Eliza said.

"Have you not heard that I am widely considered brilliant?" he said, brushing his thumb across her bottom lip very gently.

"Ah, but that is scurrilous gossip, no more," Eliza said. "You should not believe everything you hear, my lord."

They were laughing when they kissed—she could feel the shape of his smile against hers and smiled wider still, too happy to care that she was hindering rather than helping the endeavor. But then Melville pressed a hand to her jaw and tilted her head to the left and parted his lips and—

Well, a great many things felt more important than talking, after that.

34

Eliza left Bath for the final time on a Tuesday. And although it was for the happiest of reasons, the bright pink of Eliza's joy was still colored a little by bittersweet blue. For today, while she was removing to London with Perkins and the rest of their household, Margaret was not accompanying her.

But nor was she returning to Bedfordshire.

"I have told Mama and Lavinia I will not," she had told Eliza, twisting her fingers anxiously together. "They are appalled—they say they intend to never speak to me again. But I cannot deny myself a life any longer. I am going to join Caroline in Paris."

"How will you . . . ?" Eliza had asked, not knowing quite how to phrase the question.

"Those we trust, will know the truth," Margaret said. "Those we do not, will suspect us only to be companions. I shall have to allow Caroline to support me—she has sold the rights to *Holland House* for a good enough sum and as for the rest . . . we shall find out."

Margaret took a deep, steadying breath and smiled.

"I am excited," she admitted. "Even with the secrecy, it is a far sweeter future than I ever dreamed of."

Eliza had not been able to speak for a moment, pulling Margaret instead into a silent embrace. She was so happy for her—so absolutely, breathtakingly happy for her—but at the same time she could not imagine being able to survive a single day without her.

"How long do you mean to be away for?" she said into Margaret's shoulder.

"Oh, the merest moment," Margaret said. "It will be the most trifling of intervals in *our* story, you know—and when I return, we will begin our next and most exciting Act yet."

"It is to be a very long play, then," Eliza said, voice wobbling.

"Oh, the longest," Margaret said. "We are far from done."

Eliza pulled back, swiping her fingers under her eyelids to catch a stray tear.

"You will have the most wonderful adventure with Caroline, I am sure of it," she said. "It will be marvelous."

"As will London," Margaret said, pressing her hand. "In fact, I very much predict that Lady Melville is to become all the rage."

Eliza smiled. She was not Lady Melville yet, but soon, she hoped. Very soon. Since that magical hour in Hyde Park, not a day had gone by without Melville appearing at Russell Square. The very next morning, he had escorted Eliza to Somerset House to take in the view of the portrait a second time— once more early enough that they were not likely to be much observed and Melville mobbed by ladies requesting his signature.

"It looks very good," Melville said, looking up at himself. "If that is not very vain to say."

"You, vain?" Eliza said. "Surely not."

"You never charged me for the commission, you know," Melville said, grinning. "How much is it?"

Eliza pretended to consider.

"Would ten thousand pounds a year suit?" she asked.

"A little steeper than I was expecting," Melville said. "And— may I ask—is it usual to charge in yearly instalments?"

"It is perhaps better considered a rental than a purchase," she advised.

He laughed.

"I shall have to refer you to my wife," he said, still grinning. "I am reliably informed she is to be a famous portraitist, and soon rich enough to keep my poor fortune-hunting soul in the manner I am not yet—though dearly wish to be—accustomed."

"Your wife?" Eliza said, raising her eyebrows. "I did not realize you had one, my lord."

"The matter is still pending," Melville admitted.

"Pending?" Eliza said. "You ought really to resolve that."

"I intend to," he promised.

They swayed toward one another, before abruptly recollecting they were still very much in public, and still very much not married.

Melville cleared his throat and turned back to face himself.

"I do wish you would not keep attempting to lead me astray," he said primly. "I shall have you know I am not that sort of earl."

"A pity," Eliza said. "For I was hoping you were *exactly* that sort of earl."

Melville laughed. A few persons began to trickle into the room, and many did indeed make a beeline for Melville's portrait specifically, at which point Melville retreated so that he might not be observed. Eliza listened, again, as the audience discussed all the latest theories on the identity of the artist. It was all women's names in the ring now, and Eliza knew better than to think this marked progress for the respect of her gender's artistry—the rumors were circling closer to her, and it would only be a matter of time, now, before Eliza's name was attached. She did not care.

Perhaps she would even break the news to the *ton*, herself, to launch a new career. Whatever scandal it constituted, it would surely be lessened by her and Melville's marriage—one could not castigate a lady for having an affair with her own husband, surely? And even if it was not, she had everything she needed, right here, to be able to weather such storms. That did not scare her, not anymore.

"I have already had several offers from engravers," Melville said quietly, returning to Eliza's side as the group moved off, "who wish to be able to copy and distribute the image—and the publishers of my already printed titles will likely pay to reproduce, even if Paulet disapproves. It should constitute a solid source of capital."

Eliza nodded.

"I will pawn my diamonds," she whispered back. "Sell the phaeton, to hire some painting rooms . . ."

"We can sell the Berkeley Square house—find smaller lodgings," Melville added. "Let Alderley again for the summer . . ."

The *ton* would discuss them, gossip, snicker at their misfortune—but that did not scare her, either. Eliza felt as giddy and as eager as if they were discussing their honeymoon, not their forthcoming frugality.

"We will manage," she said with a fervent nod.

"We will manage *beautifully*," Melville corrected.

Economy and prudence had never been so romantic. And now, there was only for Eliza and Margaret to pack up Camden Place. In contrast to the easy manner in which they had left Harefield, this seemed a task that took a great deal more time and consideration, for in the three months they had lived in Bath, all members of the house seemed to have accumulated a vast number of possessions. In the end, they had to hire two whole post chaises in order to transport everything, for Eliza was to care for Margaret's possessions while she was abroad—and it took the better part of a whole day for the footmen to load the trunks.

It was as she was directing the removal of the easel that Perkins told her, quietly, that they had a visitor—one he had taken the liberty of showing into the drawing room. Eliza had walked downstairs and pushed open the door to find Miss Winkworth standing within—a vision in pale cambric, trailing her fingers thoughtfully over the keys of the pianoforte.

"Miss Winkworth," Eliza said, a great deal surprised. "I had thought you still in London!"

Miss Winkworth looked up.

"I asked Mama if we could break our journey in Bath," she said. "Tomorrow, we are bound for Harefield, for the . . ."

"Wedding," Eliza finished for her. The announcement had been made in the papers last week. "Yes. I am sorry to not be able to attend."

Miss Winkworth smiled, gently, as if she knew this to be a lie.

"I know that you refused to help my mother," she whispered. "I heard what you said to her, about Arden."

She sent Eliza a dimpling smile.

"She was angrier than I have ever seen her," she confessed, and the prospect did not seem to frighten her as it once had.

"I wish I could have done more," Eliza said truthfully. She looked at Miss Winkworth. It would have been indelicate to enquire after her attachment to Somerset even if she herself had not already been romantically attached to the gentleman, but . . .

"I hope," Eliza said, "that you have been able to form a genuine attachment, during your time in London?"

Miss Winkworth's rosy blush told her she understood Eliza's meaning.

"I have," she said simply.

Eliza nodded. They were well-matched, she saw suddenly, Miss Winkworth and Somerset, Winnie and Oliver. He needed someone to protect, and she needed protection. He derived value from caring, and she from being cared for. They would be happy.

"I have told Somerset he is not to contest your fortune," Miss Winkworth said softly.

"You did what?" Eliza said, unsure if she had heard correctly. "You *told* Somerset?"

"I do not like to disagree with him, ever. But you have been so kind to me, and I felt too guilty to stay silent," Miss Winkworth said, pulling a little face as if she could still not believe her effrontery.

"Guilty?" Eliza repeated. "Why ought you . . ."

"Because it was *I* who told him, about you dancing with Melville," she said, head dipping down. "I saw you, that night, and I did not say anything, for weeks . . . But after your falling out, when he and I began to court . . ."

She trailed off, her face growing ever pinker.

"I wanted him, you see," she said. "I needed him to fall out of love with you, a little."

Eliza stared at her, a little aghast. She did not know what to say. She would never have expected any of this from such a mouse.

"You certainly achieved that," she said, mouth dry and mind reeling. It was not that this would change anything—not that she would wish anything, in the end, had unraveled differently, but . . .

"Somerset has agreed to leave your fortune as is," Miss Winkworth said. "I had to make myself look very sad for a while—and my mother is not happy—but he agreed."

"You are far slyer than I thought you," Eliza said slowly, and Miss Winkworth gave an adorable, impish smile. "Thank you, I think—yes, thank you."

For whatever Miss Winkworth's motives, this was a gift indeed. She would be able to retain her staff, Melville could publish *Medea*, they could keep Berkeley Square, she would not have to sell her possessions and—and . . .

As Eliza began to think of all the many, many ways her life

was to be so much less troubled than she had prepared for, her breath caught on a gasp. She would have been all right, without the fortune. She would have been. But to be offered such an unexpected reprieve . . .

"Thank you," she said again.

"You know," Miss Winkworth said, "the wording in the will seems to me rather specific in any event. I wonder, if you no longer belonged to the Somerset family, the clause might become . . . a little void?"

Eliza felt certain, for a moment, that she could see the shades of the woman Winifred Winkworth would become in her face. She would do well, as the new Countess of Somerset. Fare better than Eliza had done. Find strength that it had taken Eliza until now to cultivate.

"Is there anything else I might do for you?" Miss Winkworth asked.

"I could not ask for anything more," Eliza said, half laughing. "I—" She paused. "Actually—the landscape in the first-floor parlor of Harefield . . . It was painted by my grandfather and I would like to buy it. You may name your price."

She could certainly afford it, now—again. Miss Winkworth nodded, dimpling.

"Good day, Lady Somerset."

She bobbed her a little curtsey and floated away.

Less of a lamb, and more of a lion," Margaret said, when Eliza told her, Caroline and Melville later that day but Eliza's eyes were on Melville. He smiled.

"I can take you to Alderley," he said, pleased—as if the news was no more life-changing than that. Eliza supposed it was not. For they could have done it, without the fortune, together, and neither would money remove all the hardship ahead. Eliza's choice in a husband would not be greeted with unequivocal approval: at the very least, a lifetime of stares and whispers awaited them, and Eliza suspected the Balfours' displeasure at the paths she and Margaret had chosen—at the persons with who they were aligning—would be far more vocal.

"And at least we will be well-dressed," Melville murmured, as if in direct response to Eliza's thoughts. She smiled, twining her fingers through his and squeezing his hand in reply.

"We must go," Caroline said gently.

Camden and Laura Place were both empty. Two carriages stood outside, loaded with bandboxes. One was bound for London, the other for Dover.

"I shall miss you, Caro," Melville said, grasping her hand tightly.

"I should hope so," Caroline said, but she touched her forehead very gently to his shoulder.

The moment felt unbearably private. Eliza and Margaret drew a little away.

"I shan't say goodbye again," Margaret said stoutly. "I do not wish my eyes to be puffy for the journey—but you will write?"

Eliza nodded, her chin wobbling. She held out her hand for Caroline to shake, as she approached, and Caroline knocked it away with a snort, pulling her instead into a tight embrace.

"Look after him for me, will you?" she whispered into Eliza's ear.

"If you will do the same," Eliza whispered back.

And they were gone. Leaving Eliza and Melville alone, at last. Melville turned to her, giving an extravagant bow and a superfluous flourish of his hand.

"Your carriage awaits," he said. "I have prepared a great many things to say to you on the journey."

"Why am I instantly concerned?" Eliza said, smiling. "I do hope they are not improper."

"How can they be, when we are to be very properly chaperoned for the entire journey?" Melville said loudly to the street at large, throwing Eliza a very obvious wink.

They set off not ten minutes later, and Eliza leaned out of the carriage window to watch Camden Place as it faded from view. It had been the first place she had ever been truly, completely, incandescently happy. But like all the best things in life, one could not enjoy them in just the same way, forever.

I will come back, she promised Bath. *Soon*.

It would always be the most splendid city she had ever seen.

"Would you prefer St. Paul's or St. Mary's, for our wedding?" Melville asked her, as Bath too began to fade into the distance.

"I was wondering . . ." Eliza said, removing her eyes from the window and staring toward her fiancé. One might think, with all the many, many hours she had already spent gazing at him, that she would be tired of the view. She was not.

"You were wondering?"

"How difficult is it to source a special license?" Eliza asked. "You seem the sort of gentleman who would know such a thing."

"The aspersions you are casting," Melville said, "I care not for them."

He regarded her, eyes twinkling and mouth smiling. If Eliza were to paint the scene, she would use only her warmest, brightest colors—but she would not. Some moments could only be lived.

"You do not want a grand occasion, with all the pomp and ceremony we can muster?" Melville asked.

"I have already had one wedding such as that," Eliza said. "I would rather elope."

"I shall have to consider the matter," Melville said. "Perhaps, now I am to be the married Lord Melville, I might decide to become dreadfully proper and dull."

"You dismay me," Eliza said, biting her lip to hide her grin.

"For now I am to be the married *Lady* Melville, I have made a very different decision."

"Is my Lady Melville to be a very dashing creature?" Melville enquired politely.

"Oh, yes—*dreadfully* wild," Eliza said. "You have my sympathies."

Melville laughed, leaning forward to kiss the smile upon her face.

"I look forward to meeting her."

Acknowledgments

Writing a second book is a very different beast to writing a first. Suddenly having real-life readers, real-life editors and a very real-life deadline has been bizarre and challenging and wonderful—and having the time and space to delve deeper into research has been the greatest joy. If you are ever passing through London and fancy seeing some Georgian art, do pay a visit to the fantastic—and free—Tate Britain, where I (under the expert and much-appreciated guidance of Sara Dibb) started my research journey, and if you are interested in learning about Britain's colonial history and the experience of Indian people in Regency England, I cannot more highly recommend the brilliant books by Rozina Visram, Dr. Arup K. Chatterjee and William Dalrymple. I love novels, but the stories of the real people living through this period are far more complex and important than any fiction. I also feel hugely privileged to have spoken both to Ann Witheridge from London Fine Art Studios and to Dr. Arup K. Chatterjee from OP Jindal Global University, who answered my questions with such grace and generosity. All errors are of course mine, and any deviations from their expert counsel were made under the influence of a romantic imagination.

More time and space for writing this year did also make room for more self-doubt, too, and so my biggest thanks must be paid to my editors, Martha Ashby and Marie Michels, who guided me from first to last draft with an impossible amount of patience, humor and perception. It's been a very fun honor collaborating with you, and I feel so lucky that, alongside my wonderful agent, Maddy Milburn (and every single glorious person at MM!), and publishing powerhouses Pam Dorman and Lynne Drew, I get to work with such a talented and fashionable editorial team. Big thanks must also go to Georgina Kamsika and Kati Nicholl for their insight and sharp eyes—they are hugely appreciated!

Next, I would love to thank the whole team at Pamela Dorman Books, Viking and Penguin, for all the shrewd, quick and highly skilled work that goes into publishing a book: thank you to Brian Tart, Andrea Schulz, Kate Stark, Mary Stone, Lindsay Prevette, Kristina Fazzalaro, Julia Falkner, Christine Choi, Paul Buckley, Libby VanderPloeg, Sabrina Bowers, Jeramie Orton, Matt Giarratano, Norina Frabotta, Chelsea Cohen and all the people in the supply chain who move heaven and earth to get my book everywhere it needs to be. Huge thanks to the book bloggers who put out so much joy with their reviews, it's always such a delight connecting with you, and thank you also to the booksellers who continue to build such glorious spaces on our high street.

I owe a great deal to my very indulgent friends, who I must thank for the following (please delete as appropriate): for the negronis, the pasta, for answering random questions about classical literature, for reading my books and then also making your mums read my books. Thank you for the margaritas, the wine, for letting me name characters after you for my own amusement, for forgiving me when I cancel plans, for coming with me on all the museum tours and for telling me when I start "speaking Regency" in a normal conversation. Thank you, I love you, let's hang out soon.

More thanks than I can give right now go always to my wonderful family, my enduring source of calm and comfort even when—most especially when—I am at my most unlikeable. To

Myla and Joey, who destroyed my first plot board with such needless enthusiasm: I don't thank you, but I forgive you.

And lastly, thank you to my readers! Hello! Thank you so much for choosing my book—I hope it made you smile at least once. I love hearing from you—I can't tell you how glad I am that you are real and no longer imaginary—so do come and say hi on social media if you have a moment.

Sophie x

Read on for a selection from
Sophie Irwin's first novel,
A Lady's Guide to Fortune-Hunting,
available now.

1

Y ou're *not* going to marry me?" Miss Talbot repeated,
disbelievingly.

"Afraid not," Mr. Charles Linfield replied, his
expression set in a kind of bracingly apologetic
grimace—the sort one might wear when confessing you could
no longer attend a friend's birthday party, rather than ending
a two-year engagement.

Kitty stared at him, uncomprehending. Katherine Talbot—
Kitty to her family and closest acquaintances—was not much
used to incomprehension. In fact, she was well known among
her family and Biddington at large for her quick mind and talent for practical problem-solving. Yet in this moment, Kitty
felt quite at a loss. She and Charles were to be married. She
had known it for years—and it was now not to be? What should
one say, what should one feel, in the face of such news? Everything was changed. And yet Charles still *looked* the same,
dressed in clothes she had seen him in a thousand times before,
with that disheveled style only the wealthy could get away
with: an intricately embroidered waistcoat that was badly mis-
buttoned, a garishly bright cravat that had been mangled rather

than tied. He ought at least, Kitty thought, staring at that awful cravat with a rising sense of indignation, to have dressed for the occasion.

Some of this ire must have seeped through to her expression, because all at once Charles swapped his maddening air of apologetic condescension for that of a sulky schoolboy.

"Oh, you needn't look at me like that," he snapped. "It isn't as if we were ever *officially* promised to one another."

"Officially promised to one another?" Kitty's spirit returned to her in full force, and she discovered, in fact, that she felt quite furious. The irredeemable cad. "We've been speaking of marriage for the past two years. We were only delayed this long because of my mother's death and my father's sickness! You *promised* me—you promised me so many things."

"Just the talk of children," he protested, before adding mulishly, "and besides, it isn't as if I could call things off when your father was on death's door. Wouldn't have been at all the thing."

"Oh, and I suppose now that he's dead—not a month in the ground—you could finally jilt me?" she said wrathfully. "Is that really so much more 'the thing'?"

He ran a hand through his hair, his eyes flicking to the door.

"Listen, there's no point us discussing it when you're like this," he affected the tone of a severely tried man holding onto his patience. "Perhaps I should go."

"Go? You can't possibly drop news such as this, and not explain yourself. I saw you just last week and we were discussing marrying in May—not three months away."

"Perhaps I should have just written a letter," he said to himself, still staring longingly at the door. "Mary said this was the best way to do it, but I think a letter would have been simpler. I can't think properly with you shrieking at me."

Kitty cast aside her many irritations and, with the instincts of a true hunter, fixed only on the salient information.

"Mary?" she said sharply. "Mary Spencer? What, exactly,

does Miss Spencer have to do with this? I had not realized she had returned to Biddington."

"Ah, yes, yes, well, she is, that is," Mr. Linfield stammered, beads of sweat appearing on his brow. "My mother invited her to stay with us, for a time. It being so good for my sisters to make other female acquaintances."

"And you spoke to Miss Spencer about bringing our engagement to an end?"

"Ah, yes, well, she was so sympathetic to the situation—to *both* our situations—and I must say it was good to be able . . . to speak to someone about it."

Silence, for a moment. And then, almost casually, "Mr. Linfield, do you mean to propose to Miss Spencer?"

"No! Well, that is to say—we already . . . So, I thought best to—to come here . . ."

"I see," Kitty said—and she did. "Well, I suppose I must commend you upon your confidence, Mr. Linfield. It is quite the feat to propose to one woman whilst already being engaged to another. Bravo, indeed."

"This is exactly what you always do!" Mr. Linfield complained, mustering some courage at last. "You twist everything around until one doesn't know which way is up. Have you thought perhaps that I wanted to spare your feelings? That I didn't want to have to tell you the truth—that if I want to make a career for myself in politics, I can hardly do it married to someone like *you*."

His derisive tone shocked her. "And what exactly is that supposed to mean?" she demanded.

He spread his arms, as if inviting her to look around. Kitty did not. She knew what she would see, for she had stood in this room every day of her life: the worn chaises huddled by the fireplace for warmth, the once elegant rug on the hearth now moth-eaten and shabby, shelves where there had once been books now standing empty.

"We may live in the same town, but we're from different *worlds*." He waved his hands about again. "I'm the son of the squire! And Mama and Miss Spencer helped me to see that I cannot afford to make a *mésalliance* if I am to make a name for myself."

Kitty had never been so aware of the sound of her heartbeat, pounding a drum loudly in her ears. A *mésalliance*, was she?

"Mr. Linfield," she said, softly but with bite. "Let there be no lies between us. You had no issue with our engagement until you encountered the pretty Miss Spencer again. A squire's son, you say! This is not the sort of ungentlemanly conduct I would have expected your family to condone. Perhaps I ought to be pleased that you have proven yourself to be so utterly dishonorable before it was too late."

She landed each blow with the precision and force of Gentleman Jackson, and Charles—Mr. Linfield forever, now—staggered backward from her.

"How could you say such a thing?" he asked, aghast. "It is not *ungentlemanly*. You're becoming quite hysterical." Mr. Linfield was sweating thickly now, twisting uncomfortably. "I do want us to remain great friends, you have to understand, Kit—"

"*Miss Talbot*," she corrected with frigid politeness. A shriek of rage was howling through her body, but she contained it, gesturing sharply to the door with a wave of her hand. "You'll forgive me if I ask you to see yourself out, Mr. Linfield."

After a quick bob of a bow, he fled eagerly from her, without looking back.

Kitty stood motionless for a moment, holding her breath as if to prevent this disaster from unfolding any further. Then she walked to the window, where the morning sun was streaming in, leaned her forehead against the glass, and exhaled slowly. From this window, one had an uninterrupted view of the garden: the daffodils just beginning to flower, the vegetable patch, still thick with weeds, and the loose chickens picking their way through, looking for grubs. Life outside continued on, and yet on her side of the glass, everything was utterly ruined.

They were alone. Completely and utterly alone now, with no one to turn to. Mama and Papa were gone, and in this hour of most grievous need, where more than ever she wished to ask for their advice, she could not. There was simply no one left to whom she could turn. Panic was rising within her. What was she to do now?

She might have stayed in this position for several hours, were she not interrupted by her youngest sister, ten-year-old Jane, who barged in only a few minutes later with the self-importance of a royal messenger.

"Kitty, *where* is Cecily's book?" she demanded.

"It was in the kitchen yesterday," Kitty answered without looking away from the garden. They ought to weed the artichoke bed this afternoon, it would need planting before long. Distantly, she heard Jane call to Cecily to pass on her words.

"She's looked there," came the reply.

"Well, look again." Kitty dismissed her impatiently with a flap of a hand.

The door opened and closed with a bang. "She says it's not there and if you've sold it, she'll be very upset because it was a gift from the vicar."

"Oh, for goodness' sake," Kitty snapped, "you may tell Cecily that I can't look for her silly vicar book, because I have just been jilted and need a few moments' reprieve, if that is not too much to ask!"

No sooner had Jane relayed this unusual message to Cecily, than the full household—all of Kitty's four sisters and Bramble the dog—descended upon the parlor, instantly filling the space with noise.

"Kitty, what is this about Mr. Linfield jilting you? Has he really?"

"I never liked him, he used to pat me on the head as if I were a child."

"My book is *not* in the kitchen."

Kitty told them as briefly as she could what had happened, with her head still resting on the glass. There was silence after this, as Kitty's sisters stared uncertainly at each other. After a few moments, Jane—having grown bored—wandered over to the creaking pianoforte and broke the silence by bashing out a jolly tune. Jane had never received music lessons, but what she lacked in talent she made up for in both fervor and volume.

"How awful," Beatrice—at nineteen years, Kitty's closest sister in both age and temperament—said at last, appalled. "Oh, Kitty dear, I am sorry. You must be heartbroken."

Kitty turned her head sharply. "Heartbroken? Beatrice, that is quite beside the point. Without my marrying Mr. Linfield, we are all ruined. Papa and Mama may have left us the house, but they also left an astonishing amount of debt. I was depending on the Linfield wealth to save us."

"You were marrying Mr. Linfield for his *fortune*?" Cecily asked, a judgmental note in her voice. The intellectual of the family at eighteen years of age, Cecily was felt by her sisters to have a rather over-developed sense of morality.

"Well, it was certainly not for his integrity or gentlemanly honor," Kitty said bitterly. "I just wish I'd had the sense to wrap it up sooner. We should not have pushed back the wedding when Mama died, I knew that a long engagement was asking for trouble. To think that Papa thought it would look unseemly!"

"How bad is it, Kitty?" Beatrice asked. Kitty stared silently at her for a few moments. How could she tell them? How could she explain all that was about to happen?

"It is . . . serious," Kitty said carefully. "Papa re-mortgaged the house to some quite disreputable people. The sales I made—our books, the silverware, some of Mama's jewels—were enough to keep them at bay for a while, but on the first of June they will return. Not four months away. And if we do not have enough money, or proof that we can start paying them, then . . ."

". . . We will have to leave? But this is our home." Harriet's lip wobbled. As second youngest, she yet remained more sensitive than Jane, who had at least stopped playing to sit quietly on the stool, watching.

Kitty did not have the heart to tell them that it would be worse than just leaving. That the sale of Netley Cottage would barely cover their debts, with nothing left after to support them. With nowhere to go and no obvious means of income, the future would be a dark place. They would have no choice but to split up, of course. She and Beatrice might find some employment in Salisbury, or one of the larger towns nearby, perhaps as housemaids—or lady's maids if they were truly lucky. Cecily—well, Kitty could not imagine Cecily being willing or able to work for anyone—but with her education she might try a school. Harriet—oh, Harriet was so young—would have to do the same. Somewhere that would provide room and board. And Jane . . . Mrs. Palmer in the town, singularly mean-spirited though she was, had always had a sort of fondness for Jane. She might be persuaded to take her in until she was old enough to find employment, too.

Kitty imagined them all, her sisters, separated and cast to the wind. Would they ever be together again, as they were now? And what if it was far worse than this already-bleak scenario? Visions of each of them, alone, hungry and despairing, flashed before her eyes. Kitty had not yet wept a tear over Mr. Linfield—he was not worth her tears—but now her throat ached painfully. They had already lost so much. It had been Kitty who had had to explain to them that Mama was not going to get better. Kitty who had broken the news of Papa's passing. How was she now to explain that the worst was still to come? She could not find the words. Kitty was not their mother, who could pull reassurances from the air like magic, nor their father, who could always say things would be all right with a confidence that made you believe him. No, Kitty was the family's problem solver—but this was far too great an obstacle for her to overcome with will alone. She wished desperately that there was someone who might carry this burden with her, a heavy load for the tender age of twenty, but there was not. Her sisters' faces stared up at her, so sure even now that she would be able to fix everything. As she always had.

As she always *would*.

The time for despair had passed. She would not—could not—be defeated so easily. She swallowed down her tears and set her shoulders.

"We have more than four months until the first of June," Kitty said firmly, moving away from the window. "That is just enough time, I believe, for us to achieve something quite extraordinary. In a town such as Biddington, I was able to ensnare a rich fiancé. Though he turned out to be a weasel, there is no reason to believe the exercise cannot be repeated, simply enough."

"I do not think any other rich men live nearby," Beatrice pointed out.

"Just so!" her sister replied cheerfully, eyes unnaturally bright. "Which is why I must travel to more fruitful ground. Beatrice, consider yourself in charge—for I shall be leaving for London."

A Lady's Guide to Fortune-Hunting
A Novel

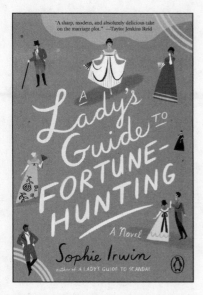

Kitty Talbot needs a fortune. Left with her father's debts, she leaves home and throws herself into the London Season to find a wealthy husband. Cunning and ingenious, Kitty knows that risk is just part of the game, but the only thing she does not anticipate is the worldly Lord Radcliffe. Radcliffe sees Kitty for the fortune-hunter that she is and is determined to thwart her plans, until their parrying takes a completely different turn.

"Bridgerton fans will swoon over this entertaining romp through Britain's Regency-era high society." *—People*